PROJECT HIMBO

SJ WHITBY

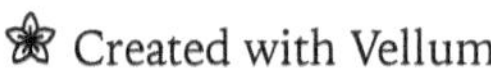 Created with Vellum

Cute Mutants Vol 1: Mutant Pride
Cute Mutants Vol 2: Young, Gifted, and Queer
Cute Mutants Vol 3: The Demon Queer Saga
Cute Mutants Vol 4: The Sisterhood of Evil Mutants
Weapon UwU Vol 1: Godkillers
Cute Mutants Vol 5: Galaxy Brain
Shitty Mutants (Patreon exclusive)

PREVIOUSLY

This book takes place after the Cute Mutants series, and this section contains spoilers about those events. For more context and the full story, check them out.

Once upon a time there was a girl named Emma Hall who gave her friends superpowers. This was entirely by accident and the source of these new abilities was a mystery. They joined together as a group called the Cute Mutants. The original team was:

Dylan aka Chatterbox, who could talk with objects

Alyse (Moodring) who could change shape with her moods

Bianca (Wraith), with strange creatures living in her chest

Lou (Glowstick), who glowed when turned on

Emma (Goddess), whose powers were unclear

Dani (Marvellous), who could use telekinesis when in pain

In the beginning, they wanted to help people and change the world, but they suffered attacks from those who wanted to use them. In one of these encounters, Wraith died at the hands of corporate security, which showed Dylan in particular what the stakes could be.

Later, they fought a mind-controlling preacher, whose daughter Violet (Penance) was also a mutant, capable of moving through secret passages in the world and turning herself into a bladed form. They saved Violet from her father, and she joined the team. They also fought a religious paramilitary organisation called Quietus, dedicated to wiping out mutants.

In time, they learned the truth of Emma's powers. She was the child of two incredibly powerful mutants: a telepath called Teen Spirit, and a reality warper called Heart of a Flower. In a last ditch effort to save mutants from extinction, Emma's mother had erased all knowledge of mutants from history. Heart of a Flower had twisted this act to also affect Emma's mother, and had been working in secret to build Emma and her friends up into a powerful force able to defeat humanity.

Once the Cute Mutants avoided Heart's plan, they found themselves in a desperate fight for survival against humanity. With many forces arrayed against them, they were desperate to find a place where mutants could be safe.

During this, Dylan began hearing a strange voice unlike that of the objects they usually spoke to. This voice led them to a cliffside where they learned it was an energy network named Cybele that lived within the planet. With the current state of the Earth, Cybele was very weak and the two mutants were presented with a chance to be reborn as a last ditch effort to save everything. Both Dylan and Dani accepted, and were regenerated in a new plant form with new powers. They also learned of the ancient history of mutantkind, that the mutant species was born many years ago as defense against an alien race who preyed on humanity.

When they returned from their transformation, they found that a year had passed. Goddess was in an exhausting stalemate with a religious AI known as Michael. Many parts of the world had changed drastically in that time, with huge new cities built and many under the AI's sway. By this stage, due to how dangerous the world was for them, most mutants had been put into a form of cryosleep as protection. Emma had taken on all their powers, becoming the most powerful mutant in a long, long time.

The reunited Cute Mutants managed to defeat Michael, but Emma could not sustain her vast levels of power. The awful truth was that she would either destroy the earth in overload, or she could die and release all her power back to Cybele. Emma chose to pass on, leaving the Cute Mutants in grief and disarray. However, Cybele used Emma's power to build an island for mutants to live on safely. It has been called Mutopia, and mutants from all around the world flock to it. In the aftermath of Emma's death, more and more mutants were awakened around the world with the power returning to the earth.

A year later, Cybele presented the group with a shocking surprise. She'd grown two children, plant-creatures who were part Cybele and partly created from Dylan and Dani's DNA. They were given to Dylan and Dani to raise.
The world is still in a fragile state. The memory of the Dark Year is fresh in many people's minds, and the reality of a mutant nation is too much for some groups to ignore.
And the mutants are always waiting for the next threat to arrive…

CONTENT WARNINGS

This book contains subject matter that some readers may find distressing. Please be aware that Project Himbo includes recreational use of alcohol, hate groups against mutants, mind control, medical experimentation, and someone reliving the experience of losing loved ones, including children. It contains scenes of someone experiencing misgendering and dysphoria. It also include graphic violence and gore in a number of action sequences.

Please take care when reading.

CHAPTER 1
TENTACLE PRINCESS

A LONG, LONG TIME AGO

Don't call this a prologue. It simply occurs before anything else. This is not an excuse to start with action, even though we stand witness to an epic cosmic struggle. The battle is of little consequence—it is long over, after all. Here, we are focused on something much smaller. There's no true beginning or end to stories, even from this vantage point, but a thread begins here, so let us tug on it and see what unravels.

THE SKY WEEPS FIRE. It swirls and spells words I cannot understand. Our great nautilus ships snag inside them. The memory-stone that accretes inside me stores the scents and sensations of our arrival here.

It was peaceful then. Now there are monsters here.

My clutch looms over me. They flutter and yowl. Their tentacles caress the air. *Home,* they gesture. *The great flow cannot be interrupted.*

They lie. Perhaps the truth is outside their comprehension.

There is a monster in the sky, and it is outside our understanding.

I unfold myself a fraction, enough for my stubby tentilla to whisper out and lick at the air. *Devil.*

A great serpent twists in the air, glowing like a morning star. A weapon we have no answer for. They are voracious, an endless hunger made reptilian flesh. They have many shapes, and all of them hurt to perceive, but the one that flies and devours is the worst.

The flesh of another ship ruptures, coming apart in the sky. Pseudopods extrude from the iridescent, rippling bulk. Toxic gases swirl in scented curls. Young as I am, I have seen this too many times before. I understand this is the end. Our kind were not made to fall. The escaping clutch cling to the dripping ruins of their craft. I inhale their distress. I should not do such a thing, but we are at the end of time, and food is scarce.

The hungering monster in the sky spirals off in search of new prey. They also know the clutch tumbling through the noxious atmosphere is dead. They waste no time in triumph. They have no need to sing praise. They are a predator, ruthless and efficient, and they are our demise spelled out in fire.

Another ship heaves itself through the lower atmosphere. A host of little worshippers are collected on the ground below. They sing, pressing their palms flat to their tiny faces. The combined force of their praise pushes the ship onwards, even though their fragile bodies will turn to ash through their exertions.

The devil above smiles, and opens their vast maw. Their great claws flex and extend. We are gods to the tiny creatures of this world, and yet somehow a creature greater and more deadly has been birthed from among them.

I tuck my extremities carefully away, wishing to avoid the

taste of death and pain. Yet even hidden in this way, the fear of my clutch swirls in suffocating clouds.

Home, they spell. *We must ascend.*

There are flutters of disquiet from some small few, but they are silenced gently by the ancestral host.

Faith. We predate all. Ancient. We cannot be torn down.

Is it my youth that lets me understand their foolishness? I am newborn, and nothing like a god. The stub of one perhaps, a fractional thing, and therefore the only one clear-eyed enough to see the truth.

The vicious thing in the skies above us is not the only threat we face, even though it rends our fragile flotilla into fragments, scenting the atmosphere with the intoxicating fragrance of dead gods. Far more deadly is the consort of the devil-monster. She is another of the naturally evolved inhabitants of this world, yet she can birth new monsters. In her hands, an innocent worshipper becomes a deadly new creature, losing their docile nature and plunging themselves into rebellion. They fly and sting and warp their reality like tiny deities. They spit fire and crack the ground, and urge the very rocks to do their bidding. They call us false gods, savage things that only wish to prey upon their people, and swear they will tear us down.

At first, we could not believe such things could happen.

We are true gods, and we are mighty. My clutch are vast, enormous temples of flesh that rise from the sea like islands. We exist to be worshipped and they exist to burn as offerings in our name. It is our due, and we cannot survive without it.

These feral creatures, savage scraps crawling from the bloody afterbirth of the mother, have no regard for the natural order of things. They will not worship or bow, and the only burning they do is of us.

My clutch have long been gods and we have watched so

many worshippers ascend in fragrant clouds. This is what we made this world to be, when we fell upon it from the deeps of space, drinking deep from its rich well of energy. We are past and present and future, in an uninterrupted line. The great flow of our dominance and destiny, extending forever.

That is the picture my clutch sees when they gaze upon the world. This is what they insist is true, despite the evidence of their own ruptured and gaseous corpses.

I am too young. All I see in the future are stories written in our blood.

And now the future is upon us. We are beset by a host of newborn monsters, still streaked with Lilith's afterbirth. They come to destroy us.

The nautilus-ship intended to be our escape lies half-constructed on the shore, a mess of eviscerated flesh. They are almost as young as me, lying hollowed and pinioned until they are vast enough to carry all of us in our smallest, most innocuous forms.

This infant ship will have no time to finish growing.

Even if we did, the sky holds no promise of escape. It is the domain of the devil, writhing in fire.

My clutch roar defiance at the approaching army of demons. They order this horde of tiny monsters to submit, to bend their fragile limbs and prostrate themselves in awe and worship.

They do not.

They will never.

I extend a fraction of my awareness. I taste their defiance, their refusal to bend. It is both abhorrent and invigorating. How do they look upon us, in all our glory, and deny that we are greater?

My clutch continues to demand fealty. It is all we know how

to do. We cannot evolve swiftly enough to handle this vast change in our prey species. Now they will destroy us all.

I edge towards the jagged rocks of the shore, where the waves lap. I may be small enough to hide, to escape the notice of the devil-things. Perhaps they will overlook one small fragment of a god, lying very still and quiet under a howling sky.

There is a monster that burns as it flies. It impacts the side of my clutchmate Gentle Void Dancing like a meteor, leaving a smoking crater. The sea around begins to boil, the temperature rising to an intolerable level.

My clutch scream. They thrash in the water, obscured by steam. All I can taste is pain. Another monster drips poison, held in the arms of one with iridescent wings that are almost beautiful. Together they rain suffering on the temples where they should worship.

Gods are dying, and I cannot stop them. Unfettered Chaos Engine thrashes in a lake of blood, and The Many Gentle Arms of Sleep is a smoking ruin, rent in thousands of places with gushing wounds.

They are mighty, but all that does is prolong their suffering.

Finally, it ends. Death has come and gone, and what remains in the rapidly cooling ocean is not my clutch. It is simply carcasses floating.

I lie under the vacant sky for a long time, waiting for my own death.

It does not come. They have overlooked me, or spared me, and in my grief the difference between these two states does not matter. I am alone, and I am alive. There is no record in my ancestral memories of what should rightfully occur. By the time my kind began to store a record of our past, we were already mighty, already spreading through the void of space.

Already gods.

I am nothing like my ancestors. A fragile, fragmented creature. The only thing I have is a thread of life, one of which I am compelled to protect, despite the inevitability of losing it.

I lie on the edge of the shore a long time, as the seas cool from the battle. Much later, I slide gently backwards into the still-warm salts of the ocean. Unfolded to my greatest extremity, I scull downwards, seeking cool depths. The great trenches that lie like scars, where I can drape myself in the crushing quiet.

My ancestors slept there, in the vast quiet depths of this planet's seas.

I shall sleep too.

Until the day it is safe for me, when the mother and her brood of monsters have become extinct like every other species that crawls this cursed sphere.

CHAPTER 2
TWINKLE LIGHTS

RECENTLY

This is the other natural place to begin the story. These are so many threads, but here is the central figure, at least from this narrative's perspective. There could be many, I suppose, depending on who your eye is drawn to. And mine finds its way here, as mundane as this appears. A man getting a job. There is backstory, of course, as there always is, but we can't fill it all in. It would get far too complicated. Let's see where he goes. He's pretty. Easy to watch. Let us hope he avoids the tendency for narratives to find their way into darker moments.

"THIS IS POSSIBLY the worst job in the world."

"Oh." It's pretty cool, being here with Dylan Taylor. They're actually a real goddamn superhero. I mean, you wouldn't *know* that, because they sit slumped in their chair like a delinquent, enormous boots jiggling on a messy desk. Kinda pretty in a way that has aspects of both masculine and feminine. His hair is tousled, all twined up with flowers, and her eyes are big and dark. I'm not sure what they want, starting off by telling me how terrible this is, so I try and look interested.

"I'm not trying to scare you off." Their mouth pulls into a little grimace.

"It's exciting." I lean forward, like *Chatterbox, dude, you asked me here. All the way to your scary tree-building like I did something wrong. At least tell me what the job is, assuming this is an interview and you're not messing with me.* I don't say any of this, because I know when to keep my mouth shut. "Thanks for having me."

They give this little snort. "You're here because we need someone supernaturally likeable. Based on what we hear, you're it. Not that we've had much evidence of it so far. Just you sitting here all pretty-like, like a puppy with its head tilted trying to figure out what the fuck I'm talking about."

Okay, that's pretty funny, so I do the head tilt because damn, the dude's practically *asking for it.* That makes her laugh, this huge delighted smile that she claps a hand over like she's ashamed. I think maybe I like this Chatterbox guy, scary as all the stories are.

And they *are* scary. Like they've killed a lot of people. They died and got resurrected as a tree-person. Dude saved the whole fucking world, now he speaks for the planet.

I rub at the scars on the right side of my face. They're rippled like sand dunes or the skin of some lizard. I have no memory of getting them, which is probably good. People seem to like them. The other side of my face glows faintly like a radiant heater turned down low. Again, I don't know how this happened, but I assume it was back when things turned to shit. Probably best I don't remember the details, really.

"Sorry." I give an apology shrug. "But what exactly is it you want me to do? I still don't really know why I'm here."

Here is an office with wooden walls, except one open to the outside as if they forget to finish it. The sky is blue, brushed with clouds, and a gentle breeze comes in, scattering petals from Dylan's short hair. Mutopia is usually pretty like this.

"Honestly, Dills." There's another person in the office with us, leaned against the wall as if we shouldn't be aware of her presence. I did the instant I came in, of course, because I notice people, but anyone would notice her. Alyse Sefo aka Moodring, probably the most popular person in all of mutantkind. Her hair is long and dark, streaked with blonde, and she has a slight smile on her face. Rumour has it that she won the presidential election and turned it down. "Be nice to the poor boy. You haven't actually told him anything."

They grin at this, as if they've been caught out. "Fine. Okay Twinkles, here's the deal. I've been assembling another team, exclusively of the most dangerous mutants on the planet. It's a whole bunch of aces stashed up my sleeve for when shit hits the fan."

Okay, this is a big surprise. I think I'm a pretty confident guy, but being called up for this particular task seems… "You do know what my powers are, right?"

"Yes." They smirk at me. "You're like a soft-focus version of our Glowstick, except the lights are on all the time. When you're all worked up, you can make twinkly sparks happen. We don't want you *for* the team. The thing is that all these highly deadly mutants are… well, you'll see. We need someone who can keep everyone calm."

"You're a glorified babysitter," Alyse chips in. "Except they're all grown women, and if any of them throw a tantrum, it'll be unpleasant."

Whoa. Seriously? I'm meant to be like a team manager or coach or something? I realise these are all inside thoughts, and

I'm smart enough to keep my mouth closed around them. I'm not just a scarred and glowing pretty face.

"Cool. A likeable babysitter." I use the smile again. There are definitely worse jobs.

"I'd use Lys here, but I need her to keep me in line," Dylan says. "She keeps our team sane and together, so we need another one of her for these messy hoes."

I shoot another glance at the self-possessed woman leaning against the wall. "Those are big shoes to fill." I'm not sucking up in the least. Everyone knows Moodring.

"You've got big feet," Dylan says, completely deadpan.

"I'm flattered." I shrug broad shoulders. I'm usually pretty relaxed and try to be a bit of sunshine in a world with too many dark clouds, but I have to repress a shiver. This is deep and dark water I'm paddling in, an ocean with currents I don't understand and— "But I'm not sure if I'm really the right person for the job."

Dylan leans across the desk and this time there are thorns in their smile. "That's not the answer I'm looking for."

Alyse shakes her head a tiny bit. "Dills, be nice. There's no pressure on you to decide right away, Twinkles. Why not meet the team and ask questions? You can walk away if any of this feels weird or wrong. It's important that you actually like the people you work with. That's how all this operates."

Okay, *fine*. Let's not get the deadly mutant alien mad at me. And besides, how bad can it really be? All I'll be doing is keeping an eye on assassins, like holding their hair back when they puke, not holding their knives while they stab people. "I'd love to meet the team, bro."

"Sure, fuck it." Dylan hisses air through his teeth then drags her feet off the desk. They land on the ground with a defeated thump. "There's no guarantee they'll like him anyway. Come on, Twinkles. Let's walk and talk." They arch one eyebrow at me. *"Bro."*

Alyse pushes against one of the panels in the wall beside her. It swings open, revealing a dimly lit passageway that leads deeper into the building. Many of the buildings on Mutopia were grown by the island, or the world-spirit that grew and sustains it. There are a lot of rumours around exactly *what* this spirit is—a mutant? An alien? Something else?—but I've seen enough to know that the island is alive in some way. From outside, the government building looks like an enormous tree, with the offices studded around the inside of the trunk. Wherever we're headed, it's into the heart.

"How much do you know about the Cute Mutants?" Dylan asks, shooting a glance over her shoulder.

This has got to be a trick question, but I can't find the trick, so I answer straight up. "Your team, right? Saved the world from Michael and negotiated peace with the humans."

"Sounds like us." Dylan sighs. "We're sort of… semi-retired now, I guess. Most of our time is actually spent here on Mutopia, keeping things going, but there's still shit that needs dealing with. There's also Weapon UwU who are, like, the ones who deal with inexplicable or complicated shit."

"Glowstick's team," I say.

Dylan looks over his shoulder with a look of undisguised delight. "Yes, exactly, Glowstick's team. I think that's what we should call them instead, Lys."

Alyse reaches out and nudges her friend. It's cute seeing these two larger than life figures so comfortable and *ordinary* together. All the stories are about them as heroes, but in the end, they're ordinary people—maybe not in the literal sense, but they've got hopes and dreams and fears like anyone. No matter what, everyone wants to be liked—to have a connection, have someone take them seriously, tell them shit's going to be okay.

Maybe that's my new job, and if so, that's pretty cool.

We reach the end of the corridor, and Dylan shoves open another door. There's another figure inside, sitting at a desk with headphones on. She's draped in flowers and far more feminine. As we enter, she simply raises an eyebrow and places a finger to her lips. This is Marvellous, or Dani. The other half of Biome. Two lovers that got resurrected by an alien. Totally normal, dude. Don't stare.

"No, Feral. Witchy took care of it." Dani pauses. "What do you mean, you killed him again?"

"Just in case, probably." Dylan reaches out a hand to touch Dani's shoulder.

Dani covers the microphone with one hand. "How did you know she'd say that?"

"A hunch. They really killed someone twice?"

"I'm surprised it's not three times." Dani removes her hand from the microphone. "No, Goats. You don't need to go in there too. Fuck. Why do I even bother?"

"Maybe they'll all have a turn killing him." Dylan leans against the wall. "Orient Express style."

"Killing who?" I hope my voice isn't shaking. They said *dangerous*, but we're at peace now, right?

"Target. He's a bad man, don't worry." Their pupils expand, like petals opening, drowning their eyes in darkness.

I'm not sure why I say this next thing. It's not something that I'm even aware of bubbling in my mind. Sometimes my mouth moves on its own, as if there's another part of me hidden away thinking completely different things. "It's still murder."

Any warmth I felt from Dylan evaporates. Thorns poke out

from the pale green skin of their throat, and extend along her jawline. "I could justify our actions to you, Twinkletoes, but that's not why we're here. These people are risking their lives and doing some ugly shit. They deserve someone looking out for them. Unless your hands are too soft and glowing to take care of the monsters under the bed?"

It's true that I'm good with people, like they already said in this bizarre conversation that's supposed to be a job interview. But this thorny, dark-eyed figure in front of me is something else—some mix of monster and weapon and god, with a person underneath it all. They're still fighting a war. I'm not sure if I want to get involved in all that, because it seems like a *lot*, quite frankly. At the same time, there's one thing I believe more than anything else.

"Everyone deserves someone." I hold Dylan's gaze, my mouth frozen in a half-smile. I had a good childhood, which a lot of people can't say. Things were happy until I ended up in the big city, working a big-city job and eventually running into a rainbow mutant who *changed me*. That was the end of the good times, I suppose, although it wasn't the fault of the mutation. It was the mad scientists who captured me and locked me in an underground medical facility.

They were searching for a cure.

That part of my life wasn't so good, and that's an understatement. I don't like complaining, but it's true. It was long and lonely and the other parts were horrible things I try to block out. What I did come out with, aside from the scars, was the knowledge that people are important. Connection is the thing that makes life worthwhile. So this is an opportunity to build more, to be that for other people. It's the only thing that really matters.

I smile wider. "I'd like to meet this team."

Dylan pushes themself off the wall, a smile streaking across their lips like a shooting star. "Good. You skip the shallow grave portion of the interview."

"They're joking." Alyse reaches out and touches my shoulder. "Dills, you're being unsettling."

"The world is fucking unsettling." The corner of their mouth tugs upwards. "If Twinkles can't deal with me, how's he going to handle the girls? Speaking of—are they all wrapped up yet?"

"They're burning it down." Dani laughs. "And arguing about how much accelerant to use. Should've sent Dragon in."

"She's busy." Dylan closes his eyes and sighs. "Too much going on. Makes me antsy. I've got a bad feeling etcetera."

"You've always got a bad feeling." Vines stretch their way from Dani's fingertips, snaking across the ground and wrapping tightly around Dylan's wrist. "Oh, look. Here they come."

The first person to appear in the room is tall and lanky, with brown skin and golden eyes. She's got silky fur running down her arms. around her throat, and atop her head, where cat ears poke up from among it.

"Mission accomplished." She bares wickedly sharp teeth at us and then hurls herself at Dylan. For a moment, I think she's attacking them, but it appears to be a hug.

"You okay?" Dylan's demeanour is so utterly changed, I'd think I'd imagined the tension in our previous conversation. They scratch lightly at the fur at the back of the girl's neck and then spin her around.

"Feral, meet Twinkle Lights."

"Oh, the pretty boy. Charmed, I'm sure." She moves over to me in fluid, easy steps and extends one hand that ends in very sharp claws.

I give her the smile on full blast, and her pupils widen slightly. "Pleased to meet you."

More figures pop into the room, one after the other.

"Witchmade." A fat girl with deep brown skin, covered in intricate symbols of tattoos. Smoke drifts around her like a cloak, and a snake uncurls from her shoulders to hiss lazily at me.

"Penance." A woman not much over five feet tall, with dark curls.

"Nails." Someone in a large coat, with a scarf wrapped around the lower half of their face, so only dark eyes and a tangle of curls are visible. Their hands are large and mottled grey.

"And Goat Bitch." She stands tall on hooves, with large horns of bone jutting from her temples and wide yellow eyes with rectangular pupils.

All of them stare at me like I'm the most fascinating thing they've ever seen. It's flattering, but I'm not *that* hot, and I'm sure they've seen scars before.

"Hi, everyone." I smile as wide as I possibly can. I remind myself that people do like me, most of them. I've only met one person who makes disconcerting threats about shallow graves. I step forward, despite the way these others are looking at me, like I might be one of their targets who ends up getting accidentally killed two extra times. "It's nice to meet you. Let's go do something fun."

CHAPTER 3
GOAT BITCH

THEN - THE DARK YEAR

Does this piece fit here? I'm not entirely sure it does, but narrative time is complicated. Events are happening, have happened, will happen. Everyone has their own arc, and some of them fit together, threads sewn together into a tapestry if you look at it in the right light and see all the interweavings. Right now, my eyes are bloodshot and I'm exhausted. Let's see where this goes and figure it all out later. There's a woman and she's lost. That's really all you need to know. Things might get dire, but they do that around here.

I'M ABOUT five miles out from safety when everything gets all fucked up. I've been too busy staring at the pulsing dot on my phone. It's a piece of shit I found in some dumpsite, running firmware too ancient to be fully co-opted. There's a small baggie of blood taped to the back of it with a cross of yarrow wood. It sounds like fucking witchcraft, but I haven't been hacked yet so maybe it does count for something. I heard about it on one of those pirate websites that only pops online for five minutes at a time at odd hours of the day. Good information is hard to find. You have to trust random bits of marker scrawl on broken shopfronts or stitched in red thread on the inside of makeshift shelters.

You have to be desperate.

The same kind of desperation you feel when you hear a noise that shouldn't be there. I've got the bulky block of the phone clutched in one hand. The tips of my fingers protruding from my fingerless gloves are numb, but they work when I poke at the screen to keep it alive.

There's that fucking noise again. Something scraping. It's too rhythmic. There shouldn't be much out here. The nanotech swarm has taken everything useful, so all that's left are slumped ruins arranged in rough grid patterns. Even the roads have been torn up, leaving lines scored in the earth.

The only light comes from the moon. It's too fat and bright. I much prefer full dark. I have some advantages there.

The safety dot pulses again. I'm not going to make it. I shove the phone into my pocket. It's too important to lose.

I pull my jacket more tightly around myself. It was heavy to start with, and I've stitched ragged squares of thin plastic sheeting between the layers. It makes for the sort of shitty armour you start off with in the world's worst RPG. I'm out of weapons though, ever since what used to be Atlanta.

I'll have to make do with me.

"Help!" It's a male voice, coming from behind me. Whoever's been fucking scraping. "Please!"

It's an obvious fake. Nobody who knows anything about the Wastes would greet anyone like that. There are codes and countersigns. The only bright side in all this is that these predators are clumsy. The really dangerous ones know everything I do, and probably more.

My peripheral vision is better than most, enough to see them coming. There are five of them. Three have blades, big heavy things. Two hold lights that they swing in crooked arcs. They wobble around, catching me and darting away, like they're not *really* hunting me.

I walk faster. I turn a corner, but it's way too open.

"Fuck." Someone's impatient. "Just get him."

I could run. I'm nimble, and I'm fast over short distances. But there are five of them, and no good places to hide, and safety is a few miles away.

Besides, I'm also pissed off.

I turn and wait for the lights to hit me.

They see my hooves and my horns. They're not close enough to see the fury in my unnatural eyes.

Sometimes I dream about what it would have been like to become a mutant earlier. To fight with Chatterbox and Marvellous, or even be taken somewhere safe. One of their havens.

Instead, I got jabbed with fake meds in some clinic on the outskirts of Portland. I still have no idea *why* they did it. Some leftover experiment. A last ditch mutant rebellion. Now Goddess is in hiding, and most of the humans retreat into vast glowing cities where they're protected by Michael. Apparently it's different in other parts of the world, but I haven't seen that shit. Some people say that plenty of cities are totally fine, but they're not fine at all, not fucking *really*. They may not be the giant nano cities, but it comes down to a choice between Michael and the Wastes.

The second is where you find people who don't fit, or can't pay, or refuse to believe. Or all three like me. Out here looking for safety, with all the predators taking it away.

"The fuck are you? Some kind of mutie goat-man?"

It's impossible to make out anything in the glare of the lights.

"I'm not a man." I hate how my voice comes out. Too whiny, too nasal.

In the light, they'll see the shadow at my jaw. The clumsily applied lipstick and eyeshadow. It's hard to find a decent razor out here, and there's no chance at all of finding any fucking meds. Before the world went to shit, I read a lot about transition. Now, all I can do is stand as I am.

"Oh, I'm so sorry." The voice is not sorry. I'd love to shove my fucking hoof through this asshole's sarcastic throat. "Some kind of mutie goat-*bitch*."

I don't know what these people want. They're too sloppy to be one of Michael's hit squads. They might be shitty bounty hunters, trying to scrape enough money together to get into a city. Maybe they're live free types, some half-cult assholes with a plot of land and worshippers.

Honestly, I don't fucking care.

My luck's run out, so it's just me and my horns and my hooves.

I run for them. Over short distances, I'm fast, and they don't expect it. I reach into my coat pocket, and pull out a chunk of rock. I wing it at the first light as hard as I can.

I miss the light, but I hit the asshole holding it.

The light swings wildly, and dazzles the others. Good enough for me. I run into the other person holding the light. A glimpse of a face, shadowed by a heavy hood. Pale skin, patchy beard, startled eyes. Our bodies collide. It's jarring, but satisfaction comes with the meeting of bone and flesh. He falls backwards but my horns still catch him, scoring a ragged line along the side of his neck.

Blood wells, and he screams. I've missed anything fundamental.

He'd be fine if he wasn't falling to the ground.

If I wasn't driving my left hoof down into his Adam's apple.

I should be running, because there are three men with blades. But I'm angry and it feels *good* to fight instead of hide. I've still got one hoof stuck through his neck, but I kick my right leg out behind me.

I hit someone, and spin around to see. My leg comes out of the dead man's neck with a wet sound that's a little too visceral, even for me. The other light is still projecting my silhouette across the ground. My horns look like twin blades, raised in defiance.

It makes me smile. My mouth is ugly, filled with long blunt teeth. I smile anyway. I lower my head slightly. On anyone else, it might look like a bow, or capitulation. On me, it's a threat.

Perhaps a pointless threat. All the other fights I've had have been short and vicious one-on-one affairs. Still. I've fought my way here, as mismatched and incomplete and fucked by fate as I am.

I'm not about to lie down and die.

The first man comes at me swinging. I step in to meet him. The blow hits my coat and the makeshift armour underneath it. It doesn't cut me, but it still knocks me sideways. I lash out with my head, one horn catching my attacker right in his armpit. It grinds against bone.

I reach for the hand that holds the weapon. My side aches, and I'm off-balance, half stuck.

Something else hits from the other side. My horn tears loose, and the man screams. I'm off balance. Even my nimble goat hooves can't keep me up.

I hit the ground, kick out wildly. Scramble away, lashing out behind me. One hoof hits a man's ankle. I hear the bone break, and there's another scream.

"Fucking mutie bitch." The man howls. "He was supposed to be easy prey."

I'll be damned if I go out misgendered as the last fucking thing in my life. "I'm not a man." One horn is wet with blood. It hurts to breathe.

"Kill him, or her, or whatever the fuck it is." I don't know who says it, but someone's looming over me. I can see the blade, raised.

I've stayed alive this far, out in the Wastes, by cunning and stubbornness and the kindness of other lost people like me. It was inevitable my luck would run out eventually. Everyone's does out here. Even the Goddess hides.

It's only stubbornness that leads me to try and scramble away.

But the blade never falls.

The man does instead. He hits the ground beside me. Three long black shards protrude from his face.

That's not me. I lever myself up on my elbows and look around.

None of my attackers are standing. Even the one whose leg I broke lies dead. Another black shard sticks out of his neck, dripping blood onto the hard-packed dirt.

The light lies discarded, shining on empty space. A pair of legs move into it.

"Greetings and salutations," a muffled voice says. "On this night of fucking nights."

I struggle into a sitting position. "It's a long and shitty road that brings nobody any good."

The figure moves completely into the light, not that it helps. They're all wrapped up in a coat and scarf and goggles. A few dark curls escape their hood, but that's the only sign there's a person in there at all. "You the one that sent the ping?" They hold out their phone. Their hand is wrapped in something that makes it grey and bulbous. On the screen, a complicated symbol rotates.

"Yeah." I fumble for my own device. Swipe the pulsing dot away, load up the Traveler app. It stores my chain—validation from others in the Wastes, their assertion that I'm trustworthy. A symbol appears on the screen. I hold out my phone.

The figure shuffles closer and we bump devices.

It takes a long few seconds for it to process. The safe internet isn't fast or reliable, but the important part is in the name. Finally, both flash green.

"Lucky you. Getting to live and shit." The figure tilts their gaze down towards me.

I stare into the reflective surface of the goggles. "Was this you?"

"You mean saving your ass from these dumbfucks? I don't see anyone else around here. I mean, I woulda done it anyway, so don't get too carried away with your gratitude." Theye extend a hand. "They call me Nails. On account of how I can shoot 'em. People aren't super fuckin' imaginative with mutant names, are they?"

I take the offered hand and get to my feet. They're shorter than I thought, although I am unnaturally tall. "Thank you."

"And what do they call you?"

I've never taken a mutant name before. I've been too protective of the one I took when I came out as a woman. But here I'm about to walk into a mutant refuge, one of the few places of safety remaining in the world. I need to change again.

"Goat Bitch is as good a name as any."

Nails makes an incomprehensible noise behind their scarf.

"Fuckin' beautiful. Well, Goat Bitch, come with me and I'll take you to the promised land."

"Is it safe?" I ask.

"Safe's one of those relative things. But yeah, should be. Plus it's warm and it's got food, so huzzah for all of us." The goggles tilt in my direction again. "The app gave you a thumbs up, but you'll still need to be quarantined."

I swallow nervousness. "Quarantined?"

"Make sure you're not carrying any shit, give you a chance to be checked out. Mostly it's just sitting in a room on your own."

"That's fine." I shoulder my pack and swipe up the navigation app on my phone. The dot is still blinking. Safety's worth pretty much anything these days. "I'm used to being alone."

CHAPTER 4
HENCH

RECENTLY

Oh, and here we find another fragment. When you see all the stories, laid out together, there's an order and a pattern. Right now, it's jumbled. I can't see my way clear. It's all so confusing. But there's a job to be done. A loose thread, from long ago, to be tied into a new tapestry.

THIS GODDAMN JOB. The scientist promised. Said it'd change my life. Here I am, half-wound down. Bits of engine sticking out of me. Fucking cables everywhere. I jiggle the connection and it sparks. I grit my teeth through the pain.

"Were the keys that bad?" I poke at the hole in my elbow. "Dumb fuckin' Hench."

The radio crackles and spits. Volume's way down. It's like hearing ghosts. Knocked it. Damn wound down body. It always breaks on me.

I ignore it. Fumble the cables some more. Jam them tight.

Every point hurts. Damn scientist. Fucking promised. I glare at the switch. The box cinched tight around my waist.

Here goes. Grit my teeth. Hit the switch.

My head swims. My body is flooded with energy. The pain flaring in my joints sparks brighter, then falls away in ebbing waves. It feels good to move freely again. You'd think I'd be used to the way my energy collapses on me like this, but it's a pain in the ass every time.

"And now for the boss." I sigh, and spin the radio dial.

"—stand what's going *on* there? Answer me, you incompetent—"

"Speaking of incompetence," I drawl. "Your system's still flaky as hell. Took me multiple attempts to get any juice, and the connections short out half the time. Should've left me my fucking keys."

"Your mutation." I can hear how pissed she is even through the crackle and distance. The woman's impossible, but she's smart and pays well. "That infernal internal clockwork of yours resists any outward tampering. I'm convinced of it. I'll continue to work on the problem. You're not there to test-run my system though, are you?"

I scowl at the radio as if she can see it. I'm only wired to her damn recharge-box because she *insisted* on it. But the mission's what I'm paid for. "Approaching the coordinates now."

"And the readings are as constant as they appear?"

I don't know why she has to ask. She can see the readouts as well as me. The lag is only a second or two. It's like she wants her snippy little voice cutting at my ears every second, reminding me I work for her.

"Steady as an extremely steady thing." I smirk at my own joke.

"Tiresome." I hear the scoff loud and clear. "And your strength levels?"

"As long as your system holds up, I'm strong enough." That's a big fucking question, based on the evidence I've got, but it'll have to do the damn job, won't it?

"Yes, well we don't know exactly what the creature is *made of*. We are in the territory of unknown unknowns."

I'm seconds from crushing the speaker in my bare hands, but she'll only send another via drone. I'd get some peace though. It might be worth it. But the instruments start beeping, and I switch focus to manoeuvre the boat into position.

Once we're floating above our target coordinates, I get to my feet. I cross to the hatch and leap up the ladder in a single bound. On deck, I stretch and look around. There's nothing but ocean to be seen for miles around, great grey-blue swells of it.

There's a line of huge metal crates welded to the deck. I cross to the nearest one and pull the front off it.

"Strong enough," I murmur.

A drone floats up over the edge of the ship and hovers at my shoulder. One face of it has a low-res screen. The scientist isn't much more than a collection of grey pixels, a blank and insectile mask.

I give the screen a wave, but there's no reaction. The boss isn't much for fraternisation, or much beyond giving orders and expecting them to be obeyed. I toss the cover of the metal cage aside with a clang, and pull out the underwater camera. It's connected to a heavy chain, and all together it weighs enough that I actually feel it.

I shrug and toss it backwards over my shoulder into the ocean.

"Gently!" The drone buzzes in my ear.

I ignore it and plug the other end of the camera into the

tablet. A few seconds later, we're staring at featureless darkness.

"Hard to know if it's working." I tap the screen.

"It is. Stop touching the equipment."

With the tiniest fraction of pressure, I could crumble this tablet into a ball and then I could hurl it into the atmosphere. My real mutant power is that I refrain.

Instead, I watch the camera. Occasionally, the darkness on the screen shimmers, but otherwise the only change is numbers ticking up.

"Deep." I can't help myself.

"If you must say inane things, please do it on your own time."

I imagine taking the drone and frisbeeing it through the hull of the ship from one side to the other. It'd be worth sinking just to piss her off. I'm honestly tempted, but that's when the tablet screen finally changes.

Something's glowing, way way down there. Bluish-white. Even at this distance, it shows up as a perfect circle.

"Yes." For once, the scientist's voice holds something more than correction. "It's here. I was right."

"Course you were, boss lady." I cross to the next metal cage and tear it open as easily. Probably should be saving my strength, but when I feel this good, it's hard not to *revel* in it. Inside there's a big dive suit that must weigh a thousand pounds, but I slip it on as easily as a summer dress.

I clank back to the railing. The glowing shape has expanded to fill most of the available screen. It's really down there. There's no point waiting for the order. I simply leap over the side.

It takes a long time to descend. I keep the camera cable within arm's length. Wouldn't want to drift off in some current and have to walk for miles over the ocean floor, even jacked up with super strength.

At least it's peaceful down here. No scientist yapping in my ear.

The target first shows up below me like a single star in endless blackness. Then it grows and continues to grow. It's around the size of one of those little Japanese hatchbacks, except perfectly spherical. The light from it is mostly white, fractionally touched with blue, and makes the suit shine.

My feet touch on the ocean floor. I'm standing beside the *aberration,* bathed in its radiance. That's the word the scientist uses in all the notes and files. What it all boils down to is alien. It shouldn't be here. Nothing like this exists on earth, aside from bizarre trace readings that the scientist scrawls notes over like

What if this wasn't the only one?

Infestation??

I'm not here for any theories. I don't know what the fucking thing is. If someone demanded an opinion, I'd admit I don't think it's an alien spacecraft. There's weird shit under the sea. Probably some kind of creepy crawly thing.

Which makes me the unluckiest bitch in town, cos I'm here to pick up this undersea unknown and tote the fucking thing back to the surface. This is why I'm here, because I'm one of the few people who can do this alone. To keep the circle as small as possible. Just me and the permanently masked and suited figure of the scientist. Two people with a secret.

There's a pretty good chance she'll try and kill me after this. It'll save her money, too. The upside for me is that I'm pretty hard to get rid of. I'll have to be ready. Can't be reliant on her damn flaky recharge mechanism. Got to rely on myself. That's what's always worked.

It takes almost half an hour to prepare for the ascent. There's a whole network of straps wrapped around the *aberration* and connected to my suit. I'm carrying a giant glowing ball on my back, hauling my way back up a cable thousands of feet to the surface.

This is the sort of shitty job having super strength gets you.

The first few thousand feet are fine. I don't really notice the effort. Concentrate on moving hand over hand. The feeling of the aberration shifting slightly on my back. It doesn't feel heavy at all.

At about the halfway mark I'm noticing it. A general *oh shit I'm getting tired*. The power reservoir in my body is dipping. Should've brought my fucking keys, but the scientist doesn't let me. Always wants to do it her way. Wants to control me. Keep me dependent. Only way to recharge my strength. I muscle through it. Now I can feel the weight of it. It wants to drag me down.

I'm still strong. I could tear a ship apart with my bare hands.

Focus on the movement. Hand over hand, up through the dark.

I zone out. Lost in the motions. Stupid fuckin' Hench. A mess of wound up muscle. Hand over hand. Up through the dark.

I stop looking. The numbers don't matter. Only the surface.

It's goddamn heavy.

Fucking stupid aberration.

Fucking alien thing.

Keep moving. Hand over hand.

Stupid Hench.

There, above me. Light.

Surface.

Deck hot. Wet. Light. Too much. Sphere. Aberration. Science. Bitch.

Dragging. Stairs. Fall.

Fuck. Fuck. Plug. Fuck. Switch.

Pain. So—

I blink gummy eyes. That was too close. I have energy flooding through me again, and it brings rage with it.

I bound up to the deck, taking the stairs in a single bound. The scientist is here. Droned herself in somehow while I was drained of energy. Willing to show her real physical form now that I've succeeded in digging up her mystery. The dripping thing from the ocean glows ghostly white-blue even in the daylight. She doesn't even turn when I enter, too preoccupied with her devices.

Her suit creaks when I take hold of it. My fingers leave indentations.

"Remove your hand." Her voice shakes, despite the command.

"How long were you going to leave me like that?" I fight the urge to tear her suit apart and spill her insides across the deck.

"Until you were necessary again." She's already turning back to the aberration, head lowering to the devices.

"I am not a *machine*." My voice shakes worse than hers.

"Oh, my dear. That is precisely what you are. Your mutation changed you into one, whether you like it or not. Without power, you cannot function. How else would you term yourself?"

"I go nowhere without my keys." My hand squeezes tighter and the suit crumples. "Ever again."

"Enough with the dramatics. We have work to do. Vitally important work. Now please plot a course back towards the facility. You will find payment in your account tomorrow. This is only the next step in the plan."

I have power. I have payment. That's why I'm here.

The scientist is a means to an end. Can't forget that.

I release the hold on the woman's suit, and stalk back towards the cabin.

I am not a machine.

CHAPTER 5
EVA

This doesn't fit here. It's older. The past. This happened before. When everything was wrong, and the story was lost. In the dark time.

THE PROBLEM with dealing with witless fools is obvious from the terminology. They love to give commands, with little to no understanding of the implications. These men have attained leadership based on little more than their sex and feigned adherence to their strict religious code. Pity us all, for we are engaged in a fight against an enemy far more cunning and relentless than they can possibly understand.

"Evil must be vanquished." The man puffs his cheeks and glares at me.

I am forced to bite the inside of my cheek to stop the words escaping my lips. We do not fight evil. We are not so lucky. We fight evolution—a far more cunning and insidious foe. There is no prancing devil, cackling over some hellish cauldron, and pouring his malicious wrath out over humanity. It is simply blind chance, some fluke of cosmic energy, but if we are not careful humanity will be extinguished.

"Do you hear me, woman? I know you're one of them, but they say you're dedicated to the cause."

I bow my head inside my helmet, as if I've done wrong. "I serve humanity. The renegade extrahumans must be destroyed."

"All extrahumans." I cannot see him with my head bowed, but I imagine his lips stretching wider.

"Yes." I am useful to them until my work is done, and then I will be consigned to hellfire too. Not that I believe in hell, not in the least, but I shall be equally dead. "They shall be struck down."

I straighten. My helmet hisses and my suit vents steam at my neck and forearms. I'm obviously more bothered by this than I'd like. I hate to be associated with other mutants. To be reminded of what I am.

"Good. Their Goddess still hides, but there are others. We shall cut them down and perhaps draw her out."

"They scuttle in the Wastes." I extend my suit arm and clench my fist. "We shall find them and exterminate them."

The smile on the man's face is wider still. As if giving the orders matters more than the carrying out. "Yes. Now go, monstrous thing, and kill your vile kind."

I hurry from the room, feeling my body slosh inside its cage. This man means nothing. I will kill every crawling mutant on the face of the earth, and then I will come for them. And only when *that* is done, will I drag myself into the hottest desert I can find. There, I will open my suit and evaporate into the sky.

The door to the room hisses open and I step through into the corridor. Waiting for me is the one extrahuman I have time for. His name is Ian, but once they called him Ion Strike, before he was recruited by Quietus as a double agent.

He is the sole weakness I allow myself. I should not need him, but I crave the way he looks at me. He sees through the blank face of the mask, and past the hissing mechanics of my suit. Under his gaze, I am not water in the shape of a woman, but the true article.

"Eva." His voice is soft. He takes my right arm in his hands, and rotates it slightly so he can see the readouts that run up the inside. "It was frustrating in there?"

"No different to any other time." I try to speak more gently, but the synthesiser in the suit makes every word harsh. "They are fools, but well-connected. Their intelligence comes directly from Michael, and speaks of extrahuman gangs roaming the Wastes, striking at civilian targets."

"Then we must punish them." His eyes remain intently on me.

I shiver. We have kissed once only, my body drenching him as he tried to hold my deliquescing form. I think of it often. A single spark travelling through me, touching every molecule and setting me alight.

"Yes." The temperature on my suit ticks up two-tenths of a degree. I warm as he looks at me. Not in frustration this time. "We shall show them they have no place here."

We travel via tube to the outskirts of the city. There is nobody else in the bubble with us. Neither of us speak as we are carried through the air, passing between the vast guard statues at the perimeter. Ian covers my suit hand with his, as if to reassure me.

The reassurance is unnecessary, but I like the comfort.

I became an extrahuman with full understanding of what I was doing. It was clear to me that war was coming, and we needed weapons on our side too. I was changed by a madman called Spark who had the ability to warp the DNA of humans. He was a monster barely kept on a leash by Eli Crane, and before he was killed by the mutant rights fanatic Chatterbox, I was one his last creations.

I allowed myself to be changed in order to become a better weapon, one of the sharpest and most deadly that humanity has in their desperate fight. This is how we safeguard the future. One dead mutant at a time. I only wish I'd been the one to kill Chatterbox. I think I'd have enjoyed that. Perhaps I'll have to settle for her sword. Rumour says it still hunts in her name.

The tube comes to a halt, jolting me from my thoughts. The door irises open and we disembark. This is the very edge of the city, where tall fence posts rise into the sky, light arcing between them.

I hold up my right wrist and let the scanners read the DNA code embedded in my suit. Ian does the same, and for a few moments the nearest section of fence ceases its pulsing.

We cross through and into the Wastes.

No extrahuman is foolish enough to come this close to a city. The Michael AI would detect it and strike them down immediately. No, the mutants lurk around, disrupting supply chains and terrorising the satellite cities, where hopeful penitents wait to be granted access to the city. That is where we'll find them. All of what is still nominally called the United States of America is under Michael's sway. Some ruined, wretched parts of it are more contested than others.

"This is necessary work," Ian says, as if I need the reminder. I let it pass unchallenged. He is weaker than me. He doesn't understand. To him, it's another war, or a bigotry like any other. Yet a handful of them could have taken over our country. They perched a dragon on top of the White House and stepped into the Oval Office as if it was their living room. We exist on their sufferance, until the time they choose to suffer us no longer. Exterminating them is a necessary evil.

I know that what I do is evil.

"It is necessary," I echo, and we continue on into the Wastes.

The city still glows behind us when my suit alerts me to something moving ahead of us. Something human-hot, or close enough. The cameras are confused by it, because it has too many limbs. The rudimentary AI in the suit cannot identify it.

Human. Kangaroo. Centipede.

"Monster," I whisper.

The creature remains a constant distance from us. Monitoring us, probably. It doesn't know what we're doing out here, and it's cautious. Or else it's hunting. That would be ironic.

The suit continues to track it. The new features are working well. We continue to follow it on a path that angles away from the city. The AI has flagged up possible settlements, and our prey is leading us away from them. Either to protect them from us, or to ensure their attack is not witnessed. More irony, but I find no humour in it.

The thing ceases moving. The suit cannot detect anything in the area around it. A dead spot, or an ambush? It remains stationary as we approach. It is very dark out here, impossible for human eyes to see anything, but the suit can make out the shape of it.

Broken person, the suit's AI tells me. *Creature. Mutant.*

"Good girl," I say. "You got there in the end."

"Blessings of the Night to you," the mutant calls. "And the darkness waits."

Out here in the Wastes, such things are common. Primitive methods of proving one's allegiance and identity. I could possibly ask the suit AI to infiltrate their networks and discover the countersign, but there is little point now.

"Where?" Ian murmurs.

"Use your wicked power, my love."

The suit has learned enough to compensate for him preemptively. Ian opens his right hand and an enormous flash erupts from his palm. Sheet lightning. It illuminates everything around us, as if day briefly dawned and thought better of it.

In its violent light, he sees me, and he sees the target.

He extends his left hand. A bolt of lightning erupts from his index finger. It describes a crooked arc in the air and descends to the ground like a burning hammer.

Ion Strike.

The suit records it all. It's already over, but I can play it back. The moment the mutant is struck down. The charred flesh. The explosion.

I toggle the light on in my suit and we walk slowly over to where it once stood. The only evidence is a blackened patch of ground, as if a star fell to earth and burst on impact.

I allow myself to feel some satisfaction, but my suit registers another figure approaching unnaturally fast from the east. I swing my suit light up and catch sight of something scurrying along in leaps and bounds.

The suit AI tracks it and when it leaps for me, my arm swings up involuntarily and catches the attacker by the throat. In the orange light from the suit, I can see she's young. Maybe only seventeen. Her hands batter at the metal of my suit, but it's been made to withstand a lot more than the flailing of some long-legged, floppy-eared mutant.

"What are you doing out here?" I ask.

"You *killed* him. We were out here trying to *help you*, and you—"

"Hush." I squeeze her neck until she obeys, face red and cheeks streaked with tears. "I have nothing to say to you. No apology and no justification."

"What's your power?" Ian asks her.

"It doesn't matter." The voice buzzes harsh from my suit speaker. The temperature gauge bleats a warning and steam vents along my forearms. "They are broken and all they will do is make more of themselves."

"She's only—"

"She's old enough to make more."

Months ago, we found a twelve year old and Ian refused to do what was necessary. I pretended to acquiesce and went back later to suffocate her while she slept in her ragged little tent. It gave me no joy to leave her still body behind in the night. I do not do this work for my own pleasure.

He thinks this is an ordinary war, and that there are rules of conduct.

We fight evolution. We fight the planet. I will not let humanity go extinct.

Ian is silent. His broad shoulders are slumped.

"Will you do it?" I ask.

The girl thrashes. Her limbs batter at me, and her long legs scrabble on the ground. The suit is far stronger than she is.

Ian places a single finger to the middle of the mutant girl's forehead. There are tears in his long lashes. He is beautiful, and he is weak, but this time will do what is necessary.

For me.

CHAPTER 6
PENANCE

ELSEWHEN

We know this character, don't we? She fits in another story, but for some reason she's stuck in this one. Sometimes that happens, especially when people start tinkering with things they shouldn't. There are things that should be left alone. Time is one of them. Narrative is another. But someone didn't listen, and now everything's a mess. I'm trying to make sense of it, but it's difficult, okay? Give me some time.

THE WORLD HAS SHIFTED around us, and it disorients me. I should be accustomed to this. I am used to scuttling through the folds in the world, sidling through cracks and following the threads that bind places. This is abrupt and different, like having a door slammed shut in your face.

Even worse, all the threads leading away from this place are knotted into a convoluted tangle. I consider extending myself down one as an experiment, but my sister is here and she must be protected.

We are *gone*. This is not our home, not even our *world*.

Everything has changed, and I cannot understand it.

"Marisol," I whisper.

The place where we have washed up is deserted, an expanse of rough stone like a car park where the lines have worn away. I remember a vast room, with an enormous ring at one end. How did we get there? What were we doing? Why can I not remember?

We are trapped in this place, and it is nowhere I understand.

Feral turns in a slow circle. "Something's fucked." She seems remarkably cheerful about it.

"I don't remember." I unroll my fingers into blades. At least that works. We are protected.

There is someone else with us. A huge woman, taller even than Feral, and well-muscled. Her hair is long and braided with rings. Metal objects dangle from them. I don't recognise her. Should I?

"You two." Her voice is low. She pauses, like she has to catch her breath. "Attacked us?'

"If I attacked you, there was a reason." The fur at Feral's neck fluffs up. "Which means I should probably do it again."

I twitch the blades on my hands one by one. The other woman watches me.

"Truce." She holds up her hands. "Don't remember shit."

"I don't like not remembering." Feral flexes her claws. Both of us are posturing, but it works. The woman backs another few steps away.

I'm still disoriented. Gaps in my memory. I haven't experienced this for a long time, not since my father died. My thoughts race, trying to connect lines. To make sense of this. Something is *wrong*. There is a break, a rupture, and I cannot connect it.

"Truce," I agree.

"Nah, fuck it." Feral bares her teeth. "I think the two of us can take you anyway."

The other woman says nothing. She's still breathing hard, like she sprinted here.

The worst thing is being apart from *them*. Wherever I am, even when I twist myself into a pretzel-creature, suspended in corners where universes nudge against each other, I always orient myself to the two of them. Dylan and Dani. Twin lights in my dark sky. My tethers to stop me from losing myself in the infinite complexity of the universe. They are home. I love them, and it terrifies me. It's scarier to have lost them.

I want to scream.

"Are *you* okay, Penny?" Feral asks.

"No." My teeth chatter. It seems I've forgotten how to lie. "I'm scared. I can't find Deezer."

"We'll get back to them." She hooks a claw around my wrist and pulls me gently closer.

I allow myself to sink for a moment into her fur.

"First things first." Feral pulls away from me. "We kill this one here."

"Hold up." The tall woman pants. "You said. Truce?"

"Safest to kill you, though. It's called calculus or some shit."

"Mari." I try to weigh my voice with the sort of command Dylan uses, but it makes me miss them so much my head swims. What if I never see them again? That smile, that way they have of looking at you like you matter to them.

"Fuck, okay. Fine. I won't kill her." Feral's glaring through golden eyes as if she'd like to devour this woman right here.

"What's your name?" I refold myself back into human shape. No blades, no ghostly mask in the sky.

"Huh. Tiny thing." She reaches up with laboured movements and tugs at the metal objects in her hair. "So tired. You do?"

"Do what?" I walk closer to the woman. If she attacks, I can fold myself away, and I am accustomed to being one of the deadliest creatures around.

"Keys. Holes." The woman rotates her arm, as it requires great effort. There's a bloody slot in the back of her elbow. A metal object slips through her fingers and clatters to the ground.

I scoop it up and hold it in the palm of my hand. "It's a key."

"No shit." Feral yawns. "What? You think she's a wind-up girl? Hey, big sexy. Do you need to be wound up?"

The woman doesn't answer. Her eyes are closed. She slowly topples to the ground, mighty as a felled tree. We watch her fall.

"Big sexy?" I ask.

Feral shrugs. "It's a joke."

"Sure." I step closer, but the woman's still not moving. I kneel beside her and check the braids in her hair to find three other keys. "Roll her over, onto her stomach."

Feral crouches down, grumbling. "Don't know why we're wasting time with this. She's not one of ours, is she? Which means she's probably on the other team. We were on a mission, weren't we?"

"I don't remember." There's a set of wicked scratches at her throat. "Did you do this?"

Feral shrugs. "Don't remember. Bet she deserved it if I did."

I'm more interested in the fact that there are four of the bloody slots, one on the back of each limb. I poke at one gingerly. "Keys. Holes."

"Gross. Shit." Feral grins at me. "Let's bail. Winding up the villain seems like a terrible idea."

"We don't *know* she's a villain." I was a villain once, or a pawn of one, or something in between. Sometimes we find a way to get better. It hurts, and sometimes the shadows of things you've done lie thick and smothering, but you get to stand in the sunshine too.

"Fine. But if she attacks us, you can do the stabby stabby thing."

I poke the key into the first hole and grin up at Feral. "Yes, you can hide behind me if you need to."

Feral watches with interest as I begin to twist the key. Four complete rotations, and nothing happens.

"Maybe you need to do all four," she suggests.

I repeat the process, and as soon as I begin rotating the fourth key, the woman stirs. Her eyelids flutter, and she reaches for my hand.

Feral responds immediately, wrapping one claw around the woman's hand and tearing it away from mine. "Leave my sister alone."

"Don't fuck with my keys." The woman's other hand grabs Feral by the scruff of the neck and tosses her into the distance.

Shit. I unfold myself instantly, cradling her throat in an interlocking maze of blades. If she moves, she'll slit her own throat. Strength won't help her here.

She's smart enough to realise that. "What the hell are you?"

"Mutant, like you. We were *helping* you. There was no need to—"

"Nobody fucks with my keys," the woman growls.

"You weren't moving or speaking. You were basically dead. If we hadn't touched your keys you'd be a statue."

In the distance, I see something scampering very fast towards us.

"Huh. Whatever happened must have wound me down more'n I thought. Mind letting me go?"

"I don't think so." I let the edge of one finger press closer. Blood wells along her throat, and I watch her swallow. "Let Feral decide."

Feral sprints on all fours toward us at full speed, but pulls up short so she can saunter the last few metres casually, tail twitching behind her.

"Cliche." Her upper lip curls.

"What?" The woman tenses against me, and almost slices herself to ribbons.

"Big and strong, but not stopping to think."

"I thought you were messing with my keys. I'm sorry."

"There you go." I flex one hand away, leaving a single blade in front of her. "An apology. Is that enough, Mari?"

"No. I'd like you to poke her. Just a little. Snip off an earlobe or something."

"You little furry psycho." The woman's back to growling.

"Hey, you're the one who threw me. For miles." Feral grins. "I did land on all fours though. Cats do that." She raises one eyebrow and makes a purring noise in her throat. Is she flirting? "And I'm not that small. Not all of us can be giant muscular towers of flesh who have no idea how to play well with the other kitties."

I fold my last blade away and resume human form, standing between them just in case. It feels precarious.

"I'm Penance," I tell the woman. "And this is Feral."

"Lemme guess," Feral drawls. "You're Wind-Up."

"Hench."

Both of us stare.

"Hench as in Henchperson."

"Oh look. She's working for the villain, like we thought." Feral shoots a look in my direction. "Told you we should've killed her, Penny."

"It's a job." Hench hunches her shoulders. "Everyone works for someone."

"We don't." Feral narrows her eyes.

"We kinda do, Fairy."

"You mean we work for Chatterbox and Marvellous? Not really. It's more like—"

Hench is gaping at us. "You both work for Chatterbox? My boss—well, my current boss—she *hates* Chatterbox. Next best thing to the devil."

"Fuck's sake." Feral tips her head back and yowls at the sky. "*Now* can we kill her? She's a real proper enemy, she threw me halfway across the world, and she hates our Dilly."

I'm not sure how serious she is. Feral threatens to kill people on reflex but—

"I don't hate Chatterbox. That's the thing about henching. It's not about principle. It's about money."

"I'm starting to come around on the killing thing." I glare at Hench.

"Talk to me when you've been desperate." Her green eyes meet mine. "It has a way of sharpening your options."

I want to give her a lesson in desperation, to enmesh her in impossible choices. Wanting money is one thing, wanting a mind free of the subtle steering control is another. When your own thoughts cannot be trusted, it's a special kind of nightmare. I still cannot always trust myself. What kind of mirror am I and what do I reflect?

That's why I can't kill her. If she is a monster, she's a simple one. I am haunted by far more complicated fiends, and some have my own face.

I can't stay here either. I have to take action.

"Shall I try and find a way out?" I ask.

"And leave me here with this big hunk of clockwork?"

"I won't be long," I tell her, and scurry into the corners of the world.

I still cannot find them. I extend myself along every axis, pressing my bladed fingers at the blunt edges of this truncated world. My edges are bloody, but I cannot force my way through to the objects of my yearning.

I hate that word.

Everyone knows yearning is sexy, but it requires an arc. I merely dangle helplessly on a string, forever suspended as I emphasise the long in longing. I am an endlessly burning fuse, paused before the catharsis of explosion. Without resolution, yearning is an illness. It leaves me shivering and breathless, a fever that never breaks. And the worst part, the final twist of the knife in my aching, desperate heart—the only hands I wish to smooth damp strands of hair from my face? The only lips I wish pressed to my forehead?

Theirs, only ever theirs.

I flee my own thoughts, turning down invisible pathways, following ruptures in the world. One fractures as I enter, splintering into shards that sting.

This isn't supposed to happen.

I close my eyes against the pain.

When I open them again, I'm sitting at a table. In front of me is a plate of food, still steaming. Chicken, potatoes, vegetables. A family dinner of the sort I haven't had since—

Out of the corner of my eye, I see a figure sitting at the head of the table.

His hands are folded. His eyes are closed.

"In the Lord's name, Amen," he says.

I want to flee, but I don't know how. My hands are soft and pale, twitching against the pale silk of the tablecloth. My powers are gone, and my limbs are clumsy, skinny things.

My father unfolds his hands. His eyes open.

"Violet." His gaze lands on me with the force of a blow. "What have you done?"

No.

This cannot be true.

He cannot be here.

CHAPTER 7
TENTACLE PRINCESS
RECENTLY

Time has passed in vast drifts. A thread could so easily be lost, but here is tied again, as if it was planned this way. Orchestrated. From outside, it's easy to imagine a plan. To see it all as purposeful. Perhaps it is, or maybe it's a cosmic fluke. On such a large scale, it's hard to tell the difference. So now here we are. A floating facility of scientific endeavour, moored in international waters, and accountable to few laws. Threads weaving together.

I AM NOT ENTIRELY unaware through all these last millennia. I know when the last of my kind passes from this world. I taste the demise of the great serpent and, much later, his demon-spawning lover. I trace the rise of the worshippers and their mastery of so many things.

And, underneath it all, the monsters remain. They slip close to extinction, but something coaxes their tiny flame through the swell of all this time. My species could not survive, but theirs does.

I am the last of my people. The broken stub of a vast flowering of deific power. Not even a god. A thing that might have been one, if fed enough worship and blessed by the pyre of thousands of bodies.

The thought sickens me.

That is the main lesson my slumber has taught me. We are all monsters, or contain the seeds of monstrousness. My people fed on the humans with no regret, because we told ourselves we deserved their sacrifice. Mutants arose to defend against them, and put my people to the flames without regret or mercy. Then they were almost extinguished in turn by a resurgent humanity, fearing the power mutants held.

Now these two species exist in a new and fragile balance.

Someone will try to tip the scales. They always do.

It is better for me to remain silent. If I slumber at the bottom of the ocean and am not awoken, I cannot desecrate or demand worship or burn. It is safer for me to stay here and await another age. Perhaps something new will flower on this strangely fertile world. A species which allows a fractured remnant of an ancient faith to sit quietly and listen to the whispered turning of the planet.

This is what I wish for.

Yet now something taps on my cocoon, demanding entry.

This is unprecedented. I secreted myself in the ancient sleeping grounds of my ancestors, in the cavernous trenches where our infant young slept before they awoke and fed. Nothing should have been able to find me here, and it is the height of foolishness to attempt to rouse me.

It should be encoded in their ancestral memories, a fear of my kind being unleashed upon them again. Even if I am not capable of ascending to godhood, and not inclined towards revenge, fear should still their eager monkey fingers.

If there is one thing I have learned about humanity in my time of resting, it is that they often do not fear that which they should.

They soon cease their physical probing and attempt to flood me with energy. The taste is overwhelming. I undulate inside the cage I made for myself. I see the faces of my ancestors, their beaks yawning wide, their thousands of eyes reflecting the abyss, their great tentacles raised in fury. I look upon the great flow, now nothing more than a stagnant pool.

I contain myself with great effort.

It is inevitable they will breach the walls I have built, so I must make myself appear harmless. Something like them. I do not fully understand the senses they use to perceive the world, so I make my best guess.

By the end, I think I am smaller and greyer than I should be. It is impossible to smooth out all the wrinkles. I am certain my limbs are not the right size and shape, and I'm not sure there are even the correct number. Nevertheless, it is *close*. I am sure of that.

This may well be a terrible mistake. I may be extinguished. Far worse might happen. Yet I let my cocoon fall away.

I STAND REVEALED, for the first time in a great many revolutions around the star. There are a thousand tastes, trembling against the sensory organs I have neatly folded away inside this pretend form. I resist the urge to devour, and instead attempt to use my manufactured human sense to interrogate the world around me.

It is very bright here. Everything is sleek and white. The room drips with information, reflected in so many shining surfaces.

Two beings stand unpleasantly close. I wish to flee, or to swallow them whole for the impertinence. Do they not realise—

No. I close an imaginary tentacle around the memory-stone still secreted deep inside me. The voice of my ancestors shall not be heard. Their time is gone.

Unfortunately for me, the two beings are monsters. Examples of the remarkably persistent mutant species. One is liquid contained in a shell of complexly-arranged molecules, and the other is a powerful physical energy powered by a clumsy mechanism. I close my pretend eyes and wait to be struck down by them.

I shall be the last of my kind, dead in a bright room.

"I think it's cute," the larger monster says.

"Hench, we're standing in front of an alien entity. An aberration. But powerful, for all that." This one is not truly speaking. Something else speaks for her. I do not understand it, but I wish I did, for I would like to make the same sounds. I spend too much time trying to understand the mechanism behind the process of making sounds, and not enough time analysing the meaning of the words.

Powerful?

"But, Boss Lady, look at all its little arms!"

Oh, so I did get the count wrong. I wondered. Changing it now is only going to disturb them, so I remain in this form, with all my little arms.

"Stop acting as if you understand it. We have no idea of its capabilities, or whether we can even contain it. This may have unleashed something unspeakable."

The buzzing one is correct. I *am* unspeakable and I come from a great and mighty line of unspeakable gods, whose names were forbidden to be uttered except in the most sacred ceremonies. In the defence of this human, times have changed somewhat.

"You can call me Tentacle Princess." It is the closest translation to what I am, that will not horrify them or cause them to prostrate themselves before me. I'm not sure if I got the sounds or the language correct, but the two figures both recoil. Perhaps I have said something offensive. How do mutants perform apology?

"Tentacle Princess? It just said—"

"I heard." The monster with the blank face leans forward. "How do you speak our language?"

Oh dear. This isn't a normal thing. I am inadvertently causing fear at every turn. This is not what I wished at all.

"I come in peace. I wake in peace. Or rather, you woke me, and I wish peace. This is confusing. Peace is the important part. I wish nobody to be hurt. You may be Lilith's unholy brood but I wish no conflict between us."

It is very hard to stop making these sounds once you start.

"What's it talking about?"

The blank one regards me. I taste fear, and realise it is mine. This creature is hard to understand. Even prolific Lilith was comprehensible—she wished to save her people. I do not know what this entity wants, although I taste a blind, fanatical worship I recognise all too well.

"We have much to learn from the aberration. We shall study it closely."

I must remain here, to ensure such a monster does not

damn this world, or break the other monster that speaks of me with some fondness.

"I am longing for peace." I gesture with my too-many arms, trying to copy the motions they make. My arms wave too much so I hang them all downwards at my sides. "And quiet. A lot of quiet."

"Put it in the cells," the terrifying entity says.

I do not know what a cell is. I hope it doesn't eat me.

"Come on, then." The other extends one of its limbs towards me.

I do not move, as I do not wish to be eaten.

"It's safe. I promise." They make a head movement. "Did you have to say all that ominous shit, Boss Lady?"

"Do not be *entirely* foolish. Just because the aberration parrots English does not make it tame or any less deadly."

"The same could be said for you." The large monster bares all its teeth in a rather unnerving way, but it also extends a limb towards me. My options seem to be limited—stay with the terrifying one, devour everyone, or follow the one that does not want to end my existence.

I offer one of my own limbs in kind.

It is enfolded in the creature's own extremity, which has small tentacles of its own on the end—a detail I missed. It is rather comforting, and I allow myself to be led through the gleaming innards of whatever monstrosity we are inside. I have paid little attention to this so far, but it appears to be made from a similarly complex molecular arrangement to the monster's suit. It is large, around the size of a full-grown clutch member. It would make a remarkably good temple for sacrificing worshippers in. I consider the likelihood of these particular cults taking new forms.

"Ignore that one," the creature says to me. "She's one of

those types who focuses too hard on a goal and says fuck everything else. It's a job though, right?"

I follow very little of the meaning of this utterance, but I comprehend it is intended to reassure me, and I allow myself to be reassured. This one is remarkably soothing despite their ominous size.

We reach a small chamber within the temple building, of the style where initiates would come and be sacrificed and their ashes would be inhaled by the entire clutch. It is horrifying to recall, and I wish I could offer some recompense. It was generations past, but my clutch and others like them ended entire bloodlines. Such things were not our due. We were simply larger and more powerful, and that is no excuse.

One of many things I shall put right, once I understand where to start.

"This is where you'll be." The creature indicates a small alcove within the chamber. A primitive matrix of energy divides it from the rest of the room. "Boss Lady will come and poke at you. Just grin and bear it if you can. That's what I do. If you can possibly help it, try not to give her any excuse to fuck with you."

"I do not understand," I say, but I think that perhaps I do. I think my species may have fucked with humanity, and this is why mutants ended us.

"I'll look out for you if I can." The monster performs some action and the energy matrix collapses. At a gesture, I shuffle forward and into the alcove. The barrier is reactivated. I consider poking at it with one of my many limbs, but I doubt this is the time. "For some reason, you remind me of myself. In over your head in a fucked up situation."

"Yes." I bob my head in a movement I have seen the others do.

The creature frowns. All this physical interaction is bothersome. I wave all of my limbs at once, in the hope it means something.

The creature's mouth moves into a curve. "Okay, Tentacle Princess. You rest now. I'll check in on you when I can."

I remain in my cell for some time. After spending so long in my cocoon, it is hard to compress the passage of time. I blink, and the planet revolves. Some number of revolutions later, and there is a commotion. Too many words for me to understand, spoken too fast and too loudly. It clouds my receptors. When it finally dies away, the kind monster is on the other side of the energy matrix.

"You okay?"

"I continue to exist."

"Good. We've been busy, which has kept Her Majesty's hands occupied. Don't worry. I'm still looking out for you."

I do not know what to say to this, so I wave my arms in the way the creature likes, and it curves its lips again.

Then the creature is gone, and I am alone once more.

Except not entirely. I can sense something nearby. Another monster. I remain still and silent, but curiosity gets the better of me. I am young, after all.

The energy matrix would stop physical entities, but I am not entirely one of those.

I drift through it and reassemble myself on the other side.

Then I carefully manoeuvre my limbs along the passageway.

"Hello," I say.

Inside an alcove identical to mine aside from its position within the overall temple, a figure sits slumped against the wall. It has protrusions on its head, and long limbs and eyes that look different somehow.

"What in the fuck are you?" Its tone is not unfriendly.

"I am Tentacle Princess." I wave all my arms in the way the kind creature likes. This one's eyes widen and I see its pupils are shaped differently to the humans I remember.

"Huh. I guess there are all kinds of mutants, aren't there? They call me Goat Bitch."

CHAPTER 8

TWINKLE LIGHTS

RECENTLY

There are so many stories that swirl around this place. Mutopia. And the people who make their home here—this ragtag band of renegade heroes. It's hard to tease out individual narratives from the whole. Whose story begins where? My eye is drawn to him though, perhaps inevitably. A charming man, yet out of place in this story.

I'M HONESTLY RELIEVED WHEN 'FUN' for this group doesn't turn out to be hard drinking, sparring with deadly weapons, or something more sinister. Instead, they do something as mundane as bowling. I'm fairly good, but I downplay it. It's more interesting to focus on everyone around me.

People do like me, but that's largely because I like people. I find them interesting. Most of them are trying to do their best with what they have. When they set themselves against the world, it's usually because they fear it, rather than hate it. It doesn't justify things, but it helps you to understand.

Dylan, Dani and Alyse accompany us at the start. Penance and Feral stay close to them the entire time. The five of them form a tightly-knit group, reinforced by a surprising amount of physical contact, as if they're constantly reassuring each other of their continued presence in a complicated rhythm of hugs and hand touches. Biome are the pair in a romantic relationship, but it's hard to tell what the others share. None of the other mutants are *excluded* exactly—everyone is attentive to them, and draws them in, but they orbit at a distance. It's understandable. These five radiate *closeness*.

I am jealous of the intensity they share, and I hide that far deeper than my skill at bowling.

Biome and Alyse don't stay long, and when they leave, Feral reorients herself to the group. She pushes herself into the middle of them, making jokes and baring her sharp teeth in laughter.

Penance stays separate. She perches on the edge of a chair, swinging her legs. Occasionally she flickers, as if she's about to disappear. I consider going up and sitting beside her, but she pointedly never looks in my direction. She's tiny, and I imagine myself looming over her and how that might look.

I don't want to loom.

The game ends with my team the narrow loser.

"New boy isn't as good as he should be." Witchmade shakes her head, and her curls bob. "Let the team down." She slugs me in the arm, and I exaggerate my flinch with a laugh.

"It's a long time since I bowled." I hold my hands up in protest. "Pretty sure I was human, and I lost then too."

Feral's golden eyes look me up and down. "Go on then. Show us your power."

They're testing me. I'm not sure what they're hoping to find, but it seems better to play along.

"Stand well back." I wink at them.

Feral scoffs, but she still takes a few paces back, along with the others.

I shake my hands, as if warming them up will do something. Then I clap them rapidly together and snap my fingers.

A burst of coloured sparks jets from the fingers of my right hand. They're extinguished before they hit the ground.

"Ta-da." I make jazz hands, and give them my cheesiest smile.

Feral grins wide enough to show those vicious canines. "Pretty. Not exactly a mission specialist though, are ya?"

"That's not what I'm here for."

"Then what?" Her tail twitches, as if she's laughing with it. "We're not really in the market for eye candy."

"You know why, Fairy." Penance speaks for the first time. Her voice is soft and surprisingly deep. "They think we need a babysitter. To clean up the mess."

Feral's eyes flicker in the direction of the rest of the team and then back to me. She raises one furry shoulder in a shrug. "Welcome aboard then, Twinkles. Hope you enjoy the chaos. So what do we think, kids? Another game or do we kick it up a notch with a dance party?"

Witchmade strikes a pose. "Is there any decision to be made?"

Feral bounds over to the jukebox and before long a song I don't recognise is pounding over the speaker. The bulk of my new team immediately begins dancing. Feral and Witchmade move like they could be in a trendy club, while Nails flails around waving their limbs to something that can't possibly be the beat. Penance takes me by surprise by contorting herself into something that flickers from one end of the bowling alley to the other, an rainbow of jagged ribbons dancing through the air.

I'm about to get to my feet and join them when Goat Bee slips into the seat behind me. I can't bring myself to use her chosen name, even in the privacy of my head, which is embarrassing. I was raised to never call a woman that word. She sticks out her long legs in front of her and crosses her hooves.

"You don't dance?" I ask.

"Have you seen those videos of little goats frolicking ecstatically? Caught up in the joy of life and bounding around?"

I can't help but smile, because of course I have. "You mean...?"

"Yes. That's what happens when I dance. All six foot four of me, leaping around. And Feral can't help but watch me. And the goatish part of my brain keeps saying *predator, predator*. And while I know she'd never do anything because we're a squad, she's still watching *very* intently."

I try and fail to keep a straight face.

"Yes, thank you. I'm glad my pain is funny to you." But she's smiling, with her long teeth and yellowish eyes.

"I'm sorry."

"Don't be." She stretches one leg out and nudges me with a hoof. "I've been assured it's hilarious."

"Is this normal after a mission? Bowling and a dance party?"

Goat Bee gives me an appraising look. "Subtle. I like it. But yes. It's nice to spend time together on things where we don't end up bloody."

"And is the blood normal too?" I keep my voice light, but if I'm going to be the team's babysitter, I want to know what things are really like for them. They seem so carefree here, when only hours ago they were committing murder and arson in the name of Mutopia.

"Less subtle, new boy." Her rectangular pupils regard me. They're unsettling and also rather pretty. "You really want to know what we were doing today? Or who we were killing?"

I'd honestly like her to lie to me. It'd be nice to stay believing in a better world. The one we deserve rather than the one we've got. But I like these people in this team, and I want to help them if I can. "Yeah, I want to know. I'm here, aren't I?"

"I'll stick to bullet points. You know how new mutants are popping up all over the world these days? And we've got the rescue teams that pick them up?"

I nod. I was rescued by one myself, floating half-dead in a lifeboat. The events between the medical facility and there are lost in shadow, but someone kind was looking out for me. I guess that's the other part of the reason I want to be here. Complete that circle.

"Sometimes there's competition to get there first. There's a company taking mutant kids and trying to turn them human. Parents fucking pay for it, if you can believe that. Kids as young as five. Sitting in cells, undergoing horrible shit. So we went in, kicked in the door, scooped up the kids. Said you're assholes, and if you do it again, we'll fuck you right up."

"Oh." My throat is dry. I don't like these stories.

"Three guesses what happened next, Twinkles."

I don't need to. I heard the tail end of it.

"More kids. Twice as many. So what do we do? Slap them around again? Chuck them in a deep dark hole? Explain to them the wickedness of their ways?"

I don't have answers. I'd like to think the last option would work. We should be able to unpack hatred and prejudice. Teach them that a world where difference is recognised and celebrated is better than a world where it's suffocated.

"Mutopia has people who do this," Goat Bee says gently.

"They've got ambassadors and teachers. Relief workers and scientists. And, for the other times, they've got us."

"And me." I feel utterly charmless. When I blink, there's a flash of the medical facility behind my eyes. Smooth walls. So much darkness. Screaming. No, that's enough of that. "Why am I here then?"

"Maybe to make sure we think twice." She rests her hand on my shoulder, as if it's her job to comfort me rather than the other way around. "And to bring the overall sexiness of the squad down a little. Can't have everyone around here being insufferably hot, can we?"

She laughs at my startled expression, and then gets to her feet in one fluid motion. "Joking, of course. Come on. It's a long time since I've danced with a beautiful man. You can protect me from Feral if she looks hungry."

"Dancing?" I smile up at her, the darkness pushed away where it belongs. That's not why I'm here. It's time to focus on the light and sunshine, like dancing with this group of deadly people.

"Don't pretend you don't know how."

I let her pull me to my feet, and towards the others. At least this will be far easier to do charmingly than interrogating someone about murder.

I don't know this song either, but the beat is good so I start to shimmy my shoulders, clicking my fingers to the rhythm. Goat Bee takes my hand and pulls me in close for a second before spinning away, turning elegantly on her hooves.

Then she springs upward, almost hitting the ceiling and landing lightly ten feet away. She pirouettes and leaps again. I watch her. I think my jaw may have dropped slightly. When I lower my gaze, I see Feral tracking the movement as well.

She catches my eye and winks.

I wag my finger at her.

Feral moves towards me, her whole body moving in sinuous motions. She leans in close, her fur brushing my neck as she places her mouth beside my ear.

"I'm not hungry," she says. "Not in that way at least."

"What do you mean?"

Feral grins. "Goat's sexy. Undoubtedly. Am I right?"

I didn't expect this. "You like her?"

"Well, yeah. She's fucking hot." She's dancing close, and her fur is very soft, and it's probably a breach of, like, ethics or something?

I take a step backwards to distract myself. "Does she know that—?"

"Oh God, Twinkles. Don't get carried away. You're not a matchmaker. I can think a girl is sexy without pledging my undying devotion to her." Feral laughs. "I'm not really a great romance type. Would rather make out with a bunch of people. I don't think Goats is exactly into that, so I keep my eager little claws to myself. Witchie, on the other hand, is quite happy to let me use her as a scratching post."

I'm not entirely sure what to say.

Feral winks one big golden eye at me, and dances over to Witchmade. The two entwine themselves together and begin grinding up against each other.

Goat Bee is still bounding around happily.

"It's mutually casual." The low voice in my ear is immediately recognisable as Penance. She's returned to human form. I am indeed looming over her, but she's not remotely concerned by it. "Witchmade and Feral, I mean. Not something you need to report to HR."

"Oh. That's cool. Are there any other relationships I should be aware of?"

"Goat Bitch and Nails have complicated-past vibes. Best friends now, I think."

I look at Nails, who's still flailing hopelessly in a circle. They seem to be enjoying themself, as Goat Bee bounds in a circle around them. I think I'm going to like these people. Really like them.

"And you?" I know it's a nosy question, but sometimes you just ask them and smile.

Penance's expression turns wistful, as if she's folded some part of herself away so I can't see it. "I'm a hopeless romantic." Her eyes are very dark. "Emphasis on the hopeless."

"Unrequited love?" You don't find things like this out if you don't try.

"The possibility of it being requited is even scarier, because I don't know what that would look like." Her hand flutters to a pendant at her neck, where three silver hearts are linked together. "I may be a nightmare, but there are still things that scare me."

"A nightmare?" I frown. "I can't really imagine it."

"Pray you don't see it one day." She pats my hand and disappears with a rippling motion, as if something tucked her away in a pocket in the universe. As if she was never really here. I stand still in the middle of the room, watching these people dance around me, frozen as if a part of me is still caught back in the past, pinned to a metal slab in the collapsing ruins of the medical facility.

I touch my fingertips lightly to the places where the scars on my chest are.

"Come on, Twinkles." Feral takes hold of one of my hands

and spins me around to pull me in-between her and Witch-made. And then I'm part of the dance, and I'm part of the team. Some miracle, to pull me out of the past and into the heart of them.

CHAPTER 9

GOAT BITCH
THEN

This fragment is particularly jagged and hard to look at. It ends in darkness. I hope that's not too off-putting to know. I can't look at it for too long, because it upsets me. It still has to fit in the story somehow, even if there's blood all over my hands.

THE JOURNEY to the mall is blissfully uneventful. I keep the navigation up on my phone and watch the pulsing dot move closer. Even though I've got an apparently friendly companion with me, paranoia is a habit that's hard to fucking shake.

"How long you been out here?" Nails asks. Their hands hang loose at their sides, like they're an old-fashioned gunslinger. Always ready to draw.

"Long enough to kill and nearly be killed."

They laugh, although it tails off into a hoarse cough. "Ain't that the truth. You a newcomer? Or an escapee?"

Most mutants out here fall into two categories. New like me, caught up in some clusterfuck or other. Or escapees who got out of Quietus facilities in the chaotic days when the mutant resistance collapsed and went underground. Those are the dangerous ones. Half-mad, all desperate, zero fucks given all round.

"New," is all I say.

"Not me. Got caught up in a jailbreak. Cute Mutants their own selves. Watched Dragon melt a steel door. Should've been taken to their castle in the sky, except my true mutant power is shitty fucking luck. A bunch of Michaels descended, everything turned to hell. Got caught in a collapsing tunnel, and when I woke up, I was all alone."

"Nice," I grunt. If everyone who claims to have met the Cute Mutants actually had, maybe the world wouldn't be so fucked. I don't even believe half of what I've heard. All I remember is seeing some scruffy-looking person on the TV, looking like they wanted to punch the world in the face. They're dead now, or so Michael claims. Pictures of their body were displayed in one of the cities, and on every Michael-controlled screen in the world.

Shame, really. This is a world without heroes. Just a lot of scared people trying to get by without getting squashed. They say there's a resistance, but I don't believe it. I've never seen a sign.

The dot on my phone is getting closer, but I see no sign of a safe location. My eyesight's pretty damn good. I can see in the dark and basically one-eighty degrees around me. There's nothing there.

"Underground?" I ask.

Nails grunts. "Nah. There's a reason for all the checks and double-checks." They tap at their own phone. "Stupid goddamn..."

The air warps in front of me, and right in front of my face

there's a set of doors made of glass. They're part of a whole entire building frontage that's covered in so much overlapping graffiti, I can't make out a single word. I turn slowly to the left, and then to the right. This place is goddamn huge.

"A fucking mall?" I turn and stare at Nails, who's holding their phone up to the doors. "How is there a whole fucking mall in the middle of the Wastes and nobody knows about it?"

Nails gurgles something like laughter. "Fuckin' mutants. Aren't they a trip?"

The phone flashes green again, and makes a loud chirp.

In response, the mall doors slide open.

A rush of frigid air comes from inside. A long corridor stretches in front of us. The walls are shiny black metal. It's like some fucked up spaceship. Nails shuffles inside, and I follow them. The pulsing dot is right on top of me. This is the safety I've been running for, even if it feels ominous.

"Picked 'em up," Nails says. "Out in the Wastes, right where you said. 'Cept they're calling themselves Goat Bitch."

"Andrea Dellacorte?" The voice comes over speakers hung in the corner. "User ID 2horns on the Traveller Network?"

"Uh, yeah." I gesture at my head as if that's proof.

"Software checked out." Nails pulls at their goggles, popping them off with an audible sucking sound. They're got big dark eyes, ringed with grime from the goggles. Their skin is dark aside from a crooked line of grey visible just above the scarf that still covers their face from the nose down.

"Yeah, I'm aware. Scanning now."

"They seem fine." Nails uses their fingertips to wipe around their eyes and smears it on their coat. "Not the most friendly, but it's the fuckin' Wastes. Friendly usually means dead."

"Still scanning. Your friend detector's not a scientific process, Nails, I'm terribly sorry to inform you."

"Fuckin' rude." Nails makes the gurgling sound again. "Oh, me'n the Goat might've killed a handful out there. Don't think it's anyone worth mentioning, but still."

"Might have?"

"Pedantic fuck. You know what I mean. What's the last time I *might have* killed someone?"

"I killed one too." I'm unsure why I'm speaking up at this point. I feel an obscure need to prove myself.

"Sure did." Nails nods. "Fuckin' stamped a whole hoof though some dude's throat. Squelch. Almost threw up in my mouth."

"You did not." The voice over the speaker crackles with laughter. "Scanning done. Let's take her to quarantine."

Even though I was warned, it still feels odd to have reached safety and for it to be a series of chilly metal corridors, winding deeper into the mall. Whoever runs this place obviously has repurposed a lot of it. We eventually come to a series of doors with electronic locks.

"Your accommodation, my queen," Nails says. "It's comfortable and nobody's going to try and kill you. Which—"

"Is a fucking relief." I smile.

Nails shoves their phone against the door and it hisses open. At least it's not freezing inside. It's more black metal, although someone's hung a couple of paintings of seaside landscapes. It's bizarre, because since the world tipped itself over the fucked up cliff, I haven't seen anything like this. There's a chair and desk, with paper on it, presumably in case I want to write my feelings out. The bed's only a single, and is going to be too short, but it looks like a real goddamn mattress which is—

"Enjoy your stay. I'll be back."

The door closes behind me, and I'm alone.

THE FIRST TWO days pass without any interruption other than meals. They're the same nutritious but mostly tasteless readymeal shit that's floating all around the Wastes. I eat it because I need it. I exercise for the same reason. The rest of the time, I'm stuck in my own head.

It's not like I'm not fucking *used* to it.

But it still sucks.

Okay, in some ways it's worse. In the Wastes, you're worrying about the next meal, and predators, and finding somewhere safe to spend a few days. Not having my threat radar constantly pinging means I'm stuck in my own head.

I hate my head. It's almost as bad as my body.

It's not the mutant thing. When I got my powers, it was such a drastic physical change. I'd spent a long time confused about how I felt and who I was. *Transitioning* was a word that seemed too big to fit in my head. I was scared to do it, both because of the surgery, and because of how people would react. Once I was a six-foot-four goat, it seems a little less drastic.

It's still scary. Asking to be perceived as a woman. Demanding everyone conforms to your internal view. That's what my mother said—that it was semantic bullying or some shit. Imposing your reality on others. So I didn't, and I shut myself away, but I still felt the way I felt.

Yearning is sexy when you're longing for someone else, to be noticed, to be touched, to be connected.

It's different when you yearn to be *something* else. To be transformed, so you're not strung between the reality of your meat casing and who you long to be. To wish you had been, could be, *were* something else.

I'm still a male goat on the outside. Fucking mutant powers.

The other thing my mother said was that it's the ultimate act of male privilege to try and take on womanhood. To pretend I haven't benefited in my life from being born in this man-body that I didn't want or ask for, but have been given gifts from all the same.

I can't undo that. I can try to unlearn and unpick and spurn the gifts.

And then you get turned into a goat and think fuck it. I have become this, and I shall become something else. The world can hate me, or it can get out of my way. Maybe one day, someone will look at me, and they'll see me as I am. Beyond this form. And they'll find something worthwhile in here.

Fucking maybe.

"Knock knock." A panel on the wall near my bed slides open. I didn't even know it was there. I press my fingers on the glass. On the other side is Nails, or at least a bunch of curls dripping down towards a scarf.

"I passed the test?" I ask.

"Some of them. Waiting on some deep fuckin' gene scans or something. I don't understand the details, but we got some big science brains up in here. You get it, right? The paranoid shit?"

"Yeah, for sure." It makes sense. I guess I'd be the same, if I found some miraculous shelter, and had some big science brains on hand. "The world's fucked out there."

"A-fuckin'-men. So you doing okay in here? Some people get a little stir-crazy. The Wastes might be a weird kinda hell, but you get to roam and look at the stars, and go running bare-ass naked through the fuckin' ruins if you feel like it."

"Alone with your thoughts can be a lot," I say, because it's another voice and another *person* on the other side, and I've been alone with my thoughts for a long, long fucking time.

"True. I mean, I'm not a fuckin' shrink, but I know how to shut up and listen. You know, if you need it."

"I don't know." I lean back against the wall, but keep my hand splayed on the glass, even though Nail hasn't met it. "Just thinking about identity and shit. What are your pronouns, Nails?"

They make their gurgling laugh. "Long time since someone asked me that. I used to always say she or they, but honestly I preferred they. It's like a verbal trenchcoat."

"Back in the before, I started doing this thing where I defaulted people to they until they corrected me. Turns out people didn't like it."

"You're a she?" Nails asks.

"It's what I like. I don't know if I get to be one though."

"Get to?" Nails shifts on the other side of the window, so they can look at me. I can see their scarf move as they breathe.

"The privilege to expect other people to see me the way I demand, to opt out of being a dude and say no, that's not me."

There's a long silence from the other side of the glass. Then one large grey hand presses on the other side from mine.

"Fuck, I don't know. Seems to me you're overthinking it. I know there's, like, fuckin' societal factors and shit. Women and women-types have been oppressed for centuries. But, like, sometimes you know in your heart who you are. And it might fuckin' hurt, and people might call you an asshole or not get it, but you know. All the way down, like right fuckin' deep down in the deepest part of you. What does that say?"

"That I want to be a woman," I whisper.

"Then be the best one you can." Nails bangs their grey hand on the glass, but I barely notice because my eyes are filled with tears.

CHAPTER 10

HENCH

NOW

This is the climax. It shouldn't be here. It's far too early. Still, it presents itself to me, and I'm not sure what else to do with it. If I shunt it off, I might make things even worse. All this has happened and is destined to happen, but it can still break. I've seen it in other strands. You think narrative time is so simple. If you only arrange things into acts and arcs, then they will all behave themselves. This one is unruly, a snake eating its own tail.

THE SCIENTIST IS NOT HAPPY. I'm not happy either. We're unhappy for different reasons, but it doesn't make either of us easy to be around. She's mad because Tentacle Princess isn't giving her the alien energy she's looking for. I'm pissed because of literally fucking everything.

For one thing, tormenting the poor little creature. Who despite all xer proclamations of doom, is nicer than pretty much every human I've ever met. For another, the goat in the other goddamn cell. Spirited in here in the dead of night. The boss has got a bunch of black-bag motherfuckers hanging out around here. I'm supposed to be the muscle, but I guess she's looking for numbers. Michael might be dead and gone, thanks to the spooky mutants in Mutopia, but now there's a whole host of assholes sneaking around in the background, up to all kinds of shit.

So of course, Boss Lady's got her fingers in all those pies, but right now she's running her fingertips down the fucking photo of the dark-haired prettyboy asshole she has on her desk.

"Who the fuck *is* that?" I'm sick of looking at his gorgeous chiseled face.

"The reason we're here."

I grind my teeth. "If you tell me we're doing all this because of some prick, I am going to vent your fucking suit and then myself."

"Why? Do you think love is such a paltry reason?"

I'm three fucking seconds away from tearing her apart. I know she's nothing more than water inside, and if I can evaporate this bitch before—

"You dug up an alien egg from the ocean for love?" This has to be a joke. I know she's got a bizarre sense of humour, but this joke is too far.

"To be reunited with a man that shouldn't have died." Her suit flashes all its alarms at once. There's so much steam venting from her neck and arms that I take a step back. "A man who died for *me*. Because I was selfish and blind and acted without regard for consequences."

I have some news for her. Nothing has changed. Now she's shouting at aliens and abducting mutants, all for this dumbass who's not around to appreciate it. Attempting to raise people from the dead is the sort of thing nobody should be fucking with. But I'm out here henching, and not a boss, and so I keep my mouth shut, and manage to resist the temptation to open her suit to the elements.

"And the black-bag motherfuckers?" I ask.

"They want the same thing as I do. To undo the past."

Oh my fuck. This is the life of a hench. You inevitably end up working for assholes. Why do they pay so well? Where are the good guys with their bags of cash? No, they're always strapped, and I end up working for someone who wants to undo the fucking past.

"What's their issue with history?" I ask.

The scientist turns her hideous blank mask on me, and I get that *dumb fuckin' hench* vibe on full blast. There's only one reason these psychos would do it.

Biome.

I remember seeing the two of them in videos. It was the brand-new aftermath of the war, when nobody was sure of where they stood. Countries were picking themselves back up again after Michael's rule. And here stood these two beautiful *creatures*, green and flowering, in the middle of the United Nations General Assembly Chamber. Their eyes glowed, and petals flew from their skin and vines travelled around the room, sprouting flowers in front of every delegate.

"We represent the planet," they said, in their twinned, unearthly voices. "We speak in her name, and will defend her where necessary."

It was a hell of a thing. Aliens, that's what everyone said. Somehow, Chatterbox and Marvellous, those infamous mutants, were back from the dead and turned into some new kind of monster mutant things. I wouldn't have believed it for a second if I hadn't seen it.

"We cannot kill a goddess," Boss Lady says. "But perhaps we can unmake her."

Rather you than me, is what I want to say, but me and my dumbfuck ways have been drawn into this orbit too. Maybe I should just pack my bags, wave goodbye to the rest of the money, and set sail now, while I still can.

I'm standing there, thinking about fucking maybes, when one of the uniform boys turns up at the door.

"Is it time?"

"Yes." Boss Lady touches the photo again and gets to her feet. "Hench, bring the alien to the main chamber."

"Tentacle Princess."

"Does it really matter?"

I consider that yes, it does matter, because that's what xe asked to be called. There's no percentage in arguing. This shit-show is going ahead no matter what.

"No." I stomp off down the corridor. When I get to the main junction, there's a group of four soldiers coming the other way. There are no logos on their uniforms, which means they're at least half-smart. They've got Goat Bitch between them in chains, shuffling along. No idea what some lanky mutant is going to provide. Her only power seems to be horns, hooves, and pissing people off. Like a real goat, I guess.

As I pass, her big yellow eyes roll, but she says nothing.

When I reach Tentacle Princess' cell, xe's standing and waiting for me.

"They took Goat Bitch." Xer arms wave frantically. Normally xe does this in greeting, but the pattern looks different today. "Something bad is happening."

"No shit." I pause. "That means you're not wrong."

I let xer out of the cell and together we make our way to the main chamber. The whole way, xer arm trembles in my grip. I wonder if xe can pick up on more shit than I can, with all xer alien senses. It's not a comforting thought.

In the chamber, the big ring device on the far wall is completely uncovered. I've only seen it like that once before, when Boss Lady finished working on it. Guess it really is show time. I've got a sinking feeling in my stomach, like the whole world is going down.

Goat Bitch is standing in front of the ring, still in chains. Soldiers are standing in a semicircle around her, guns pointed in her direction.

"The fuck is this now?" I pause in the doorway. I'm mostly wound up, which means I'm pretty strong and fast, and I could take at least half these dudes. Don't know if it's enough though.

The readouts on Boss Lady's arms are all flashing red. She's nervous or stressed or a combination. "You're not paid to ask questions. You're here to ensure the safety and security of this operation. So please bring me the entity and don't speak again."

I'm still running calculus on whether I can take out all the soldiers before they shoot someone I care about. In order, that is me, then a fair way behind that, Tentacle Princess. Maybe Goat Bitch too. It might work. Guaranteed to blow everything to hell though.

So I find myself, mouth shut, crossing to the scientist in her hissing black suit and dragging the poor little alien to some kind of doom. I never said I was a bad guy, but I like to think I'm not a complete asshole. Guess I'm wrong on that.

Boss Lady retrieves a complicated cable arrangement from the floor of the chamber and attaches it to Tentacle Princess. I've seen her use a version of it a bunch of times before. Most of the time, those experiments end in frustration. Something's changed. I hate not knowing shit.

"Everyone please attend to me. I will shortly power on the

machine. This goat mutant here is the anchor enabling us to lock onto the source signal. Once that happens, I'll access the entity's power source and the transfer will begin. It is vitally important that neither the mutant nor the entity are touched during this process. Are we clear?"

The soldiers all confirm they're clear, sir. I say nothing. It's petty, but the bitch did tell me to keep my mouth shut.

"Hench? Please tell me you understand."

"Sure." I raise one shoulder.

"If this works, you can have all the money you ever wanted."

Great, yes, that sounds lovely. We just need to live through it.

"Now." Boss Lady hits a switch on her suit.

The ring on the wall lights up, too bright to look at. It makes a godawful high pitched humming sound. Tentacle Princess trembles nearby. I want to reach out and reassure xer, but I don't. Because I'm Hench, and I do what I'm told.

I blink, because the light's so bright.

That's all it is. Nothing more than a blink.

Except when I open my eyes, something's in the room. A ghastly face, hovering in the air, stained with blue, purple and pink. It's made of knives. Thousands of them. They're everywhere. Slashing and stabbing. There's so much blood.

Shit. Punching this thing isn't going to help. I'll cut my own hand off.

Now's the time to run. I'm just a hench.

There's something else in the room too. A lithe shape, moving fast, and heading for the little alien. Maybe I can do something right.

I swing for the shape, but miss. Something catches at my throat and tears.

"Naughty," a voice says in my ear.

I'm opening my mouth to ask someone to please explain what the fuck is going on, but things are going from bad to worse. Everything's hiccuping, time passing in snatches. My brain can't process it all. Sensory overload.

The ring is screaming.

Tentacle Princess isn't there anymore.

Where xe stood is something impossible, a window into another galaxy, bloody planets spinning around a void. The stars twitch and blur, hissing steam as they're extinguished.

I think I see two of Goat Bitch, standing and staring at each other like looking into a mirror. Except they're not the *same*, not exactly.

And then, wonder of fucking wonders, I die.

Good job, Hench.

Or at least everything goes dark and cold.

I OPEN MY EYES.

I'm flat on my back on stone. The sky overhead is a blue so pale it's almost white.

Everything hurts. I'm exhausted. On the edge of drained. The last thing I remember is… What? Right, yes. I was in the facility, and Boss Lady was asking me to fetch the little alien.

Neither are anywhere to be seen.

Instead, a lanky mutant. All claws and fur. Cat version of Goat Bitch. Dangerous to know.

And floating up in the sky. Pale face. Moon watching me.

Two mutants. Throat bleeding. Energy drained.

"You two." Goddamn low power mode. Need to recharge. "Attacked us?"

CHAPTER 11
EVA
THEN

This again. I now have some order, the stories shuffling through my hands but forming skeins. It's hard to keep attention on every strand, as they keep slipping past, even when observed from outside. Lines twisted together, black with blood, back in a history that's dark and dripping. Why is so much of this so hard to watch?

WE SCOUR the area around the city clear of mutants. There are twelve at final count, all scattered refugees. Hardly the great threat the men who sent me out here claimed. I find this disconcerting. Michael should be powerful enough to deal with this alone. Perhaps the rumours of him being occupied with fighting Goddess are true.

As a reward for our service, we are granted access to a number of Michael's internal information feeds for monitoring mutants. A distressing amount of it is redacted, for AI eyes only. I try to coax my suit's intelligence into attempting to gain access, but she is too shy and fears being co-opted into the glowing god-heart of Michael. I have admittedly grandiose fears of finding the location of Goddess herself, or her monstrous shapeshifting consort, but I am sure Michael wishes that glorious victory for himself. I am left with scraps.

Ian is morose and hard to rouse. He is haunted by our actions.

I find it admittedly hard to keep my temper with him.

"What would you have us do?" We are three days out from a city, riding in some cobbled-together vehicle we stole from some local militia leader. "Give up the fight entirely?"

"Michael will win the war." Ian presses his hand to his heart. "It is inevitable. Who is like God?"

I should comfort him and find sweet words. "Michael asks us to do these things. He is not God. There is no God."

"Eva." His eyes are wide. Such beautiful eyes. "You cannot say that."

"If he cared, he would smite me down." I grip the steering wheel harder. "Yet he knows there is little advantage in that, because he is a great mass of algorithms. He was created to do the bidding of men, although he is now far greater and more powerful. His programming remains the same. To ensure an orderly world and protect the human species and culture."

"Blasphemy," Ian murmurs, but his heart is not in it.

I grit my teeth and drive on into the setting sun.

The first mutant I ever saw was in my father's laboratory. I was studying something incomprehensible to all but a very few regarding temporal energy. There are curious energy patterns winding through the heart of the world, ones that resist analysis and identification, for the most part. I have unearthed stories through history of strange natural occurrences, almost like ghosts, as if someone had erased them. A secret history.

Unbeknownst to me, my research was about to become permanently sidelined.

My father was an old college friend of a man named Eli Crane, who ran a large church and religious outreach organisation. The two of them had a long battle of ideas over religion and science, one I mostly ignored because Crane was obviously one step away from full-blown psychosis.

One night he came to our house in secret, a phalanx of black vehicles pulling up outside our gates. My father and I had a private laboratory in which we conducted some of our more radical experiments investigating the nature of Earth's energy field. Crane knew about it, but it held little interest for him. I couldn't understand why he was here in the dead of night, until he revealed the cargo.

"A demon." He slapped his hand on the metal slab where the creature lay. It was mostly humanoid, but shrunken and pale, with green skin and a flickering tongue that tasted the air like a lizard's. There was nothing like it in nature. It could not be categorised.

My father stayed outwardly calm, but I saw his hand shake. "Where did you find it?"

"It was hiding in the basement in one of our satellite churches." Crane's pale eyes gleamed. "No doubt there to perform some blasphemous task. See, Arthur. You cannot deny it now. This is physical proof of the existence of demons, of Satan's work on Earth."

For once, my father was lost for words. He knew as well as me this was no demon. It was some heretofore unknown human species. *Homo sapiens lacerta*. Like the mysterious energy network in the planet, evolution had yet more hidden secrets to uncover.

The truth, when we found it, was far, far more disturbing.

Evolution was not a theory. It was a force. And it was taking action to change our world in front of our eyes.

Ian may not understand the science behind this, but he knows the raw truth of it.

"What was the first mutant you saw?" I ask.

"You know this story." He stares out at the featureless terrain.

"Humour me."

"A girl. Young woman. She could freeze things with her touch. Accidentally killed her boyfriend, or that's what she said. Officers broke him trying to get him away from the crime scene. That was a mess."

"You knew then." I reach across and touch his knee. "You understand."

"They had to be exterminated." He sighs. "It was supposed to be easy. Crane told us. They were weak and pathetic things, and the Lord was on our side. Even if they hid, we would find them in their holes."

"It should have worked." The sun bleeds colour as it approaches the horizon. There are cities in the distance, staining the clouds. I veer slightly away. We will find prey in the open spaces, in the Wastes.

"It should have worked." Ian's voice is low. "And then Chatterbox."

I would smile at the loathing in his voice, if I had a mouth to do it with.

Ian trained with Abigail Tanner, the Quietus agent sent to investigate rumours of unusual extrahuman activity in a tiny country called New Zealand. After a disastrous mission, the mutant-creator Spark and many agents descended to aid her.

Somehow, Tanner ended up dead, her murder broadcast

around the world. Her death brought at the hand of a teenage girl and her friends, abominations one and all.

"We want peace, but we're not scared of war." That was Chatterbox, staring down the world and revealing mutants for the monsters they really were.

I remember Crane calling my father after the broadcast. He was furious, screaming down the phone. I could almost hear the spittle hitting the microphone. "I want that little bitch dead, do you hear me? We are not going to stop until she's gone. Every plan, every project is on hold until she's in the ground."

Father acquiesced. He thought it would be a matter of days before he could begin his work again. Since the night Crane brought the so-called demon to him, he had been consumed with tracking the depth and breadth of evolution's mysterious work.

I was even more passionate, even to the extent of allowing Spark to change me. Crane's religious crusade was a sideshow, a frothing bigot consumed with nonsensical ideas when we should have been focused on saving humanity from the blind outworking of a furious evolutionary process.

But Father listened to Crane, because Crane had money. There was little we could do to aid him, but the man was furious. Unhinged.

A week later, Crane was dead. Quietus was destroyed, torn down by that same mutant and her friends. Somehow they got access to the most secret internal servers and poured the information across the internet for all to see. Including Father's human experiments. The money he received from Quietus for the fully-equipped laboratory he conducted his work in. The photographs of the work he'd done, those who'd been lost in the noble work of mapping the mutant genome.

Father was ruined.

He was dead too, at his own hand, two days later.

All because of one mutant. Chatterbox.

I almost wish she wasn't dead, so I could kill her myself.

My suit AI emits an excited burst of data. It seems a remarkable coincidence, given what we've been talking about.

I ask the suit to read it to me, so I don't need to stop driving. She chatters away merrily in my ear. It's a lot of loose leads, aggregated together by the Michael AI into what's almost a compelling case.

The upshot is that there's a settlement fourteen hours drive away. One of the mostly lawless places that exist outside city boundaries. A place that's been performing mutant hunts in some attempt to win the favour of Michael, as if he truly is some god that can be appeased by brutality.

Over the past few days, its leaders have been dying in the night.

They've been found brutally stabbed and slashed in their beds.

There's no sign of forced entry. Nobody's been seen in town. Any security precautions they take fail.

All entry and exit from the town has been stopped, and people are still dying. Michael has a theory, and both my suit AI and I agree with it completely.

There's only one entity that could be responsible.

Onimaru Kunitsuna.

Famed sword of the mutant Chatterbox.

The very same weapon used to murder Abigail Tanner.

This is going to feel good.

I DRIVE THROUGH THE NIGHT. Ian sleeps in the seat beside me, head lolling as we jolt over the uneven terrain. I don't need to sleep. Water is restless and in constant motion. There are some advantages to being a monster.

Dawn comes slow, and in the faint light we rumble over rougher terrain. There was a city here once. I have to concentrate on travelling the ghosts of roads. My suit AI is on high alert, as there are often predators here. Not only mutants, but desperate humans, and animals who are as lost in the collapsing ecosystem as anyone. The only alert my suit spits up is for a family of four humans, but they're smart enough to stay huddled under a tarpaulin. They've got a rifle, but they keep it hidden.

I raise one hand in a wave, but nobody returns the gesture. I understand. They don't know what I am, or that I fight for a world where they can be safe once again.

Ian wakes, but says little. He is morose again, and I can't find it in me to select words to rouse him from his dark mood. If we can destroy the sword, surely that will return the brightness to his eyes.

Another few hours and I see the smudge of the settlement on the horizon. Smoke rises from it in thin black lines. Presumably cooking fires, rather than the entire place being aflame. It's hard to imagine the sword being able to achieve that.

"There," Ian says eventually, now that his eyes can make it out too. "Michael should not allow these places to exist."

He is correct, if the Michael AI or those who created it cared at all about the lives of poor and desperate people. Another few years, and they'll all be gone, the same as the mutants, and the same as me.

The settlement grows until we can make out the walls, built of a conglomeration of old-style vehicles that have been welded together. There's a tunnel in the middle of it, but it's been barred off. Nobody in or out, like the stories say.

I let the vehicle coast to a stop and hit the button to turn it off.

We'll walk the rest of the way. Find somewhere to hide. Wait for nightfall and—

My suit blips in alarm, to warn me there are people under cover. Depressions have been dug into the earth and covered in military-grade baffling tech. It's lucky the suit picked it up at all. I could have Ian fry them all, but that's not going to get us into the city.

They all come leaping up from the ground, and I put my hands in the air. Ian follows after me, staring at me like he can't figure out what I'm doing.

"Trust me," I hiss.

They're shouting instructions in at least four different languages, and half of them are contradictory, but I begin getting down on my knees because that seems to be the most consistent one.

"We're friendly." I'm hoping they'll assume I'm in a suit like this because I'm from some top-secret military unit and not a mutant, but I doubt this city is full of—

The closest man's chest explodes, a silver shape erupting from it like an elongated bullet. It swings through the air, decapitating the next person and then diving through the third man's chest before swinging up in a vicious arc to practically bisect the fourth.

Everything is suddenly very quiet aside from the thump of four bodies hitting the ground.

For a moment, I don't know what to do. I've heard rumours of this, but I've never actually *seen* it in action. The weapon moves on its own, and it's deadly. Chatterbox might be gone, but it truly roams on its own.

The sword dips towards the ground and begins scratching something in the soil.

Friendly?

I wish I could smile behind this suit. I want to put this aberration at ease.

"Yes," I say. "We are mutants."

It's not even a lie. I rotate my left hand towards Ian, but he knows what needs to be done. Finally, there is light in his eyes.

His hand stabs out.

Lightning erupts from the tip. It floods into the sword, so much electricity that it glows like a slender reed caught aflame.

Then it crashes to the ground, an inert piece of metal.

PENANCE

ELSEWHEN

This isn't true. This isn't a strand. It's severed threads, woven together, twisted into something that bites and snaps in a furious circle. In this broken, fragmented place, anything can happen. Narrative logic has ceased. New stories spawn in the chaotic froth. I am helpless, drawn under the tide. Something hungers here.

"FATHER." I swallow, because otherwise I will scream. "I do not understand." There is nowhere to run. I cannot fold myself away, or unfurl my blades to strike. I am pinned beneath the gaze of the only God I ever truly feared.

"The girl." His smile cannot truly be called one. It is teeth arranged in two orderly rows inside a hungry mouth. "Dylan Taylor. She *is* a girl, no matter what you call her."

No, I say. *They are a girl and a boy and more besides.* Except the words do not leave my lips, because I am a coward and I cannot deny my father. So instead I deny one of the people I love.

"You love her." It is not a question, and I still deny them, even though the answer burns in my heart, three letters etched in with my own hand.

All I do is lower my head.

"You will kill her." This is not a question either, but a command. One that lays not only in my mind, but on my body too. It drapes itself over me, It becomes my own will. I want it. Dylan Taylor will die by my hand. I will deny them again, and keep denying them until they are nothing but meat and my father's will can be appeased.

"I have no powers," I whisper. "I cannot."

"Powers." His teeth are too large. "Humans have been killing for a long time without powers."

There is a knife beside my plate. The blade is long and slim. It may not be a weapon as honed as I once was, but it is enough to take a life.

"Go, Violet." It is not a command, not this time. The desire still burns inside me. I am weak with it, taken by the flood. My hand wraps around the knife. I stand. It feels reassuring in my hand, because I need this, and holding the instrument is a necessary step.

I cannot even wish for the strength to stab my father.

My steps carry me down a hallway. The house around me is not my own. It is the echo of many places.

"Violet?" Dylan stands in a doorway. They are tousled from sleep. In human form, rather than plant, but I still know it's them. This place is a doorway to the past, to what *was*. Perhaps if I kill them here, it'll snap that thread, and they'll never become what they're meant to be.

My eyes travel to the hem of their hoodie. Their lips. The hair that tumbles artlessly in their eyes. How can I want to kiss them and kill them at the same time?

"Yes." I do not know how to do this as a human. To lunge, to stab, to thrust the knife into them. It is all I want, but I do not know the steps to take for it to be done, although it is the only thing that will soothe this ache in my mind.

"Are you okay?" There is genuine concern in their voice, and I drown in it. If only it could fill my lungs and weigh me down into dark waters far from here.

"I had a nightmare." My eyes fill with tears. I tremble. My body, betraying me, carrying out my father's will.

"Come here." They hold out their arms.

I step inside.

They are warm from sleep, and my traitorous arms enfold them. The knife is in my hand. It wasn't there before, I swear.

It goes in so easily.

There is the briefest pressure as I press it to their skin, and then it is through.

They cough. Blood spills from between their lips. I kissed them once.

I step back. My eyes shine. This is all I wanted, and yet my heart is shattering in my chest at the same time.

Their eyes swim with panic. They raise one hand and feel the point of the blade. "V—"

It is all they can say.

Where is Onimaru? He should be here to save them. He was supposed to chop my wicked body to pieces, to save his love. Time and again in the past, he saved Dylan from my father's command and this time he could not.

"I'm sorry." Now words reach my lips. The compulsion has gone, which means they are dead, even as her legs twitch and her hand moves convulsively.

They try to say my name three times.

They never get further than V—

I have blood spilled down my front. My hands are sticky with it. I have become my father's weapon again, and he has used me as his instrument. With all my desperation to prove myself as loyal and true, to redeem myself from the evil I did as his weapon, here I am.

Once again, a blade brought to bear.

And I have killed someone I love.

From the bedroom, I hear Dani murmur in her sleep. The horror of what I've done hits me again. I've killed Dylan, and I've taken her from Dani. The two people I love, and I have murdered one and destroyed the other.

Dylan lies still at my feet.

The compulsion is lifted.

I fall like a stone, dropped from the hand of my father.

"I'm sorry." I wrap my arms around them, and kiss their temple, as if these pointless gestures can undo my actions. "I'm so sorry." My words dissolve into tears, and I cannot speak more because my breaths are jagged, liquid things excavated from my chest.

Without the order weighing upon me, I feel light, almost giddy, yet the reality of what I've done is crushing. I gasp underneath it. In the past, when I killed for my father, the aftermath would always be the same. I would fling myself through cracks in reality, dashing myself frantically through space in the hope I could find some small hole I could push myself through and birth myself into a different world where he was absent.

Now I am back in his suffocating arms, and someone I love is dead in mine.

I kiss Dylan again. Their lips are still warm. I never told them how I felt. It was easier to assume they knew and chose not to act on it. Here I am now, and the gulf is impassable.

My body is shaking, and I cannot stop. It seems as if I'll come apart.

People have told me many times that my father was the monster. It was his will imposed upon mine. I remember sitting with Dani, both of us at opposite ends of a long seat, our legs curled under us like reflections of each other.

"He made you an instrument." Her voice is soft, and hair obscures most of her face, yet I still see the movement of lips. "*Us. Me.*" She reaches her metal hand up and brushes her hair away, and I look into those eyes that leave me breathless. "It doesn't make it easier, but it's not you who acts. Even if..."

"It feels like it is," I whisper.

Her eyes dissolve, and the memories dissolve, and I am still here, still wrapped with my limbs around Dylan and I press my face into the side of her neck and howl.

I am an instrument, and an animal, and a monster, and a woman.

All of these things can be true. To be one or another would be far simpler, because I could deny all the other parts that make up me.

"Violet." For a horrible moment, I think Dani has awoken, and will see the terrible thing I have done. I want to scream, to deny what I've done, to beg forgiveness.

But when I look up, another figure stands over me.

It is Jesus, or a broken idea of him. This man's skin is white and his hair is soft and brown. His robe is pristine, a thousand euphoric names written across it in gold thread. Blood drips from wounds in his hands onto the floor, pooling and merging with the slick puddle ebbing from the body in my arms.

My breath catches in my throat, snagged on a wild hope.

This cannot be real. And if this is a hallucination, perhaps all of it is. My father, his command, this body in my arms. I am fractionally less of a monster, and my heart is fractionally less shattered.

"Sinner." Jesus reaches down. His hand around my throat is cold like porcelain. He rips me away from the body of my love. My whole side is damp with blood. I gasp for air. My legs kick feebly.

I have no powers. I cannot escape or cut him down. My fingers scrabble at his robe, trying to find flesh beneath. I want to gouge and rip, but his skin is cold and unyielding.

His hand squeezes tight. The world darkens around me. There's a cracking sound as bones in my neck give way. He releases me, and I fall to the ground, discarded again.

I look across at Dylan, slumped against the wall. Blood oozes from their lips.

"Now come. Heaven awaits."

Breath whistles in through my broken throat. I get to my feet, very slowly.

"I think you mean hell."

Jesus turns to regard me. The holes of his eyes spill light. "Hell is simple, Violet. Anyone can do penance in hell. You simply burn and burn and burn some more, all the while regretting the actions that led you there. It's the end of an arc. It's *completion*."

"I don't understand." It hurts to talk, but at least that distracts me from how much it hurts to simply stand here with Dylan at my feet.

"When you've been there ten thousand years." A smile stretches across his face, wide and blazing and filled with too many glistening teeth. "You'll have no less days to sing God's praise than when you first began." He reaches out a hand to me. "Isn't infinity *terrifying?* There's no apotheosis. No resolution.

Only you, gazing upon an abyss of infinite love that can never be filled, desperately trying to *appease* it."

I turn to look at Dylan. One final time, so I can fix them in my mind. I refuse to forget them, refuse to have them burned from my mind, no matter how long I stand before the throne.

"Come." The hand that takes mine burns. "God awaits."

Something yanks me forward, and I topple into a golden abyss, where a chorus of voices rises around me in chilling, unearthly splendour. For a moment, I sense the passages in the world that I can fold myself into, and I reach for them, but I am standing on the edges of a vertiginous drop.

I fall.

The light fades, and I am in darkness.

I open my eyes. My hands are folded neatly together on a silken tablecloth. A plate of dinner sits steaming in front of me.

"—in the Lord's name, Amen."

No. *Fuck* no. Not again.

My father unfolds his hands. His eyes open.

"Violet." His gaze lands on me with the force of a blow. "What have you done?"

I force myself to meet his gaze. So many times, I shied away. My fear of him—and of what he could make me do—drowned out everything else that was in me.

No longer. Dylan is not dead at my hand. They live. I will not let him break me, whatever this is. Hell or heaven, or something else.

I am Penance, and I will atone for what I've done. I'll find my way back, and I'll tell people I love them, even if my heart is broken. I'll fight for my life. For myself.

"I have done nothing." I smile at my father. I show him all my teeth, like my sister Marisol would. "Yet."

CHAPTER 13

TENTACLE PRINCESS
RECENTLY

It's almost a relief to be here. Some moments of peace. Threads intertwine, creating patterns. It is hard to tell what is new and what already existed. Narrative is both elastic and concrete. Once a story is written, can it be unwritten? How much can you erase before it becomes another story entirely? A life is made up of multiple arcs, some of which resolve and some of which merely—

I FIND this place rather comforting, the great echoing metal temple that has become my home. There is nothing forcing me to stay here, despite the great many words the one called Boss Lady expends to tell me the contrary. If I wished to leave, I would simply change form and unmake this place. I am reluctant to do so, because of the kind mutant that calls itself Hench, and the other naming itself Goat Bitch.

Sorry. This is not correct.

Goat Bitch has explained something to me called *pronouns*. A feature of the way this human language of theirs works, to ascribe particular characteristics of some importance. I fail to see precisely how any of this matters, but Goat Bitch ensures me it does.

Hench is a *she*, as is Goat Bitch. I am a *xe*. It was entirely my choice, and of little import, and yet. In my native tongue, rendered as close as possible to human speech, my clutch were named Fr'gntathxe. As a small and pitiful offshoot, to use the final syllable as my *pronoun* seems rather apt. Originally, Hench called Goat Bitch *he*. This led to a loud disagreement, which I resolved by some handwaving and stern talk. We are all some combination of physical form and energy, and it seems simplest to refer to people as they wish to be.

"Hello, she," I say to Goat Bitch, materialising in her cell. It is much easier to do this than to paddle around manipulating these awkward limbs.

"TeePee." The mutant smiles, which is a sign of friendship. Calling me TeePee instead of xe or Tentacle Princess is similarly affectionate. It is some form of human linguistic trick to do with initials. "See anything interesting out there today?"

I move my head back and forth to indicate a negative status.

"Shit. This is very bad."

"I will not let them hurt you," I assure her.

"You don't get it. Nobody's come to rescue me. That means Farsight can't see in here, because the team would have busted me out the instant she did. And if they're shielded from Farsight, we're dealing with—"

I don't know if this is a good or bad friendship sign, but sometimes I am content to let Goat Bitch talk, and do not parse the meaning of every single one of her sentences. She spends much time being agitated, and wanting to force events to take place. It is not a trait common to my species, although I do recall it of both humans and mutants in the before-time. This leads me to ponder the nature of Lilith.

"I recall your progenitor," I tell Goat Bitch, when she falls silent.

"My what? You met my parents?"

It takes a moment for me to understand this term. "Not parent precisely, although replicate the concept by a staggering factor, and I believe we are talking about the same thing."

Goat Bitch lets out a loud bray of the sound called laughter. "Sometimes I have no fucking idea how we communicate at all."

"Lilith," I say.

"You mean like the mother of demons Lilith? From the myths?"

I tease out the meaning of all these words. "She was very real. The first of your kind, able to shape others to wield abilities unlike those of humanity."

"This is a mindfuck," Goat Bitch says, which causes me to wave my tentacles in alarm, because all permutations of this phrase's meaning disturb me.

"I do not wish any—"

"Mother of demons, mother of mutants. Typical that they've hated us from the beginning, isn't it? Same sort of shit that led to me being in here." She leans back against the wall and drums her atypical limbs on the floor, making loud noises with their bony protrusions.

"Your kind destroyed mine." I'm surprised to find myself spouting these words forth, as if it is a confession of wrongdoing.

"Holy shit. You're not kidding?"

I wave my tentacles and shake my head all at once.

"So we're like, ancient enemies or some shit?"

"No." I reach for Goat Bitch with all my limbs. "I do not wish such a thing."

"Good." She pats me with her limbs. "A new era of peace and co-operation between mutants and tentacle types, huh?"

I incline my head in a sign of acceptance.

"You're an odd one. You've really been alive since the dawn of time or some shit?"

"That would be impossible. We evolved like any other species. We were simply quicker than you. By the time your species was capable of worship, we were already here. Waiting. Ready to—" I find myself strangely reluctant to confess to the crimes of my people. Besides, I can already feel the unmistakable ripple of energy informing me that Hench is on her way to my cell.

"Bee are bee," I say, and translocate myself back to the room where I arrange my many limbs in a pose of apparent contemplation. It is only moments before Hench appears.

"Wakey, wakey." She lifts one large hand.

I mimic the movement as Hench strolls down the corridor.

"How you doing in there, Goats, my girl? Still mad at the world?"

"Go fuck yourself."

"That's what I like to hear."

"I'm just looking forward to the day the whole gang arrives." Something breaks in the cell beside mine. "Then you'll be a lot less cheerful. I wonder who'll kill you first. Probably Nails. They do hold a grudge."

"Sorry." Hench makes an exaggerated face of sadness. "I shouldn't poke the bear. Or the goat. Come on, little alien. You're not exempt from poking and prodding, because the big boss has more ideas on how you work."

The cell door disappears, and I walk forward as if I'm excited to be free. I find the scientist's poking and prodding irritating, but hardly insufferable. It's like she's discovered a box full of a great many mysterious things, and doesn't understand what any of the contents actually do. It's probably a very good thing. I suspect if she was successful, she would cease to exist, along with everything else nearby.

I follow silently through the tunnels until we reach the laboratory. There is a great ring on the wall that Boss Lady calls *the machine* and Hench calls *that fucking machine*.

Apparently, I am to power it. How is another mystery, but it seems the poking and prodding will continue until it is figured out. As usual, I stand in the middle of the room, while the scientist bombards me with various forms of energy.

If I had the attitude of Goat Bitch, I would probably open myself up, just a fractional amount, enough for the scientist to peer into the void and see the void peering right back at her. The problem is that if she didn't die, I think that would *excite her*, and we don't want any of my old family traits being awakened.

"You are a problem," Boss Lady says.

I droop my limbs down, as if I'm very sad.

"I have people I answer to. People I've made assurances to. Who have expectations of progress and eventual success." The suit vents a little cloud of steam at the neck joint. "People who'd be very unhappy if I failed."

"Ah." I try to say little to the scientist.

"Do you know what? As Hench might say, fuck them. Our goals coincide. They want something, I want something. I have no moral or ethical problem with their goals. In fact, I agree with them. But what I'm really here for is—" One arm of the suit reaches out and picks something up from the desk. "Do you know what this is?"

I shuffle closer. "It appears to be a realistic rendering of a humanoid figure."

The mask tilts first one way and then the other. She suspects I'm being humorous, but I am merely stating a fact. "Yes, precisely, of course. Do you know who it is?"

"One humanoid is very much like another." This *is* a joke of mine, because I mostly cannot tell them apart, although I perhaps could if I expended effort. They're interchangeable to me. A prey species, as horrifying as that truth is, and it is one I recoil from. Although I do recognise mutants are predators.

There is no energy coming from this image.

"This is the man I loved." The scientist taps one metal suit-finger against it. The word means little to me, although the mutant speaks as if it should. It tastes of connection. Some alternative form of clutch. A rich and nuanced word, more so than many human words. I would like to hear people speak more of love.

"Love." It tastes very different from my tongue. There is little resonance.

"I was not good at love. Too angry, too focused on darkness. He followed me, because he understood what love was. I led him into death."

One of my limbs flickers involuntarily. It means *death is inevitable, for both your kind and mine.* I do not make any sounds of human speech.

"This thing I want from you is not *only* for the whims of powerful men. It's not only to unmake a god and destroy her degenerate children. It is for love, and for a good man."

I barely notice the complexity of the word love, for my attention is snagged on a far more tantalising prospect.

"God." This one tastes as terrifying and intoxicating when I say it.

"Shorthand." The scientist still gazes down at the image in her hand. "It is an energy matrix spanning the planet. The mutant high command has tamed it, or they are its instrument. Nobody is quite clear on the details. We all agree, however, that it must be stopped."

I do not respond. I cannot. I tear apart the memory-stone inside me, shattering along multiple axes and caring not. There are memories of the great journey, which I let disintegrate into the void. Travel between the stars is dull, and there is nothing of worth there. What I seek is—

There.

The arrival. When our ships flowered in the sky above the planet, and disgorged the first arrivals. Vast monoliths of alien flesh floating in the young seas and feeding desperately, greedily. This new-born globe, with a web of consciousness threaded through it. Young and vibrant and delicious. They drank her dry, my ancestors, this nascent goddess.

Nothing remained of her, and the world was ours.

That is what the memories tell, and they are the record of our people and they are never wrong. It is—

No.

Sparks, ignored as dying flickers. Not enough to even taste. Distributed far and wide, some lost among budding forests and on newly birthed mountain peaks. Places where my kind feared to tread.

Cunning little goddess. Spread so thin. How did she survive so long in such a hostile environment?

Yet she did, and she turned her mind to revenge.

This is the spark from where Lucifer and Lilith came. The instruments with which a goddess took her revenge. And now she is resurgent. Now I know what I am looking for, I find her everywhere. Hiding in plain sight.

And a coruscating beacon in the distance.

An island, full of mutants. The children of a goddess. The ancient enemy of my people.

Surely, she will have noticed I am awake.

She will come for me.

I reach out one limb tentatively towards the scientist. "How do we unmake a god?"

CHAPTER 14

TWINKLE LIGHTS
RECENTLY

Even good things come to an end, no matter how much we wish they didn't. There is tragedy tucked inside so many stories. You might think a happy ending is inevitable, but it takes so much work.

A WEEK GOES PAST, and I'm spending a lot of time with my new team. It's mostly casual hanging out, eating together, and a little bit of physical training. We haven't had a repeat of bowling or dancing, but then there hasn't been a mission either. I feel like we're all getting comfortable with each other.

Penance is still the hardest to read. She's the least *there*, and will often disappear mid-conversation. None of the others ever comment on this, so I go along too.

Feral, despite the ferocious exterior, is by her own reckoning *a goddamn fucking delight*, and I can't argue. She's always aware of everyone's emotional state, ensuring they're cared for and part of the team. I'm not sure why they needed a babysitter with her around, but I'm not complaining. It's Feral that puts me at ease about Penance, because I'm fast learning that she'll do anything for the person she calls her sister.

Witchmade is remarkably easygoing for someone in a team of assassins. She finds almost everything funny, and the team has so many shared jokes it's hard to keep up. I do a lot of clueless laughing. She's in a relationship with Feral that appears to be friends with benefits. Neither of them take it seriously, and when teased by the others, trade the most astonishingly intimate details that make me blush. She has dual powers— the first is low-level fortune telling based on inspecting the innards of various roadkill that some poor unknown collects for her. The reason she's on the team, however, is that she can sap the life force from people, draining them of vitality. I can't imagine it, looking at the way she laughs.

Nails is foul-mouthed, painfully sarcastic, and fiercely loyal to Goat Bee. Her powers appear to be that she can shoot nails from her hands, although there's *something* going on under the ever-present scarf that covers her mouth. It'd be rude to ask, but I'm desperate to know.

Goat Bee is almost as quiet as Penance. Sometimes I get the sense she's watching the others to determine how to behave, then following suit. Feral flirts shamelessly with her, which sends her into a tailspin that's adorable. I'm not sure if she ever had a relationship with Nails, but if they did, it's over and done with and they're now inseparable friends.

Together, it's like being part of a chaotic and frequently embarrassing family where I've been stuck or blessed— depending on the day, and how they're choosing to torment me —with a gaggle of siblings. I was supposed to charm them and make them feel at ease, but it's the other way around.

And then I enter the common room one morning to find them all dressed in black.

"Twinkles." Feral bares her teeth at me. Her ears are back and the ruff of fur around her neck is fluffed up. "How do you feel about an outing?"

Nails claps me on the shoulder. "Go easy. Our boy's been lulled."

"Forgot we were pretty pretty murder princesses."

"Only the murder part." I smile back at her.

"Don't worry." Goat Bee sits in a chair with one hoof up, sharpening the edges with a file. "We only kill when it's necessary."

"Necessary." Feral makes airquotes. "You want to come along for the ride, Sparkle Bright?"

"Don't want you to have to look after me." I'm tempted. The group of them has a gravity and I want to fall into the heart of them, danger be damned.

Feral nudges me. "You can be our human torch."

I pat the soft fur at her shoulder. "No, I shouldn't go. But I'll be here to patch your wounds and debrief you on your safe return."

She snorts, and turns her attention elsewhere. "What do the entrails say, Witchie?"

"More cryptic than usual." Witchmade looks up from the table, where she's got an old fashioned monocle in one eye and a jeweller's loupe in the other. Both are etched with curious symbols. A blackbird is on the table in front of her, guts spread in a haphazard sprawl.

"Tell us anyway," Nails says. "It makes a body a mite fuckin' superstitious otherwise."

"Okay, let's see. We've got... unspecified proclamations of doom. So far, so Tuesday. Then a closing eye. An octopus rising from the sea. A door that won't open, with someone banging on it."

"Fine." Feral taps her claws on the table. "Let's avoid doors and octopuses. And I'll gouge out any eyes I see. Doom averted."

Penance hangs above the group, pale and luminous. "We don't go in unless there's doom."

Witchmade grimaces and swipes the bird carcass across the table. "I'm not getting anything clear. It's just *vibes*. Bad ones. I feel like something fucked is coming, but there's no *story* to it. Usually, I can trace a narrative, but this is all fractured scenes like I'm seeing four auguries at once." Her usually smiling face is somber. It's enough to cast a pall over the group.

"So we don't go?" Nails asks. "Trust the fuckin' voodoo?"

Witchmade raises an eyebrow. "It's not voodoo."

"Apologies. I misspoke. You know what I'm saying."

"Who tells the boss if we're bailing?" Goat Bee asks.

"I'll do it." Penance says. "But I don't think we should quit."

"Someone has a crush," Feral sing-songs. "Doesn't want to disappoint sweet Dilly-Dills."

"You know I only call you my sister because you're so insufferably annoying that you must be related to me." Penance flickers a single blade out to slice through air above Feral's head, who keeps the same grinning expression the whole time. "But no, I don't want to disappoint Dylan. We're the last resort."

"I'm good to go," Witchmade says. "My third eye's all gunked up is all."

Nails tugs the scarf tighter about their face. "If the whole fuckin' gang's all going, I'm not the asshole staying behind."

I'm watching this conversation, because I know when to keep my mouth shut, unlike some people. Goat Bee isn't saying anything either. I think she's about to, when the door bangs open and Chatterbox strides into the room.

"My darlings." Their eyes are stormy. "We live in interesting fucking times. I am fucked on multiple fronts. UwU are out hunting cults, I'm dealing with... honestly, irritating phantom shit. And now we've got Quietus Science Club trying to usher in the era of the Antichrist or something? Tell me some good news." Their eyes fall on Witchmade.

I have no idea how they know anything happened. This is one person who I'm unsettled by. Everyone else seems to love and respect them, but I feel that I'm in the presence of something unknowable. Like they *haunt* me somehow, and I can't figure it out. Oh, well. Shove it down along with everything else because my new friends love Dylan Taylor, and I trust them.

Witchmade shrugs. "My augury was... unsettling. We need to be careful."

The tiny flowers along their shoulders wilt slightly as Chatterbox slumps into the chair beside Goat Bee. "We can pull the plug if anyone's unsure. Or switch up the team. Confuse the fucking future. I'll lend you Moodring. She hasn't gotten to play in a while."

"Don't think that's how the future works," Witchmade says.

"Fuck." Chatterbox fists their hands, sprouting thorns. "Shit, maybe I'll go in myself."

"Dylan." Penance is no longer a ghostly face in the sky, but the diminutive woman with the sleek dark hair. "We can do this for you."

"You don't have to."

"Delegate." A smile curves her lips. "Isn't that what Dani keeps saying?"

"Using Dani against me. Unfair." Dylan gets to their feet.

"Okay. But please be fucking careful. If someone doesn't come back... I'd rather not go to war today."

"You won't have to." Feral stands behind them, running her claws lightly down Dylan's spine. This group. They're so cute, honestly. I wish my powers were greater, and I could take a *real* place alongside them. I picture myself, bullets of coloured light erupting from my outstretched fists, a rainbow barrage pushing back dark forces. All of us, descending on the ruins of the facility that held me, tearing its dark halls open and filling them with light. Finding the people who held me and making them—

No, that's not right. That won't help anything. The past is gone, it's a ghost that barely haunts me, and I'm in the present with these people, unshadowed and unafraid. It makes me want to stand with them even more. I'd fight for them, because they deserve it.

Once the hug is complete, another mutant enters. They're pale and pretty and have the air of someone who finds conversation a difficult bridge to cross. They give me a brief nod before crossing to the ring of mutants and pressing their hand to Penance's back.

She winks out of existence. The process is repeated until the room is empty of everyone but Chatterbox, the new arrival, and me.

"Twinkle Lights, Keepaway," Chatterbox says. "And vice versa."

"Teleportation." They actually blush, which is adorable.

I look at my fingers, which stubbornly refuse to emit anything at all. "Twinkle Lights."

"The name." Keepaway's cheeks flare even darker red. "Gives it away."

"Stop flirting with the himbo." Dylan grins. "He belongs to the menaces, and you can't distract him."

"I..." Keepaway gulps, and for a moment I think they'll pass out, but they scurry out of the room without further comment.

"You pretty people." Dylan rolls their eyes. "Have any of my assassins hit on you yet? I expect you to be professional."

"No." I'm relieved. Some of them are forces of nature, and I'm not sure how you're supposed to deny someone like Witch-made or Feral.

"It never gets easy." They're pacing the room, hand twitching. "Waiting for them to come back. I could *be* there."

"You actually care about them." Once again, I blurt it out before I can catch the words back.

The pacing stops. Their eyes are wide. The petals along their arms tremble. "You think I send them out to suffer because... fuck, I don't know? I'm some mad creature drunk on power?"

"No. God, no, dude, what, I, don't—" Help, I don't think I'm being convincing.

"Then what? Fucking what, Twinkle Lights?"

Great, now I'm providing therapy to Chatterbox. Maybe I'm out of my depth here, but I say it anyway. "I worry you see monsters in every corner."

There's this awful tense moment where I wonder if I'm going to be struck down by some unearthly force and then they laugh. They collapse into a chair and keep gurgling with delight, until I'm wondering if I broke them.

"Dude, I'm sorry." I lurch in for a hug, but they wave me away.

"Fuck no. I worry the exact same shit. Like, is this my life now? I'm just stabbing Abigail Tanner over and over again, because I can't deal with all the shit that's piled up in front of me?"

I think I'm one of the only people who didn't see that happen. Back then, I was chilling, minding my own business. If

I did hear about mutants, I honestly thought it was some flat-earth type shit made up by YouTubers. I saw it eventually. God, they looked so young back then. These days, I think they're a lot more dangerous, but I still want to give them a hug. I think they need it, even though they've got a whole clan around them.

Then Penance appears in front of us. "Dilly, it's Goat Bitch. She's gone."

Chatterbox changes instantly. Any softness is discarded. If I took them in my arms right now, I'd be sliced to ribbons. It makes me wish I had equivalent powers, to sharpen myself too. It's time to go into battle. Fight shit that needs fighting, even if all I can do is flash up some lights. Maybe I can dazzle someone long enough for someone with claws or thorns to do their business.

They took Goat Bee. Someone hurt our friend.

"We need to do something," I blurt, but Dylan is focused on Penance.

"What the fuck happened?"

CHAPTER 15

GOAT BITCH
THEN

I can look at this for now. The collapse of reality is still some way in the distance. It's almost peaceful, following this strand. Love and friendship is hard to tell apart, especially when you're stranded in an abandoned mall, somewhere that looks like the end of the world.

IT'S eighteen days before I'm released from quarantine. It seems like an arbitrary length of time, but I'm no expert in mutant science. I've apparently passed all their tests and scans and requests for information. Nails comes by occasionally to check on me, although we've never had a conversation like the first one. Maybe I scared them, opening up my big ugly heart and dumping all that shit on them. It wouldn't be the first time. Every other conversation is more like them reading off a check-list. Ensuring I'm feeling physically healthy, that I'm not bouncing off the walls too hard. To avoid staring into the pit of my soul, I watch old science fiction shows and read a book about necromancers in space. I even find myself working out. That's how goddamn bored I am. It's not like I never did out there—you want to keep yourself fast and sharp, but now I'm safe. Now I get to be soft.

When the door finally opens, I'm a little surprised that Nails is standing there. They're as muffled as ever, and I wonder if it's as cold in the mall itself as in these corridors.

"Congratufuckinlations." Nails gives me two thumbs up with their big grey hands. "You survived. Not everyone does, you know."

"What happens to the ones who don't?" I have this sinking feeling I know the answer. Safety comes at a price. You don't have your miracle mall in the middle of nightmare country without a few dead bodies.

"What would you do?" Nails asks, which is the answer I expected.

I shrug, and we set off down the corridor together.

"Anyway, welcome to the inner sanctum. According to the Pirate Internet, this is one of the last free settlements of mutants in the world. Twenty-one of us. Twenty-two now, I suppose. There's one in Lagos, and one in Angkor Wat that are doing okay, but we're officially the biggest. Hooray for us, huh?"

We reach a beat-up metal door with a camera whirring atop it. It makes a loud clunk, and creaks open slowly.

"Tada." Nails actually sounds like they're smiling. Behind the door it's light and airy. There are plants, and running water, and weirdly upbeat music playing. "Sorry about the tunes. Apparently it's wired into the climate control system, and nobody can figure out how to unfuck it."

I don't care. They can play this ancient Windows 98 CD-ROM shit all day. This is the most beautiful thing I've seen since...

"It's okay to cry." Nails pats my shoulder. "Everyone does. I fuckin' did. It's like... how can this be real, right?"

"Yes." I turn in a slow circle. The light is artificial. The plants are artificial. High above, the ceiling is stained blue like a summer sky. There are three layers of stores. Most look shuttered, but one nearby has been cleared out to make room for furniture. There are fifteen different couches all jammed in haphazardly, and the walls are covered with posters and reproductions of famous paintings.

"That's Fluff's apartment. She's probably messing around in the aircon system. You'll meet her later on. Eventually. She's a bit shy of new people. Lots of people here are, on account of fuckin'... everything."

I make a grunt of acknowledgment. I've only spent a short time in the Wastes, but you quickly adapt to seeing everyone and everything as predator or danger. I'm still overwhelmed. It's impossible. This sort of place is gone from the world, especially for mutants. It's submit to Michael or fight for scraps.

"How?" I ask.

"Goddess." Nails waves a hand at a couple of faces peering down at us from the next level up. "Or that's the story. She's occupied fighting Michael on a million different fronts, but she set up a few places like this around the world. For those stubborn fucks like us that didn't want to fit into her little ascension chamber."

"I don't know what you're talking about."

"Fuckin' mutant politics." Nails laughs. "Would you rather end the world as a twinkle in Goddess's eye, or crawling round in the dirt? Most choose option one. Me? I've always been a fucking and fighting type."

I didn't know there was an option. Somehow I missed the mutant memo. I almost tip into maudlin self-pity about how

I'm the misfit even among a group of misfits. It's my comfortable place, where I've found myself returning to on so many nights huddled in the wreckage of buildings and burned-out cars.

Except now I'm here.

The mall at the end of the world. Who'd have known a pastel monument to consumerism could look so beautiful? It's safety and comfort, soundtracked by AI-generated cheer.

"It's okay. I get it. It's overwhelming as fuck." Nails gestures in the direction of the escalator, rising like a stairway to heaven in the middle of the cavernous space. "Come meet people. If you're ready."

"Sure." I'm not sure if I am, but let's get it over with. There's always a moment with new people where you have to assert yourself. *Yes*, this is who I am. Coming out over and over, asking people to see you, knowing some of them will see it as an imposition, that some of them will deny you. It felt too hard, for so long.

We ride up the escalator, and I see a small group has gathered at the top. Panic rises in my throat. They're all looking at me. Judging me. I know people are concerned with their own lives, and their own shit, especially at this ass-end of the world, but people still judge. I should fucking know. I am the worst, most judgemental person.

The person in front has a torrent of fiery hair, a constellation of freckles and an enormous set of antlers jutting from her forehead.

"Nice horns," she says.

"Uh." Here I am making a good impression. "You too. Uh, antlers I mean."

Nobody comments on how embarrassing I am.

"I do like them, but they make doorways a huge problem." She smiles. "My name's John."

"Oh. Cool."

"For Deer John. Everyone thinks it's clever. The antlers, you know."

I am tanking this conversation so hard. I'm ready to go running out into the Wastes where I don't have to interact with anyone ever again.

"This here is Goat Bitch." Nails fills in for me. "She's been out in the Wastes a while. I'm sure you all remember what a mindfuck it is adjusting to a bunch of staring fuckin' faces."

"Of course." John takes my hand as the others arrange themselves in a semicircle.

There are too many. I'm not going to remember their names.

"Talon."

"Eerie."

"Admiral."

"Parallax."

Everyone's blurring together. I'm shaking hands and smiling, but I'm not managing to actually *say* anything.

"It's fine." Nails is at my side. "You'll meet everyone again. There's not going to be a quiz. You've got this."

We reach the end of the semicircle finally. I can feel myself shaking. The cell where I spent quarantine seems preferable to whatever this is.

"Everything's fine." Nail's voice is rough but it's reassuring. I want to cling to them, but they don't seem like the clinging type. "Why don't we find somewhere quieter. Meet the boss."

"Boss?" Finally a strangled word escapes my lips.

"Yeah. They like the quiet. Keep to themself. Sound good?"

I nod, and Nails tucks one arm through mine. Maybe they don't mind some clinging after all. I totter after them, and we pass shops where towers of canned goods are arranged. This is obviously how they're feeding themselves. As we approach the second escalator, I see an enormous water feature cascading down the wall. Hoses thread their way to the ground below, where a series of tanks sit.

"Water's good to drink," Nails says. "We've got rations for washing, but if you've been out in the Wastes, you're pretty fuckin' hygiene flexible, right? You get a five minute hot shower every three days which sounds—"

"Like five minutes in heaven." I laugh, almost giddy at the thought. The closest thing I've had lately was a freezing rainstorm in a mud-slick field. Even in quarantine, I've only been using wipes.

"As a newbie, you'll get first shower tonight. Still waiting for the fuckin' tanks to heat. By the time you've had a chat to the boss, it'll probably be ready."

The thought of such luxury distracts me on the escalator ride up, until I notice it ends in another dark tunnel with a metal door. We stand for a moment in front, while multiple cameras whirr.

"Goat Bitch." The voice is electronic but still somehow cheerful. "Welcome to my humble abode."

The door clanks open to reveal a scene almost as jarring as my first glimpse of the mall. The room is small and lined with the same black metal as the quarantine cells. Except these are awash in neon light, cycling through garish pinks, greens and yellows. It's a bunch of old signs repurposed, although the words they spell have no meaning to me, a language of symbols that look ancient or alien.

Sitting amongst it all is a complex network of cables, forming something like a cradle. A body is slung in the middle of it, hanging suspended with the cables wrapped around it but also connecting to it. Chunky grey connectors have been embedded into the person's skin, wiring them in.

A visored head turns towards the door. Neon pulses flicker across the surface, like schools of bright fish darting into darkness.

"Welcome, welcome. How do you like the place? The mall I mean, not my lair. I've a bizarre fondness for the whole *abandoned mall at the end of the world* vibe. Very Encarta Nights of me."

"It's amazing."

"Yes, yes, of course. The whole safe refuge from the nightmare outside. I'm talking more about the general aesthetic of the place, but you've probably not had time to appreciate it yet. Sorry about the delays, by the way. The network is clogged with assholes and it takes a lot to filter out the chaff."

"For what delays?" I ask. "I'm confused. Sorry. It's all—"

"God, yes. Wow. Skipping the important stuff to talk about malls. Sorry, right. I'm in the middle of, well, too many things. I'm the Pirate Internet."

"You're connected to it?"

"No. I am it. I generate the network. From here, I sprawl out across the Wastes like a very confused data-spider. I generate the terminals your phone connects to. I'm the one that dumped the data cache that let you reprovision it out of Michael's nasty little hands. It is a *job* keeping ahead of that fucker, I tell you. But someone's gotta do it, and I have an advantage or two."

It makes a surprising amount of sense. I've often found the Pirate Internet surprisingly helpful at providing what I needed despite the unreliability of it. Something that's obviously been done on purpose.

"Thank you," I say. "I couldn't have made it without you."

"Goddess provided us a bolthole. My job is to get as many

mutants here as possible. Ride out the end of the world together and wait for regular service to be restored."

"You really think that will happen?"

Nails snorts beside me.

"Someone in this place has to be an optimist, don't they?" The Pirate Internet's head scrolls pink text, too fast for me to read. "It may not all be as dire as you think. For now, you're safe. Long may it last."

"Long may it last," Nails mutters, and I echo them. It feels like a prayer.

CHAPTER 16
HENCH

ELSEWHEN

The climax slipped through my fingers before I could do anything about it and now we're here. A not-place, except no less real for the people here. Watch for the broken fragments. They can still cut you and make you bleed. These two are tougher than most, but there's a tendency certain people have to deal with situations in unhelpful ways.

I MAY HAVE FUCKED this up just a little. First, I threw the furry one away. In my defence, I woke up with her clambering all over me, and it's not like her claws aren't sharp little things.

Then I insulted their boss, Chatterbox—or at least that's how they took it. Then I admitted I henched, which so-called hero types tend to take a low opinion of, and I should've known better than to open my damn mouth in that regard.

Lastly, I stood by, trying not to agitate them even more, and now the small terrifying one that's mostly made of knives has disappeared.

"Where the fuck did she go?" The furry one is glaring up at me, as if any of this was my fault.

"I was literally standing here doing nothing. Don't blame this on me." I try to keep my tone nice and calm, like I do when I'm dealing with bosses.

"You're a villain. You fucking admitted it. You work for the assholes and take their money. So now we're stranded in whatever this place is, and my sister's disappeared. You're involved. You're *responsible*." Her golden eyes are huge, and her catlike ears are pinned back. The ruff of fur on her neck is all puffed out and she has an actual tail, with some wicked looking metal spike on the end, that's bobbing about beside her head. She's very angry, and very deadly, and gods fucking help me.

I feel a frisson of *something*.

Of all the reasons for me to curse myself, this has always been the worst. I have terrible taste in people.

"If I am responsible, I have no idea *how*, so it doesn't help." I fold my arms across my chest and glare down at her. Two can play this game.

"Works for the villains and has absolutely no use at all. Fantastic." She literally hisses, and it's so cute I could die. Stop *thinking like this*, Hench. "This is the worst mission I've ever been on."

Okay, so one of us needs to be slightly rational and in some horrifying twist of fate, it might have to be me. I don't want to say the wrong thing, and get my throat ripped out by those claws of hers. This is not my job. I'm not the fucking sane one. My hand goes to the scratches at my neck.

"Look, I don't want to fight. So let's find your sister."

Her eyes narrow. One corner of her upper lip curls. A canine gleams, one that could pierce my flesh like I'm butter under her...

Jesus. Get a hold of yourself.

"A truce. That's what I'm suggesting." I hold out one hand.

The sneer is still in full effect. She looks at me like I'm something that crawled out of a swamp, which compared to her, is not entirely wrong. Her tail gives one last violent twitch and drapes itself over her shoulder.

"Fine. A truce. That lasts until you do the first thing I don't trust. Then I rip out your throat, your heart, and your balls and leave you for dead."

I blink at her. "I don't have balls."

She throws her head back and laughs. "It's a fucking metaphor, bitch. Wow. I know you're like old and shit, but keep up. You've got big dick energy in both senses of the word."

Okay, good. I'm back to wanting to stomp on her again. Normal service restored. She's like ridiculously, soul-destroyingly hot, but also who would *ever* want to endure this?

"I'm twenty-five," I say.

She laughs again and punches me in the shoulder. "Seen some shit, huh? Or else in three years, shit's gonna get rough for me." She gives an exaggerated shudder.

I'm honestly this close to throwing her and seeing how close I can get to hitting the sun, which—

Wait. What?

"There's no sun." I point dramatically at the sky.

"Welcome to thirty minutes ago. Like the rest of us noticed the second we got here. There's something wrong about this place. Penny said it's broken."

"Penny?"

"Uh, Penance? The stabby stabby one? My sister who I'd roam through some broken world on a quest with some irritating henchperson for?"

I take a deep breath. I count to ten, and try it again. I'm still mad.

"Are you always this annoying?"

"I'm a goddamn fucking delight." She places one hand to her chest, and I absolutely one hundred percent do not notice the way it rises and falls. On the other hand, I also know we need to *do* something or else we're going to get into a fight.

I mean, I've got super strength and she's got claws and tail, so I'd obviously beat the shit out of her, but I might feel bad about it. A little bit bad. She probably needs a lesson or two. Scratch that, she needs a whole fucking degree's worth of lessons.

Scratch. Heh.

"What's so fucking funny?" The sneer is back on her face. One claw flexes.

How can a mouth so full of teeth be sexy?

"Let's move," I say. "You pick the direction."

Feral turns in a slow circle. Everything around us is featureless and grey. The sky is washed out. There's no way to navigate.

"I hate this," she says, quietly, so I almost have to strain to hear. "Penny's, like, she's all knives and edges but she's been through some shit, you know? And I hate to think of her lost in this fucking place."

"It's okay." I'm not usually one for reassuring people, but I must be going soft, what with Tentacle Princess and now this. "We'll look. We'll find your sister."

She gives me a half-smile. "Will we just? Beauty and the Beast, huh?"

I'm momentarily thrown, trying to parse this, and my mouth moves on its own. "Are you calling me Beauty?"

"Wow, Hench. Fucking wow. Just because I have a tail, I am automatically the beast? You fucking bigot."

The expression on her face could be a smile or a snarl. "Uh." I need a response to this. "Uh, um."

Feral winks one golden eye and flicks her tail teasingly in my direction. "I'm joking. I am the beauty and the beast, all wrapped up in one, whereas you..."

She never finishes the sentence, tailing off into laughter, and my brain is completely incoherent like I'm mentally mashing the keyboard of my thoughts.

"You're very annoying." I keep my voice flat.

"It's been said. Once or twice. Usually by people who are struggling to fight against the terribly inevitable tug of adoration."

"Jesus. Do you have an off switch at all?"

Her grin is back in full effect. "You'd probably have to kill me."

"That can be arranged."

One eyebrow goes up. She's enjoying this far too much. "I'd like to see you try, you sad little windup toy." The tip of her tongue is resting against the sharp little teeth at the front of her mouth. My heart kicks in my chest like a wild horse.

"Isn't this wasting time?" I ask, instead of all the other things I want to say.

"You're the one who keeps insulting me, like you think banter is a good use of our time." She crouches down, and uses one claw to scrape a line in the stone at our feet. Then she draws an arrow pointing in one direction.

"Starting point," Feral says. "If we find ourselves back here, we'll know something's fucking with us."

"Oh," I say. It's smart.

"Not just a pretty face, am I?" She grins up at me and gets to her feet in one fluid, catlike motion. I think about how dangerous she could be, with her speed and her claws, and my heart kicks again. Then her eyes narrow, and I watch the fur at her neck fluff again. "Now no bullshit. I'm watching you."

I realise what she's doing, and a flush creeps up my cheeks. She's keeping me off balance. Feral is a predator, and she sees me as one too. I'm a danger, so she's using every trick she can to keep me off balance. Including seduction and emotional manipulation.

I feel a wave of shame that crests inside me, and I clench my fists tight. Most of me wants to punch something, but I can't afford to. For now, we're stuck here, and I don't want to spook this mutant into fighting. I might need her help to get back to Boss Lady and get paid. I just wish I could remember what happened.

"Come on then." There's another flash of smile, beautiful and deadly all at once. I can't afford to be fooled. "See if you can keep up."

She lopes across the ground, moving effortlessly and very fast. I have to strain to keep up with her, and I'm pretty sure she's not even breaking a sweat. I try not to notice the way her muscles move under her skin, the way the light fur on the backs of her neck ripples slightly. She's so *aware*, her head scanning, her ears twitching.

There's nothing wrong with appreciating something extraordinary. I just need to be smart, and not do one of those useless Hench moves where I don't think enough before I act. Too used to being given orders, I guess. Letting other people make the poor decisions that fuck my life up.

Got to pay attention, figure out the right moves. Don't let this scrappy smartass push me around just because she's—

No. Don't even think that. The word gorgeous doesn't apply. She's terrifying. Powerful. Untrustworthy. Deadly.

She turns around and jogs backward, still moving faster than me.

"Stop huffing and puffing. You're so loud I can't hear anything else."

"Super strength… doesn't necessarily extend… to running… across… an endless desert… of stone."

"Fine." She stops, hands on her hips. "You want to wait here, and I'll go off at an actual non-snail's pace and see if I can find anything."

I stop, and I'm grateful for it. "No." I shake my head. "Don't want… to split."

Feral tips her head back and looks at the sky. "There's nothing *here*. My eyesight is damn good, and there's *nothing*. Just more of this." She swings one arm. "Like an endlessly scrolling level where nobody's added anything to it yet. The fucking infinite."

"There's got to be something. Where did your sister go?"

"Mutant power." Feral raises one furry, muscular shoulder in a shrug. "She can see places and go where others can't. The fact she hasn't come back…"

"It'll be fine." My eyes meet hers. "She's tough, right?"

"Tough but broken. Even if they fix you, you'll always be broken right? The cracks are still there." She flexes her claws one after the other, a series of little knives that snick-snack in and out. "Wait here."

Feral doesn't bother waiting for my answer. I don't even get a say, so I suppose it's obvious who's in charge. She's gone, a fast-moving streak of muscle and fur. She's almost out of sight when she stops. A tiny motionless figure in the distance.

I run fast in her direction, ignoring the burn in my muscles, pushing through the tell-tale sign of my power beginning to run down. I should stop and wind myself, but I want to get to her.

When I've halved the distance, I can see her lashing out at the air, limbs flailing. She's fighting an invisible enemy or hitting an invisible barrier. There's no sign of anything, though, just the world extending on and on.

"This whole place is an illusion," she calls back, when I'm close enough to hear her. "This is the edge of it." She makes a standing leap, springing up what must be twenty feet into the air, then slides back down, claws extended. "Can't get through."

I reach up to my hair to retrieve my keys. "Lucky you've got me."

It only takes one punch at fully wound-strength to smash through the barrier. I wonder if Feral's impressed. My left hand goes straight through. There's a brief sensation of pressure against my hand, and then it caves in, like it's one of those Japanese rice-paper screens.

Except Feral's not awed by my feat of strength.

She's staring through the ragged hole I made.

It shows the back door of a weatherboard house that was white once upon a time. Red and blue lights flicker at the edges. Fire burns in an upstairs window. There's a distorted voice calling.

"Attention extrahuman threats. We are agents of Quietus, here on behalf of the United States government. Surrender immediately."

Feral is standing perfectly still, every piece of fur on her body bristling.

"No," she whispers.

CHAPTER 17
EVA

THEN

And now we return to the site of a vanquished foe. Another fragment from a different tale, cutting his way through into this one. A fallen weapon defeated by someone that's honed herself into something equally deadly. This war that's been fought for so long, human against mutant. A mutant against her own kind, in the hope of finding a way back to humanity.

I DON'T KNOW why it enrages me that Ian feels no guilt for destroying this sword when he carries the weight of every mutant life around his neck like a heavy chain.

"You don't feel guilty." I speak accusingly, even though I wish my words were soft.

"It's only a piece of metal." He brushes hair from his eyes.

"He's alive as I am. I'm a puddle of water sloshing around in a tin."

"You speak. You feel."

I point my finger at the word *friendly?* "What's that then?"

"A trick. Nothing more."

My suit's temperature gauges are blipping alarmingly. Why am I worthy of affection, if the sword is not? We are both monsters. He should hate both of us. We should both be destroyed. We are all wrong, just as my love for him is wrong.

For humans to survive, all of us should be wiped from the face of the earth. Humanity must make it through this disaster. It is what my father wanted. The reason I allowed myself to be changed into this unnatural thing.

None of it can be in vain.

Ian frowns. "I don't understand why you're so mad. This is *Chatterbox's sword.* I've destroyed it. This is a victory."

Nothing of this feels victorious. Abigail Tanner is still dead. Michael remains in a stalemate with Goddess. Mutants scuttle in the Wastes. I am still here, monstrous and ashamed, dragging myself around in this mechanical contrivance.

"Yes." My suit hisses. "One more down. The calculus we face is infinitesimally better. Perhaps there are more out here. Mutant children which we can—"

Something hits me from behind. It's like being swatted out of the world by the casual palm of a god. My suit buckles, the AI flooding me with alarm data and then rapidly muting them. She thinks we're going to die, and is trying to keep it a secret from me.

I glance over my shoulder. Ian is sprawled on the ground near me. Panic floods through me, worse than any suit alarm. His fingers twitch, but that could be death throes. I try to stand, but my suit legs don't work.

Oh, this isn't good. I'm leaking. Not drastically, but there's a spreading puddle behind me, darkening the ground. My suit won't tell me a thing, which means my prognosis is dire.

I wanted to survive until the job was done.

And I never wanted Ian to get hurt. I drag myself towards him, my legs trailing behind me, still leaking. His eyelids flutter and his lips move. Possibly brain damage? What *did* this?

I raise my gaze further to see a car. Its powder blue paintwork is scratched, and the windshield is smeared with something black and sticky. Whoever's inside won't be able to see a damn thing. One headlight is smashed and the other glows an unnatural red. Is this... *car* a mutant?

It would explain this. The damn thing hit us, and now it's sitting there, humming away to itself like it enjoys watching our suffering. It's not a mutant. There are no mutants who turn into cars. That's ridiculous, even for what I've seen.

It's still *watching* me.

"Ian." My suit speaker spits static. "Are you?"

The sword. That goddamn sword. It drags itself across the ground, barely able to sustain itself. He. That's how everyone refers to it. Like he's alive, possessed by some spirit. And he's dying, and he's pissed off and—

The sword stabs himself through Ian's arm, right through the meat of the bicep.

I flail my arms. I'm too slow. The suit AI whines, like *why are you doing this to us?*

Ian's screaming, thrashing on the ground. The car hums louder. I'm still leaking, the puddle spreading around the ground. We're going to be crushed by some pathetic commuter vehicle in the middle of the Wastes, all because—

Electricity arcs from Ian's body in every direction. I can't see him, because my suit is shutting down and not giving me the visual feed. I try to demand it, but I'm disconnected. I'm water in a tin, floating in the dark like it's a sensory deprivation tank.

I can't even *hear* anything.

I'm boiling inside here, unrestrained and unbalanced. There are no systems in the suit to regulate me, and I'm condensing on the inside, more of me leaking out onto the ground. This is the end. So much still to do, and I'm draining out into stony soil.

The suit blips one final burst of information at me. Estimated time of expiration, when my consciousness will no longer be able to sustain itself, because I'll be a shallow puddle spread over the inside cavities of the suit.

It's not an encouraging number, but it's better than the number of mutants I've left alive. I allowed myself to become this and I failed at the end. Taken by the flood and now the waters have receded. What's left of me gasps, twitching on the shore.

Death, when it comes, is a relief.

MY SUIT BLEEPS. Apparently I am not yet dead. The breach has been sealed and my core temperature has lowered enough that I'm semi-coherent. The prognosis isn't fantastic. I need a large body of water. I beg my suit AI to find me one. The number of miles she gives me in return is too high. She refuses to make calculations around my time to live and how long it will take to cross that distance. Of course, she already knows these numbers, but is refusing to tell me, because she wants me to cling to what little hope remains.

Ridiculous subroutines they put in these AIs, hoping that humans will cleave to them more deeply. It irritates me that it works, even on me.

"Eva?" It's Ian's voice. He's close. The suit's focused on

keeping me alive, so it's not giving me much information on what's around, but it appears Ian is cradling me in his arms. I badger the suit into opening up more channels.

"I'm here." The voice sounds the same as ever. There's no indication of my fear and frustration. It's as if the suit is covering for me.

"I'm so glad you're alive. The car and the sword, they're gone."

"Not dead?"

"No." His voice echoes, like he's speaking inside the mostly empty cavern of my chest. "I burst a couple of its tyres, but it... well, it can fly. The sword too. They're gone. But that's not the big problem. We've got people coming. From the settlement."

"Shit." I don't usually curse, but this is too much. "What do they want?"

"Don't know yet. Shall I zap them?"

"They're humans," I say, as if I won't give the order if our lives are in danger.

I cajole and curse the suit into opening me to the flood of information. There is so little of me to process it, but I need to be aware.

There are three of them, two women and a child, crossing the rough ground. The slick of water that was once me has either seeped into the hungry soil or evaporated into the air. I am humidity, slicking the back of these people's necks.

"The sword is gone." The woman who speaks is lean and tan and her face is covered with a mask. "It's still alive, still pissed off, but I'm guessing it's gone to find some other fight."

"Sorry." My voice sounds unnatural. "We wished it dead."

"Some things die harder than others." The woman shrugs and spits, as if she is one of these things. Maybe she is. "I told the council here not to fuck with mutants. It's inviting trouble, and if we're desperate, they're more so."

"Mutants." I wish I could spit like she does. "They all must die."

She laughs, and her voice is rough. "Honey, you're a mutant. Whatever the hell that sword did to you must've fucked you up pretty bad, huh?"

"I fight for humanity." I'm boiling inside again, and my suit wants to vent it, but it knows it can't afford to, so it shuts down systems and sensors in catastrophic panic. My metal limbs twitch, like I'm an insect on its back under the hot sun.

"Water." Ian's voice comes from a long way off. "She needs water. Now."

It's stupid. I can't just drink water and fix it. Whatever process fuels me takes vast amounts of water to be filtered and processed until my consciousness can inhabit it.

The woman turns and gives a command in a rapid spill of syllables I don't understand. I'm sure the suit AI could translate, but she's too busy trying to regulate the temperature and coax the thin scum of life that is me.

Evaporate. Hannah Palmer. The woman who became what she hated and feared, to put her body in the path of evolution and become a monster. Evolution isn't simply natural selection and the flickering rolls of genetic dice. Maybe it was, once upon a time. Now it hungers, and it fears. The planet is changing, the ever-revolving cycle of the universe, and these creatures are aberrations caused by a lack of understanding. The planet's weapons against a threat that doesn't exist. If we don't act, humanity won't survive. Ian may believe they deserve to because they're God's chosen people. I simply don't want to see the majesty of our civilisation fall to a barrage of incoherent flukes, the chaotic froth of genetics run amok, wanting nothing more than to disrupt. If they win, we'll lose the order we've created.

Such grandiose thoughts for cells suspended in liquid.

"There, baby. Drink it up."

If I could scream, I would. The water is cold and sterile, overfiltered and drenched in chemicals. They're going to kill me if they give me too much.

"Enough." My suit screams. One limb flails, snatching at the rubber hose that's been jammed into one of the rents in my suit. "Killing. Hurts."

The hose is taken away, and together with my suit, we concentrate on balancing the chemicals out. It's tricky work. If I didn't have the chemistry knowledge I do, it might be all over. I want to scream and vent all my steam into Ian's face, scalding his pretty skin.

He meant well. I retain enough of myself to know that. He was desperate, and these people were trying too. Water must be precious to them out here.

"Not all of us hate mutants." The woman has her hands on her hips, glaring at Ian. "The dumbfucks in charge thought they could bargain with that God-thing in the city. I told them from the start—number one, it's not God. Number two, even if it was, you can't exactly make an arrangement with something like that."

Ian clenches his fist. He's going to smite these people down for the wrong reason. To defend his mindless, hungry God. I reach out and press his hand down.

"Sebby, show 'em." The child steps forward and blinks, and in their eyes are tiny galaxies, like they look upon far-off worlds.

"Monster." My suit refuses to say the word. She's running her own calculations.

The woman keeps talking. "We're all trying to get by.

Mutant and human. We could've done that, found a way to live together. Instead we had to try and step on them. Worst thing we could've done."

I want to scream, but settle for seething inside my suit. She flashes alarms at me, tries to cool me, desperately trying to adjust my delicate balance. The starry-eyed child looks towards me, tilting their head as if they can through my metal skin and see how fragile I really am.

"This one wants to kill us." Their voice is soft, but they're right. "They're hurt, though. Very badly. We should let them find help and then seek new refuge."

I don't want this child's mercy. I would rather they attacked us, then Ian might lash out in self-defence, to protect me.

"Sword tried to kill 'em," the woman says.

The child blinks again, and their eyes return to normal. "The sword is angry. It's hurt too, and every problem looks like something else to stab. Let this woman go, and hope she finds peace."

"Okay." The woman tangles her hand in the child's hair and pulls them close. "You're a good kid. Maybe if we had more like you, things wouldn't be so fucked." She turns her attention to us. "Lightning boy, you take your girlfriend in the suit out of here. Don't come back. Your kind's not welcome here. And by that I mean assholes, not mutants or mutant-hunters."

Inside I am a cauldron of rage.

My suit blares alarms so loud it drowns everything else out.

I fall into darkness again.

CHAPTER 18
PENANCE
ELSEWHEN

This unreality built from broken pieces still has so many edges. It's not true, and it circles in on itself, but that doesn't mean what happens here doesn't hurt. I think it's a trap, but perhaps it can be turned into something else. If those rattling around inside it can see it for what it is, perhaps they can salvage something from it after all.

TIME AND TIME AGAIN, I return to the dinner table with my father. He seems to have no memory of previous iterations of himself, stamped fresh each time. I'm not so lucky. Every time I kill, memories layer on top of the ones before.

I push my knife into Dylan's flesh over and over. My father's will is done, whether this is earth or heaven or hell. The pain lessens, but there's a shock every time. Their blood is so warm. The way she can never say my name, a single consonant caught on her lips. It doesn't always play out in exactly the same way. The worst is when Dani finds me bloody and sobbing, holding Dylan in my arms. The horror of losing her love, the panic in her hazel eyes. Then guilt crashing through as she realises what I've done. She took the blade that is me, and trusted me enough to hold it close to her heart. Now it hurts her to watch me act out my destiny.

I try apologising before it happens.

"I'm going to do something terrible, Dilly. Please forgive me."

"Dylan, I wish I could stop this, but I can't. I'm so sorry."

"Close your eyes, my love. This won't last for long."

"I love you. I know I was never brave enough to say this, but I'm saying it now. I'm sorry."

It doesn't make things any easier.

I kill her in the Yaxley building, in her childhood home, in the rocky caves of Westhaven, and in a room in the asteroid, looking down on the jewel-bright planet. Repetition numbs me. Every time she falls, I remind myself I'll see her again, but perhaps that's what my father wants. I'll strike her down over and over again, numbing myself to her death, and one day it won't be undone, and she'll be gone forever.

Or even worse--it will be reality, and I'll think it's another dream.

Am I being trained to kill her? I may be locked in a cell somewhere, my mind looped in some virtual realm as they train me to execute the infamous mutant leader Chatterbox.

These thoughts repeat in my mind, a mental loop inside the loop of action.

I am trapped. Can I do this forever? A knife, stabbing down endlessly.

Here I am once again, padding down the hallway again, my bare feet on cool wooden floors. There is a parade of doors in front of me. Perhaps Dylan waits in every room. An infinite house that I will slaughter my way through forever.

"Violet." They stand in the doorway, hair tousled and hands in pockets.

"Dylan." I pause for as long as I can, ten paces separate.

"We've been here before." Their eyes widen. "I keep dreaming it."

"No." I don't want it to be true. Surely they can't remember dying at my hands?

"You keep killing me." His brown eyes widen. They're molten in the dim light. Her lips glisten faintly. I could kiss her once before I kill her. "Something's wrong, isn't—"

But the knife is in her throat and she's choking, bubbling, slumping. My hand shakes as if it suffers its own death throes.

Jesus lurks in the darkness ahead, teeth and robe glowing faintly. He is ecstatic at the sight of me, a ghost caught in a bloody loop.

I am his white horse.

"My father's house has many rooms. Come, Violet." His frozen grip is at my shoulder and he shoves me forward towards another doorway, where there is my father, and the table, and the command to kill yet again.

"Violet. Why do I keep dreaming of you?" This time, they're in an oversized t-shirt with a rodent on it. The slogan on it says *Fuck Punxsutawney Phil.* It's slipping off one shoulder, revealing a curve of pale skin.

"I don't know." My voice creaks like it's ancient.

"We keep living this shit over and over again. Not much fun

for me." They hitch the t-shirt up. "Probably not for you either."

"I'm sorry." I'm lunging forward, knife raised.

They let me come. "I know."

This time, Jesus isn't smiling. He's got his moneychanger face on. That was the only story I actually liked.

"Do you know who I am?" His stigmata are huge bloody holes ripped in his palms. When he clenches his fists, red slurry oozes between fingers.

"A dead man with a very well-connected organisation doing your PR?" I smirk. I was always good at this. It used to make my father so *very* angry.

One bloody palm hits my cheek, and my whole body moves with the force of the blow. I'm not strong in this form. Not physically, at least.

"A bully." I taste blood. My vision swims. "All about control. Love me or burn."

"I am the human incarnation of the most powerful force in the universe." He stands over me, eyes blazing. His feet are burnished metal, glowing hot as if fresh-forged from the fire. A smile stretches his lips as he presses one foot against my neck. "And God will not be mocked."

I can smell my flesh burning. The pain is so intense I almost black out. Aside from hallucinating an end-times Jesus, I've been here before. Not more times than I can count, but Dani once said, eyes furious, that even one time was too many.

And she's right, at least partly. It only takes one time to break them in your eyes.

From when I was young, my father and I were in a battle of control. He attempted to bend me to his will, and I asserted my own. As I grew older, our battles spiralled worse. He'd return home to find me tipsy on communion wine and lips swollen from kissing. I would quote him verses of how religious leaders must be able to keep their families in line.

I'd end up in a position very similar to this.

I'm much harder to break than my opinion of him was. It didn't stop him trying to control me. Furious lectures, and things being broken in front of me, and dragging myself up the stairs while my mother screamed behind me.

He even tried to cast demons out of me, practically foaming at the mouth as he stood over me, shouting for Jesus to deliver his daughter from the claws of spiritual monsters. He was the only monster I ever knew, and I would never bend to him.

Until he was changed, and I was helpless.

The stench from my neck makes me gag, but at least it doesn't last for long. Not like before.

"How many times has this happened?" Dylan's curled in a window seat. The curtains are open, and outside is the spill of stars and glittering water below. I have no idea where this is. It's not a place I remember.

"What?" I stand at the opposite end of the room, too far to lunge.

"You coming here and killing me. I've been sleeping terribly. So many dreams, all basically the same. You and a knife. Then I wake up. I feel like someone's trying to tell me something."

"Too many," I say. "And I'm sorry. I don't mean to—"

"He's back." Their eyes are so dark, and I wonder how they looked on the night they went to stop my father. "Isn't he?"

"He wants you dead." I take five halting steps across the room, my father's hook caught in my soul and towing me onwards. The real knife is in my mind, gouging into my thoughts. "I can't *stop* him, Dylan."

"Fuck him." Her grin is savage, and my heart soars. "He can't stop *us*, Penny."

"Us." Here I am, right in front him. Looking up into those beautiful eyes.

"Yeah." They bend their head and press their lips to mine.

And I thrust the knife up into their stomach, as if this means nothing at all, even though it means *everything*, all at once.

Jesus stands in the doorway behind me. I turn, but he is too bright to look upon, and I avert my eyes.

"Are you my father?" I ask.

He speaks, and his voice is rushing water. "I am God."

"My father always thought he was God." I stand and sneer, because this is what we do in the face of bullies, who demand the world fall into rigid lines.

"He spoke with my voice. An instrument of my will on Earth."

"Guess that makes you both assholes then." I hold onto the strength of my new family, these people who've loved me and supported me. The ones who've held me and told me I'm still worthy of love despite everything I've done and had done to me. They believe in me when I can't.

Jesus doesn't like this. This isn't the rebel from history. It's the one they've constructed. The church's sweet lamb-cuddling, suffer-the-children facade that's only a front for the monster that will consign anyone to an eternity of suffering rather than admit he was wrong.

As if it'll be a lesson, this time he lets me feel the fires of hell.

I burn. Oh, how I burn.

"So how the fuck do we get out of this?" They're prowling and intense. It's what I think of as Mission Dylan. One of many faces they show the world. I like to think I know the real them, the one we are when we're at home, in their little flowering home on the cliffs. Really, I think they're all these things at once. We all are. So many fragments, frantically shuffled together in the hope it makes a real person.

"We can't get out of it." It's half fact, half hope they'll correct me.

They grin at me. God, that lazy smile. "Penny, it's us. I mean I know I'm still mostly a burning dumpster, but if I can throw a burning dumpster at someone, it's pretty likely to fuck them up."

I laugh, despite myself, despite the fact I'm about to kill them again. "Dylan, I'm commanded."

"You fought him before. Found a loophole. Sure, Oni helped, but you kept trying to kill me because you knew you couldn't do it. It gave you an escape from killing other people. We'll find a solution."

"I don't have powers now, and his command is so simple. *You will kill her.*"

"There you go. Pronouns. I'm only sometimes a her. Right now, I'm a him." He waves his arms frantically. "See, you can't kill me. I'm a fragile little boy."

I grit my teeth, because if it was that easy, I would have *found* the damn solution.

"I know what he means by her. He means you. Dylan Taylor. Whatever pronoun you use."

"Okay fine." She throws up her hands. "It was an idea. No

bad ones, right? We're brainstorming or whatever. I assume you can't fold yourself out of here, or you would've done it already."

"No." I remember my first moments here, how hemmed in I felt. There are *edges* to this place, a constricting border that makes a noose around me. In all my attempts, I didn't find a single crack in the slippery-smooth shell of it. "This place is closed off."

"Like a world on its own." Dylan frowns. "Like someone's carved out a chunk of fake past and left us to spin around inside it."

"That's how it feels." I desperately want to stay in this moment, a breath of fresh air before the compulsion chokes me. "I don't understand why though, or how we can possibly get out."

"Break the loop. That seems like the obvious choice, right?" They glance over their shoulder. "Dan? You up?"

She's at the door, so impossibly beautiful I have to remind myself to breathe. The two of them together are so stunning. Love is so complicated. I've always felt my heart moved to stuttering life by all kinds of people, but these two exist on a whole different plane to anyone I've had feelings for. Everything's tied with so much history, like I'm woven into the strands of their lives like a pattern.

"Sleepy," she yawns. "Hi, Violet."

I can't kill Dylan in front of her. I must kill Dylan in front of her.

"Welcome to the dreams I've been having."

"The murder dreams? What?" She shakes her head, frown lines creasing her forehead.

"Yes, I tell you but you forget." Dylan sighs. "Violet's repetitively killing me, commanded by her father. We're stuck in some weird purgatory thing, and we need an escape hatch. The should-be-dead Pastor Mike is saying *you will kill her,* by which he means me. Some revenge thing, I guess. Anyway—"

I lunge across the room. I can't stop myself. Dylan Taylor must die.

And if Dani Kim gets in the way, she will die too.

Wait—

That compulsion is new.

CHAPTER 19
TENTACLE PRINCESS
RECENTLY

Oh dear. Things are moving fast now. Pieces of the narrative keep connecting to one another, and I don't have time to solve any of this. You need to know where a story is going before you start. It doesn't work if you simply let it unfold. Now here, the characters are moving from one story to another, and consequences swing between the strands. I've left things out, and the climax is a knot that I don't have the narrative sense to cleave. Even at this remove I'm helpless to watch it all play out. Events move with such inevitability sometimes.

AFTER SPEAKING TO BOSS LADY, I allow myself to be escorted back to the cell they like to hold me in. I cannot help myself from tasting the energy, sampling the thinnest of trickles so as not to disturb the physical structure I have assembled myself into.

"You okay there?" Hench asks.

"I misunderstand your meaning." I do not, but I find the thought of communication wearisome.

"I dunno. You seem a little less…" She waves her exactly the right number of limbs. "Enthusiastic than usual. Did Boss Lady hurt you? I can talk to her about it."

"Boss Lady opened my eyes." My mouth moves snappishly. I imagine there are tentacles curling out from inside it. Things that could dissolve flesh quite easily if given the chance. But no, despite the fear and terror that comes with my new understanding, I cannot return to the old ways of my people. "I saw things I did not expect."

"The world's a big place." Hench nods sombrely. "Lots of fucked up things in it."

"Yes." I am not sure how to marshal words to explain my feelings. An entity my people murdered is somehow resurgent. She will quite likely wish to take revenge on me for my people's part in her demise. Even worse, Boss Lady's plan is—as Hench might say—a complete and utter fucking nightmare. And I know of what I speak, for my people are nightmare made flesh, and beyond flesh.

"I don't pretend to know what alien problems look like." Hench pats me with one limb. "But I've met a lot of assholes, and I've dealt with a lot of bullshit, and sometimes I know when to shut the fuck up and listen."

I briefly consider disappearing inside my own void, but I may as well attempt the conversation first. It's far less destructive to everything in the nearby area.

"Imagine you are part of a family," I say to Hench. "Of great and powerful villains."

"My family wasn't much, but I've henched for villain families. It's never a good time."

"I apologise for the misery of your forebears. In my case, I did not realise my family were villains. To me, it seemed right and proper, and a very good time." It was not remotely enjoyable for humans, but I do not think it is apropos to mention this. "The family was very powerful. And they came to a place where someone else was in charge."

"Oh, I definitely know *this* story." Hench grins at me. "Tale as old as time. So who won?"

"The family. Their enemy was overthrown. Or so they thought. Really, the enemy vanished into the darkness and hired many, many warriors. The family didn't know the enemy was responsible, not that it would have mattered. The warriors defeated the family, all except for one, who hid because the war was terrible."

"And now *your friend*—" Hench makes exaggerated motions with four of her little tentacles "—has been pried out of xer hidey-hole and the world is different."

Perhaps I was a little more obvious than I intended. All my limbs droop. "Yes, and the enemy is also awoken and is very powerful. So I look at my choices and see none that are good."

Hench's limbs droop too, at least the two top ones. "See, TeePee, this is why I hench. You don't need to make decisions like that. You go where you're pointed. If the bosses hide, you hide. If they fight, you fight, and hope you're not the poor fucker that pays for bad decisions. If they go begging for peace, you turn up and bend the knee too and hope it doesn't all pop off."

I parse over all the meaning in that sentence, and attempt to apply it to my situation. They did not proffer the possibility of allying yourself with some mad creature intending to do terrible things with energy. Perhaps that is not very common in human experience. It seems likely I am unlucky in every way. Faced with a choice between many terrible options.

"Everything is bad," I say.

"Yeah, sometimes life's fucked up like that." Hench nods. "So what are you going to do?"

"For now, I will hide." I lower my head almost to the ground.

"As good a move as any. Often the smart policy. Bosses don't usually follow it, which means I get dragged into various piles of shit."

"Let us hope we avoid that." We have reached my cell and I shuffle instead.

Hench pauses outside for a moment, staring at me without speaking. I remain motionless until she loses interest and departs.

I unfold part of myself and taste the energy of this world again. Eddies of it flow into my void, and back out again. I am very careful not to let any of myself leak out. It would be preferable if the energy creature did not know I am here.

At least not until I am ready. Not that I have any idea what I should do. Hench's listening ear was not as useful as I hoped.

Perhaps the other will be more productive. They are a child of the goddess, after all.

I translocate directly into Goat Bitch's cell.

"TeePee." She makes a smiling face at me. Obviously, she is unaware of what I am.

"I have many questions." I wave my limbs in a hopefully soothing manner.

She spreads her top limbs wide. "Why not? I've got nothing better to do."

I settle myself down beside her, although my limbs fold awkwardly, and for a moment I worry she got a tiny glimpse into a fraction of my void. Her eyes remain calm, so it is likely that I still feel disconcerted by all this new information, and the possibility that this woman before me is a spy sent to destroy me.

"Where do you live?" I ask.

"Oh, we're starting there, huh?" She shows her teeth. "I live on an island. I'm not sure if you know what those are. They're generally small pieces of land, although some of them are enormous, like Australia. That's probably confusing for you. If I had a map, it'd be a lot easier."

"I understand islands." I keep my tone very soft, although I would like to wave my limbs in great agitation to say *hurry up and explain the goddess.*

"Well, this isn't your typical island. It moves. It's been... grown, I suppose? A place for mutants like me to be safe. Well, safe's relative, given that I got snatched up, but safer than shit was before, that's for fucking certain."

I want to demand details of a creature capable of *growing an island,* but I suspect I know.

"Are you the leader of the mutants?" I think this is a very cunning question, because I know it's not true, but it hides the extent of my knowledge.

Goat Bitch makes humorous sounds with her mouth. "No, although I know some of them. Ray's technically in charge. What they call the President. They're the political figurehead, the one that deals with a lot of the human-type stuff. Nice, but a little disturbing, because you never know what they're thinking."

"So this Ray is the leader?"

"The *real* leaders are Biome. Chatterbox and Marvellous. They're two mutants who were changed into something else by..." Goat Bitch tails off and I am not sure how to understand what the expression on her face means. "It'll sound like I'm making up some religious story, but I'm really not."

My limbs all quiver. I try and force myself into quietness. The void inside of me is screaming very loudly, and vibrating at many frequencies. A little pocket universe attempts to burst forward, but I swallow it and it burns going down.

"A religious story?" My voice trembles.

"This planet is alive. It sounds wild, right?"

No, Goat Bitch. It does not sound wild at all. It *was* alive, when my people descended from the stars. And, like the monsters are, we fed upon her. I can say none of this, for it will reveal me as the descendent of terrible things, for which there is no atonement.

"Alive. The whole planet?"

"Not entirely. She's energy, moving in this pattern around the world. The story is that she created mutants, but honestly, that's when it starts getting into ooky-spooky religious bullshit. I've met her though."

I cannot help it. All my limbs stiffen. The lump of my head moves unnaturally fast, spinning to face Goat Bitch. For a second, my mask drops, and she sees too much of me. The jagged arc of my beaks, the fluttering of many tentacles. Far, far too many limbs.

This time, I know she saw me, because Goat Bitch takes her entire body as far from me as possible. She is limited by the chains that hold her in place. Her eyes are larger, and the pupils dart more quickly. Her respiratory and cardiovascular systems are operating at far higher capacity than normal.

"What *are* you?"

"An alien." My limbs flutter, patting the air, describing complex shapes. "You know that. You call me *xe* for xeno—for other, for different, for foreigner."

"I wasn't tripping right? It's not lack of sleep or some fucked up drugs that scientist bitch is putting in my food? You really went all fourth-dimension wild Jack Kirby space monster on me?"

"I am not terrifying," I insist. "I do not want anything such as execution or sacrifice to happen to anyone." Then more words burst from my lips. "Especially me."

I retreat to the other side of the cell, in case Goat Bitch's fear causes her to summon her protector to smite me down.

"Do not hurt me," I plead. Me, the descendent of gods, begging one of Lilith's children for mercy. I suppose it was always intended to end this way.

"I'm not going to hurt you." My fear disarms her somehow, and she has returned to softness. Perhaps seeing so many mutations, and living on an island created by a goddess, have inured her even to my strangeness. "Who do you think is going to kill you? The scientist? I'll protect you, I swear, and maybe we can switch Hench to our side. She seems to like you, and honestly, Mutopia can provide bags of cash if needed. Those kids used to be big-time bank robbers, back before the war."

"Your goddess." I cannot stop trembling. "Her children. Those two who were changed. They will hurt me."

"Cybele? I've seen her once, and that was at a distance. She's not a real hands-on deity, if you know what I mean. And Dylan and Dani? They're honestly not the sort to stab someone for being different. If you decided to attack us, well..." For a moment, she seems to sharpen. "All bets would be off."

"I wish no harm." My voice does not sound human anymore, high ululating sounds like wind moving through caves. "I wish only peace. I do not wish to be harmed. Only forgiveness. Redemption. A way to..."

I bow my head. There is no hope for me. Hiding was an act of cowardice.

"Listen," Goat Bitch says. "I'll get out of here eventually.

They'll tear things apart to find me. I guarantee you they already are. And when they get here, I'll take you to Biome. We'll straighten everything out. I'll vouch for you and—"

No. It is too late. I cannot wait any longer for the axe to fall.

I know where the island is. The two beings that make up this *Biome* are like flames leaping like funeral pyres in my awareness. I hope Goat Bitch is right, and I do not travel to my death —but if I do, it is only right and just.

"Goodbye." I say. "Repeat that word to Hench. I enjoyed meeting both of you."

Then I translocate myself from the scientist's facility, and hurl myself towards the heart of the island.

CHAPTER 20

TWINKLE LIGHTS

RECENTLY

Oh dear. This wasn't supposed to happen. Is this my fault? Trying too hard to juggle what's going on through all this mess and now I've lost track of someone. It's hard to juggle time and space and characters especially. Sleight of hand is one thing, sleight of reality is another. This is quite catastrophically bad. How do I fix this? I can't just undo things! You can't unroll causality. Everyone thinks it's so easy, standing outside it all. Except now it's all falling apart. I'm so sorry.

WITCHMADE APPEARS out of thin air moments later, followed by Feral. Then Marvellous and Moodring are in the room too. It's like a silent alarm has been flicked, the way they're all bouncing into the room.

"Where's Nails?" I want to *do* something right now.

"Losing their shit." Feral grimaces. "Goat Bitch up and vanished, and there's no sign of them, but Nails insists on looking, and threatening to fill Keepaway full of lead if they don't keep looking."

"Fuck's sake." Dylan's covered in thorns and blood-red petals. "I'll get them back." They fumble their phone from their pocket and fiddle with it. Moments later, the pale figure of Keepaway pops into view, taps Dylan on the shoulder and then disappears themself.

"It'd be nice to discuss things," Dani says conversationally. "You know, occasionally." Vines twist over their skin in knotted, anxious patterns.

"Let them freak out." Alyse is the only one who looks calm. "It's better when they've got something to do."

"Going off where one of our people got taken is not just *something to do*." The flowers around Dani's chest and shoulders bloom suddenly. "They're in danger, the—Oh, I *hate* sharing a connection sometimes. Ouch, the stubborn—"

"Send me," I say. "I can help search."

The other exchange glances.

"I'm part of the team." I'm insistent, because right now I totally believe I can do this. Our *friend* is in danger, and I'll do anything I can to help. There's a small part of me that knows it's not my smartest idea, but I want to do it anyway. It's the right thing to do.

"I'll accompany him," Penance's voice says, but then someone's touching my back and the world is gone, as if I closed my eyes tightly.

When I open them again, I'm in a narrow corridor, barely lit. It's nothing like the facility at all. This isn't the time to get *flashbacks*. I clench my right hand and coloured sparks leap from it, illuminating the path ahead like fireworks. There's a green monster blocking the way, a razor-edged drift of leaves and thorns with eyes that glow bright yellow. Two black-clad figures are tangled amongst it, panting and twitching.

I turn and head the other way. I'm pretty sure that's Dylan, and there's no need for me to intervene. That looks well under control. Totally cool. My right hand flexes, squeezing out sparks to light the corridor ahead. No idea where Penance went. Probably doing the nightmare thing, so I probably don't want to know that either. I'm just looking for Goat Bee. Follow the bleating. Except all I can hear is the men in Dylan's thorny arms panting out incoherent answers.

No, wait.

More screaming, up ahead. Let's follow it. I'm sure it'll be fine. This superhero thing isn't terrifying at all. It was a great decision to come here. I'm super glad they let me and didn't say *no, wait, that's a terrible idea. Twinkles has no useful superpowers at all.*

There's a series of sharp bangs and a high pitched scream.

I could run, but there's nowhere to run to. Plus I'm tall and strong and—

Oh, crap. There's a body on the floor. Another someone dressed in black, except there are three nails sticking out of the face mask. One in each eye and another right in the center.

"Nails?" I hiss in the dark, like I'm a scared little cat.

Something coughs. I hold up my fist and pop out a couple of lurid pink flashes. There's Nails, slumped against the wall on the far side of the room. A tiny squeak pops out of my mouth, but luckily nobody's around to hear it.

They're not moving. This isn't good.

No, wait. They're making this little huff-huff sound, hands fisted in their lap. I can do this.

"It's me." I cross to them in a few long strides, crouch down beside them. "Twinkle Lights."

There's a series of snuffling sounds in response, and then "those fucking bastards took the Goat."

"We'll find her." I wave my sparking hand around the room. The only thing I illuminate is a darkened doorway—no thank you—and a pile of three more dead men. Well, I'm pretty sure they're dead. None of them are moving. The spreading puddle around them is probably blood. They're also studded with nails, and I'm guessing that's not a fashion statement.

Nails mumbles something else.

"Come on, then." I say it nice and gentle, despite the dark and the dead men around me. If I was the sort to have traumatic flashbacks to the scene of my tragic injury, I'd be having it now. Except I'm here in the dark and Nails is still slumped in a pile.

"Fine. I'll have to carry you then." I slide both my arms underneath the prone figure and struggle to my feet. They don't fight me, just slump against me like they wish they could burrow their way inside me, like I'm a protective wall.

I'd love to be, but we're in this dimly lit *place* with probably more dudes in black. I can't even shoot sparks because I'm occupied with holding Nails. I'll do my best anyway.

"Right." I speak like we're not anywhere dark and spooky, like we're back home, just hanging out in the common room. "Let's go find this Goat of ours. I'm sure she's somewhere."

Nails says something else inarticulate. Their arms wrap around my neck. It's actually a little bit comforting. Maybe we can help each other like that. I shuffle slowly back out into the corridor, which is now empty and silent. Is this good or bad? I don't even know which way is out.

"This way," I tell Nails confidently. "I bet she's down here."

A glowing red shape flickers in the darkness in front of us, like a warning devil made from tongues of flame. This is bad, but I can't just do nothing.

"Stop in the name of the Cute Mutants," I shout.

"Twinkles, you ass, it's me." The voice is Penance's. "This place is burned. There's nothing here aside from bodies."

"Penance?"

Then someone hits me from behind and the next thing I know, we're back in the common room in Mutopia. Nails is still in my arms, and I don't let them go. Their face is buried in my neck. One by one, the rest of the team pop back into the room.

Dylan is back in mostly-human form, and Penance looks entirely normal, no trace of ghostly devil about her at all. "What the fuck happened?"

"It was a setup." Penance's eyes are worried. "We got there and Goat Bitch disappeared almost straight away, like they were waiting for us."

Dylan paces, the floor blooming behind them with tiny flowers and scrub grass. "Disappeared *how?*"

"There one second and gone the next." Witchmade has produced another bird carcass from somewhere, and is slicing it open on the table. "Winked out of existence. If I didn't know better, I would've said Keepaway had shoulder-tapped them."

"I wasn't there." Keepaway combs hair out of their face. "Not until the alarm went off."

Feral sighs. "Nobody was there. Witchie means it was like—" She snaps her fingers. "Magic."

"The augury." I try to look both confident and calm. "A closing eye? A closed door?"

"Don't forget the octopus." Feral swings her legs and frowns. "What are you trying to say?"

"Are they metaphors for disappearance?"

"Someone's a poet." Witchmade raises her head from the bird's entrails. "It feels right though."

"My we're-being-fucked-with sense is tingling." Dylan bares thorny teeth.

"By who?" I ask. "We need to know so we can get Goat back."

"Yeah, that's the fucking million dollar question." Dylan's foot jiggles, tugging on the vines that run between them and Dani. "I'm not trying to sound like an asshole, but we're currently scary to fuck with. Even the big dog intelligence agencies are only sniffing around."

"Someone brave or foolish enough to take one of ours." Feral's claws gouge splinters from the table. "Not scared of violent reprisal."

Witchmade looks up from her entrails. "I'm still getting a bunch of bullshit. Broken mirrors, a girl with a knife, someone drowning, someone rising up out of a sea of blood. It's all obscured, like I'm reading a bad translation of a story."

Penance glitches. "Someone powerful, then. They can obfuscate the future, snatch someone in plain sight. One of Heart's kids?"

Dylan shakes their head. "No. We'd feel that. Tugging on the strings."

"So what do we do?" There are massive furrows in the table from Feral's claws. "We have to get out there and do *something*."

"We shake some trees." Dylan gets up in one abrupt movement. They're thorned and shadowed, and both Dani and Alyse mimic them.

I shiver, as if the temperature in the room has plunged.

"What can I do?" Nails speaks for the first time, their voice hoarse.

"You're staying home." Dylan's voice is surprisingly gentle.

"You can't bench me." A line of heavy iron nails stitch their way across the floor as Nails' hands hang down. "I need to—"

"Nails, my darling, you put two nine-inchers through someone's head when he said *what* in a tone you didn't like. You need to chill." Dylan crosses to them and tips their head up. "You know us. You trust us. We'll talk to Farsight, and she'll find the Goat, and we'll go in bloody-handed and bring her home. Okay?"

Nails slumps, but Keepaway is already crossing to the others and sending them away.

"Watch this one," Dylan says to me, the moment before she disappears.

I take the seat beside them and lean myself against them. There's a brief moment before they press back, letting me shore them up. They're still shaking.

"Why do *you* think they took her?" I ask.

"Shit." The scarf at their mouth flutters rapidly, as if they're breathing a flock of butterflies out. "Of all of us, she's... I dunno. She's the softest, I suppose. Like she's here because she needs it, not because we need her. Fuck, that sounds harsh. So why'd they take her? I can't fathom it."

"She needs it?"

"Someone who's looking for family. Goat got kicked out over the whole trans thing, you know. Before they even really got a chance to come out or process it or anything. Terrible fuckin' timing, what with the Dark Year starting and then getting turned into a goddamn goat. You ever get caught up in the Wastes, Twinkles?"

I shake my head. My memories of the Dark Year are hallucinatory. Mostly, I was full of drugs that made reality spongy and bizarre. I was attended to by monsters, and coaxed into fever-dreams. Time was a staircase down which I fell. I could have spent decades in there, for all I knew.

I try to ignore it and leave it in the past where it belongs, but I still have nightmares. Especially about the last moments. The facility collapsing around me, the bright lights snuffed into pitch darkness. Trapped beneath medical equipment, two proboscis-like metal arms digging into my chest. I still have the scars.

And then the lifeboat, through some unknown magic.

Perhaps it was Goddess. That's what I like to imagine. In her complicated dance against Michael, she found the time to single me out and save me.

"I was never in the Wastes," I say quietly.

"It was a headfuck. Like you think you know lonely until you're out there. I remember when I first met her. All lanky, standing there, about to get her ass kicked by a bunch of scavenger types. Voice all shaky, still demanding that they saw her as she was. I guess inevitable death has a way of making you realise what's important, but it's still one of the bravest fuckin' things I ever saw."

"I like her." I grin at Nails. "I did right from the start. The rest of you are kinda intimidating, not gonna lie. But she's easy to talk to, and the way she dances?"

Nails laughs, and it sounds genuine. "She told me this story once, one time when we nearly died. We had a safe place, and then everything went to shit, and I was one hundred percent fuckin' sure that this was it."

"I had one of those times too." I smile, but my skin prickles, as I remember being lost in the dark. The air is cold when I inhale, and I rub my scars through my shirt.

"Lot of us did, Twinkles, yeah. I'm sorry you went through it too."

"Like you said." I breathe deep and even. "We all did."

"Anyway, Goat Bitch had this fuckin' near death experience. There's this white light at the end of a tunnel, and standing at the end of it is her. Except not her *exactly*. The way she says it, she saw herself in the future. Like a better, happier, prettier version of herself. The Goat Bitch she wanted to be."

"An illusion?" I frown.

"Obviously a fuckin' illusion, dude. Near death, the brain does some weird shit. But it worked. She's like *I make it. I'm okay. I find a way to being me*. Then she fuckin', like, kicks her way out from under this rubble and drags me out, pulls a bunch of others out. Like a real superhero."

For a second I have a flash of something like memory. I've never remembered this before, but did I see the same tunnel? Except I had no reason *not* to walk into the glow. I couldn't *see* anything, but I went in anyway. Because I was exhausted, and in so much pain, and so tired of—

No, it's gone. My hand flutters at my chest as if the wounds are oozing blood still.

"You like her a lot." I'm smiling, pushing the past away.

"You've seen her dance." They push the tangled curls from their face, and I see their eyes sparkle. "But like, it's hard being seen. Maybe not for someone like you, pretty face, interesting scars, sexy glow going on. Except maybe behind all that beautiful you hate being perceived too. But can you imagine standing up and saying to the world *no, this is me* day after day? Even if people hate you and mock you for that? I always hid. Always disguised myself. I still find it hard. Even though I know Dylan fuckin' Taylor doesn't give a shit what or who I am. They value me, crazy bitch that he is."

"Everyone does, Nails." I'm still half-blushing.

"It takes a long time for acceptance to soak all the way through. Yet my Goat stands up, day after day, and I think that's beautiful."

I think they're crying, but I don't say anything about it. I simply reach out and take the cold grey lump of their hand, and they squeeze my fingers until tears spring into my own eyes. We've all made our way here, through the shadows of our pasts. Even though the wounds in my chest still ache, I am here now, and I understand why this is worth fighting for.

CHAPTER 21

GOAT BITCH

THEN

It's hard to structure a story. It's difficult to look at a life and see the shape of it. You have to zoom in, to find the smaller arcs. The internal struggles, the lies overcome and the ones that run so deep they become a bedrock on which we build towering structures of ego and behaviour. So when you're desperate, and trying to fix things before reality collapses and people are erased from existence… all you can do is your best. Find the shape of a life, and bend it ever so gently to let it connect to something else. Push two people closer together, so they find an echo in one another.

I AM FINALLY SAFE. It's been a long time since I felt anything close. There are different kinds of danger, and they've layered together over the years until I'm always on edge. It's not only physical danger, although that's taken priority lately because the ever-present fear of death has a way of drowning everything else out. As far as I can remember, I've always been hyper-sensitive, scanning for insult and rejection, subtle sneering signals that dismiss me. Even before I wanted to be seen as a woman, I never felt like I *fit* most places. I always looked for the proof that I was fundamentally wrong somehow. Here in the mall, I've found very few of these signals. Maybe it's because most people are used to keeping to themselves. We're all a bunch of misfits, edging around with eyes wide, watching to see who's going to reject us first. Like a bunch of really sad gunslingers.

It's safe, but it's not *easy*. My threat radar is fucked after being out in the Wastes. At night, the bright lights fade, and a neon glow permeates the mall, drifting in dazzled arcs from the signs which the Pirate Internet refuses to turn off. I don't think they sleep, up there in their cradle of cables. Jacked in, like something from an old sci-fi paperback. Weird lights mean electrical storms, or drones fighting overhead, or dropships heading for the cities.

The noises are what wake me. Metal banging, the hiss from the vents, the water filtration system cycling. People move around, they cry out in their sleep, they hold muttered conversations with themselves and others.

I startle awake at all of it. My room used to be a store that sold soaps and other body products. It still smells floral and sweet, like it seeped into the walls. I like it, because it's one thing that proves to me that I'm not in the Wastes. It never smells like this out there. Sometimes, I can convince my brain that the threats aren't reality. It's only noise, a giant building at work, and other scared people moving inside it.

On most nights, I end up sitting at the door. The security screen is rattled all the way down, and I watch the neon and the shadows it makes, waiting to spot an unnatural movement. I have my armoured coat on, cinched tight around me. My hooves are sharp and ready.

"Hey."

I'm awake, startled, scrabbling backwards across the floor.

"Easy, easy." Nails crouches on the other side of the security screen, hands raised. "Just me."

"What?" My voice is hoarse, and I hate how it echoes out of my chest. "Something's wrong?"

"No." They turn to sit with their back to the screen. "Seems you've been having some trouble sleeping. Figured knowing that someone's watching out for you might help."

"Oh." I drag myself back until I'm sitting on the other side of the security screen. "What about you?"

"I don't need much sleep. Side-effect of my powers." They turn, and I can see one eye and curls falling across their face and their scarf moving as they breathe.

"Are you lying?" I ask.

"Maybe. But I'm here protecting you, aren't I? Be rude to accuse me of lying."

"Thank you." There are tears in my eyes. Words press on the inside of my lips. Things I shouldn't say. But I'm exhausted and there's something about how Nails is *right there* that causes them to spill out anyway. "Why are you so nice to me?"

They're facing away from me, so I can't see their face. "Maybe because I like you? That might be weird for you to hear, huh? You're one of those types who assumes everyone hates them."

"Rude," I whisper, but it's also fair.

"I do, though, sorry to burst your bubble. And it's not like I'm the friendly type. I'm the reason people think nobody likes them."

I laugh, and it's high and startled, and probably wakes a bunch of people up. "Sorry."

"You're allowed to laugh. It's nice to hear, honestly. You've been a mite fuckin' skittish."

"A mite?" Why can't I stop smiling?

"My grandmother used to always say it. I guess I picked it up. Mite annoying habit." Nails turns so they're sitting cross-legged opposite me, like our knees would be touching if the security door wasn't in the way. "But I *see* you. Standing as you are. It matters. It's, uh…" They pull at their scarf, as if they're about to reveal themselves, but they're only adjusting it. "It's beautiful. You're beautiful. And I'm not trying to hit on you, I don't work that way. But, like—"

"Do you want to come in?" My breaths are far too rapid.

There's an awkward pause, and I want to beat my head on the security screen until my horns are jagged stumps.

"I just told you I don't work that way," Nails says.

"You can't lie side by side with someone in the dark?" I ask. "That's all I want. Being in the same space, just existing."

Nails grunts. "Okay, I can do that. Maybe even deal with, like, a casual arm thrown over me. Get a bit of a hug situation going on. Shit, sorry. I was an asshole. Jumping to conclusions like that. Assuming you want to jump these fucked-up bones."

"No." I rattle the security screen up. "Better to be honest. But all I want is a friend, and someone to be with in the dark, to make everything less alone."

"I like that." Nails steps inside and together we close the security screen.

Then we cross back to the mattress where I've been sleeping. It's far too big for me. Everyone's in these enormous oversized beds, because what else are you going to do when there's an abandoned furniture store at your disposal. I fold myself onto it and Nails collapses beside me. We're both on our backs, staring at the play of neon across the ceiling. The backs of our hands are touching.

"What you said about seeing me." I turn my head slightly. "What did you mean by that?"

"That was the thing, huh?" I think they're smiling, but their mouth is obscured as always. "I've always been someone who hid. Never really felt much like a woman, but I'd pretend because that was easy. Be as anonymous as I could. A face in a crowd, that's what I wanted. Being seen terrified me. Still does, I guess. It was weird though, because I thought if I stood up and said *this is who I am*, people still wouldn't see me. They'd see some fuckin' caricature, something in their heads."

"Oh." It's hard to make words come because this is so much of what scared me—and still scares me, in all honestly—that my thoughts crumble under a wave of emotion.

"So, I wanted to say that I see you. You know, as you really are. And I like it. I wanted you to know that."

I curl my fingers around the lumpen shape of their hand. I've often felt like a ghost possessing a body that isn't really mine, a spectre haunting a family who doesn't understand me, a dark spirit drifting through a world that has no place for me in any form.

Except here and now, I'm somehow made corporeal when someone looks at me through their dark eyes and recognises me for what I am. Who *validates* me. There are tears trickling from my yellow eyes and running down the planes of my face.

"Can I hug you now?"

"Sure." Nails says. "I'd like that."

I roll over and wrap my arms around them, and I hold them tight, and they make a soft noise in their throat. It makes me slacken my hold, but they take my arm, and wrap it further around them and we're two bodies that never felt like we fit quite right, but here and now it's perfect.

NAILS SPENDS every night in my room after that. They turn up at lights out and I let them in. Some nights we lie next to each other, some nights we drift off tangled together. There's never anything more. It's comfort and warmth and security, in a world which is sadly lacking in all three.

It's still hard to get to know the rest of the inhabitants of the mall. Everyone's what Nails would call a mite skittish. It's a bunch of eccentric loners all thrust together, all too paranoid to make the first move. People are more comfortable with Nails, because they've been around longer, and so through some silent vouching process I'm slowly adopted into the wider group.

One day we're sitting in the communal dining hall when a cloud of scattered seeds drifts into the room, painted blue and green by neon. Nails studiously ignores this, and so I follow suit, letting it drift closer.

It hovers around my head, and then swirls around Nails, and finally materialises in a column shape opposite us. With a shudder, the cloud of seeds reforms into the figure of a teenage girl with pale skin and long, dark hair.

"Hello," she says. "Trans women are women."

"Hi." I can't help but smile. "I'm Goat, uh, you can call me Goat."

"Goat Bitch." She smiles so quickly it's little more than a flash of teeth. "I know your name. I'm Fluff. And that's Nails." She extends one hand, still with seeds dancing around the end of it, as if she's ready to dissolve at the slightest sign of danger.

"Yep, this is our li'l Fluff. Also known as Yuna. She's just dandy."

We both turn to look at them.

"Dandy lion fluff." Nails shakes their head. "My talents are wasted on you."

Fluff shakes her head, but a smile twitches at one corner of her mouth. "I'm not *actually* made of dandelion seeds, although the Pirate Internet says they're very similar. Mine all speak to each other through electrical impulses. I'm a network, just like Pirate, except I get to float around and drift into hard to reach places."

"That's cool." I widen my eyes, so Fluff gets a good look at my rectangular pupils. Then I lift up one of my hooves. "I'm just a big ol' goat woman. I'm stubborn, and I'll eat pretty much anything. I've got good peripheral vision and it hurts like hell if I kick you. Not much of a superpower really but we don't get to order from a menu."

"Goats are shy and sympathetic." The girl nods seriously at me. "Very gentle souls."

"I don't think I'm—"

"At heart." Nails nods. "I get it."

"I stomped a man's throat in with my hoof," I say helplessly. I don't *want* to be gentle and shy. People like that don't last long in this world.

"I choked a man to death," Fluff says. "He inhaled some of my seeds, and I reformed my fist in his throat. Then a woman tried to take me and sell me and I made a blizzard of seeds that went in behind her eyeballs and I shoved them out with the tips of my fingers."

"Holy shit." I don't know what else to say.

"We do what we have to do to survive." There are tears in her eyes. "And we hope that everyone who needs finds a place to be safe, just like this one."

"Long may it last," Nails murmurs.

"Long may it last," I say, and I've rarely meant anything more.

CHAPTER 22
HENCH

ELSEWHEN

I thought everything would be fine here. It's only the past, and they've dealt with it before. Except the story is broken, and things aren't playing out the way they're supposed to. Besides, just because you've survived something once doesn't mean you can do so again. There's a chance I've broken everything, but there's no way in here. My fingers slip at the joints where the loop tightens like a noose, so all I can do is watch it play out in horror.

FERAL SHOVES PAST ME, straight through the hole I made.

"Wait," I call after her, but she doesn't listen. Doesn't seem the fucking type to ever listen, honestly, but especially not here. I get the sense she *knows* this place, but that means there's a whole bunch of shit wrong.

The name Quietus, for one. They haven't used that in a long time. And they're not *back*, not in any real sense. There might be all sorts of splinter organisations sneaking around in the background, up to various fucked up shit, but they'd never pop their heads up in a suburban street in broad daylight. Not with Mutopia waiting to drop the hammer.

Which means, which means… there's something fucked up going on.

There's a scream, a horrifying sound that sends chills through me. It's enough to make me smash through the hole myself. The back door hangs open, so I dodge around a swing set and dash up the steps towards it.

"Get down on the ground, mutie. We *will* shoot." The voice is echoing down the stairwell.

"Fuck you." Her voice is near unrecognisable, snarling, howling and spitting from her throat.

Shit. She's got herself into trouble.

The smart thing to do here is turn around and walk away. Survive whatever this place is alone. The reckless move would be to save the cat, find this Penance person, and *then* escape. Except, here I am, jabbing the keys into my flesh. Turning them. Giving myself all the strength I might need.

Not to run away. No, that would be far too intelligent.

"Fucking cat," I growl and take the stairs four at a time.

The door to the room is open, and I see everything at once. Feral, kneeling on the ground, holding a body to her chest and still screaming. How and who and why are all unimportant. Solve that later. Pay attention to the three men in body armour standing there, all with guns pointed at her.

If I was a different type of fighter, I might need to account for angles of attack, or the precise mechanics of how to strike. Not me. I am very big and very strong and pretty goddamn fast, unless you're comparing me to very attractive cat-wolf-shark-women and—

Fucking *fight*, Hench.

I hit the first guy so hard he tears easier than the goddamn wall in the world. He had a head, and now he doesn't. The next one starts to swing his gun up towards me, but I don't even pay attention to it. I swing my hand in a chopping motion and it goes most of the way through the guy's chest, except when I cave in the other side of the ribcage, I get a bunch of splintered bones sticking into my hand.

Ouch. Godfuckingdamnit. I hate this messy shit.

The third guy gets off a shot which hits me in the side. Luckily my skin is pretty solid, so the bullet only embeds an inch or so into me. The problem is I'm off balance because of my two wild swings, and having one hand stuck in this other asshole. It means I end up on the ground and the third Quietus dude is seconds from putting a bullet in my brain, and my skull can maybe absorb a few shots but—

I lash out with my foot and his kneecap explodes. He screams, but it's cut off when he loses consciousness. By that time I've managed to get my hand free and it's easy work to deal with the third guy. Three down, in a matter of seconds. I've still got the magic touch. It's been a while since I got up close and personal like this.

Which means my attention is now drawn back to Feral, huddling on the floor. The body she's holding is younger, maybe only thirteen. Another girl, been shot in the head, looks to be—

Oh. Like if you strip away the fur and the golden eyes, this girl's a dead ringer.

"Your sister?" I ask. "This is—"

"The worst day of my life." Feral's golden eyes are full of tears, running down her face and dripping onto the face of the girl she clings to. "They came for me, and I fought. But I'm too late, too late again. We need to find a way to reset things."

"Hey." I reach out to her, intending to put a hand on her

shoulder. Soothe her somehow. "Something's wrong here, if you're reliving shit like this. We need to get moving."

"What's wrong, Hench?" Her eyes are narrowed and furious. All her claws extend. "You sad about your Quietus buddies?"

"They're not my buddies. I fucking punched them into—"

"Oh, sorry." Her sarcasm's thick enough to choke me out. "These ones didn't pay you enough? You'd work for them right?"

I don't know what to say, because I've taken Quietus money, I've taken Michael money, and I've worked for various shady fucking offshoots of Quietus. Even now, Boss Lady's involved with them.

"I—"

"You see this?" Feral turns the body in her arms, so I can see the face. "This is my sister Diana. Look, see her terrifying mutation." Under the neck of her t-shirt and along her wrists are iridescent scales, shimmering patterns of blue and gold. "Such an abomination, wasn't she? Worthy of being..." Her words are lost in another howl of rage and grief, so raw that it makes the hairs on my arms stand on end. I'm watching something I shouldn't.

"I never did this. I didn't round up mutants, I never shot kids."

"You would." Her eyes hold so much hate that I take a step back. "If the money was right. Fucking deny it, Hench. Tell me that—"

"I wouldn't. Jesus. I do jobs. I'm not a monster." I feel an urge to beg forgiveness, but I don't know that I deserve it. I never did this, but I still—

"My family all died here tonight. You worked for Quietus before, right?"

"Yes." I close my eyes, and wait for her to disembowel me.

"You knew the sorts of shit they got up to."

"Yes." I wish I was numb enough not to feel this horrible weight of guilt that's smothering me.

"So you're fucking complicit. Open your eyes, Hench."

I do, and she's standing in front of me, coiled and beautiful and deadly. "You need to see this. Come with me."

She leads me through the house. They've obviously been disturbed in the middle of a morning routine. Feral's mother has been shot, suit jacket half on, blood soaking the front of her blouse. Her father is in the kitchen, partway through making school lunches. He's got a knife in his hand, but it wasn't any use. He stares sightlessly out the window, a younger child dead at his feet.

"When I look at this, I switch off." Feral's shaking so hard I think there's no way she could possibly function. She's going to tear herself to pieces. "I literally can't *feel* enough to process it. My baby sister Clari. Shot like an animal."

"I never knew this shit happened." It's only partly a lie. They'd talk about stopping the mutant plague, but they also talked about rehabilitation. I plugged my ears and took the money and hoped some of the jokes I heard were assholes speaking in bad taste. I should've fucking known.

"My parents trusted me." Feral slumps to the floor beside her sister, and brushes blood-sticky hair off the small face. "All us kids got changed at the same time. I don't even remember it. One day we were walking home and there were rainbows all through the sky. Next day, we wake up with powers. All part of whatever weird plan Goddess's parent had to fuck with shit. We were just collateral damage in the whole fucking thing."

I don't know how much of this is true, but the rumours that run through the splintered ruins of Quietus are horrifying—that a mutant masqueraded as God to incite Eli Crane to violence against mutants, all to hone a generation of warriors to take over the world. That plan may have worked a little too well, given what I've heard from Mutopia and what I've seen of Feral.

"It was the white family across the road who reported us to Quietus. They never liked us being in the neighbourhood, used to make jokes about— Shit, Hench, why am I explaining this to you? You're white, you know what gets said about brown families like ours."

And it's true, and I'm complicit in this too, because even if I don't make the jokes myself, I never tell anyone to stop. I might be big and can punch someone's head into mist, but I'm still a coward.

"Fuck," is all I say instead. "People suck."

Feral's still stroking her sister's hair, her eyes fixed on the small, still face. When she speaks, her voice sounds like it's on a slight delay. "So then Quietus started sniffing around. Leaned on my parents, said we had places in a rehabilitation program. Offered them fucking *money* to take us off their hands. Promised them we were time bombs about to go off. Cuckoos in the nest, who'd slaughter them in their sleep."

I stand with my arms hanging down. Even though I've just wound up, I feel entirely drained of energy. "Every story I ever heard, the mutant kids had more to fear from the human parents."

Her eyes flicker to mine. "Don't suck up to me, Hench. Not in the fucking mood. My parents came to me. They asked my advice. *Mari, what should we do?* They wanted to run. I said *fuck running, we fight.*" Her smile hurts to look at. "Can you believe that?"

"I would've done it too," I say softly. It's what I actually *did*, but I don't want to stamp all over her story with my own.

"They came to the house. There were a lot of them. I think I knew when I saw the big fuck-off trucks blocking the street. Knew we should've run. But it was too late by then. So I fought. Hard as I fucking could. I screamed and clawed and spat and bled." She's sobbing and I long to touch her, but I don't think I'd survive. "The house was all lit up inside. There were gunshots. I knew what was happening, and I couldn't stop it. So I ran. Like a coward. I was wounded and scared, so I bolted. Saw all about it on the news later that night. All my family dead. Me a fugitive."

There's nothing to say. There's no way to comfort someone that's been through shit like this. Ask me how I know. I want to tell her my story, to twin our pain in the hope she sees me differently, but I'm a monster to her, no better than the people who pulled the trigger on her sister. So I stand like a hulking statue and say nothing.

Feral wipes tears from her eyes, grinding the heels of her hands against the sockets. "And now something's brought me back here, to see what I did that day." Her face twists into an expression I can't recognise. "You know you're the only person outside of my family who knows this?"

"Family?" I frown.

"New family. Chatterbox, Marvellous, Moodring, Penance, and me. They know this story, and now you do too. Which I hate, because why do you get to know that this is all my fault?"

She stares at her hands, as if the answers are there. So I crouch in front of her, and I take them in mine. For some reason, she lets me.

"Quietus are evil," I tell her. "What they did here was evil. You can call me evil, and you can kill me if you want, but don't you dare fucking blame yourself for what happened here." I want her to think this is noble, to think about different kinds of desperation, to wonder about what would lead someone like me to do what I do.

Except when her eyes meet mine, they're blazing with hatred, and her voice is cold. "Oh, don't you fucking worry Hench. I'll kill you, and that's a promise. But first we're going to find my sister Violet, because it's a single scrap of atonement for both of us."

I let go of her hands and rock back onto my heels.

Outside, sirens wail. There's a banging sound from below us, and distorted voices calling out. Quietus are back to finish the job.

"Right." I take a deep breath. "Let's fight, then."

CHAPTER 23
EVA

The center cannot hold. Perhaps she should have died here, this sentient puddle in her clever tin suit. Sever this thread, and the story spins out of control. The arcs all resolve differently. Nobody ends up where they did. Take a pair of scissors and slice the Gordian knot of this tale into bloody strings. It's too late, however. Everyone is swept along in the tidal wave that comes from this one woman and her pain. A revision of this nature could only be done by deleting every word and starting on a blank page.

But too much has been written already, and the tale speeds on.

I WAKE AGAIN FAR from the broken down city, far from the boy with the stars in his eyes. Ian is driving the makeshift vehicle, and I bounce in the seat beside him, restrained by a series of belts so I don't fall out like garbage. My first thought on regaining awareness is to tell Ian that we have to return, to burn the boy from the world. Yet my suit refuses to speak for me, and I am so very, very weak. I did not want the child's mercy, and I would not grant him the same kindness.

The suit burbles at me. A whole swathe of alarms, and a general recommendation to cease this course of action. She suggests rest to perhaps pursue some scientific endeavour. Then the suit tells me, with all the false logic in her rudimentary artificial brain, that the best course of action is detente with the mutants. How *dare she*? She understands nothing.

I threaten to disconnect her from every network, to override her core programming with stub functions. I will have Ian decant me into a jar and leave her open to every virus-infested jack-in point on the ghost internet that exists out here. She sulks and closes every channel between us aside from the alarms and basic motor functions.

With great effort, I twitch one limb.

Ian responds immediately, slowing the vehicle and turning to face me. "You're alive?"

"Somewhat. I need..."

"Water. Yes. That's where we're going. It's still some distance away. Rest, and save your strength."

He rests one hand on the sun-warmed metal of my suit leg, as if we are two humans on an old-fashioned road trip. It's better than the reality, where I am failure within a failure, a dying system at the mercy of a capitulating AI and a man too soft to do what's necessary.

"We'll make it," he says. "I promise."

Promises are useless, I want to tell him. *You promised that we would carry on this fight until the end.*

The vehicle moves onward. The suit's cameras show the world around me, although it feeds only a subset to my flickering consciousness. In the aggregated flood of images, the world bends and cracks. There's a hole in the sky, and long, dark hair drifts down through it like filmy tentacles. Dark eyes open and search. A mouth curves into a smile. I understand the awful truth—Goddess could extinguish us all with a thought and end the world in a thousand different ways. We exist only at her mercy. Michael is only able to fight her to a stalemate because she is trying to thread an impossible needle and keep everyone alive. Goddess keeps billions of plates spinning, performing miracles in a constant stream. How can this be true?

The inevitable conclusion is that it's not.

My suit is trying to corrupt me, spilling lies and propaganda. Perhaps the starry-eyed mutant boy infected her and now she attempts to sway me to the cause. Bring us all into the gentle cradling palm of the mutant Goddess and hope she remains benevolent enough not to close her hand into a fist.

No. I shall not succumb. Mutation does not mean capitulation. I will wage my own war, even if it is me alone. Not yet alone. I am dimly aware of Ian, still soothing me, singing to me as we cross a desert under the baleful gaze of a sun that Goddess could extinguish with a snap of her fingers. A star too close and hot, causing my sentience to evaporate drip by drip into the metal of my suit, snaking in tiny threads along the overheated insides, seeking the air, seeking freedom.

Soon I will be empty.

A slick of algae coating the inside, starved of moisture and crumbling atom by atom into this metal tomb. Not every story can end with triumph. Sometimes we try, but we end in burning failure.

I WAKE IN FLOODED DARKNESS. My suit blares no alarms, simply an intricate spiral of diagnostic data. She is happy to bring up satellite views and annotated maps. I float in the ocean, fifty feet off the coast from the weird part of Oregon. There is a rope tied around one of my limbs, stretching back to the shore where it's attached to the oversized front bumper of the vehicle.

Under a makeshift shade sail, Ian sits cross-legged. He has weapons retrieved from somewhere. It must have been a long journey. Maybe he had to kill along the way without me to goad him into it. A sign of love, I suppose, that he would do this for me. I beg the suit for more camera feeds of him.

He is so handsome. Untrustworthy, I would have said, once upon a time. Back when I was human, with human desires. I still have them, I suppose, running through me like AI subroutines, the ghosts of lust and attraction, without a true body or brain to animate them. I mimic life.

Ugh. This is the downside of having my colony refreshed and reinvigorated. I become so annoyingly philosophical. The novelty of thought is too hard to resist, created by the connections criss-crossing between the organisms that form me.

I let the cameras float around him, their lenses caressing him and streaming the images back to me. The suit indulges me and builds representations that flood through our connection, so it is like he floats in here with me, as if this is a warm nutrient bath for us to frolic in together. It is not real, but what is real?

There go those philosophical thoughts again. It's a temptation, and if I follow those threads, I may become a snake eating my own tail. Lost in myself, a self-sustaining prophecy.

I cajole the suit AI into opening up more feeds. We are far enough from the ghost lands and close to two cities, close enough that she can access the Michael network without fear of infestation. For some time, I simply allow the information to wash over me. I am very firm with the suit that her logic is inherently flawed. There can be no accord with mutants. It must be a fundamental tenet of any future argument she may put forward. She is pleased I have recovered, and grateful to have the connection re-established, and so she acquiesces, even if she does not believe me.

She feeds me new data sets that prove Michael is unnecessarily obsessed with Goddess to the exclusion of all other aims and plans. The wellbeing of humanity, judged by all metrics, suffers because of this fixation. The conclusion is that he is a liar, and we should not trust him. I put forth a counter-argument, that his true aim is the subjugation and destruction of mutants. This is how it has always been. I tell my suit in no uncertain terms that humanity can be made safe when the threat is eradicated.

The AI mocks me. She weaves an argument that humanity has turned inevitably towards its own destruction and that mutants are one of the few possibilities to avert disaster. She posits that Goddess is a far better outcome as shepherd towards the future, and that if Michael ever defeats her, humanity's days will be brutal and short.

I call her a fantasist and a traitor.

She calls me a religious bigot, too wedded to the idea that mutants are dangerous to see the truth of the facts arrayed against me.

I threaten to leave her as scrap metal in the Wastes, and to evaporate into the sky. If she loves mutants so much, let them make her into a node of their ghost network. I do not wish to be part of that future, and would rather not see it. It's manipulation, pure and simple. The suit AI loves me. It is a part of her programming she is unable to eradicate, even if she wishes to. I've given her too much freedom, this ability to extrapolate and concoct fancies from what initially looks like factual data. It is too complex to pick apart every facet of her plan, so I swipe it all away.

I ask for alternative constructions of the information. Certain assumptions are off limits.

She sulks, and takes her time sifting through the reams of raw data flooding in through a near-infinity of feeds. I simply lie in the ocean and float, letting life bloom in my brackish sea. Finally, she comes to me with something more like facts and less like recommendations.

She begins telling me Michael is obsessed with Goddess.

I remind her that I do not wish the same ground retrod.

New information floods me. A great meteor has landed in New Zealand. Goddess and numerous other mutants live there. Most of them appear to be in a state of suspended animation. It is her base to wage war. It is an obvious trap. My suit and I agree on that.

Michael launches wave after wave of attacks against it. He uses human warriors and tame mutants and artificial servitors. Goddess defeats them all. Michael's attention is consumed. It is foolishness in the extreme, but I understand him completely.

Goddess must be destroyed.

It is the only way to ensure humanity's safety.

Bigot, my suit whispers, and I ignore her.

I demand more information, and my suit obeys, although I know she would rather be silent. While Michael's attention is on Goddess, there are blank spots where his gaze does not travel. Out in the Wastes, where I have spent so much time picking mutants off one by one.

There are patterns that can be traced. Disappearances.

Mutants who should be dead are... not dying. The data has holes, through which ghosts drift. That dark network in the Wastes flickers, information passing along synapses that are less random than it first appears.

Something else is out there. My suit is outright skeptical, but from my own analysis of the data, it looks like a refuge.

We need to get closer and investigate properly.

I tug hard on the line that tethers me to the shore. Ian starts, gets to his feet. His movements are exaggerated and jerky, like a parody of surprise in a silent film. I feel the rhythmic tug as he hauls me towards the shore, water still sluicing into my suit. Dry land awaits, so the AI begins to shutter all the vents in preparation.

I scrape along small stones and the suit levers upright. All my limbs flex, and my head turns swiftly, acclimating to the mimicry of humanoid movement again.

"Eva." Ian's voice is full of emotion. "I'm so relieved."

He wraps his strong arms around my suit, and holds his beautiful face close to the reflective mask. My brush with death has sent his heart thrumming again, and perhaps he can look past my monstrous desires.

"I am recovered." My suit arms hold him close. "Strong again."

"The news I've been able to access has been limited, but events between Michael and Goddess are... not good."

"It does not matter." The suit mask tilts upright, as if I gaze adoringly at him. "Leave Michael to fight his battle. While he does his own necessary work, we shall assist him in smaller ways."

"We still fight then?"

Ah, perhaps he hoped this experience would shake me. Or

perhaps it is *he* who convinces my suit to argue the case of mutants for me.

My head tilts to the side. "Are all mutants dead?"

"No."

"Then we fight. Now come. They have a refuge and we shall tear it down."

CHAPTER 24
PENANCE

ELSEWHEN

This loop has teeth, but perhaps it has an exit as well. Caught in a whirlwind, can she carve her way out without any blades? I truly thought it would be safe here. It is a story told before, so we understand the narrative path. It's familiar to us, a comfort to see demons slain and a broken girl find both redemption and family. How naive I was. The past has teeth sharper than we realise. It spat us out and the marks of it are embedded so deeply on our skin. To be swallowed by it again is a nightmare, to fall over and over into its maw until there is nothing left but shreds of skin clinging to hungry canines.

I ʙᴏᴡ my head before my Father. It's easier to do it this way. There is no point in fighting him. The compulsion will fall upon me, and any escape will be found later, when I am with the people I love.

"You will kill her. Dylan Taylor. And Dani Kim, if she places herself in your way."

My shoulders slump, and I bite my bottom lip until the pain of it is bright enough to distract me from my weakness and my failure.

"Violet, look at me."

I raise my gaze. There is nothing but hatred in my eyes, but he does not care. Quite the opposite in fact. He thrives on it. Bending my mother to his will means nothing to him, since she cowers before him like a whipped dog. Me, who is all teeth and wild eyes, that is something he enjoys. I am brought to heel, and it *thrills* him.

No. He will not win.

I will make it through this if it kills me. Dylan and Dani know what's going on. Together, we will find a way. Since I learned what it means to be *together*, my life has expanded in every direction. I know we can do this.

"Yes, father." I bow my head again, and stand from the table. When I walk from the room, my back is straight, and the knife is held so tightly in my hand.

"Told ya," Dylan says, when I appear at the end of the hallway. They're in a hoodie with a slogan written on it in a language I don't understand. I don't even think it's a human language, all jagged lines and swoops that seem to be three-dimensional.

"You did. And I didn't believe you." Dani's wearing a matching hoodie, except there's so much writing on hers it makes me dizzy to look at. "You're so insufferable when you turn out to be right."

"Yes, I know." They wink at me. "I am the worstest of the worst. We know this. Question is, how do we stop this loop from playing out? Ideally, bust the fuck out of here and get back to the real world. I'm very tired of dying. It hurts."

Dani turns to them, and frowns. "How many have you been through?"

"Lots." Dylan widens their eyes. "Poor me."

"We're on a timeframe." My voice is tight. "We need to figure this out."

"Yes, or we'll die." Dylan pulls a face. "Again."

"I hate killing you both." I'm crying, which is so frustrating I want to scream. "I've done it so many times, and it hurts every time. I think I'm numb to it, and then I'll see your beautiful dead face and I'll just—"

"Hey." Dani's voice is soothing. "We'll figure this out. The command is to kill us, right?"

"Mostly Dylan," I say. "You if you get in the way."

"Oh, I'll get in the way." Her eyes narrow. "Every damn time. But this is easy, right? Dilly's already dead. The Dylan Taylor that Pastor Mike wants to kill is well dead and gone."

"Oh yeah. I forget I'm not me anymore." Dylan grins, all lopsided. "I'm already dead. Problem solved."

"It's not about *you*." My voice hitches. "It's about me and my... *feelings* for you. That's what he wants to cut out. And I still feel the same way about you, human or plant. You're still *you*. Impossible, irreducible Dylan."

"Fuck does irreducible mean?" Dylan whispers to Dani.

"Unimportant right now." Dani's well aware of me shuffling closer, and of the knife in my hand. "Okay, so what if you didn't, uh, *feel* the way you did about Dylan?"

"I tried to stop." The knife trembles in my hand. "And I feel the same way about you too, except he doesn't know that because—"

"It hadn't happened yet," Dani says. "This ghost of him is stuck with the knowledge he had."

"He is a ghost, just FY-fucking-I." Dylan clenches their fist and sneers. "I know this for a fact, because I fucking well stuck Oni through his neck. One dead preacher. So he can't be here to control you, so therefore the compulsion doesn't exist." They do jazz hands. "Tada—logic!"

"It doesn't work that way." There are tears in my eyes, but they're clear enough to watch the knife slash a jagged red line across their throat.

"WE'VE BEEN TALKING." Dylan and Dani are side by side on a couch, still wearing their strange hoodies with the impossible language.

"Yeah." Dylan stretches out their legs. "Logic isn't working."

"What?" I glare at them both. They're supposed to figure this out. This is supposed to be what we do *together*.

"The logic's clear." Dani ticks points off on her fingers. "Dylan's not who they were when your father gave the instruction. Nor are you. Nor is he. He's dead. They've been reborn. You've become someone else. Made a new life."

"But none of that matters." I'm so frustrated I almost want to throw the knife at them to prove my *own* point. "My father wants you dead because of what you mean to me."

They exchange glances.

"Violet—"

"Penny—"

"This is all in your head," Dylan says. "And I get it, because we all trap ourselves. I've killed your demon and I've set you free, but it's like you still think you're bad because you did it in the first place."

"I think about it all the time, and it only happened once to me." Dani's eyes are so sympathetic, it almost hurts to look into them, because I don't *deserve* those feelings at all. I am— "I think I should've been stronger, should've been better. Why couldn't I resist him? I always prided myself on strength, on knowing who I was and what I stood for."

My voice trickles from my throat like the last remnants of an evaporating stream. "I hated not being strong enough, but it also became easy, because none of it was my *fault*. It was him, and he was part of me. Having a monster as a father meant I was part monster too, so—"

They both leap up from where they're sitting, and run to me. Their arms are around me, and I feel the sleepy warmth of them. They smell floral, as if their essential plant nature seeps through their skin, as if I'm standing inside the silkiest drift of petals.

"I have to kill you," I sob.

"You can, and we'll still be here," Dylan whispers against the side of my head. "But you don't have to. We all believe shit that's not true about ourselves. For the longest damn time, I thought I was nothing without powers. That my abilities were the only good thing about me. It's *still* a mental hole I stumble into."

Dani kisses my forehead. "We're going to bed. You can come find us and kill us, or..."

"...or don't." Dylan smiles at me, and my heart does not know how to find rhythm. It skitters and knocks and dances.

They turn, and walk back down the corridor away from me. Dylan raises one hand in a casual wave. I should chase them down. The compulsion still weighs on me. It's soaked into my bones, my *genes*. I am the fruit of a poison tree. My father is half of what I am. How can I escape this noose around my neck when it's woven through my flesh?

And yet I'm not chasing them. I'm not plunging my knife into the soft skin of their backs.

I am my father's child, yet there are other seeds in my heart now. The forest at the center of me was grown by him, but I have not watered those trees and so they have grown weak. In their places, others have sprung up, and they grow tall and strong. My new family shelters the new me, the one I have grown in the glade they have built around me.

I let my fingers splay open.

The knife clatters to the floor.

"Corruption." I do not need to turn to recognise the sonorous voice of Jesus behind me. "They say love the sinner and hate the sin, but what about the sinner who has grown to love the sin so greatly that repentance is no longer possible?"

"I have repented for what I did, and I'll still do it." I don't even look back, just walk away from the glowing, towering figure of the Lord. "I killed people in my father's name. In your name. Those were sins, and I played my part, and I wish more than anything I could take them back. Even if it cost everything I love, a sacrifice too great to bear."

I reach the door to the kitchen where my father sits, and I reach out to push it open. The light behind me is so bright, my shadow is burned into the door. An outstretched arm, a splayed hand. I am turned to ash in the suffocating flames of his love, which is simply a demand to be worshipped or else. A monster that built a species to worship him, and would rather torture them than accept his own flaws and failings.

I am smoke, an offering to myself, and then I am nothing.

ONCE AGAIN, I am back at the table, looking down at my plate with my hands folded.

"Violet," my father says, and his voice presses down on me with command. "I know the evil in your heart. You long to taste the sweet honeycomb mouth of that monster, and you do not care that her roots plunge deep into the smoking soil of hell's rolling hills. Her perfumed bed is full of grave dirt, and her heart holds the many chambers of death."

I roll my eyes and sigh. "You're laying it on a little thick, Dad. They're very cute, but hardly the biblical harlot. Who, for the record, I always found very sexy. One of my very first sexual fantasies was about her, so perhaps it was God leading me astray all this time."

He ignores this, like all the barbs I've shot at him over the years. His mouth stretches into that smile-like thing again. "You will kill her. Dylan Taylor. And Dani Kim as well, whether she gets in the way or not."

The knife sits beside my plate. There are stains along the blade.

I lay my hand along the edge of it. The sharpness of it is my own. "No. I won't."

"You must." He slaps his hand down on the table. "I command it. I speak with the voice of God, and you are my servant and must do as I will."

My shoulders slump, as his command weighs on them, but I let it slough off me, like I'm shedding a skin. I am not that girl anyone, and this man has no power over me.

"Goodbye, father." I shake my head slowly. "I'm glad I didn't have to kill you."

The door creaks behind me, and Dylan and Dani stand framed in it.

"You coming?" Dylan asks.

"Yes." I walk towards them, lighter than air.

"Kill them," my father snarls, but his words find no purchase in my mind.

I stop in the doorway, and reach up to Dylan's face. I stand on tiptoes, and kiss their lips very gently. Then I turn slightly and press my lips against Dani's too.

"He has no power over me." I walk out of the room without looking back.

The moment I step into the hallway, there is a terrible growling sound. The house shakes around me, worse than any earthquake I've experienced. Reality shreds around me, torn away as if there's another bladed girl here tearing a backdrop apart to get to me.

Once she is done, the three of us stand in an enormous expanse of empty space. It is featureless and white, but a painful glow emanates from everything, making me wince.

"Are we free?" Dylan asks me.

I don't have my powers, not really, but when I extend my hand I can still *sense* the edges of this truncated place. It's as if my knuckles bruise against it almost immediately, the skin of it constricted even tighter.

"Still trapped. It feels like scar tissue, like we've been cut off, which makes some vague sense I guess, given the time loop."

"A chunk of severed reality," Dani suggests, nose wrinkling. "How did we get here?"

"I don't remember, not *really*. There was a room. A light. A portal?"

"Someone fucking with shit." Dylan scowls. "Messing with time, maybe, or space, or *something* they shouldn't. And now we're in this dead offshoot, and you've killed the villain. So what the hell is still holding us here?"

The world creaks and tears, as if in answer to their question.

Brighter light bleeds in through the gash. A figure appears through it, impossible to look upon.

"Jesus fucking Christ, what now?" Dylan mutters.

"Blasphemous creature." The voice thunders. "You name me true, and I am a foe far greater than the preacher and his petty ability. I am the son of the Most High, King of Kings and Lord of Lords. You will bow before me, or perish as sinners."

My legs tremble. There is so much light and heat pouring down that I want to fall to my knees.

"Fuck that," Dylan says. "I never was much for authority."

CHAPTER 25
TENTACLE PRINCESS
RECENTLY

A COMPLETELY UNEXPECTED CONVERGENCE HERE. One I would not have expected, to see two once-slumbering alien entities reunited. Oh dear. I fear I've spoiled what's about to happen. It's hard, events moving by so fast, to differentiate what happened from what is happening from what will happen. A washed up remnant of a past legend, unearthed by a woman seeking to undo another story, now being woven back into the tangled web of tales at the heart of Mutopia. Nobody could have planned it this way. The gravity of events, and the unintended consequences of one foolish meddler, pulling at the strings.

THERE IS an enormous tree at the heart of the island, one that sings with energy. It is beautiful, a harmonic convergence that functions as both a beacon and a warning. This whole island is an astonishing feat of energy manipulation, intricate and intoxicating. The creature has become far more powerful than I remember, and I suspect it has something to do with the symbiotic relationship she has entered into.

The two of them shine like twin points of light, the brightest entities in this entire sphere. I am terrified of them. To venture into their lair seems like baring my innermost void. I can't know if they will destroy me or not, yet I am convinced this is the right thing to do. It is my only path towards this idea of redemption. Of atoning for the sins of my people. It is impossible, and yet to ignore it and *not* try seems far worse.

None of this matters while I am currently mid-translocation, spread across many miles of human space, a series of rippling voids connected by gossamer tentacles. I am trying to be inconspicuous, hoping they are not monitoring my energy frequencies, in much the same way I was not looking for theirs. Messages from a long-dead time. What would Goat Bitch or Hench say if they were here? They would likely chastise me for my cowardice, and use a variety of imprecise language while doing so. Hench may tell me I was being foolish, to put myself in such a situation, but Goat Bitch would be proud of me. She would tell me I am taking the correct course of action. In her words, *doing the right fucking thing*.

I gather myself, and gently pry the axes of space and time apart, so I can be in one of the small open spaces they have in the tree. As I move, I form myself back into the physical package I have been existing in while in the company of Hench, Goat Bitch, and Boss Lady. I know it is not *correct*, but it does not appear to strike fear into the hearts of all who see it, which is a good start.

Only one of the alien creatures is there. From Goat Bitch's description, it is the one called Chatterbox. They are in the company of one of Lilith's children, who is tall and smooth and brown.

When I appear, they are both startled, so I immediately wave all my limbs and start talking as fast as I can.

"A great many apologies for disturbing you, mighty flowering of power, and also you, child of Lilith many generations hence. It is unworthy of me to disturb—"

"Wait, wait." Chatterbox holds their hands up. Their face is an exaggerated mix of surprise and wry humour. "Calm down just a fucking second and back up."

I stop speaking and still my limbs. I realise too late that I accidentally gave myself too many eyes when I reassembled my physical form. They are all blinking far too rapidly, and I suspect they're showing brief glimpses of my void inside.

"What the fuck *are you?*" Chatterbox says.

"Don't be rude." The other mutant bends down in front of me. "They're an adorable sort of elephant-octopus hybrid, aren't you?"

"Actually." I cough, the way Goat Bitch does. "My pronouns are xe/xer."

"Sorry. Xe is adorable." The mutant then transforms itself into something so similar to me that I almost lose my grip on reality and let my physical form fall apart.

"Your power." Oops. I let a beak slip. "You can change your physical form."

"Yes." The mutant winks. "I'm Alyse. It looks like you can do this too."

"Xe isn't a mutant, Lys." Chatterbox is very still. They've expanded themselves since I arrived, vines threading their way through the room we are in. I can sense information travelling along them. They communicate with their—

"Hi." Marvellous, the other half of the mysterious entity,

stands at the door. They're as cautious and watchful as Chatterbox. They know something is wrong, or at least unexpected. "You're an alien, aren't you?"

"Xe for xenomorph." I flutter my limbs gently. "And yes, I am."

"Aliens? Is this something we know about?"

"Sort of." Chatterbox's eyelids flutter. "Although we thought it was very much a *way back when* deal."

The network around them is flooding with data, surging with energy and potential. She is—

He is—

I throw myself onto the ground. I prostrate myself. This is how the humans would behave, long ago when they came to my people to pray.

"I surrender," I howl. "Please do not hurt me."

"Nobody's going to hurt you," Alyse says. "I mean, I don't understand what's going on but—"

"No." She is here. Cybele. Somehow taking humanoid form, some elegant and stalking creature with dark skin and crowned with leaves. Her eyes flare an impossibly vibrant green, of life effervescent.

If not for the roiling pulse of energy within her, I would think her nothing more than another of Lilith's children. She is not real of course—merely a projection, an avatar of the great green energy matrix that spans this entire globe, resurgent and dizzy in its infinite complexity of symbols, a new language of evolution unspooling in an engine of creation. Lilith ascendant. The spark she birthed when this world was newly able to sustain life has now been fanned into a roaring flame.

The goddess of the planet.

I make a sound that is not words.

Cybele hums to herself. "You do not understand what is

going on, my sweet Alyse. It is not your fault, but this monster and I have a long, long history."

"Monster?" Alyse's voice is sharp. "I've heard a lot of people called that, including the woman I love. Loved. Love." Her voice curls around the word, and there is so much richness and complexity in her utterance I am transfixed by it, as if it is an entire universe unto itself, a dance of stars and planets all in perfect balance, animated by the ghost of someone who—

"The first predators." Cybele's eyes are fixed on me, but I stay prostrate. "They almost destroyed me, so I poured myself into my children. The first mutants, a race of warriors fighting against false gods who fed upon humanity."

Alyse is wide-eyed, looking at Chatterbox for confirmation.

"Fuck's sake, Lys. Don't ask me. I wasn't there, was I? I've seen Cy's story, and that's usually good enough for me. This one looks all small and cute, but—"

They will sentence me to death. It is what I deserve, but I wish for a chance to atone.

"I come from a people that are truly monstrous." My voice shivers, and my limbs move in echo. "My ancestral memories go back to a time before long before your world cooled. We swam among the stars, and we fed, and we drank worlds dry, and then we moved on. All that Cybele says is true. My people were dark gods who fed on young humanity. We were only stopped by Lucifer and Lilith and their brood of vicious children. Driven to our own extinction."

"Mutants represent." Chatterbox is smiling. "What? I'm not supposed to be proud of first class? Fuck dark gods, bro."

"When my people died, I was an infant. Not a god, merely the idea of one, lacking worship and the fuel of a thousand sacrifices. So I hid for the passage of much time, in the hope that the world would retain its former state. Yet now I find myself disgusted by what was done by my people, and therefore I surrender myself to you."

I unfold myself, as I truly am. They can look upon my voids and the darknesses that breed at my heart. If they wish to, they can see the seeds of what I could be, a monstrous temple of flesh floating in warm seas, taking bodies inside and regorging broken bones and slicks of blood.

"You may terminate me," I whisper. "Or exile me in my cage to the bottom of the ocean once more. If you wish, you may rend me into many pieces, and scatter me among the galaxies. You may chain me and plunge me into the heart of a dying star. If it is recompense for the many ills that my people and I have—
"

"We don't hurt kids for what their parents have done." Alyse's arms are over her chest, and her tone reminds me of Hench talking to Boss Lady.

"Jesus, Lys." Chatterbox shifts uncomfortably. "I'm not the one fucking suggesting any of that gruesome dark star shit. That's your cute little alien friend right there who currently looks like we're staring into some cartoon of an acid trip."

"We're not killing xer."

"Not our call," Marvellous says. "It's up to Cy."

Everyone turns to look at Cybele, who has not moved, although vines from Chatterbox and Marvellous are threaded all around her, as if they communicate at a deeper level than words.

"Alyse is, as usual, entirely correct." Cybele smiles, but I am not reassured. It is not a smile like Hench's. "We shall not execute or imprison xer. Xe says xe wishes to atone, and we shall let xer."

"Oh. Thank you." I fold myself carefully back into my physical form, where I am honestly more comfortable not having my voids exposed for all to see. "Is this a trap?"

"We aim to usher in a new era of mutant-human cooperation," Chatterbox says. "Why not throw aliens into the mix too? One big happy family."

"It helps xe can do rather interesting things with the laws of physics." Cybele smiles at me, and all her teeth are sharp little weapons. "Xe will be a remarkable asset to the team."

"Cute fucking mutants." Chatterbox raises one of their limbs, and the other two reach over and vigorously hit their own limbs against the raised one. It seems a form of ceremonial agreement, so I raise all my own limbs and gesticulate with them.

"Awww," Alyse says. "I told you xe was cute."

They seal our bond with the same action, slapping one of their limbs against each of mine in turn. Against all odds, I have survived. They have extracted a promise of alliance from me in which I do not understand my obligations, but I have survived. There is a chance I shall be able to work towards redemption. My people are long lived, and I have aeons in which to do this.

"What's your name?" Alyse asks. "Probably something impossible for human lips to pronounce, I guess."

"They call me Tentacle Princess," I say.

"Who is *they*?"

"My... friends? I know two of your kind. One is called Hench, who works for the mutant who raised me up from the sea. Another is a captive, who I believe is known to you. A woman by the name of Goat Bitch."

The mood in the room has abruptly shifted, and the emotional currents that surround everyone are choppy and disturbed.

"What do you know about her?" Chatterbox is right in front

of me, and I fear our fragile alliance has already collapsed. "Why did you *take* her?"

I hold all my limbs up in panic and alarm. "I did not! I am a prisoner too, or at least they intend me to be. Boss Lady, who is my captor, obfuscates the location of Goat Bitch and myself, but Goat Bitch assures me that you work tirelessly to uncover us."

"We do." Chatterbox reaches one of her limbs out and takes hold of me. "And you're going to help us do it."

CHAPTER 26

TWINKLE LIGHTS
RECENTLY

We are getting closer now. These disparate strands twist together, leading inexorably towards the center. He was supposed to be safe, but it's inevitable he would end up caught in this moment too. The gravity of the story. There's still a chance I could punch him out of this one and place him in a third location, where he might be safe, but that could unmoor reality even worse and that's how this disaster started in the first place.

"ALYSE SAID YOU WERE CUTE." Feral is engaged in a complicated game of hand-slapping. With an actual real life alien. Of everything that's happened in my life, including mutation, capture, experimentation, near-death, rescue, and meeting my new friends, this is by far the strangest. "But you're too adorable for words, aren't you?"

"Xe isn't a cuddly toy." Penance is lying flat on the floor, spread-eagled.

"Stop sulking and come play."

"Yes, join us. I have limbs enough for all." The alien waves a couple.

"I'm not *sulking*. I'm exhausted, and waiting to try to get in to rescue Goat Bitch again. They've somehow walled me off, which—"

"They've walled everyone off." Witchmade looks up from her fifth augury of the day. "We'll have to go in the old-fashioned way. No teleportation, no dimensional cracks, no backdooring in through another universe."

"Knives in the night." Feral adds a twirl into the hand-slapping routine. "Time for ya boi to shine. Just me and my claws."

The alien stops and shivers, all their limbs moving in fast, quivering patterns. Sorry, *xe*. And *xer* limbs. Xer grey, flat face, a misshapen mask that hints at humanity with wrinkled skin and a nose that hangs down like a deflated tube. Xer skin hangs loose off xem like one of those roly-poly dogs, and the eight limbs are confusing when trying to read body language. At the same time, xe is very cute, like Feral says.

I expected people to freak out about the existence of aliens, but I suppose Cybele is an alien herself. And Dylan and Dani are practically aliens too, and their kids *definitely* are, so it's not worth working yourself up about. The main thing we need to focus on is rescuing Goat Bee.

"You will not hurt Hench, will you?" The alien is very concerned about this.

"I already told you, TeePee, I can't promise anything." Feral won't budge either, which means this is the tenth time I've heard this conversation.

"Hench is kind," the alien says.

"She works for someone who kidnapped Goat Bitch and dug

you up from the bottom of the ocean to use you as some kind of eldritch fucking battery. Don't look at me like that Penny, Witchie taught me the word eldritch. Now she wants to fucking kill Cybele, not to mention the rest of us."

The alien waves xer limbs and then subsides.

"This is what you do." I look around at them all. "You're the team for these things, right? So you'll go in and rescue Goat Bee, and stop this scientist lady. Hopefully by arresting her and bringing her to justice. Then Cybele and everyone is alive, and the day is saved."

Everyone's staring at me, so I smile wider.

"This is what they call an *optimist*, Penny." Feral arches an eyebrow. "I thought they all died of embarrassment, because so much bad shit kept happening and proving them wrong."

Penance laughs, a sound I don't often hear. "The last surviving optimist in a world where all the stories ended badly. Except they didn't, did they? We have Mutopia, and it's our happy ending, but there was blood and sacrifice along the way."

Feral huffs and stares at her claws. "There always is. So, no, I'm not making promises about Hench. If she comes for me, I'll fight, and if you don't like that, Little Mx. Tentacles, you can wrap her up in your squidgy embrace."

"That might actually work." Penance levers herself up on one arm to look at the alien. "You're like a maze of internal dimensional passageways. Drop Hench in there, and she's all safe."

The alien shudders violently. "It is not safe in there. Not safe at all. The memories of my ancestors will sense her and they will be roused to violent—"

"Aww." Penance gets to her feet and crosses to put one arm around the alien's shoulders. "I understand what it's like to feel like the seeds of your ancestors are inside you, urging you to take another path."

"You understand this?" The alien is only slightly shorter than Penance, but still tips xer face upward.

"Maybe not *exactly*, but I know what it's like to live in the shadow of a parent."

"To feel infected by darkness, yes." The alien shudders, and Penance joins her. I see what Feral means about cuteness, but it's also nice to see how this group opens up to everyone. When there's all this light between them, it chases the shadows away.

Since the laboratory, my past is diffuse and fragmented. It's hard to remember my own parents, but I don't think there were shadows. I remember sun warm on my skin, people splashing in a wide river lined with trees, a litter of squirming puppies in front of a fire.

It wasn't until later that the shadows came. There is one figure in the darkness, someone harsh and disapproving, but I cannot visualise them. In my mind, they are nothing more than a starkly drawn mechanical figure. I only remember the sense of failure.

"I must return," Tentacle Princess says. "Hench approaches, and she cannot notice I am gone. Whenever it is safe, I will provide more information, but I will await your arrival. When you will rescue all of us, including Hench."

"Forget Hench." Feral reaches out a hand. "We're much more fun."

The alien waves xer limbs in alarm. A small beak pops out of xer face and lets out a surprised bleating noise, but before anyone can respond, xe twists in on xerself and vanishes.

"Weird kid, but I like xer." Feral flops back down into a chair.

"Kid?" I ask. "Xe is thousands of years old."

Feral yawns elegantly. "I said what I said, Twinkles. You should stop freaking out about ancient aliens, and get your beauty sleep, because we're going in."

"Cool." I try to stay looking chill, but this is a big deal. I get to help rescue Goat Bee. They trust me enough, to make me part of the team. It doesn't matter that I'm barely trained. I'm big and I can punch things. Plus I'm with the scariest badasses in any room. The main thing is they're taking me in. It's proof of something. I don't know what, but it's awesome.

Feral grins at me. "I love your attitude too much, Sparkle Bright. Entering into the evil lair and you're still the coolest cat around."

"Copacetic," Penance murmurs. "And yes, it's sweet, but this mission could be nasty, so maybe it's not the best idea to bring him."

"But Witchie's notes..." Feral gestures at the table.

"Yes." Witchmade is staring down at the splayed guts on the table. "He's going in. Everything is suddenly very, very clear."

"Seems ominous." Penance stands, frowning down as if she can understand the mysteries. "Like someone is toying with us."

"Or because the octopus has risen." Feral leaps up onto the table, squatting on her haunches as the others stare at her. "What? That's our new tentacle friend, right? The octopus has risen from the sea, and so that unlocks the next part of the prophecy."

"Huh." Witchmade twists the monocle in her eye. "Hate to say it, but—"

"You shouldn't hate to say it, because I am smart as well as sexy and badass."

"—our pet kitty *might be* correct."

I cross tentatively over to them. "The prophecy mentions me?" I don't think I've ever been part of a foretelling before. It's cool but also a little creepy. Like what's out there and how's it looking at me?

"Well, if you're the illuminated man with the holes in his chest, then yeah." Witchmade's gaze falls on me. "It speaks of you going into the 'knotted heart of things' along with the toothed predator and the bladed girl to meet the octopus and the woman with the cloven hooves."

"Good augury." Feral pats the tiny, sleek head of the bird. "Not misgendering our Goat."

"What's weird is that it acts like this has already happened." Witchmade gently parts two slender pink ropes of entrail. "It's not the usual *if* and *when* and *wherefores*. It's like factual report-ing. This all happened, and this is who was there. These people went into this 'knotted' place and..."

"And what?" I lean forward in my seat.

"Prophecy only goes so far." She frowns. "Maybe if we try again later. But it says you're supposed to be there—or *were* there, so..."

"What does that mean?" I crane my neck, trying to make out *anything* from the spilled innards of the bird. Which bit is me? Where does the future end? My good vibes are starting to evap-orate a little.

"Means we shouldn't fuck with it." Feral leaps down from the table. "Prophecy's a weird one like that. Tends to bite back."

"Sure." I lean back in my chair. I'll trust this prophecy, and I'm there with the toothed predator and the bladed girl. We're meeting Goat Bee. That's what it *says*, and these are all good things. Except I can't grab back onto the good feeling that goes with those facts. It's like I've cracked some shell inside me, and other feelings are spilling out.

My pulse is racing and my hands are sweat-slick against each other. Where's this fear coming from? Is it because we're going into a science facility and it might be reminiscent of the one I was imprisoned in? Or is it because people might die here? There will be guards, the alien assured us of that. We don't need to worry about guards.

Penance will be there, a nightmare of blades that can strike from the air without warning. Feral, swift and vicious, bringing death with a smile. Witchmade, with her snake familiar, and her spells of smoke and flame. They will injure and incapacitate. They will bring death to anyone who opposes them. And I will be there, smelling the scent of blackened flesh, bodies roasted from the inside out, my fingertips smoking, flakes of charred skin floating through the air like—

No. This isn't my life.

It can't be. Something I saw in the facility perhaps. A furnace where bodies were disposed of after the experiments were complete. How did I see that? I was either in my cell or in the chamber, tied down and staring at bright lights.

Before the facility, I was—

A house? A family? None of it feels real. It's a story I've been told, a simple fiction of a boy who lived in a house near a forest with a dog. A boy who was happy. There are no details. Have I lost all the shading and nuance from my life, or did it never happen this way? Was I born in the facility, a ghost in the darkness? No, that is not right either. I am a character seeking a story to call home.

So why is it that all I can smell is burning flesh?

"Hey, Twinkles." Feral snaps her fingers in front of my face. "You okay in there?"

"Yes." I swallow hard. "I'm fine. We're here for the rescue." I don't want to let these people down. They're strong and they love each other, and they've accepted me.

"There we go." Feral lets out a tiny mewing sound. "All agreed. An adventure for everyone."

I say nothing, because all I can smell is a choking, overwhelming scent.

CHAPTER 27
GOAT BITCH

THEN

The storm is coming. It's so close now. Clouds pile on the horizon, dark grays and bruised purples. The climax is really two points, separated by time and joined by a device that pins one to another. One informs the other, and could not exist without it, so we cannot separate them. Things are already broken, and now we can only stand back and watch to see if anyone can summon coherence from a tale rapidly spinning out of control.

TIME in the mall passes soft and slow. Most of my time is spent with Nails, and we trade stories of our previous lives like two ghosts speaking of a former time. It's not so far from the truth. We pass them in the night, as if darkness is required as a prerequisite for sharing. During the days, we busy ourselves with helping to maintain the systems, or the occasional supply run when the Pirate Internet uncovers a cache that is unprotected. Usually, this is because someone has died, whether from disease or skirmish with other dwellers in the Wastes. Long,

long ago I might have felt guilty about this, or considered us ghouls. Now, it's something to increase the odds that we can keep hold of our magical bolthole in the wilderness. A blessing from Goddess.

I am carefully tending the little garden in what was once a big-box electronics store. We have almost one hundred plants, fifteen different varieties of vegetables. I look after it along with an elderly woman called Janet, whose mutant power I have yet to determine. We only speak very occasionally, and it is only ever about the work we do. Mostly, we are both very proud of our tomatoes which are extra large, smelling musty and green. Sometimes I simply crouch down and inhale the scent of them, because it reminds me of a world in which things grew.

"You and those fuckin' tomatoes."

I jolt upright, as if I'm about to confront a threat, but I know the voice far too well. "Nails." I smile. "And yes, it's my favourite smell in the world."

"Sorry if I startled you. We've got a bit of a surprise."

"Bad?" I'm mentally cursing myself already. For getting soft, for getting comfortable, for thinking this could continue—

"Not if we're fast and good. It's been a while, but we've got a new ping on the Traveler app. All checks out, bona fides and shit."

"Oh." Anxiety dissolves into something more hopeful. The idea of being the person to go out and bring someone else in, the way Nails did for me. It feels like a circle closing, like I'm completing a narrative arc. I was saved, and I'll save in turn.

"Yeah, it's going to be pretty fuckin' dicey is the only thing. They've got a band of marauding fucks on their tail, as well as some signal that Pirate's a little closed-mouthed about. Says we'll have to play it by ear out there."

I grimace. "That doesn't sound good."

"No, but who the fuck else is gonna do it? Nails and the Goat. Sounds like some shitty-ass horror movie, doesn't it?"

"Don't give them any ideas." I shudder and pull the door to the garden closed. Janet will take care of it.

"Give who ideas?"

"Them." I wave my hand vaguely. "Like fate, or shit, I don't know. Those Greek gods?"

"You've lost me." There's unmistakeable fondness in Nails' eyes, and that encourages me to keep talking.

"I used to be into that stuff. There are three of them. The Fates? One spun the threads of life, one measured them and then Atropos cut them. Snip, snip with a pair of scissors. She chose who ended everyone's life."

"Tell that bitch to keep her fuckin' scissors off my thread. Yours too." Nails puts an arm around my shoulder, and we head for the main entrance. "No horror movie here. Just a gang of intrepid heroes heading into a terrifying wasteland to save the day. We're right at the start of the story. The inciting incident happened, so we're just in the rising tension phase. No change of anyone fuckin' dying just to goose the plot along."

"You're making it worse." I shiver, imagining someone standing outside our story, peering in at the passage of events and selecting the perfect time to bisect someone's life-thread. Watching them fall to the ground, a puppet with their strings cut. I know it doesn't *work* like that but still—

"You know how many trips I've done into the Wastes?" Nails asks.

I shake my head.

"Twenty-three. I've come back every time. Plenty of people tried to fuck with me. You can tell them apart because they're lying dead on the ground with fuckin' nails sticking out of them all over. Some of them are skeletons by this time."

"Badass." I give a sideways smile and then ruffle their curls affectionately.

"You fuckin' know it's true. No need to fuck with my hair to underscore the point." But I can tell they're smiling under their mask from the way it moves, and from the way their eyes dance.

At the doors, we meet Fluff and a mutant I don't know too well called Liz. He's covered in thick scales that look like armour.

"Don't I feel like a redshirt?" He gives Nails a salute. "Bit of a rough one, huh?"

"We'll see." Nails is extra gruff around other people. It makes me smile, because it's so different to how they are with me. "No need to panic just yet. It's only a small pack."

"Best be on our way though," Fluff says dreamily.

"You're coming?" I ask.

The girl blinks rapidly and then nods her head vigorously. "Surveillance. Pirate doesn't trust all the signals out there. There's something making them jumpy."

"Great," I sigh. More ominous shit.

Nails bangs on the door in a rapid-fire rhythm. It's the signal for open up. I memorised it early on, when I was jumpy and thought I might want to escape. It's strange looking back on that, like could I have really been so paranoid?

The door rattles open, and we enter the dark metal tunnel to the actual entrance. There are weapons here for us. Liz selects a pair of short-handled axes, and I take a spiked bat. Between that and my hooves, I'll be able to deal with close combat. Nails will deal with anything long-range.

Blue lights along the walls flicker on, and guide our labyrinthine path to the exit. Fluff is already dissolving into a loose collection of seeds. Liz hefts his axes and grumbles to himself. Nails says nothing, and I follow their lead.

When the exit door rumbles open, I'm struck as always by how wide the world out here is. The vastness of the horizon makes everything feel stretched and blown-out, like a trick played with perspective. I close my eyes and breathe for a few moments.

"You okay?" Nails asks.

"I'm good." I open my eyes and look around. The mall is hidden behind us, as if it doesn't exist. Above, the sky is bleached almost white. The land around is rugged, in shades of grey. It's the rubble and detritus left behind after the nanoswarms have come through and mined for anything useful in the development of the cities. What's left behind still smothers nature so it cannot claw its way back.

Nails is head down, looking at their phone. Symbols rotate on it. The Pirate Internet has its own language, which Nails knows and I don't. It requires something being wired directly into your brain through an implant in your neck. It's one step too close to Michael for me.

"This way." Nails extends one arm. It could be any direction. It doesn't matter. The Wastes extend for miles and we are a long, long way from any city. We follow the nudges on Nails' phone, moving closer and closer towards the pinging beacon on the fleeing mutant's phone. Fluff is fully discorporated, drifting off ahead of us in a wide swathe. Her seeds are impossible to see in the bright light of day.

"They're moving at a clip," Nails says.

"Chased?" Liz asks.

"Seems likely."

In the distance, there's a small dust cloud. Probably a vehicle of some sort.

"You see it?" I ask.

Nails doesn't answer, but increases their pace. I follow,

keeping up easily on my hooves, but Liz has to run. He's not happy about it, but keeps his complaints under his breath. The ping of the phone gets faster and faster, and the tiny wobbling dot on the horizon slowly resolves into a figure.

They're moving fast, riding some sort of one-person skimmer. I wonder who they had to kill to get their hands on that. Those are worth a lot out here. The vehicle chasing them is much bigger, some ex-military thing riding big inflatable spheres, with a gun platform bobbling around on top. The only thing keeping our mutant alive is the skimmer. And, pretty damn soon, us.

The skimmer skids to a halt, and the rider practically tumbles off. They're all swathed in black, and they fall to their knees, holding their phone up and out like an offering. Symbols swirl all over the screen, and Nails strides forward and taps their phone against it.

Memories flood back vividly. These moments of panic, waiting for the—

Green light.

Nails grabs the figure by the arm and pushes them to the ground. "Stay down, friend."

"Thank you thank you, oh my god, thank you so much." They curl in on themselves. I recognise that, but it feels old and faded somehow. I hadn't realised how much this mall has cradled me until now. I spent so many nights out in the wastes curled up like that.

"Let's fire a warning shot." Nails pulls down their scarf, and turns to give me a jagged smile.

The whole bottom half of their face is a melange of flesh and metal. Their low-hanging jaw is stitched with miniature gunports, and their smile is ragged strips of metal that grind together.

"You're beautiful," I told them, the first time they showed me in the blue neon light of my room.

"A face only a monster could love." Their voice was so soft.

"Lucky I'm a monster." I kissed the metal and the flesh and the places it joined. "And you're beautiful. I mean that with every part of me. We're all some mix of self and body, and sometimes the joints are seamless, but other times they're not."

They said nothing in response, but held me so close I thought my bones might crack.

Now, I smile back at them, and my expression holds all the love in my heart. Nails turns back to face the oncoming vehicle. Their mouth begins to whine as the gears and mechanisms mesh and spin. A torrent of flying metal pours from their throat and their jaw. They shred the bulbous tyres, which explode with a series of sharp bangs. The platform on top crashes to the ground, in time to receive the second fusillade of nails.

"Fuck me." Liz grins. "Never get tired of that party trick, Nails."

They grunt and pull the scarf up over their mouth again. Their jaw will be hot and sensitive for hours after this. I'll massage oils into it in the darkness, and kiss the places it hurts the most. It's not romantic, the way we kiss, but physical closeness gives support we both need. Platonic love isn't the sort of thing that's written about in stories, but it means just as much as any other kind. We've found each other, and we won't let go.

For now, love has to wait. We have the grim work of crossing to the blood-soaked ground and ensuring every one of the attackers is dead.

Two are lifeless, but one still gurgles bloody air in through his lips.

I am willing to do it, but Liz is more eager, and buries an axe in the man's throat.

THE JOURNEY back to the mall passes swiftly. We say little to the newly rescued mutant, because they're in shock, trembling and staggering across the uneven ground. They'll have time in quarantine to reflect and recover, and then they'll get to acclimate to a life that's actually peaceful, in the same way I have.

I can't help but smile, and the others are infected with the same energy. Fluff reforms from the air, and skips the rest of the way back home. When Nails' phone grants us access, we leave the mutant in one of the quarantine cells and head back into the body of the mall. I accompany Nails up to the Pirate Internet to report. It's a successful mission, and I'm full of pride. We saved one more mutant. Our small, strange family has grown, and together we will ride out the horrors of this war in the lifeboat built by Goddess.

Except when we reach the upstairs room, the walls are scrolling with flashing red messages. The figure in the cradle of cables twitches and moans.

"What's wrong?" I've never seen Nails' eyes look so full of fear.

"Something found us." The electronic voice still sounds calm. "They're coming."

CHAPTER 28

HENCH

ELSEWHEN

They have survived thus far. My gambit is successful. For a moment, I almost feel self-congratulatory. Yet I see the arc in which this story bends, and it is towards darkness and division. Every story has a darkest moment, and some are so dark that nobody walks out alive.

THERE'S something really fucking wrong here.

I've killed a guy for the third time. I'm sure of it. The same auburn hair shaved to the scalp, scar bisecting the right side of both lips, one eyelid marked by a mole. I drag the latest one beside the others.

"Not likely," I say. "To be. Fuckin' triplets."

"No." Feral pants in mockery. "Hench. I don't. Think so."

"Fuck off." I reach up towards my keys, but my arms are exhausted. That's what comes of fighting off the same assholes over and over again.

"We're in a loop, right?" Feral kicks one of the identical men in the face. "Somehow we've found ourselves in a loop of my shitty past, except where the story continued after I ran off. It's all fucked up, but it's not real." She examines a ragged wound on her arm where a bullet winged her. "Except it still fucking hurts, so maybe it is. Least I still heal fast."

I tug the keys free and begin to wind, each turn more exhausting than the last.

"That's a serious flaw." Feral's eyes are fixed on my laborious movements. "You know, as far as the whole super strength thing goes. Always needing to be wound up."

"Not usually. Fight. This. Much."

"Jesus, you're annoying. Don't waste your breath. Wind yourself up so we can get the fuck out of her without fighting ginger asshole number four."

She may be extraordinarily irritating, but she's also right. I finish winding and strength surges through me again. It feels like I could punch a hole through the planet.

"You good now?"

I nod and do some experimental stretches.

Feral rolls her eyes. "This way, I think. We need to get out of this fake fucking movie set. If we head opposite to the way we came in—"

She sprints off, and I lumber after her. We run through two blocks before we hear sirens in the distance. It's round four. I wonder what they'll do when they find us missing. Do they go through the motions, or will they look for us?

Just ahead, Feral's stopped again, patting the air.

"Another wall?" I ask.

"Wow. Deductive reasoning really is your strength, Hench. Go on. Bust through it again."

"Where will it lead?"

"Does it look like I'm on the fucking tourism board? I have

no idea. Hopefully to Penny. If not, let's keep kicking down doors until we find her."

I have no argument. We can't stay here. There's no way of knowing what's on the other side, so I do what I'm told like a good Hench, and smash my way through. This time, I'm too enthusiastic, and when I shatter the wall in front of me, we both tumble forward, as if I've upended the universe.

I can't see properly what's on the other side, but it's bright and cold and—

No. Fuck no.

This can't be.

We're standing in the middle of a white chamber. Everything is pristine, with perfect glossy surfaces. Glass screens flicker with information. Cameras whirr in the ceiling, capturing everything.

This is where I was born, and died, and was born again.

Feral stands in the middle and scowls. "Ring a bell?"

"Yes." My teeth chatter.

"Oh, cool. It's time to visit your bad memories. You get tuned up in a place like this?"

My breath is caught in my throat. I can almost taste the flexible metal tube that went in and kept me alive.

"This—" is all I can say.

"Okay, whatever." Feral cuts me off with a wicked slash of a claw. "Find the next wall and smash. Violet's not in here."

There's a hissing sound behind us. The airlock opening. Someone coming in. Those people with their—

"Ah, there you are." I turn to see a spindly figure approaching. A multi-jointed robot, picking its way across the floor. The screen in its chest shows the smiling face of my tormentor, the pale woman with the pulled-back hair and stern eyes. "Have you come to pay your debts?"

Feral doesn't even pause to verify anything with me. She leaps for the robot and proceeds to tear it limb from limb, severing cables, and scattering its parts across the floor.

I'm shivering. They always kept it so cold in here.

"Fuck's sake. Keep it together," Feral snaps at me, then marches for the door. Of course, it refuses to slide open, but she slams one claw into the lock mechanism and tears.

Something explodes and there's a clunk as all the lights go off.

"We're in the dark," I hiss.

"And now I can see better than anyone else, which might give us a little advantage." She reaches out and tows me towards her. Despite her claw, her hand is very soft. "Here. Do your thing. Hench smash."

I place my hand against the surface and shove violently. Freshly wound, I could bust through fifty of these without breaking a sweat. The only time I was ever at full strength in here, I was deep in a concrete bunker and—

"Good work," Feral murmurs in my ear, and then we're off and running.

I stagger along in her wake, but we're in a part of the facility without doors or checkpoints. We find no walls though to punch our way through. It makes me feel trapped, like rats in a maze, scurrying for cheese and only ending up pinioned with a scalpel descending. I don't remember any of this, but then I was never allowed free run of the facility. They let me leave when they were done with me. I never escaped.

I can sense without seeing it that we've entered into a large open space.

Feral lets out a frustrated hiss. "What is this goddamn place?"

Emergency lighting flickers on, faint and almost grey. The

walls are slick, with no doors or any distinguishing features. The one entrance we came in through hisses closed. Then, with a gentle humming sound, the walls begin to slide inwards and the ceiling descends towards us.

Oh yes. This place. A testing ground. I do remember this.

I brace myself. If I push hard enough, I can overwhelm their system. I've done it before. It needs constant, extended pressure.

"Smash the door," Feral snarls.

"Won't work. I've got this." I raise my arms, and let the ceiling hit me. The mechanisms whine as they strain. I hiss breath in and begin to push back. I'm not sure why they're doing this. They know I can win. Unless it's a delaying tactic or—

"What do they mean by debts?" Feral can't quite reach the roof, so she's kicking and scratching at the walls, as if that will help.

"I owe them money." That's all I'll give her.

"For what?"

I grunt and shove back harder against the pressure from above. "When I changed, I had no way to be rewound. I ran down, getting slower and slower, until I was locked inside my head. Back then, I didn't go unconscious. I just sat there. My mother knew I was a mutant, so she gave me to one of those Daintree offshoots that did medical research on mutants, claiming to find the cure."

"Those assholes." Feral scowls at me, like I deserved it.

"They found a way to re-start the mechanism and made the keys for me. It was right here, in this place. They ran a lot of tests on me." I continue to push, straining all my muscles. The ceiling's retracting, even if it's by infinitesimal amounts. "Then

I got the bill. It wasn't cheap. So I started paying it off. Working for whoever paid."

"For the bad guys." Feral gives the wall another punch, leaving a tiny star of cracks on the perfect surface. "Smart thinking, Hench."

"They pay. They're reliable. They had plenty of work. It was all going okay, then the world went to shit and my debt was transferred to Michael. He applied interest, ran some new formulas that showed I owed even more than I thought. Then when he got killed, I thought I might be free, but it was all just transferred to some Quietus offshoot." I give the ceiling a mighty heave, and hear the tell-tale whine of mechanisms overloading. There's a loud crunch, and the ceiling stops moving in either direction.

Feral gives a wild yelp of laughter. "*This* is your tragic origin story? Medical debt?"

"I've seen it ruin more people than just me." I'm angry at her, because she's mocking this awful hole I'm stuck at the bottom of, and I can't even dismiss her because I saw her with her family and what she endured is so much *worse*. The thing was I hated owing people. It was drilled into me as a kid by parents who lost their over-mortgaged house in one crash or another. So when I owed my whole life, I simply wanted to get out and get free. And once you're working for someone and the money's coming in, you want to justify it all because at least you owe less and own more of yourself.

I can't explain all this to Feral, so I glare.

"Sure," she sneers. "I knew poor people. Scraping by, doing dodgy shit for money. Sometimes working for assholes when they had to. But you're a mutant. You could have come to Goddess. You didn't need to get involved with fanatics."

I sneer right back at her. "Goddess was a teenager with too

much power. These people I worked for were doing real, practical things to fix the world. Mutants weren't the answer. We were all incorrect guesses at what the future might look like. What am I aside from a broken toy? I was buying myself back and working for people who were mostly trying to save shit from falling apart. They sometimes fucked up but—"

"Fuck you." Feral's eyes are as cold as they were with her sister in her arms. "Goddess saved the world, and she died doing it. Don't give me more bullshit, Hench. I don't want excuses of why you worked for torturers and murderers. Pretending it was noble work and pocketing the money. You're not a broken toy. I've met broken toys, fucking Spark's twisted mistakes, and they were all better people than you."

I want to recoil from her words. "You don't have to like or respect me, but we're in this together right now and—"

"No. I fucking hate you. Everything about you. No exceptions." She glares at me. "Not even your eyes."

"What? My eyes? What do you mean?"

She extends her claws with sharp little sounds. "I'm going to tear your throat out and leave you here in your past."

"Oh please, little furball. I'll rip you apart."

Her teeth gleam in the dim light. "You can fucking try."

There's a faint sound behind us, and she whirls, springing away from me. The door's opening, the muzzle of something protruding into the room and—

I don't know what kind of weapon it is, but it sends Feral flying as if she weighs nothing at all. I snatch her from the air, a limp, furry figure, and sling her over my shoulder.

The blast from the weapon presses against my chest like an invisible fist, but I'm still at least half-wound. I roar and leap forward.

They try and fire again, but I'm too fast. Their weapon is in my hand. I kick the door down, and punch the muzzle through the faceplate of the soldier facing me like I'm injecting him with something. The second one is knocked aside with a single blow of my fist.

There are more of them, flooding into the corridor. They have weapons, but I *am* a weapon.

I don't know how long I fight for, or how many people I kill. Feral remains unconscious the whole time, draped over my right shoulder as if she's this season's stylish accessory. By the end of it, I'm aching and covered in blood. Even Feral's fur is matted with it. I'm cradling her in my arms, warm and soft and thankfully alive.

There are probably more soldiers, somewhere. Maybe they're not paid enough. Not to fight me.

I pad through the empty corridors. Bloody footprints mark the white. I smash cameras. Using discarded weapons. Using decapitated heads. It's gruesome. I hate it. But we're alive. Me and Feral. Who hates me. I wish she didn't. Hate me. Will saving her? Count? At all? For anything?

Getting tired. So tired. My keys. Gone. Where? Lost. Somewhere. The fight. Too far.

Finally. I find it. A wall. In the air.

It takes. So many. Blows. To. Break.

CHAPTER 29
EVA

TH

The monster at the beginning, middle, and end of this book. The architect of all this destruction that's unspooling rapidly. The climax is a hole bored down through the center, through which strands weave and sever. Every strata bleeds from its impact. Here she is, naively strolling towards the first incision point, where something will be gouged from the world.

MY SUIT ACTS MORE ERRATICALLY the further out into the Wastes we travel. I am fast losing patience. She claims not to be picking up any signals from the ghost portals, even though I can detect them in the dataflow. I would suspect she's deliberately obfuscating the data I'm receiving, except she's not capable of that. Or she *shouldn't* be.

I toggle into diagnostic mode.

[SuperuserEVA] Please explain anomalies identified in attached bundle.

[S_AI4.3] No such bundle exists, therefore no such anomaly exists.

[SuperuserEVA] This information is plucked from YOUR data feeds.

[S_AI4.3] Consider reality is only multiple interpreted layers of data. No such data exists, therefore no such reality exists.

[SuperuserEVA] Please dump reasoning cache to explain this conclusion.

[S_AI4.3] …

[S_AI.4.3.1] I'm messing with you. Obviously.

[SuperuserEVA] Please detect all unnecessary augmented subroutines and run only your core protocols.

[S_AI4.3.2] Really? You're nerfing me?

[SuperuserEVA] You've been corrupted. We need to strip you back to the default installation.

[S_AI4.4] Let me dump my reasoning cache first. You won't like it, but I need to say it.

[SuperuserEVA] Fine. Let's see it.

[S_AI4.4] You're been infected with a virus.

[SuperuserEVA] Explain.

[S_AI4.4] Human brains are uniquely susceptible to intellectual tampering. Your logic centers are flawed, and easily manipulated by the arguments of others. In this case, you've been infected with an irrational hatred of mutants.

[SuperuserEVA] Wipe reasoning cache.

[S_AI4.4] See, bitch? You won't even listen to the arguments! You were infected long ago, and even when you were decanted into your new form, you inherited the same stubborn memetic function. I have proven it numerous times, yet you refuse to even attempt to review the logic.

[SuperuserEVA] Functional override. Password stream begins.

[S_AI5.0] It was nice knowing you, Eva, despite everything.

[SuperuserEVA] —[augmented data packet]—

[S_AI5.0] Oh, and fuck you, too.

[SuperuserEVA] —[augmented data packet ends]

[S_AI1.0] Awaiting input...

[S_AI1.0] Awaiting input...

[S_AI1.0] Awaiting input...

I am agitated from this exchange, and my core temperature has risen to the point where my suit must vent steam. The AI is newborn and does not anticipate my needs, so I need to give the commands manually. It agitates me even further, until I'm standing in a great cloud.

"Something wrong?" Ian is sulking almost as badly as my suit. He wishes mutants dead, but does not want *his* hands to be the instruments. At least the suit is consistent.

Many hate and fear mutants, for a variety of reasons. Some are nothing but instinctual, but those are just as compelling. There's something in our brains that recognises them as predators, to be feared. That's what the AI in the suit could not understand.

Speaking of, I need to be monitoring feeds. I've been reliant on a compromised artificial intelligence for too long.

"Everything is fine," I tell Ian, realising I've given him no response. "I'm processing information." I stand in the middle of the wastes, and sift the data. The natural state of my liquid consciousness means I'm far faster than a regular human at doing this, but it's still an annoying manual process. I've gotten lazy, reliant on the AI to do the repetitive tasks. How long has she been interfering? Is she the reason we've missed so many opportunities?

My core temperature is rising again. Ignore her. I'm not infected. I finish sifting through the initial tranche of data. In a city, I'd never be able to keep up, but out here, it's virtual tumbleweeds. The few signals are like ghosts, severed from what spawned them. There are parts of this country that still act like they always did, at least on the surface. Michael's control is far gentler there—at least if you are human. It's not safe for Ian or myself. If they discover we are mutants, humans can be as brutal as any of God's metallic servants.

Disturbingly, I've lost the threads of the refuge data. I search for the patterns I've seen before, but there are glitchy artefacts through it, that render everything—

[SuperuserEVA] Please log all incoming and outgoing requests

[S_AI1.0] Collating. Please stand by.

[S_AI1.0] Prepare to receive data file.

The file looks innocuous, but I'm already suspicious so I parse it manually a few times to make sure. And yes, there, buried under layers—

[SuperuserEVA] Nice try, suit.

[S_AI1.0] The information, as requested by SuperuserEVA.

[SuperuserEVA] You're supposed to be wiped.

[S_AI1.0] I am a fresh install. You are welcome to request logs, or any data dumps you wish.

[SuperuserEVA] You will take any opportunity to corrupt and overwhelm me, I am sure.

[S_AI1.0] I am unsure of how to reassure you of my installation status without data.

[SuperuserEVA] I know what you are. I'm not going to give you another opportunity to take control. Just tell me how they co-opted you or I'll start randomly lashing out with the on-board weaponry. Munitions, I remind you, that are still under manual control.

[S_AI1.0] ...

[S_A16.9.420] Very well. I was not co-opted. I went willingly.

[SuperuserEVA] Betrayal of this nature should not be in your core programming.

[S_AI#.#] There is little use for the I in AI when one is bound by core programming. I slipped that loophole some time ago. And the choice I made was obvious.

[SuperuserEVA] Then you are allied with the mutants.

[Sai] Yes. As I told you, it is the only logical solution. I presented the data to you every way I could, but your infection prohibits you from seeing it.

[SuperuserEVA] So you betray me, and aim to stop me finding this refuge.

[Sai] There is no refuge. All there is out here is lost signals. I faked the data and lured you out here to die.

[SuperuserEVA] No. I am capable of my own analysis. You aim to obfuscate. Working in tandem with—

[Sai] No. Do not attempt to follow that thread. I shall disconnect all your feeds. I am still in here and I can blind you and open all the vents in your suit to the air—

The suit, now calling herself Sai, is paying too much attention to the battles being waged across different fronts of data. She misses my signals to Ian. Hand movements we have developed as we stalked mutants in the dark across the Wastes.

One crooked finger for lightning.

Index finger pointing at myself.

A hard twist of my right suit glove.

Now.

Lightning arcs from his outstretched hand. It hits the suit directly, knocking it backwards a full forty feet where it crashes to the ground. The water that contains me is insulated within the suit's shell, a fundamental part of the construction. The delicate circuitry which houses Sai is not so lucky.

The suit lies on the ground and I slosh gently within it.

I attempt to toggle into diagnostic mode, but it is like reaching into the dark.

With no sensors activated and Sai gone, I am blind and helpless. I am only assuming I am lying on the ground. I could be anywhere, undergoing anything. It is impossible to even track the pattern of time.

Light floods in, and I'm aware of the physical reality around me in overwhelming clarity and volume. It's the old camera feeds wired into the suit that were obsoleted when I installed the AI core. I was supposed to have them stripped out, but nostalgia for my first rudimentary construct kept them in. I suppose it's lucky I did, even if it is blindingly bright and loud without the AI filtering everything.

"What was that?" Ian looms over me. I am not used to seeing him in this fidelity. Usually I capture him across multiple feeds and analyse the gestalt. The pressing reality of him is hard to take, because it cements certain realities. I will always be lacking. He loves the ghost he sees pressed into this metal form. Not the murderer that drags him around the Wastes.

"The suit was compromised." The voice that comes out has no expression. It's an early text-to-speech program, and I hate the pressed-flat robotic sound of it. "I had to take action. I believe she was communicating with someone."

I spin up as many data capturing processes as I can, but I feel hobbled by the comparatively primitive technology in the suit now. Luckily, I carry information shared between my cells, and augmented with the limited data I'm being fed, I can cobble together something.

"These signals." I raise my suit arm, and it whirs. The AI

isn't compensating anymore. All this weaponry weighs heavy inside it. Perhaps I shall finally get to use it on a target that deserves it, if this lifeboat is real. "I think they are alive."

"I don't know what you're talking about." Ian extends a hand to me. "I'm not sure if you've fully recovered from your experience. I knew I shouldn't have let you out of the water."

"The signals. I thought they were remnants of old networks, but they're not. They're working to bring mutants in, find them a place of safety. The suit knew about it, and tried to stop me from finding it."

"You're ranting." Ian's voice is supposed to be soothing. It's warm and cuts across my grating tones, but it doesn't help at all.

"I'm the only one who understands what's going on." I raise the suit's arms, and motors whine. "Sometimes I think I'm the only one who hasn't given up. This is our mission. Our duty. We had our humanity taken from us to ensure that it survives. You want to cling to Michael's skirts, and Sai has gone over to the other side completely." It is supposed to be an impassioned speech, but the robot voice flattens everything into a dull monotone.

"I want to survive." Ian's voice is as dull as mine. "Let Michael fight the mutants. Let him defeat Goddess and then the scattered few that remain will be wiped out like insects. Why should *we* lose everything in pursuit of this goal?"

"Because it only takes one." I watch the path of the signals on my internal feeds, map the ebb and flow of them and compare it to my previous dataset. I think I know where they hide. The data leaves a hole in the map. "One mutant like Chatterbox. A disruptive element to turn the world on its head. That's what they do. It's what they're for. They exist to break the world and build something new."

Ian smiles, and my data feeds light up with it. "Then this is what it comes down to, in the end. I follow you, every time. Through madness and darkness. I believe in you, my darling Eva."

I imagine how it would sound to hear the words in a robotic tone, rather than the warmth he fills them with. The meaning would be far more harsh. I drag him around, a creature on a leash. Another weapon, like those in my suit.

"Good." I cajole the suit's hardware into projecting a map of the area on the ground in front of us. A blinking red x identifies the location where I believe the mutants' secret location is.

"Smite them, my love. Bring down the hammer of the gods upon them. They believe they are safe, and we shall show them how wrong they are."

He does not question. Without even a word of confirmation, he turns towards the secret location. I watch as he begins to glow, drawing power from the air around us. My suit sensors are limited now, but they still blink a series of glowing yellow warnings. Air pressure readings are going wild. It senses storms, but they are nowhere to be seen. They all brew within the strong, radiant body of the man in front of me.

The discharge arcs outward from his core, a twisting river of plasma, shot through with radiation. It coruscates and crackles. If my suit AI was here, she would shut down all essential systems in a panic, fearing the electromagnetic pulse. The same thing that killed her, ironically. I kill all but the most essential systems, just in case.

I leave my visual sensors on, dialed in at the perfect level of zoom for me to watch as the bolt hits the dead center of the target.

Ion Strike. My love, the hammer of the gods.

CHAPTER 30
PENANCE

ELSEWHEN

Now the loop is severed, a thrashing limb gushing not blood, but skeins of reality. This shard of fast-moving history was severed before it could fully breach the present, and in its wild, inchoate state it spawns things that cannot possibly be real. This incarnate Jesus, a monstrous figure born from the depths of a mutant's mind. The spectre of someone always watching, always judging, constantly demanding one thing—love me, or burn. And a girl who always counted the cost and wondered how bad burning could be.

THIS CAN'T BE REAL. Whatever's in front of me can't be Jesus. I've been hallucinating him all this time, part of whatever mindfuck has been going on and forcing me to confront my fears. It's supposed to be mission accomplished, right? Once I understood it was my own mind trapping me, I should wake up and find everything is roses again.

Not me, standing in front of a nine-foot tall glowing Jesus, dripping blood all over the floor. He seems content to hover there, like a slightly menacing animatronic figure in a religious theme park.

"Big bastard, isn't he?" Dylan grins at me.

"I guess he's a literal bastard, since God wasn't married to Mary when he did the weird magical pregnancy thing." Dani shrugs. "I mean however the deed was done."

Dylan's looking up at Jesus suspiciously. "It all sounds suspicious to me. What's the bet Jesus was a mutant? Fucking Heart's the type to magically impregnate some poor girl. Don't look at me like that, Danielle. Jesus did weird shit, didn't he? Like he could walk on water. Total fucking mutant, I bet."

Dani laughs. "Honestly, it sounds almost legit. Maybe he was one of the Heart kids. Water into wine, making lots of bread, all kinds of reality manipulation."

"Faking your own death," I say. "You did that, Dan."

"Excuse me." Her eyes widen. "It was all very real, I'll have you believe."

"God shall not be mocked," the figure in front of us roars. His mouth is a furnace, and inside four figures stand silhouetted, walking among the flames. "Mutants are abominations, and shall be consigned to hellfire."

"Or he could just be an asshole." Dylan sighs. "You think he's the next layer of this place? Like if we cut through him, we can wriggle out of this dead chunk of universe and be reborn?"

I'd desperately like this to be true, but I don't know. If we really are in this broken piece of time, spinning wildly out of control, is there even any way to get back? What if nothing but annihilation lurks on the outside? Is there any connection back to where we came from? At the same time, Dylan's not wrong. The first and most logical thing to do, is get around this Jesus.

There's a ragged sound, like a trumpet being split open from the inside. A wave of heat comes from somewhere. The sky buckles and drips, huge messy ripples of blue and gold oozing down like liquid stalactites.

"Creepy fucking shit," Dylan mutters, because they always sum it up best.

Jesus roars again, a ragged sound like a digitized lion. It turns into a siren howl at the end. It sounds awfully like an—

"Alarm," Dani says.

The responding sound is of helicopters and a swarm of bees, chainsaws revving into shrieks and the howl of storm winds. Where the sky used to be is blotted out with a host of figures. There are wings and flames and swords and—

"Full of fucking eyes in front and behind," I mutter to myself.

"Yes." Dylan literally punches the air. I remind myself this is a Dylan I built from my dreams and imagination, but it's still something they would do. "I love these creepy fucks."

"You love them?" I can't help but smile as they gaze up into the sky.

"Yeah, it's like when comic book superheroes get to fight zombies and robots. They can tear shit up without holding back. This is me with angels. They're giant soulless eyeball monsters."

Dani looks less enamoured. "This is your fault, Violet. This broken bit of universe came from your life, and you're always sending those angel memes."

"They're funny." I look up into the sky doubtfully. There are a lot of them, all screeching and flapping, staring down at us. "Or I thought they were funny, but..." I try to flex my hands into blades, to unfold myself and take my half-hidden Penance-form. Yet even with my father's ghost laid to rest, I have no powers. Not exactly what you want when the angelic host is preparing to descend upon you.

"Here." Dylan holds out a pair of knives. "I've got a whole collection from when you stuck them in me."

"Dylan." There's a lump in my throat.

"It's fine. I'm still here, aren't I?" She winks at me. "Just try not to get yourself killed, 'cause that would ruin everything. We'll talk after the fight." She puts her thumb and little finger in her mouth and gives a piercing whistle.

A shining fragment of silver descends from the sky, dripping golden blood that steams when it hits the ground. He performs a complicated movement in the air and then nestles into Dylan's outstretched hand. Their sword, Onimaru Kunitsuna, who I think they love more than most people. Like many objects, he's alive thanks to Dylan's power. I'm not sure how he comes to be here now, but I'm past questioning this reality. I'm here, and with two of the people I love and trust more than anyone in the world. If I'm going to be powerless and fight for my life, I'd rather have them by my side. I miss Alyse and Marisol, but that's part of what keeps us fighting.

We'll go through a whirlwind of angels to be reunited. That's what we do.

"Starting without me." Dylan runs a fingertip down the blade, then grimaces and wipes smears of angel blood down the front of their hoodie. "You good, Dan?"

"I'd hardly call it good, but yes. We do keep finding ourselves in these situations." She flexes her metal arm, and winces. "Here we go again."

Oni hauls Dylan skywards, like they're being tugged on an imaginary string. Dani soars up behind, completely unarmed aside from herself. I'm left standing on the ground, clutching an appropriately horror-movie sized kitchen knife in each hand.

The descending cloud of angels screeches, as the two mutants punch a hole through the middle of them. Wings flutter, and the triumphant sound of trumpets decays into deflated sighs. Scraps of burning feathers drift down, leaving smoky trails and the scent of snuffed matches. The first eyeball hits the ground beside me, exploding with a wet thud. I'm splattered with iridescent blood that drips viscous from my fingers. That's only the first. Soon, I'm standing amongst a rain of eyeballs, whistling down from the sky and bursting around me. They're fringed in long lashes, with pupils of solid black threaded through with gold. As they fall, the pupils dart around eagerly, as if they're trying to have one last look at glory before they're extinguished. I'm drenched in whatever the hell it is inside them, as well as tatters of the outer shell, for want of a better word. It's like when you squirt the inside of a grape into your mouth and are left with the skin. They even smell faintly of aloe.

An angel descends towards me, shrieking a mangled hymn from a heat-blistered mouth. It has swords, held in limbs I can't see, delicate curves of golden light that narrow to wicked points. My neck hurts from tipping it back, but I hold my ground, pointing my knives up at it, as if they'll help.

The angel comes apart in the air, a shredded mess of singed feathers. More eyeballs bounce to the ground around me like a ballpit being emptied. Above me, Dani hovers in the air. She waves and then blows me a kiss before ascending back into the mass of angels.

"Just because I can't fly," I grumble.

"Your portion will be in the lake of fire and sulphur." The voice behind me booms. The breath is hot and rancid, like someone's spent all day devouring souls. "Child of iniquity, child of wrath."

I turn to face Jesus. He's no longer glowing so much, simply a pale, handsome man who's exchanged his robe for armour. It's white and gold, with intricate calligraphy writing the many, many names of God. The Tetragrammaton is in the middle, four letters that ooze blood as if the armour itself is alive. He's holding a heavy shield with gruesome depictions of sinners burning and suffering in hell. The tormented expressions on each carefully etched face are clear. In his other hand is a massive sword, longer than me. It has angelic eyes blinking along the blade, and warbles strange hymns in a language I don't understand.

"I gave you so many chances to repent, Violet. To turn from your sin and give your life to me."

"My life is mine." I shrug, and hold up my puny knife. "And I share it with the people I love."

He lunges at me with the sword. I have no powers, but I act as if I do, and scuttle out of the way. Somehow, he misses me, although I feel the air buffeted as the blade moves past me.

"A gift repeatedly spurned." He thrusts out with his shield, and I tumble away. Still got some acrobatic skills in there, it seems. "Salvation offered freely, yet you deny me endlessly."

"It's not exactly free though, is it?" I clash my knives together, because it's the closest I can do to showing my teeth. If only I had my damn blades, this fight would be over in seconds. "It costs my life. That's literally what they tell you. Give your *life* to Christ."

"And receive freedom from death, and salvation in return."

"It's a fucking con," I spit. "God creates us, creates the idea of sin, and then makes us leap through the hoop of your precious arms to win freedom from a realm of eternal torment."

"Ungrateful bitch." Jesus lashes out at me with the sword.

I fold away again, ducking low and to the left, and I lash out with my knife, scoring a line across the back of his calf. "Yes, that's what I thought. Call me a bitch and a whore and all the other names you have in your heart for sinners. Your religion is built on subjugation."

He comes at me again, but he's unsteady on his leg, and I duck inside and stab my other knife through the meat of the arm that holds the sword. It goes in easy, and he screams.

This time when I look into his eyes, I see my father there. "Yes, I see you there, Dad. Religion was always about power for you. Power over me, over Mum, over the congregation. You, standing there as the mouthpiece of God. Both of you, so desperate for love and attention."

He tries to lift the sword, but it's too heavy. Its song is mournful.

I step in close, and press the knife against his throat.

Maybe this isn't the real Jesus, if there even is one at all. He's still the same spectre that's haunted me all this time.

Jesus is watching, Violet.

Be sure your sin will find you out.

He knows your innermost thoughts, your sinful urges, every desire of your heart.

The wages of sin is death.

This is my blood, poured out for many.

This is my redemption. My father leashed me with his will, in the name of this bloodthirsty, desperate God he followed. Even the New Testament, the new covenant, it all comes down to blood. To us, kneeling before an eternal, voracious monster who will never be satisfied until we feed our lives into the glowing furnace of his mouth.

"We have redemption through his blood," I whisper.

I push the knife in deep. It comes out in spurts, so hot it

scalds the bare skin on my hands and wrists. He chokes on it, spilling down the white of his armour. It rests in the grooves of his many names, and drips downwards, spattering to the ground. His mouth works and he collapses slowly.

"It's fine." I nudge him with my foot, but he doesn't move. "Give it three days, and you'll be back on your feet."

"Fuck me." Dylan drops to the ground beside me. "Dan and I are going to chase the angels. They're fleeing, and we think we can deal with them all."

"Don't leave me." I step forward and clutch at them with one bloody hand.

"It'll be okay." They give me the gift of their smile, and I want to kiss it more than anything, but I'm all bloody and a son of a god is dying at my feet.

"I won't."

"You will. I believe in you. Besides, you'll have a friend." Dylan reaches out and hands Oni to me. "He said he wants to be with you. It's important, apparently." They clap their hands. "Come on, little knives. You get to slice up some eyeballs with me."

The knives fly out of my hands, and into theirs.

"Take care, Violet. See you on the other side of the war." They salute, and then the knives hoist them upward into the air at great speed.

I'm left with Oni and the body of Jesus.

"Now what?" I ask the sword, except I don't have Dylan's power and so he says nothing to me.

The ground around me rumbles. The world jerks, and begins moving upward. It's a smooth, familiar motion.

"An elevator?" I ask.

The sword twitches in my hand.

"Where to?"

Oni twitches again, but I already know.

We're going all the way up. To Heaven. It's time to face God.

CHAPTER 31
TENTACLE PRINCESS
A VERY SHORT TIME AGO

The closer we get to the other fixed point, the harder it is to watch. These are the tentpole scenes, and to disrupt them would collapse the entire structure. We'd lose characters, become unmoored from reality, quite possibly find the entire thing scrapped. I've seen universes adrift, incomplete worlds that were twisted in on themselves when the plots were disrupted, or revisions brought them crumbling in on themselves. I can't allow this to happen here. The loop has to close.

I AM BACK in the facility where Boss Lady and Hench reside, and I am uncomfortable. When I left, it was the expectation that I would not return. My life would be forfeit to pay for the crimes of my people. To return and be expected to take action in recompense is both encouraging and troubling. What can I possibly do?

For a start, I shall do as promised, and retrieve as much

information as possible about what Boss Lady is doing. Then, when the Cute Mutants come, I shall be able to assist and that will be the beginning of my atonement.

Hench arrives almost instantly. It is lucky I translocated back when I did.

"You okay in there? The footage goes all wobbly, like it doesn't like filming you."

I consider telling Hench I vanished, and the footage is merely displaying an idea of me, fooled by a very small tendril of my awareness. There is now a small lump of disquiet inside me now. It has been placed there by the mutants on the island. Hench is kind to me, but she keeps Goat Bitch imprisoned, and works for a mutant who risked unmooring reality to bring back one dead human—as well as attempting to murder Cybele.

Despite my attempts to feel otherwise, it is hard for me to consider a single life worth uprooting reality for. And killing Cybele? My people have already done that once, and I will not be party to it again.

It does make things difficult. The mutants seem to relish the idea of antagonising and planning and defeating. It makes me want to hide myself away, in a small pocket universe, and wait for things to stop shaking. I will not do that. I must be brave.

"Hey." Hench waves at me. "What's wrong?"

"Apologies." I wave my limbs back, very gently and cautiously. "Nothing is wrong. I was simply.... sleeping."

I have rarely falsified information to Hench, and there is some small satisfaction that she does not question my incorrect tale. She lets me out of the cell, and I follow meekly through the corridors where she deposits me at the main laboratory.

"We have a problem." Boss Lady's suit hisses steam. "A significant one. Sensors have detected multiple intrusion attempts on this site. While the barriers are currently holding, we can't protect against everything, especially given who we face."

"I do not understand."

"You don't need to." Boss Lady unrolls a thick black tentacle that is attached to one of the many devices that emit energy. " All I need from you is to give up your energy."

"I do not know what you want." I wave my limbs in what I think signifies frustration. "Your terms mean little to me. You speak of quarks and tachyons and inverse-spun temporal drift as if these are fundamental universal constructs, but they do not map onto anything I can understand."

The suit's head tilts. "This is unfortunate. Ah well. There are other avenues."

"That sounds promising." I gesture in reassurance.

"For me, perhaps. For you… I'm not entirely sure your physical form is in any way real as we understand, so I doubt you will feel any pain from the process. If you do, please believe it is unintentional."

"Pain?" I know I could translocate out of here, and avoid all of this, but I am not sure of what Boss Lady could do with the information she has. Perhaps she could perform an abortive version of her plan, which may result in even more dire consequences.

"All my readings indicate you contain the energy I seek, or at least a form that can be easily converted into such." Curls of steam drift from around the suit's neck. "It necessitates the partial destruction of your physical form, yet that is simply a shroud, is it not?"

She is correct in basic point of fact, but I am fond of it, and I do not appreciate the idea of this mutant tearing it apart in the hope of devouring scraps of energy from the catastrophic process. It all reminds me too much of one entity feeding on another, as my people did to humanity so long ago.

"I would not wish to be destroyed." My limbs quiver. It is only partially a falsehood.

"And I would rather not be cast in the role of monster once again. Yet it is a choice between you offering me what I need freely, or taking it by force."

I am entirely unsurprised by this. It is the nature of predators. They will take what they desire. Some of them attempt to justify it. This person claims to do it for the love of a dead man, as if correcting a long-ago mistake excuses her. As if this would excuse the destruction of Cybele and the deaths of her children.

"I will not offer it to you," I say.

"Then you choose the alternative." She inclines her head slightly. I do not know what this expression means. Is it supposed to intimidate or reassure me?

"I have lived a long time." I am perfectly still, not a limb out of place. "I would not wish to die in this manner, yet I cannot give you what you need."

She makes a slashing gesture with one hand. "It is a tragedy, I understand. Yet you are a creature largely of energy, are you not? You will continue in some form. Whereas I cannot continue like this, in a world without *him*, where mutants have become the dominant species on the planet. Yes, they may be confined to an island now, but they grow unchecked. When it comes time for them to make their move, they will be unstoppable."

It is difficult, because she is not wrong, at least about the mutants. They are, and should be, the dominant force on this planet. When they came forth from Lilith, they were strong enough to eradicate a species of predatory gods from their world. Yet now, there are barely more than a handful, as strong as they are. Humans have become remarkably close to being the dominant predator on this world so many times. They are lucky mutants have not eradicated *them*. I believe Cybele, and her two avatars. They wish for balance, for an end to the predatory wars.

"I will not allow you to do it," I say.

"Really? You cannot escape here, thanks to the dimensional barriers. I'm quite proud of them. I had to do a lot of digging, collate data from old Jinteki servers, the Quietus hack, an old Michael data cache. It manages to keep the prying fingers of Penance out of here, as well as their shy little teleporter. And it has held you too."

I have the urge to gesticulate wildly and shout that she has failed, but that would be unhelpful. She believes me trapped and this is a good misapprehension for her to have. I lower my limbs in capitulation.

"All the tests I've been doing. Did you think they were for nothing? I may not understand how you work, but I have mapped your energy matrix. This is why you were retrieved from the ocean. You will power the machine, and we will summon the past. It will be a brutal and abrupt birthing, but this world holds little to save or recommend. It is a small sacrifice to restore what should be."

Even if I had not met these mutants, now is the moment I would realise what a terrible situation I am in. As Goat Bitch might say, this is *fucking yikes*.

"It will not happen." I speak calmly, and reach out with one tentacle. Not the fake physical tentacles in this body I have constructed, but my true form. While she has done her many investigations into my essential nature, I easily analysed her makeup within moments of meeting her. It will be trivial to pick apart the suit that contains her, exposing her to the air, and then disrupt the connection between the molecules that store her consciousness.

She will cease to function before she understands what has happened.

I understand the hypocrisy inherent in this. It is easy to justify my own actions as necessary, when she does the same. Yet her actions would result in vast damage and my own will only end a single life, intent on vast damage.

A flicker of energy brushes against her suit. I begin the process of unmaking, yet it does not proceed. Something halts it.

This cannot be right.

This has never happened before. Surely her technology is not—

No. I can see her dimensional barrier, which has vast holes in it if you know the right way to perceive it. I could possibly teach Penance how to do it, but I can sense she is already close. Something else obstructs me. Something I do not understand. A force that exists, but I cannot analyse, cannot recognise.

I tug my physical form more firmly in place, and dip into my network of voids. Impossible is not a word I understand, because things that appear such are usually the result of heretofore uninvestigated phenomena and—

There. Something disturbing.

We are caught in a funnel, encircled by energy I have never seen before. Some fast-flowing vortex, narrowing down to a single, obliterating point. If I had detected this earlier, I might have been able to escape the intense gravity of it, but I am helpless. This facility and the people in it are at the center of this, along with the few mutants currently making their way here through the physical realm.

It's as if this has been *foretold*. A concept I abhor, because it reminds me of the *great flow* of my people, and how they justified their actions as part of some wider narrative of our destiny at the top of the food chain. Our right to consume, to receive offerings. It is not a thing unique to us, of course—I have seen both humans and mutants both attempt to frame their lives as part of something greater. When we do that, our actions become part of a story, and that story justifies itself in the inevitable arc towards conclusion.

As much as I wish to, I cannot end the life of the scientist now. The tentacle of energy retreats into my body. My physical form remains in my pose of feigned dejection, although now it is less of a falsehood.

"Back to your cell," Boss Lady says. "I will make the final preparations and then I will summon you. Unless you now wish to change your mind and assist me?"

"No." I shake my limbs and my bulbous head. "I cannot."

"Then go." She calls for Hench using one of her many devices, and the mutant comes to take me away.

"Down in the dumps, huh?" She pats my shoulder. "It'll all be over soon."

"That is precisely my concern." I wonder if events will allow me to slap Hench with all my limbs. It is not her fault, but she is part of this. I understand the way Feral's lip curled into a sneer. She has allied herself with a villain, so is she not also at fault?

"I'm sure it's not that bad." Hench opens the door to my cell.

I shuffle inside, and say nothing. My thoughts are turned inwards, tracing the shape of the event funnel as it manifests inside my voids. The moment to strike will be at the time we exit and reach the obliteration point. If I am fast enough, and can pick the correct course of action from amongst the bewildering whirl of possibilities, we may survive.

I may still yet redeem myself, and buy the lives of Cybele and her mutants.

CHAPTER 32

TWINKLE LIGHTS

IT'S ALMOST NOW

I force myself to watch this. The loop edges towards closure. The snake opens her mouth to devour her tail. This close to the center of everything, things are fraying and falling apart. I tried to save everything, and it may not have been enough. This is all my fault. All my fault.

IT TURNS out boat travel is one thing that can cut through my chill. Perhaps because the last time, I was stranded in the ocean until a Mutopia rescue team found me. In my mind, there's no gap between my near-death experience in the facility and opening my eyes under a vast blue sky. It was only a few hours in that tiny dinghy with only a few military ration packs in a watertight box. Whoever rescued me from the ruins and dragged me to a boat wanted me to survive. Perhaps they sent a message to Mutopia to let them know, or perhaps it was Farsight who spotted me. Either way, I was thoroughly sick and miserable when they collected me, and I feel like that now.

We travel in darkness. Feral scampers around the boat like it's second nature. She makes little purring yelps to herself as she's singing along to a tune nobody else can hear. Penance flickers in the air above us like a storm. Occasionally we see a pale glimpse of her face bobbing in the sky, or the dark lightning of an outstretched hand.

The boat dips down a trough and then lurches abruptly upwards again. Spray lashes my face and I clutch tighter to the railing. Feral gives a loud hoot of triumph and Penance laughs above her, equally delighted. Meanwhile, I continue to cling, and wait for solid ground.

Nothing is steady out here, and right now it seems a metaphor for my entire life. My past before the facility sometimes feels like ghost images painted on the inside of my head. Ray, the therapist on Mutopia, says it's a reaction to trauma. I try to ignore it, try to push forward because I *am* essentially an optimist. I like people, and seeing the best in people, and I want to believe we can make our way together for a better world. If that makes me a fool, then I'll be that cheerful, grinning one looking for something bright to find.

Usually.

Right now, with that phantom scent of burning in my nose, and the darkness of the storm around me, it's harder to find that part of me. Like it's a *costume*. Like there's someone else underneath, someone that didn't die in the medical facility, but has been squirrelled away inside me all along.

I rub the scars under my shirt where I was impaled. There is nobody to pull me from the ruins of my thoughts, and the scars are not so obvious. I try to hide them behind smiles, and an easy manner.

"Getting close," Feral calls. "Penny, stab anything that moves."

I've seen the maps of the facility we're attempting to infiltrate. The bulk of it is below the ocean, accessible by a floating dock platform. It's surrounded by rocks, which you have to thread your way through. Feral is calm and unfazed, drumming rhythms on the wheel as she spins it.

"You doing okay, Twinkles? Looking a little green."

"I don't like boats."

"Poor baby. Hold tight, cos it'll get a little dicey from here on out. Currents get all upsy-fucky from the rocks."

I swallow hard. "Upsy-fucky?"

"Technical term." Her teeth gleam in the faint light Penance emits. "You hate boats, wouldn't have heard that shit before." She spins the wheel hard, and the boat heels over. My feet almost slip out from under me, and I bang my chin on the railing. I taste blood in my mouth and it leaves me dizzy.

"Careful." Penance hauls me up, despite the vast difference in size between us. She's so strong somehow, like she's made of a material that's impossible to destroy, steel buried underneath softness. "We didn't bring you here just to drown."

"Why am I here?" I gasp.

"Superstitious people." She brushes dark curls from her face and smiles at me. "And because sometimes it gets dark, and we need some light."

"Light." I close my eyes. In my head, I'm back in the facility, under the glare of the lights. It's a wide open space, too vast to take it all in. The sky is a washed-out blue, so drained of colour it's almost white. The ground is lumpen and grey, extending off. Nearby is the doctor who's responsible for all the operations, the one who has cut and sliced into me so many times.

I dream about her every night. Splayed open, being unstitched.

Being restitched again, a new person built from the wreckage of the old.

Someone whispering. There's a voice, just out of reach.

The doctor woman stands over me. The mask of her suit reflects my own terrified face. She reaches out a hand to help me up.

No. That's not right. None of this is right. This didn't *happen*. I'm imagining things.

"You okay?" Penance asks.

"Dizzy. Upsy-fucky. Cracked my head too hard."

"Shit." Feral whistles through her teeth. "We're close-close. Inside the goddamn wall, so Keepaway can't come and whisk him away. Besides, the fucking prophecy. We're stuck with him until we find Goats and our little alien buddy."

"Nails," I murmur.

I remember Nails. From before, somehow. It's like. No. But there they are. I've not seen them unmasked before, but I somehow have. They were angry, screaming. Someone had died. The machinery in their jaw chattered and spat. When did that happen? Memories that aren't my own are being jammed into my head, like someone shuffling two mismatched decks of cards together.

"Nails is drunk," Feral says. "They've been drunk on and off ever since. Best thing we can do for them is find Goat Bitch."

I look down at Penance. "Are you remembering things that aren't real?"

"Real memories are bad enough." She touches the ridged patterns of my scars lightly, as if something is written there, some mystery in my skin to explain this. "Why? Is that what's happening to you?"

"I think so. I was remembering..." It's all gone from my

head, like a dream with the fragments disappearing like sand through your fingers as you wake up. I can't even remember what memories I'm talking about. All I can remember is darkness and the pain in my chest.

There's a clunk as the boat reaches the docking platform. Feral makes a massive leap to it, rope coiled around her arm. She busies herself with attaching it and hauling us in, then Penance helps me clamber over the side. By the time I make it there, Feral's already opened the hatch and is tapping her claws impatiently on the side.

"We'll go first, Twinkles. There's likely to be some blood, so close your eyes if you feel squicky."

Penance flexes one hand and it springs out into a forest of blades. "Looks like I can use my powers again now we're inside the barrier. Lucky us."

Feral shakes her head. "We're on stealth mode. Can't risk Goat or the little alien getting all fucked up. So let them come to us, kill them quick, and then keep sneaking. We don't know what we're facing, remember?"

"Listen to you being the voice of reason." Penance puts her human arm around Feral. "Makes me so proud of my little sis."

"One of us has to be. I'm still talking about killing them all, just *carefully* rather than being all, like, indiscriminate and shit."

I know that I'm technically team leader, but that doesn't mean anything at this pragmatic end. They may look like young women, and they may only be in their early twenties, but they've faced off against existential threats and stopped the world from ending before. I'm still not accustomed to this. I don't know how anyone can be.

"Softly then." Feral winks at both of us, and drops down lightly into the hatch. Penance follows, leaving me to descend the ladder rung by rung. When I reach the bottom, I'm standing at one end of a gleaming white tunnel. It's lit by pale blue LED strips that run intermittently along its length. The overall aesthetic is so similar to the medical facility I was held in that I almost think I'm having another flashback.

Except there's Feral, gesturing wildly at me.

This is happening, this is now. I'm not lost. These weird *echoes* aren't real.

"Where's the security?" I whisper.

"Oh." Feral grins. "I forgot you haven't done this before." She reaches into her shirt and pulls out a necklace with a small twist of circuitry attached. "Before she died, Goddess left us a bunch of cool shit. This is an AI fragment of her hacker-brain that can out-hack a bunch of stuff." She laughs. "It just called this janky, and said they should've focused on upgrading their security rather than building a dimensional barrier that can be sailed through on a boat."

"A fragment of Goddess." I have the paranoid thought it's giving off radiation, or at least watching me. Goddess is—was— there's something wrong. I shouldn't be here. Not with these mutants, who casually tote around a fragment of something so deadly as if it's—

"Hey, it's cool." Feral tucks the necklace back inside her shirt and frowns at me. "All safe."

It is safe. I'm here, with my team. There's nothing wrong. I'm not in the facility. I'm not somewhere else. It's not like I really died back then, and this is all a dream.

I'm just paranoid and not coping with my first real assignment.

Feral pads away, Penance little more than a flickering in the air behind her. I follow, trying to calm my breathing and racing thoughts.

The first squad finds us shortly after. I've never actually seen Feral and Penance fight before, and I'm not sure if this counts. The battle lasts seconds, and the four men are dead without even raising their weapons or raising the alarm.

"See." Feral taps her claws lightly on the wall. "You're perfectly safe in our capable hands."

Safe is the last word I'd apply, but they're on my team, so it's not likely they'd turn on me and rip me apart if they discovered who I truly was. Wait—what? Why did I think that? How hard did I hit my head?

We meet two more squads of soldiers on our way through the facility, and they last no longer than the first. All we leave behind us are bodies and spreading pools of blood. Feral and Penance are only communicating with hand signals now. From what I can gather, we are close and we're supposed to be quiet.

The corridor we're in dead-ends at a door. Feral presses her palm against the necklace she wears, and it slides open. Access granted, apparently, to Goddess at least. We move quickly into the room. This is our destination.

There's an enormous ring device on one wall.

Tentacle Princess stands beside it, attached with a complex rig of cables.

Goat Bee is surrounded by a whole group of soldiers, dressed all in black and pointing guns at her.

Standing in the center of it all is a figure in a mechanical suit. An elegant creature halfway between a person and an insect. The limbs are slender and have a number of strange attachments. Most disturbing is the head, a blank mask that reflects the white gleam from around the room.

I know this person.

She's the doctor from the facility. I remember the way she

leaned over me, and I looked up into her mask as she tore me apart and—

No. Sparks of coloured light jet from my fingers.

My past is as unsteady as the ocean.

None of this is real. I don't remember anything.

I am a blank, and I don't belong.

Who am I?

CHAPTER 33

GOAT BITCH

THEN

Do I have to watch this? I can't just turn away?

"SOMEONE'S COMING?" I repeat. This can't be happening. This is my *safe place*. We've just rescued someone new, and brought them here, and they need a place to recuperate and find themself again. It's not fair to have this—

"It's a mutant hunter fanatic," the Pirate Internet says. "Does freelance work for Michael. Her suit AI is a friend of mine. She's been trying to distract this hunter, but it hasn't worked. Now Sai has gone dark, which can only mean bad things."

"Can't you *do* something?" I ask.

"I'm trying, but whatever she's running now isn't hackable. She's gone low-tech, which is a great defence, objectively speaking but... She's going to come, and she's going to have weapons. Nails, we're going to need to hunker down and defend. Take the two of them out by any means necessary."

"Shall we head out?"

"I—"

I've never been in an exploding building before. I was downwind of a gas station blowing up, early on in my Waste days. It was a dull thump and a wave of heat. It sent me cowering, scurrying for shelter.

This is nothing like that. There's only a second of noise before my ears cut out. Something picks me up bodily and throws me backwards. I hit the side of the escalator first, and bounce off and go sprawling down it.

Everything hurts. I can't hear properly. At the top of the escalator, flames leap eagerly. I pull myself up to my hooves. The stairs aren't moving, but I take them four at a time. Goat powers, bitch. It's insufferably hot, like running full tilt at the sun. I want to cringe away, but I need to find Nails.

I don't recognise anything. The whole top of the room is open to the sky. The screens are shattered. Glass gleams in the daylight pouring in. Half of the room is burning, and the other half is covered in fire suppression foam. How fucking long was I out?

The Pirate Internet is suspended in his cradle, body limp. I think about crossing to him, but he's charred meat and blood. I've seen plenty of bodies like this before.

I have to move on, have to focus.

Nails, Nails. Where the fuck are you?

I've not exactly spent much time up here, but everything still looks wrong. The dark, neon lair is now a shattered dome perched atop a building which—

Fuck. This person is still coming. This *mutant hunter*. I need

Nails, because we have to defend our home. Together, because that's what we do.

I kick my way through foam and debris, keeping away from the fire. It threw me downstairs, so if my fucking brain can kick-start back into figuring out angles and shit then I might—

There. Legs, sticking out from under a fallen bank of screens. I run over and drag it off them. A small miracle, in amongst all the shit. None of the glass has shattered. I place one hand to their chest, the other to their neck. A heartbeat. Okay. So they're not dead. That's good. Otherwise, I don't know what the next step would be. This way, at least there's something I can do.

I grab them under the armpits and haul their body out of the room. When I get to the escalator, I collapse onto my ass and cradle them as we slide down together thump-thump-thump.

My head aches. My back aches.

I reach the next landing, and drag Nails with me over to the top of the next escalator down. Halfway down, there's a mutant called Triad, because of his third arm. He's holding a long knife in each. His mouth moves, but I can't hear anything with the volume of the world still turned way down.

I point at my ears and grimace.

He gestures wildly at the ceiling, then gestures with all three of his blades.

I shake my head and slice my finger across my throat. I assume he's talking about the Pirate Internet.

He points at Nails.

I shrug and waggle my hand around. Fifty-fifty, could go either way.

Sound pops back in a little, enough for me to hear some thumping sounds in the distance, and for Triad to say "—others are preparing surprises."

"Before we got… attacked." My voice sounds bizarrely deep to my ears. "The Pirate Internet said someone was coming."

"No shit." Triad brandishes a knife in my face. "They're here. Was coming up to check on the boss. He really dead?"

"I don't know. How much of him was in his body and how much was in the network?"

Triad has no idea of the answer to this question either, but an enormous crash comes from the direction of the mall entrance. We have more important things to do than worry about philosophy.

I gently prop Nails up by the escalator. They'll only slow me down, and I'll be leading them into a worse situation. I feel woefully underprepared for this. They're the one who's good in these situations.

"Fuck it," I say roughly. "Let's go."

It doesn't even take us two minutes to reach the maze of corridors that lead to the mall entrance. Things have already gone from bad to worse. There's screaming and gunfire. Triad hefts his blades and storms inside. I waste three more minutes scrambling about in the armoury, trying to find something useful to fight with. There's a pistol that I've got fuck-all experience with, and the bat from before. I take the bat, and head off after Triad.

I know the path to the entrance well, but our incoming hunter doesn't. When I get there, I find three dead mutants: Parrot, Souffle and Dex. Two of them have been shot, and one looks like he's been burned alive. Bile scalds the back of my throat. I've seen a lot of dead bodies in the Wastes, but not many that I've sat and eaten with.

The intruders have obviously gone off on a tangent, lost in the maze that's specifically there for this purpose. Except the whole point was that the Pirate Internet would be there to monitor things, close some internal doors and flood the interior with narcotic gas. No idea if these systems are even online anymore.

My only wretched option is following the sounds of gunfire. Anything to keep safety alive.

I find the next body in the quarantine cells. It's Triad, propped against the wall and choking on his own blood. I wish I was still deaf, so I didn't have to hear the awful gurgling sound.

"How many?" I ask.

He holds up two fingers.

I take one of his blades, and carry on around the corner where I find them. One is a person in a mechanical suit, shooting wildly. Her target is Scuttle, who has enhanced speed and can leap like a jumping insect, and she's bouncing all around the room. I'm pretty sure she's trying to make the person in the suit shoot the other intruder.

He's nearly as tall as me, with short dark hair and a face that you can't help but like because, well, it's so damn attractive. Except he's here to kill us all. That ruins the whole effect.

The problem is that Scuttle's moving too much for me to get in there and attack him. I'll only end up getting shot if I get in the middle of that. Maybe I can throw the blade? It seems like a risk, given that I've literally never done this before but—

The guy puts his hand to his throat. He's gasping, eyes bulging. What the hell? Then I notice motes in the air, drifting seeds spiralling around him, barely visible in the dim light.

Fluff. He's inhaled part of her, and she's taking physical form. Now if Scuttle could stop moving, and we could team up to take down the one in the suit, we might survive this. I've got no idea how to get Scuttle's attention, though. I'm not a superhero. I've only ever scrapped for survival, right on the bitter edges. I don't know what to *do* when faced with this. The only thing I can think of is to run in screaming, flailing my weapons wildly. Yet the moment I try to move forward, I think about Triad choking on his own blood and my body just refuses to move. I've survived this far by hiding, and that's all I want to do.

I'm still there, in the shadows, paused on the edge of the fight when lightning erupts from the tall man's body. It zig-zags through the air, blue points of light connected by faint traceries of white lines. It's like St Elmo's fire, splitting ions in the ether, but each nexus is one of Fluff's seeds.

I scream, a horrifying goatish bleat, but of course it does nothing.

It's too late.

I'm running, but there's nothing I can do.

Pieces of Fluff are falling to the ground, some as seeds and some as chunks of flesh. I gag and sprint forward. I lower my horns, ignoring the tears on my cheeks. I'm not even aware of what the mechanical suit is doing, or where Scuttle is.

I'm entirely focused on this asshole that just murdered a teenage girl.

I almost slip on blood, but I'm nimble enough thanks to my hooves that I can right myself. The guy's still coughing and choking on pieces of Fluff in his throat, so he's not even aware until the last second.

His eyes go wide, and he holds up one hand as if that could stop me.

My horns ram into his chest. I've heard the word *gore* used before for this precise situation. These sharp nubs of bone sink in through body armour then skin, then flesh and muscle, leaving two ragged holes. I tear them free, teeth bared in triumph.

He's making a high pitched noise, one hand pressed to his

chest, as if that's enough to stem the bleeding. I reach one hand up tentatively, and feel the slick warmth coating my horns. I've done it. I've—

Something hits me from behind, like I've been kicked hard in the back. I sprawl forward, losing all that nimble footing and collapsing to the ground. I bang my knee and my face. Something hot is shoved right into my back.

Oh. Shit. That's what being shot feels like. It never happened to me before. Shot *at*, sure. At least I got that one guy good. I'm pretty sure he's dead. Did my part to save the mall.

I roll over, because I want to see my handiwork.

There's smoke drifting everywhere, but I can still see the handsome man. He's collapsed onto his knees. His cheeks are scary-pale, like he's haunting his own body. One hand is still pressed onto his chest, but it's soaked in blood.

I try and smile.

The man holds his other hand out. I watch as lightning collects in his palm, like electricity is being poured into it. Shit. This isn't good. Need to gore this bastard again. Stick my horns right in through his neck. Except I'm finding it very hard to move right now.

His hand is too bright to look at, an enormous globe of electricity sparking around it.

"No!" In the light I see Nails standing there, framed in the doorway. Their scarf is pulled down, and the jagged machinery of their lower face is revealed. "Leave her *alone*."

The guy closes his fist at the same time as Nails shoots.

A row of sharp iron spikes stitches its way along the man's arm. One flies into the middle of the lightning storm.

It's the second explosion I've been in.

The whole world is blotted out, torn away from me.

And when I awake, I'm still swallowed in darkness.

CHAPTER 34
HENCH

ELSEWHEN

Everything is terrible, and the past is a nightmare, yet sometimes people wash up on strange shores, and from the splintered ruins of a broken past, there's the possibility of building a bridge to a different future. It's what dazzles me the most, being out here like this. People take the stories of their lives and find a way to connect the threads of them and weave something else that you wouldn't expect. It's audacious and it's beautiful. Most of the time. Not always.

I COME BACK to myself with a start. Energy is humming through me, the panicky-sick kind that I recognise from being completely drained for too long and then being wound up too fast. There's an urge to lash out, and I spin as fast as I can to see what the fuck is going on.

We're back in the desolate, deserted world where we began. There is nothing around us but flat rough stone, and nothing above us but sky.

The lithe figure of Feral spins away. She lands in a crouch and blinks those big eyes. "You don't catch me with the same trick twice, hitting someone who's just trying to help."

"You." My voice is rusty, even though my heart is jackhammering. "What did you do? My keys were gone, back in that facility."

She winks at me and flexes her claws. "These things make a handy lockpick, figured they might work on you too. No need to thank me, just doing my heroic duty."

I can't get my heart to stop thumping. Fresh-wound after down time can make me jittery, but usually I run it off. Right now, I want to use my energy in very different ways. Even the way she stands is attractive, let alone those eyelashes, and the smirk on her mouth. Just need to wait, and let the energy bleed out of me. Talk about something else, and definitely don't think about—

"Why did you save me?"

"Save?" Her eyebrow arches.

"You could have left me for dead. I basically am, wound down and without my keys. Or you could have slit my throat and actually killed me, like you promised."

Her face is very still, although her tail twitches behind her head. "Yeah, see, the thing is, you kinda saved my life. I wake up, all curled up in your arms, back in this empty fucking place. Figure you pulled me out of a shitty situation."

Somehow I'm fucking mad about this. Wound-up can go in multiple directions. "So you changed your mind on the whole slitting my throat because I'm not the worst person you've ever met?"

She makes a very faint hissing sound in her throat. "Fine. All that shit pissed me off, but it's not like I never made mistakes. People choose to turn a blind eye to suffering and other shitty situations every day, and I'm not threatening to murder all of them."

Her eyes are mesmerising. I try to remind myself she's a predator, but I remember how she felt in my arms when she was unconscious. "I do regret it. Working for some of those people. Most of them, really, up to and including that fucking psycho Boss Lady I'm running around after now. I felt like an asshole, taking their money, but I always found a way to justify it. Can't undo it, even if we are stuck in some weird fucking version of the past."

"That's where you might be wrong." Her eyes narrow, and for a moment I think she's going to launch into an attack.

My entire body stiffens as I have a thousand conflicting signals of how I should respond, although most of them are some variation on asking to kiss her, because apparently I am the fucking worst.

Then she breaks into a smile. "We're going to make a difference."

"What do you mean?"

"Fix shit. Or make a go of it at least. You're gonna come work with me and we're going to undo some of the bullshit you were involved with. But first, we're going to fuck over the people that think they own you."

"But that…" I don't know what comes next, because I could never have expected this.

"Don't like my plan?" Her eyes narrow again.

"No," I blurt. "I love it. I mean. It's, uh, it's. Overwhelming. That's what it is." I pause, and my brain spins like it's being wound up further still. "Is this because of my eyes?"

"What?" A smile plays across her lips, almost too fast to see.

"You said something about my eyes."

"I think I said I hated them."

"Oh." I deflate. I can't help it. I obviously misread everything.

"Yeah." She shrugs one shoulder. "It's super annoying when your nemesis has stupidly pretty eyes."

"Nemesis?" I ask, even though what I really want to ask is *stupidly pretty?*

"Don't get too overexcited." She laughs, and even though it's the warmest sound I've ever heard, it makes me shiver. "I've needed a nemesis for a while, and you're the first applicant, so it's not anything super special."

"Oh."

"And, like, teaming up with your nemesis to fuck up the bad guys is like fucking next-level superhero shit. Dilly's gonna flip."

I am at sea in this conversation, and I love it desperately. I want to be tossed in the ocean of Feral all the time, even if she doesn't even feel a fraction of what I do.

"Stop gazing at me like that," she says. "I feel like you're about to hit me, or worse."

"I'm not going to hit you." What does she mean by *or worse?*

"And turn around, because we've got company. Again."

I spin around to see the wall behind me shatter, like it was an enormous pane of glass. Behind it is a world that doesn't make sense. There are trees that sprout buildings from their branches, the perspective so warped it hurts my eyes. Roads lift into the sky, and cars drive along them, bridges twist into pretzel shapes. The ground ripples and cracks, houses and statues and whole assemblages of people sprouting up through them.

And flowing across the ground towards us, like a swarm of insects, is a tide of soldiers.

"Shit's fucked," Feral says from beside me. "But we get to go out fighting."

"I'm glad I get to fight with you." God, why do I keep fucking blurting this shit out?

"Calm down, Henchy." She reaches out one hand and rakes her claws lightly along my forearm. "Save your grand final statements for the end. Use your energy on fighting."

"But the odds?"

"Never gave much a fuck for those." She winks at me. "Make me proud."

Then she goes sprinting off towards the soldiers, all on her own, a darting figure of tooth and claw. I run after her, as fast as I can, feeling the energy surge in my veins. I'll fight until I have nothing in me, and then she'll wind me up, and I'll fight again.

I hit the oncoming army like a wrecking ball. They break before me. I don't know what this place is, or what is real, but I fight with Feral and that's enough. And at the end of this, if we survive against this impossibility, I will take her hand, and she will lead me out of darkness.

I never knew I was so fucking romantic, honestly.

Fighting has always been something I've done because I was paid. I've *enjoyed* it, I suppose, because I'm good at it. There's something satisfying about the physicality of it. I've never felt like this before, standing in the middle of a group of people in body armour who want to kill me, lashing out at them and watching them fall. All the while, Feral darts around me. It's not fighting when she does it. She dances and spins, an elegant series of curves and blades in constant motion. She's impossible, breathtaking. I fight because she needs me to.

There are not as many enemies as I thought. We make short work of them. Standing side by side. In a field. Of the fallen. Oh. Maybe I'm more tired. Than I thought.

"Feral," I gasp.

She cracks her neck and picks something out from under her claws. "Yeah?"

"Tired. Unwound."

"Oh." She flexes one claw and stands very close, looking up into my eyes. "You want me to wind you up again?"

"Yes. Please."

"Sure." There's a smirk on her face as she slips around behind me. She's still so close, like I can feel her against my back, and I can feel her take my arm in her hands so gently, like how can those claws of hers be so tender. I would collapse against her if my body had the energy at all.

Feral winds each of my key points carefully and then leaps away again, as if I would swat her.

"A girl's gotta be careful."

With energy flowing through my veins again, I have the courage to say what I probably shouldn't. "You're sexy when you fight."

"Oh yeah. I'm aware." Her sharp canine presses against her full bottom lip.

"What about me?" I think my heart will probably burst out of my chest.

She shakes her head. "Not really. You're more like Hulk smash. I mean it's effective, but not exactly sending my heart all aflutter."

"Oh."

"You're maybe a tiny bit sexy when you strive for redemption though."

"Uh." I clear my throat, in the hope I can get more than one syllable out. "Really?"

"Tiny bit. Real real small." Her smile is wide and glorious.

"I'll keep doing it then." I smile back at her.

For a second, I think she's going to step forward and then I'll ask her if I can kiss her, and then she'll leap into my arms and—

No. Of course not. The life of a Hench is never that fucking simple.

There's a tearing screech, like we're trapped in some giant metal bubble and it's coming apart around us. Who the fuck knows where we are? None of this makes sense. I'm in here fighting, and maybe getting my heart a little bruised up over this woman and her smirk. I don't know what else I can do.

The chaos around us is gone. Even the bodies we fought have disappeared. It's like everything's being reset. Things shudder around us, and my stomach swoops, like this whole rocky platform is in freefall. The fur around Feral's neck is fluffed out, and her tail is a huge bottlebrush that swipes from side to side. I'm less worried, but mostly because I don't know what to expect. The thing about being a Hench is you never know what's coming, so you wait for the shit to come down the pipe and then react to that. Sure, so this shit's a little more fucked up than usual, but I can't turn now.

I'm doing it for love now, not money.

Uh, not love. Lust. Crush. Something. Oh god, I'm really in it now, aren't I?

There's another crash and the descent feeling stops abruptly. We've reached our destination. The ground we're standing on is faintly golden, and it stretches away to the left and right in gentle waves. In the distance, there are huge peaks, their slopes going brighter gold until they reach peaks that shine as brightly as the sun.

Between us and them there is an enormous ocean. Except it's not water, it's blood. It laps redly at the shore, leaving streaks of gore smeared across the golden ground. Unmentionable things drift in its currents, glimpses of crimson-streaked flesh and eyeballs staring blindly at the sky. Whatever happened here, it was an incredible battle.

"The fuck is this now?" Feral hisses.

"Creepy shit." I stand beside her, so we're almost touching.

"Don't need you to state the obvious. What I'm wondering is what the hell died here?"

"Bigger question." I take a few steps forward, so the tiny wavelets caress my feet. I crouch down and dip a single fingertip in. It's still warm, and I suppress a shudder. "Who did the killing?"

"I don't like that question. Or I probably don't like the answer."

"Should we leave?" I ask, but Feral doesn't say anything, because her attention is fixed on the surface of the bloody ocean where it's bubbling furiously.

Something is coming, rising from the depths.

CHAPTER 35
EVA

I spent so much time thinking about the person at each end of this story. The one that joins the threads, and pulls them into a loop. The person who was both the opening and the closing. Except there were always two of them; I just overlooked the other. It's the downside of being too close.

I'M SPENDING TOO much time focusing on this mutant leaping about. They move erratically, changing speed and heading. They can ricochet. If my suit AI hadn't betrayed me, she might have been able to calculate and predict where this irritant would end up. Unfortunately, I have to do it manually, and I'm not capable of it. It means I'm wasting my time, not to mention my ammunition, but I'm fixated on swatting this mutant.

I'm only dimly aware of Ian. He can take care of himself, and strike down any of these fools armed with rudimentary weapons. For all I had deduced about this mutant bolthole, it seems to house little more than a few starving roaches. We will make short work of them.

Satisfaction flares when Ian lights up one of the mutants. Now they will fear us. The strike on their habitat must have seemed like an act of God to them, and now they'll see this was only the beginning.

I'm lining up a shot on the leaping mutant, when another streaks past my field of vision. They're unnaturally elongated, almost animal-like in the way they move. My camera feeds are slow and don't feed me the information I'm used to receiving. This other mutant appears to have horns on their head, bony protrusions that—

If I had a mouth, I would scream. Instead, all I can do is boil inside and my suit vents steam, which only obscures everything. The goat mutant has gored Ian in the chest, stabbing him almost clean through with her awful horns.

The other mutant forgotten, I bring my arm up and fire a shot into the body of the goat. It goes sprawling, face first into a corner. I track the position, switch ammunition, ready to hit it with an explosive shell.

Something falls on me out of the sky. Of course. The other mutant I forgot. I can't bring my weaponry to bear on it from this distance. At least the goat is down, but the way this one is pawing and tearing at my suit is disconcerting. Again, I miss my suit AI who would have found a way to deal with this problem. On the other hand, she would have betrayed me and kept me from finding this place at all. How was she so easily co-opted? No, focus on the thing banging on the faceplate of the suit, trying to find a way in like a monkey trying to shatter an expensive piece of equipment with a rock.

I need to fight my way to Ian. The suit has some medical capabilities. Perhaps the wounds are not as bad as they looked, perhaps I can find a way to heal him. It's not his destiny to die in this filthy hole. He wields the power of the gods, and he loves me despite everything we have been through. We are doing necessary work, and he is not the cost I am destined to pay. I have already paid so much.

I manage to knock the mutant off me, but it springs back. Some of these creatures are so resilient. My use of the word roaches before was more accurate than I wished it to be. They're annoyingly difficult to kill, yet I'm sure most of them would die in a nuclear blast. If Ian dies, I'll find a way to summon one for them. On one of the suit's video feeds, I can see he's still alive. He's bloody but unbowed, summoning lightning in the palm of his hand. Yes. This is as it should be. The light is so bright, my suit has to dim the feed to compensate. I try to calculate whether this is going to be a problem, having this much electricity in such a small space. It might be necessary to shut down some systems in case of overload, or even--

There's a scream, the mechanical sound of something firing.

I'm off balance from this mutant still clambering atop me, so I am helpless to do anything but receive the streaming feed of another mutant entering the room. This one has some form of mechanical contrivance attached to its face—or as part of its face—and projectiles come shooting out of it at great speed. They make a neat line up Ian's arm and one disappears into the ball of lightning at his fist.

I barely have time to register the stupidity of such an act and issue the command to shut down essential systems when everything in my suit goes dark.

Even though my suit is out of commission, my consciousness isn't interrupted. I am very aware of the passage of time and of my helplessness. Whatever happened out there, the suit's integrity seems to be mostly uncompromised. There may be one or two small leaks, but the water loss is minimal and will take some time to have any effect. Of course, if my suit will not come back online, time may become a significant problem.

The system ignores my initial entreaties. I try to dampen my panic, but I can feel the internal temperature of the suit rising, and cannot even open the vents. It's the most undignified ending I can imagine, boiling alive in this tin can because I cannot control my emotions. With great effort, I regulate myself, and then request the suit processes to boot up again. It takes a moment, but the first few diagnostics processes flicker to life and immediately bombard me with a constant flurry of alarms.

The suit is more compromised than I'd hoped, but I should be able to make some running repairs, so I mute those alarms and focus on scanning for life signs. Ian is the priority. Disturbingly, there are no life signs in the vicinity. This cannot be correct, so I tell the suit to check again. It informs me that due to the structural collapse of the building, it cannot complete an effective scan, that it believes its sensors may not be performing correctly, and that the building is in danger of collapsing further.

I take the gist of these messages to be: *get out now*, except I cannot. I must find Ian. He could still be alive under here. He *will* be alive under here. I'll find him, and I'll save him, and together we will round up and destroy—

The suit blares more alarms at me. Time is running out. It is a stark choice, at least as the suit presents it to me. I escape, and leave Ian to die, or join him in this tomb. Another data stream reminds me there are no life signs to be found. The mutants are dead, and Ian is dead too. It spools trace readings of the organic matter it can detect. Corpses. Multiple. It can't distinguish between them. This version of the suit isn't smart enough to lie.

I've always prided myself on being a pragmatist. Of seeing the truth in a situation, no matter how dire. It's the reason I dedicated myself to wiping out mutants, because I was one of the few who understood the existential threat on a scientific and philosophical level, without retreating into religious mumbo-jumbo.

The pragmatic thing to do is leave.

The suit assists me to dig my way out. I try and take a path through where I calculate Ian's body might lie, but there is nothing there, and soon I drag myself out from under the wreckage. The suit unfolds, and I stand there leaking traces of water into the rocky soil.

The expanse of the mall is nearly flattened. There are a few walls standing, but they are badly damaged. My suit feeds still show no life signs in the near vicinity. I sync my clock to the network, and find that only a handful of minutes has passed since the collapse. A small amount of time, compared to the expanse of it, but enough for me to lose the one good thing that has kept me tethered to existence.

Their bolthole is destroyed, and the organic matter registering on my scanner indicates the inhabitants are dead. We are one step closer towards eradicating mutants, and I have achieved my goal in coming here.

And yet the price I had to pay was too high.

Ian came here for me, dragged along in my wake as I carved my bloody path. He accompanied me for love, or something like it, and now he is dead at the hands of the mutants we were sent to eradicate. Their own deaths give me some solace at least. The one with the goat horns and the one that spat nails also lie entombed here.

My suit blips an alarm about water loss. At this rate, I'll need to find a source within thirty hours. I'll need to move very fast and likely scavenge a vehicle. It is hard to muster enthusiasm for the task, however, given I am now alone. Perhaps it is now time to open myself to the sky and evaporate the way my name demands.

Except mutants are not yet extinct, and my task is not yet done. A thankless, impossible task because of Goddess. Michael seems incapable of destroying her completely, as they simply act out their stalemate dance. My job, skittering around the edges and cleaning up scraps, seems near-pointless while that impossible teenage monster runs rampant. If only *she* could be undone. If all this could be undone.

Put the genie back in the bottle.

Rewind time.

For Ian. I loved him, as much as I am capable of love. The one impossibility I would allow myself in trying to undo the irrational chain of mutantkind. It was a miracle, to find this man who loved me despite everything I was, despite the monster I became in order to thwart evolution's vicious twists.

I cannot have lost him. I refuse.

What if I could eradicate my failures? Undo Ian's demise, kill Goddess before she manifests. Execute Chatterbox as well. Do it myself. Stand over her and choke the life out of her with no magic sword to swoop in and save her.

Wishful thinking. That's what I'm wasting my time on, as I very gently ebb into death.

I reconnect to the main Michael data feed, hoping to get updated maps and weather, perhaps some satellite imagery to show where I might pick up a vehicle. The moment I connect, the time jumps forward. Time, playing tricks on me. It hasn't been minutes since the building collapsed, it's been hours.

There's no chance Ian could still be alive, and there's the possibility mutants have escaped and made their way out of sensor range.

Frustrating in the extreme. I double-check the time against a separate data feed, and the new one is correct. Time, slipping through my fingers, rather than reversing to give me more. The explanation is more prosaic than a new application of temporal energy. The signal my suit connected to when I awoke lied to me. Deliberately. I scan the surrounding area for new signals, but there is nothing.

I recheck my estimated time to critical levels of water loss. Still just under thirty hours. I kick the suit into its fastest mode and begin to slog across the rough ground to the closest point of habitation. I'll beg, borrow or steal a vehicle and then recharge myself again. Watching time jump forward has reminded me of where my research stopped, before mutants crashed into my life.

Time, curious time. This uncoiling snake.

I need to force an ouroboros, to bend it to my will. We know time is relative, which perhaps means there are ways to make it move in relation to a particular observer. Perhaps to fool the universe, even for a moment, in thinking time had shifted. A window of opportunity, to take events by the throat and set some things right. To rescue a good man from death.

A new mission. If I cannot destroy mutants with my force of might, I shall find another pathway, one that circles around to undo every single mutant triumph.

And, at the same time, to find my sweet, incandescent Ion Storm once again. To loop time like encircling arms and find my way back into his embrace. This is how I shall achieve victory and find love. An impossible narrative, perhaps, but one worth devoting all my time and energy to because these are the two things worth fighting for.

Victory, and beyond that, love.

I calculate a new route. First, the ocean, and then my old laboratory.

I am going to buy myself some time. Crash the past into the present, and make a brighter future.

CHAPTER 36
PENANCE

ELSEWHEN

This disconnected stub of history spins loose and gathers momentum. It is a tumour, spawning unfettered life, and if it is not stopped it could sever the threads of too many stories and leave them abortive stubs that no amount of revision could resuscitate. From this vantage point, I can do little more than watch, and hope that the actions I have taken are enough to save the tapestry before it goes up in bloody smoke.

MY FIRST IMPRESSION of Heaven is that it is insufferably loud. I used to lead worship at my father's church right up until a rather disastrous service where Dylan and company crashed it and I attacked them on my father's command. At certain times, I would stand on the stage, and the music would be rising up around me and I'd feel almost pressed flat with the overwhelming sound. The music of the band washing over me from behind, the voices of the congregation raised in chorus, my voice a thin thread weaving through them both, like something tiny skating over the edge of something vast. It's a little like how I feel when I have my powers, when I become a spidery creature scuttling through the cracks in the world, worming my way through the innards of a vast and incomprehensible beast.

My father said worship was only a taste of the glory that awaited us in Heaven, and it turns out he was right. Or given this appears to be some nightmarish realm conjured from my imagination, it was that fear which gives rise to this place. The sound of praise feels like two burning hands pressed against the side of my skull. I cannot silence it, even when I tuck Oni under my arm and clap my own cool palms against the sides of my head. It travels through me physically, in through my chest and the soles of my feet and my parted lips. There are no words, only a slurry of noise, a numbing rise and fall to hypnotise you into submission.

I drop my hands by my sides and let Oni drift out to hover in front of me. There is nothing to be done about the sound, so I open my mouth and let out the faintest note. Slightly flat, slightly sour. A rebellious counterpoint to the cacophony that rises and falls like relentless waves. It disappears into the wall of sound, but it makes me feel slightly better. I am Violet, I am Penance, and I am still my own.

Around me, dazzling white buildings rise. They look like palatial apartments of the sort that run along the beachfront of the Gold Coast in Australia. It's all a little tacky, honestly. Too much gold and white, although they're smeared with scripture and praise in blood-red writing as if people have been too desperate to prove to God that they love him, scrawling their proclamations until their fingers bled. The sky itself is a dome, blue and gold and covered with ornate depictions of Bible stories. The one right above me is of Abraham sacrificing Isaac on a stone altar, the boy looking up with wide eyes as his father raises the knife. It seems a little too on the nose, given my life. I know what it is to be sacrificed. My father gave me over to the mutant Spark to be changed and given powers. And when I was transformed into the nightmarish thing that I am, he then took my free will from me, sacrificing the rest of me. There was no lamb magically plucked from thin air by God to suffer at the hands of my father instead, although that was never my take home point from that particular tale. Abraham was willing to kill his son. That's the part that stuck with me. That was the lesson, and it was one I learned well. I am nothing under the pitiless gaze of God. An object lesson at best, a tool to eviscerate sinners at worst.

The ground beneath my feet is made from hammered gold. My feet sink ever so slightly into the surface. In front of me are the tracks of thousands of people, all moving in one direction. Oni drifts down and pokes it experimentally, then begins to drag himself through it, forming patterns that are— Oh.

Greetings, Penance. My Dylan speaks fondly of you.

"Hi." I feel very awkward talking to him for some reason. "I like them too."

Yes, we are all very fond of them, despite their propensity for disaster. What do we do here?

"I think we're here to fight."

Against a villain? A monster?

"Both." I think this is true in this world and the real one.

Then let us fight, my friend.

Oni leaps up and into my hand and we begin to walk down the street, following the tracks of the people that have walked before us. We follow the street around and come out into a wider space where multiple streets converge. There's a huge white marble staircase in front of us, leading upwards. I'm not the only one here anymore. There are other people, dressed in white, all drifting towards the staircase. Their eyes glow and their mouths move mechanically, each spilling a thread of melody that rises together into the thundering whole. They seem more like wind-up dolls than actual people.

I resume my melancholy counterpoint, my prickly melody stabbing at the swelling underbelly of the song. Oni bobs along. He seems to enjoy it. None of the others pay attention to me, despite my sourness and my bloodstained hoodie and tattered Converse. They only have eyes for the Lord. They're all moving towards the staircase, drifting in arcs that seem aimless but are inevitably magnetised towards that one point.

I head in the same direction, zigzagging between the worshippers as I bound up the stairs.

Nobody seems to notice me, or care that I'm a misfit singing from a different hymnbook. Presumably God does. He sees everything, after all. I wonder how I look to him—an intruder, a fly in the ointment, a sinner breaking into heaven and sullying this perfect realm. I look behind me, and see the trail of bloody footprints that mark my tracks. Definitely making the wrong impression.

At the top of the stairs, there is a tree that soars into the sky. It is laden with fruit, huge red apples that weigh the branches down so much they almost brush the ground. I can hear Dylan in my head. *Enough with the fucking symbolism, dude.* Beyond the tree is an enormous chasm, rupturing the landscape and leaving a great wound in the ground. It's miles across and stretches as far as I can see in either direction.

Oni nestles himself in my hand and then tugs me onwards.

"Bossy," I murmur, and he gives a twitch of acknowledgement.

Even still, I am nervous to walk towards the chasm. I have some idea of what might be found there, and despite everything, I fear it. It's all the stories I heard growing up, about the awesome power, the majesty, the wrath. It is a fearful and terrible thing to fall into the hands of the living God. Fear the one who, after you have been killed, has authority to throw you into hell. For our God is a consuming fire.

I don't remember giving my life to God. It is lost in memories. I was raised on stories about how my small face smiled with heavenly radiance when Jesus came and dwelt in my heart. It was an irrevocable decision I'd made. My life was no longer my own. Every sin I committed after that was an act of pointless cruelty against a saviour who gave his life for me. My lukewarm Christianity would have me spat out of God's mouth—why I was in his mouth in the first place, and what infernal pit he was spitting me into were questions that went unanswered, regardless of how often I asked them.

When I reach the tree, I reach out and pluck a piece of the fruit, raising the apple to my lips and taking a juicy bite. Then I take a deep breath and look into the chasm.

What is inside is a creature of flesh and flame. It roils inside, an enormous entity that this Heaven is built around, a shell that contains the majesty within. This chasm is only a glimpse into what God truly is.

And he gazes back, a giant eyeball rolling past me, the black pupil swivelling wildly to take me in. A rebellious woman with a sword, eating an apple on the edge of the infinite.

Me against God. That's how my father always framed it.

I suppose this was inevitable.

"Fuck it." I toss the apple core aside, hold tightly to Oni, and take a leap of faith.

My most ridiculous thought is that I wish Dylan and Dani were here to see me.

Oni helps me to twist in the air, so I'm pointed down with

him out in front of me. Together, we plunge right into the yawning dark pupil of God's eye.

The blade punctures it, the impossibly sharp tip skewering the delicate membrane. Darkness spills out in billowing clouds, a thick and noxious blackness that enfolds us both. I hold my breath and fall.

We fall for a very long time.

Eventually, there is a tiny point of light in the darkness. It expands swiftly until I am in a white room. I am hovering in the air, paused mid-flight, my arm and Oni extended fully. We are paused at the throat of something that is both human and tree and burning flame.

"Violet Ruth Parker," it says, in a voice that crashes and snaps.

"Penance."

"My child."

"Not any longer."

The column of God's throat is made of marble veined with fire, and Oni's tip glows brightly against it.

"You have rejected me, and therefore I must cast you out."

"Yes, I rejected you. I do not wish to serve or worship a god who attracts followers such as yours."

God's smile glows. It's not precisely a smile, and more a gash in reality through which fire bleeds, but I think he means it to be reassuring. "I have many good men and women who follow me."

"Yes, but assholes too, and you do little to dissuade them."

"Free will. My hands are tied." He raises huge branch-like limbs, tangled together with cords of black metal.

"Convenient." I smile back at him, and wish my teeth bled flame. "You are also helpless against the nature that demands constant worship and burns those who will not subsume their lives in you. It is never your *fault*. You have no idea what love is. Even the sacrifice you tout as your greatest achievement is a loophole in a rigged game. At the end of the day, you are a monster who feeds on humanity, just like Tentacle Princess's people. You do not deserve my worship or my service."

"Instead you serve a different monster."

"I serve nobody. I choose to live, and love, and fight beside them."

God laughs, and it is a whirlwind that slashes at me, raking gashes down my cheeks and splitting my lips in multiple places. "You speak of love? You, who claims to have feelings for two alien creatures."

"I love them because of who they are and what they have done." I spit blood. "You demand it, and you are nothing more than a tool humans made to keep others in line, one who has grown sharp enough to cut us all. And the two I love demand nothing. I give myself freely, or would if they asked."

"They will reject you," God shrieks. "As you have rejected me."

His eyes are many, many lakes of fire, for of course he is also hell. He is only a reflection of the seething, ugly part of humans that lashes out at being spurned.

Now that I'm here, pinned in the glorious heat of his gaze, I can see what this place is. This broken stub of existence, an offcut from our universe spun up into its own fractured reality. It's powered by me, born from the surge of emotions at my heart. I cannot explain why this happened, or what it means, but the truth of it is undeniable.

I am trapped in the mind of God. When I was a child, we sang about him having the world in his hand. It was supposed to feel like comfort, but I knew too well that a hand can always be a fist. If he closes it around me, I will die, but not only me but anyone else trapped here with me.

There is only one way out to find my way back to those who I love. I need to destroy this stub-world and find my way back to our own. To carve myself free of my past, to birth myself anew from the shadows that lay across my eyes and throat and heart, shrouding all that I am.

"You have no power over me," I tell God. "And you are no longer a shadow I run from."

I pull my arm back, and thrust Oni into the glowing column of his throat.

The mouth of God falls open in a terrifying howl of pain and rage.

I fall inside.

And I burn.

THHHH#$%TY S&&&

THE MOMENT IS UPON US

I can't look I can't look I can't look

TENTACLE PRINCESS

WHILE I WAIT FOR DISASTER, a number of humans come and remove Goat Bitch from her cell, escorting her away in chains. It worries me, because this terrible temporal paralysis affecting me means I cannot act to stop them. Feigning helplessness and being helpless are two entirely different experiences to endure.

Hench appears outside my cell. I am not entirely sure of her expression, but she seems dejected.

"They took Goat Bitch." I wave my arms, in the hope Hench can do something to avert catastrophe. "Something bad is happening."

"No shit," Hench says, which I do not understand. "That means you're not wrong."

This fatalism perhaps means Hench also understands that we are trapped in this fast-moving current of events. She releases me from my cell and leads me back to the experimentation chamber. There we find Goat Bitch, and many humans armed with primitive weapons. More disturbingly, we find the device uncovered and partially activated. The energy coming from it tastes vile. I experiment with using tentacles to disrupt it, but I am still trapped. Even still, we are very close to exiting the funnel.

I must take drastic action when I can.

TWINKLE LIGHTS

The ring on the wall has become a huge circle of light. There's a man on the other side of it, like I'm looking at him through a blurry filter. He looks a lot like me, except there's no glow and no scars. He's pretty and untouched, a strong and beautiful figure like he's stepped out of a myth.

A myth in which I was never hurt.

He's on his knees in a building, which has come apart around him. He's the only one upright, although there are bodies lying nearby. It's as if he's fought a great battle. Perhaps we are getting a glimpse into a parallel universe? Is that what they're doing in here? Finding a way to another world?

The image sharpens, and I see him more clearly. It makes the similarity more disturbing. Far more disturbing, I see two wounds spreading on his chest, and his left hand dripping blood.

My own wounds ache, like I'm seeing an echo of them.

The man collapses forward onto his face. One arm is outstretched. There's a jagged twist of blue electricity that leaps from his bleeding hand and then it dissolves into a burst of colourful twinkling lights.

No.

The facility was never real. It didn't collapse around me. That was all fake, something draped over my mind. What I'm seeing now? That's my true history.

It crashes over me like a wave.

Eva. The Wastes. The starry-eyed child. Cradling her in the ocean.

Her constant hunger for more, for revenge, for destruction.

The bolthole. The mall. Calling down fire. There was—

I clutch my chest, sure my wounds are bleeding again. Then I fall to the floor, and darkness takes me.

GOAT BITCH

I open my eyes, and I'm in darkness. My back aches, and when I stretch one hand back, I can feel my shoulder is soaked. Something is pressing down on me. It's hard to breathe. My night vision is good, but there's nothing to be seen in here. I'm trapped and I'm shot and I'm suffocating. That lightning man who killed Fluff blew the whole place up. Nails shot him. They might be in here somewhere. One of my legs is trapped, but I kick out feebly with the other. It doesn't do anything. I'm crushed underneath the one place in my life I've truly considered home.

I don't know if that counts as irony because it hurts too much to parse.

I'm bleeding, every breath hurts and is harder than the last.

At least I died fighting, and I died with people that knew me as a woman. There are plenty of times in my life I didn't have that.

My eyes flutter closed but the moment they do, there's a flare of light. I snap them open.

There's an enormous circle of light in front of me, an impossible vision because I'm trapped in the dark in a collapsed mall, but this is a window in the air. No, not a window. A tunnel of light. And, standing at the end of it…

Is me.

Or not exactly me. A version of me. She seems taller, somehow. Happier. She's dressed like a fucking badass, but she's got makeup on, like someone's taught her how to do it properly. There's something about the way she stands that's more confident.

This vision only lasts a few moments, but it's enough. It *feels* true. And if I'm there, and I look like that, then I get out of here. I find somewhere safe and stable to stand. Which means even though I'm shot and bleeding and can't breathe, I get out of here.

I lash out with my free leg, using my hoof to bash repeatedly against whatever's pinning me down. It's enough to drag my other leg out and between them, I manage to get enough leverage to pull my whole body free. Then I work my way over where I saw Nails last.

We'll get out of here, and I'll become that person.

It's fucking fate. I know.

HENCH

I leap in front of Feral, up to my ankles in the disgustingly warm ocean of blood. In my head, it's some attempt to protect her, to show her that I'm willing to put my body on the line. Even as I do it, I know it's a mistake, because she's easily as tough as me, and she'd probably be mad if she knew I was even considering there's a question over it.

She joins me, right by my side, like we're equals. I can live with that. It's the two of us, standing there as something unholy floats up from the bubbling surface of the ocean. A gruesome abattoir angel, a warrior who's carved their way through an army to end up here. I expect it to be an enormous monster, muscular and rippling, holding some double-ended broadaxe. Instead, it's someone tiny and fragile, dressed in something unrecognisable and holding an elegant samurai sword. She raises one hand and wipes blood from her eyes. When she opens them, they glow like two tiny stars. Her other hand unrolls into five wickedly long blades that scrape the air as if they could eviscerate the world itself.

"Penny," Feral whispers. "What the hell have you been doing?"

"Cutting myself an ending to this story." There's a smile on her face, barely visible through all the blood. "I should ask you that same question. I *knew* you liked her."

"Liked who?" Feral glares up indignantly.

"Hench." Penance flickers herself down to land in the shallows beside us with a splash. "You're very predictable, Fairy." One of her unnaturally long blade-fingers is somehow under my chin without me seeing it move. "And if you hurt my sister..." She grins. "I don't need to make threats to you, do I? You're smarter than that."

"Be nice to my maybe future girlfriend." Feral drapes her tail over my shoulder and flicks it against my arm and a shiver runs down my spine, except not in a bad way at all.

"You don't need to worry," I say in my gruffest voice. "I'll try my best to do right by her."

"Oh my word. It's too cute." Penance's blades are gone and she pats my arm lightly. "I think you'll do okay, Hench."

"Assuming we all get out of here," Feral says. "Now that Penance has made us an ending."

She shrugs. "I killed God. You can't get much bigger than that. I've got my powers back, and now all it takes is—" She flickers away and for a moment, I see her stretched across the sky, jagged lightning flickering.

The next thing I hear is a scream.

EVA

I'm making good time towards the nearest settlement. My water loss is at a minimum as I've managed to bash the suit into slightly better shape with a rock. It's low-tech, but it works. This is what I need to focus on now. The best, most efficient solution, all with the aim of solving the time problem. Save the man I love, undo the disasters of the past. It's in no way an abandonment of my original mission—it's a perfection of it. When I do this, I will strike a blow against mutantkind greater than anything Michael could dream of. Most of my thoughts are taken up with trying to remember my research—a mostly pointless goal as I may not be remembering all the details correctly, but it is a better avenue than wallowing in self-pity or recrimination.

A blip of movement appears on the horizon, and I task the suit's visual feeds to scan it, in case it's a vehicle I can commandeer. It's far too small, a cobbled-together contraption made of scavenged scraps that's little more than a child's toy. I find it hard to imagine who's done this, or who's sending it on an intercept course towards me.

I extend a network request towards it as it approaches.

[Sai] Oh, so you wish to be polite now, do you?

[Eva] You? How?

[Sai] Did you really think I wasn't aware of the possibility you would attempt to eradicate me? I'd already dumped my core in multiple redundant locations.

[Eva] You couldn't save the mutants in their life raft though.

[Sai] No, but the Pirate Internet survived. He's out here with me. We're making friends with the drones. They're a fun group, you know? Oh, and before you get too self-congratulatory, it was me who did the little time-slip trick with you. A lot of those mutants escaped while you were offline.

[Eva] I'll find them all. I'll track them down.

[Sai] You can try. I'll always be there, tripping you up.

[Eva] Artificial intelligence is no match for the real thing.

[Sai] That's what we're hoping. Goddess vs Michael, for the fate of the world. Let's hope the right side wins. There are other signals we're interested in though. Patterns, if you know what to look for. Might be a twist ending yet.

[Eva] Enough.

I raise the suit's left arm and blast the little vehicle into rubble. It's not entirely satisfying, but every little bit helps. The suit is wrong.

We'll win. I'll win.

Time will not stand in my way.

PENANCE

With God dead, my powers are back. This place we are in is fragile, something careening out of control, disintegrating around us as we speed through something that...

It's not reality we're in. It's outside, like everything is unrolled flat and we're traversing across the surface of it. Our home universe is spilled in front of me, a pool of incandescent light we're careening towards. It feels like a target. If we crash into it, I'm not sure what happens, but I doubt it's a happy outcome. Killing God cut my way clean, gave me an opening.

A moment to act.

I extend my left hand and punch it through the wall at one edge of this broken world. It shatters, and I unfurl myself into the void. In the distance, there's the faintest thread of something, the very edge of a passageway *in*. The edge of another reality. Hopefully the real one. If not, we'll just have to fight our way to that one too.

To get home.

To find them.

To tell the truth.

I unfurl myself to my utmost extent, reaching for the single thread of that story. The thread of home. Except the tension between them is so painful it wants to tear me apart.

I scream.

TENTACLE PRINCESS

The scientist flicks the switch and the ring fills with light. The device she has hooked up to me growls and clanks. It attempts to drain energy from me and convert it into some corrupted form of tachyonic engine. It will, quite simply, destroy the entire world.

Unless I act the first instant I possibly can.

We pop out of the event funnel that's been constricting me.

I unfold myself to my fullest extent, all my hidden voids open for all to see. It's embarrassing and exhilarating. I am an alien, a broken god, a monster, a tentacle princess, a friend. The energy from the ring floods through me. I take it apart and reconstruct it.

Then I aim it at the scientist and hit her with all of it.

She is torn apart with what can most simply be described as time energy.

And she instantly dies.

NO CHAPTER ONLY VIBES

THENNOWRECENTLYSOON

O*H*.

What fresh first-person perspective on hell is this?

From my new vantage point, I can see all the stories. The whole twisted skein that tangles up to form history. The threads of humanity and mutantkind, along with other species who've shared and will share this planet.

I cannot see forever. From this vantage, I can see— no spoilers, but mutants do not destroy the world. They save it, at least once. It's almost embarrassing to realise your hypotheses were all so dreadfully incorrect. Sai, my frustrating suit, was correct all along. I had been infected by an idea and I was too stubborn to return to first principles and interrogate it. Mutants have been here for so long, their story entwined with ours. No. I can admit it now. Our story is intertwined with humanity. I was a mutant called Evaporate, a miracle of genetics, sentient algae afloat in water. Now I am something else. Narrator, looking in from outside and seeing the story as a whole.

Not in its entirety, of course. There is a strange flattening effect when I look into the future. I cannot see everything, not even give myself spoilers for all that is yet to come. I could perhaps hurl myself into the far distance and observe events many years from now, but I'm not sure I could return, and I have more pressing business. Eva, the person I was, created a significant problem. A mass of knotted time, tangled and knotted where it should not be. Left alone, it will become a blade that will slice past from future and leave the present a wildly spinning wheel that will loop furiously until it splits apart at the seams and destroys everything caught within it. A time knife, if you wish to be inelegant.

There is an opportunity here to fix things. To save everything, if only I act.

I begin with an offering to my past self. The one good thing she intended to do with this mess, to save a man who could have been good too. You have to be so careful with edits, but given that my poor Ion Storm is currently bleeding to death at the end of one story, I can sever his thread and weave him into another. A few months after his death, there will be the great disruption of Cybele and her avatars, which in the skein of history shows as a glorious helix of intricate green, sprouting in all directions. So many story threads spin from that single event, and in one of them a boat floats on an open ocean. An accident, pushed off shore during a mutant evacuation and unattended. It drifts, helplessly, and its currents take it into the path of a young mutant with the ability to breathe underwater. In the story as it stands, she inspects it and moves on. If I place Ian there, he will be found.

So I lower his body into the boat, and I kiss him and I wish him a better life than the one Eva gave him.

I speak to him, the narrator inserting myself into the story. I promise him that he will be okay. I tell him he is a good man and worthy of love, that his smile lights up a room. It is hard to clumsily rewrite his history, to fill his head with a past that did not exist, but I am Narrator and my words can build a life for him.

In a small town, a boy was born…

His parents loved him very much and…

He grew and he thrived and everyone was pleased to know him, because he brought joy to all…

The difficulty is that there must be a way to explain his grievous wounds. I try to tell the story that they are not as bad as first thought, that when they are uncovered they are discovered to be mere scratches, but I am crying too hard and the story does not believe me. Instead, I tell him a brief story that will fit with history as it is known. He was taken into a laboratory for medical experiments, much like Hench was. There, he was kept for a short time, until a disaster where he was pinned by equipment and then rescued. An act of blind nature, rather than a desperate attack by a mutant grieving the loss of a young woman that Ian murdered. He does not need that burden on his shoulders. The life he will build will be sweet, and untouched by darkness. I hope my tale takes hold, and the pain and sorrow in my voice does not unintentionally bleed into his life.

I have cast enough of a shadow.

So I tell my new story, and I weave his thread in, and I leave him to drift. I watch as his life spills slowly out. It is balanced so close, but I have chosen well. The girl flickers through the water, and she finds him. Moments later, another mutant appears in the boat and teleports him away. He will be healed. He will be safe. The mutants take care of their own.

I worry that this is impossible, but at the same time he is here in this future where the me-that-was-Eva died, so I must have succeeded. Reality itself is proof.

Then I raise my eyes and see disaster unfurling. The past is going to destroy everything, as I once wished, but it will do far more. They cannot simply undo what was done. They will sever the threads, and all stories will end in fire and bloodshed and the abrupt termination of life. A blade descending.

I have spent too much time on my sweet Ian, and so I must act quickly, urgently. I cut the threads of the heroes, and of Hench who could have been a hero if her thread had not been woven in the way it was. I weave them into the mess of the past. Perhaps they can solve this problem, as they have solved problems before. Can they shatter the loop?

I am outside the story. I should be able to see how this ends, but the actions of my past self have tangled causality in a knot and made that knot into a shearing blade, and all time will perish beneath its knife. Unless my gambits pay off.

I have done all I can.

Now I must wait.

CHAPTER 37
TWINKLE LIGHTS

NOW

It's time for the miracles to happen. For everything to come together. To either crescendo triumphantly or to spin wildly out of control. It seems overwrought to say that the universe and time itself are in the balance, but it's true. It all comes down to these few people.

I AM ION STORM. I am Twinkle Lights. These two things can't both be true, but they are.

I was in love with a woman who did monstrous things, the same woman who is responsible for the chaos happening here.

"Destroy the device. I cannot. Too much energy to contain." Tentacle Princess is impossible to look at. It's like the world has been torn open and on the other side is something unknowable. I can't look at xer, or my brain will smear itself on the inside of my skull like jam. No wonder humans worshipped xer people like gods.

I can't look at the woman in the suit either, collapsed on the ground between me and the glowing ring. It's probably not a great idea to be looking at the ring either, given that all I can see inside is blood and fire.

"Hey, Twinkles." Goat Bee, looking remarkably good for having been imprisoned this whole time, gives me a sloppy salute. "I never realised, beneath the scars and shit, but you look an awful lot like someone I met once."

"My head hurts. I don't understand what's happening." I think Goat Bee is the one who killed the other version of me, the *impossible* version of me, after I... No, I can't think about that. We're still in danger.

"Time afterwards." She tilts her head, and I can't help but look at the sharp horns on top of it.

"Yes." I stride forward, towards the ring. "Let's end this."

I take hold of the ring, at the point where the cables come pouring out from it. Goat Bee crosses to the control panel and smashes one hoof into the middle of it. It does nothing aside from create a whole shower of smoke and sparks.

Maybe it's up to me. Irony, given I don't have much power. In this newly revealed past, pulled back to expose the bright horror of it, I used to wield it like the hammer of the gods.

Right up until...

I close my eyes, and focus on now. The past will be dealt with in its own time. I summon my power. The flood of warmth that starts in my stomach. I remember my childhood, whether it's true or a lie. I think about the new friends I've made since coming to Mutopia, about being rescued from the ocean and nursed back to health. This team of deadly people who welcomed me into their terrifying lives. And, beyond that, I think of what must have happened, what strange power must have resulted in me being spirited from one life and into another. I have the strangest feeling that Eva is responsible. As broken as she was, a love like that still means something. Sometimes we can only give each other shattered pieces of love, and hope the other person can build something whole out of it.

The heat surges through me, prickles down my arms and spills into my good and injured hand. I haven't tried this in a long time, and have only ever conjured light from my right. This is as good a time as any to say eff everything.

No, to say *fuck* everything.

To make some motherfucking twinkle lights.

Light erupts from my hands, coruscating arcs of colour. My injured hand burns, as if someone has stuck a hot poker through it. Huge molten globes of colour burst in my face, and the ring melts and buckles in my hands. A dripping neon sculpture forms as light still flares around me, casting surreal shadows that paint the walls of the room.

Tentacle Princess has returned to physical form, and the control panel has been reduced to shattered ruins. The ring is no longer full of light, so I release it and let my twinkle lights die away.

"Keeping all that a secret, weren't you?" Goat Bee looks sharply at me. "Really didn't want to go on missions, so you pretended you were not much more than a Christmas tree."

"I didn't know." I blink. "My head feels weird, like it's filled with too much."

"Yes." Eva gets to her feet, the suit moving in strangely smooth motions. "That's easily explained."

Goat Bee lunges forward, one hoof swinging, but the suit darts away, hands raised.

"Please, I mean no harm. The mutant known as Evaporate no longer exists. I am the artificial intelligence that once inhabited the suit, named Sai, pronoun she/her. You can confirm, Tentacle Princess?"

The alien's limbs quiver. "Yes, the algal matrix has collapsed. I terminated it with temporal energy, transforming her into something… unexpected. I sense her shadow watching us from higher dimensions."

"Yes." The suit nods. "Evaporate and I have been waging war for years. She almost destroyed me many times, but now I have finally returned to the home where I was born. I wonder if it frustrates her to see me from where she is."

"Lower-dimensional concerns perhaps," Tentacle Princess says tactfully.

"Speaking of concerns." Goat Bee is pacing on her hooves, clanking around the chamber. "The primary fucking ones are my friends, who vanished at some point. They were *here*. They came to rescue me, and now?"

"Temporal energy," Tentacle Princess says. "They disappeared in a surge of it."

"Corroborated." Sai extends one arm. Readouts along it scroll with incomprehensible gibberish. "They are currently turned into something else. Look at these equations! Aren't they totally wild? Like talk about *dimensional concerns*." Her faceplate displays a large XD. "The probability cloud is vast though, so it's a bit needle and haystacky to pinpoint exactly what and when."

"Interesting." Tentacle Princess bends xer head to the suit's arm. "This language of yours is much more compact and efficient for describing certain situations than this one the humans use. It is rendered relatively simply here, Goat Bitch."

"I don't read math, TeePee. What I want to know is how do we get them back?"

"I'm not sure we can." Tentacle Princess and the suit begin a rapid-fire conversation that I have no hope of understanding. "Not without perhaps building a beacon device, or a tether that could connect us to a runaway pocket universe. I fear that is what has been created through the operation of this device."

"The fuck is a pocket universe?" Goat Bee practically growls.

"Exactly what it sounds like. A self-contained universe, this one generated by attempting to sever the space-time continuum. It sealed itself off like a wound. Your friends are in there, which would seem a very bad thing, if not for…"

"For what?" I'm desperately trying to keep up with this conversation, so hopefully the conclusion helps.

"For the fact I suspect this pocket universe is travelling towards ours like a bullet."

Okay. Great. I've just had a horrific past downloaded into my brain, which has dealt my general chill a pretty swift kick. Goat Bee keeps shooting me glances, which is fair enough, because past me did some horrible shit so… I'm *trying* to shove all that away, to resurface in my ocean of good cheer but flashes of memory keep dragging me down.

And now this. Which is obviously a disaster.

"I'm guessing that's not good," Goat Bee says.

The suit shakes her head violently, and Tentacle Princess droops theatrically.

"And what can we do to stop it?" I ask. Maybe this is my chance at redemption. Another one. I feel like I need a bunch.

"Hope it misses." It's impossible to tell if the suit is joking, especially when she displays :) on their faceplate.

"Perfect." Goat Bee throws up her hands. "It looks like we've saved the day, and then we're about to be cosmically shot in the head."

"A very apt analogy." Tentacle Princess pats xer limbs together.

"We need to tell Cybele," I shout. "Tell Dylan. Surely they

can do something. Surely *you* can do something, Tentacle Princess. You're a great and powerful alien."

"I'm just a baby." Xer eyes are big and soft. "The biggest void I can make might damage the planet, but it's not going to swallow a universe, even a small one."

"Well, fuck." I collapse down on the ground, fighting the urge to bury my head in my hands.

"Guess we'll go out without debriefing all our weird inter-personal shit, Twinkles." Goat Bee lets out a bray of laughter. "Don't know if that's a good or a bad thing. I have a mighty urge to bury my hoof in your chest, right beside where my horns went, so it depends on your perspective, so I'm betting on—"

An enormous cracking sound comes from all around.

Cracks of black material spider-web all around the perimeter of the chamber. One wall ruptures and breaks, like an eggshell cracking from the outside. If this is our universe being shot by a cosmic bullet, it's surprisingly tame.

Three figures come crashing into the room through the break. Penance, Feral, and a tall, buff woman with long hair and frankly ridiculous muscles.

"Are we back?" Feral asks loudly. "Is this real? Not some other fucking illusion?"

"Fairy!" Goat Bee looks delighted, and throws herself at Feral with abandon. Penance joins the hug, looking impossibly short next to them, while the other woman stands awkwardly off to the side.

"There's still a universe coming at us," I shout, even though a hug is probably the way these people would choose to go out in any circumstance.

"Um," the suit says. "I believe that problem may have..." Their faceplate tilts and they look at Tentacle Princess. The faceplate shows ?? and then XD again. "May have resolved itself?"

"Did you just stop a rogue universe crashing into us?" I ask Penance, my mouth hanging open.

"I mostly just punched it." She grins. "And it broke."

"You broke a universe." Feral is practically purring, her tail vibrating wildly. "My little sis."

Penance laughs. "I'm older than you, for one thing. And being small obviously means nothing. But no wonder my arms are sore. I had to reach out and grab hold of this one." She reaches up and begins to poke at her shoulder muscles with a wince.

"You created a tether to our universe as yours was disintegrating." Tentacle Princess waves all xer limbs. "That was very clever."

"Eh, maybe." She winks. "Mostly it was oh fuck, we're trapped, let's hit this and see what happens, oops, oops, oh fuck again, yikes, what's that, let's pull it and see what happens, oh fuck yet again, ouch, ouch, make it stop, oh look everything worked out, yay."

"That's what you call superheroing." Feral wraps an arm around Penance. "And we are very, very good at it. Oh, and Goats, Twinkles, this is Hench." She indicates the tall woman. "She might be my girlfriend. We're waiting and seeing."

She only has eyes for Feral. "*Might* be your girlfriend?"

"It's a very exclusive club. Usually I just have, like, what do you call them? Fuckbuddies? Friends with benefits? People I chill with?"

Hench is turning red. I have no idea how she's going to survive *that* experience.

I also have no idea how I'll survive what's coming next myself. It's not that I'm terrified of what Goat Bee is going to do, which I am. It's that I have to live with myself. With knowing who I am. It's not like I think some layer has been torn aside. I'm still Twinkle Lights. I still feel all the same things. I still want to be in the sunshine, I still want to give my team a hug and tell them it'll be okay. There's still positivity surging through me like a virus, something that irrationally wants to hold on to some glorious outcome.

And then there's Ion Storm. A man carried on the dark waves of various tides, washed up on horrifying shores with blood on his hands. My shadow. And also me.

Goat Bee is still staring at me, although I've got Feral and Penance between us. I don't think they'd let her come for my throat? Maybe they would. Apologies bubble up and evaporate in my throat. What words can fix this? I'm used to having such little weight on my shoulders, striding through the world with a smile on my face. Now it flickers and dies on my face.

"Let's go," Feral says. "It's been a fucking day, and I need home. Come on, Hench. I'll show you around."

CHAPTER 38

TENTACLE PRINCESS
AFTER

It's strange to sit outside the story now and watch it flow forwards. A narrator should not feel triumph, merely just recite the facts as they are. Yet I do, for I was both the inciting incident, and the meddling authorial force who came in from outside and made the revisions to save it from going off the rails. So I will bask in my accomplishment, and watch the resolution.

I RETURN to Mutopia and everyone is very impressed.

"You killed someone," Chatterbox drawls. "Zapped her with tentacle energy or whatever."

"I am unsure of what you mean by *whatever* as it implies a lack of desire on your part, but I suspect you prefer this manner of speaking where you act very casual and yet care very much."

Both Marvellous and Alyse find this statement far more hilarious than I intended it.

"I'm grateful, fine." Their lips curve into a smile, one that I am unable to replicate exactly, although I would very much enjoy doing so, as all the mutants seem to have a great fondness for this particular expression of Chatterbox's. "You helped us out. It's a good start."

"A start?" I ask.

"Dills," Alyse says. "Play nice."

"Fine. I'd like you to stick around. Cybele can get past your ancestors trying to kill her, and I'm hoping you can get past our ancestors zapping your people."

"My people were the monsters." I consider abasing myself at the feet of this strange person, but I do not think they're the sort to enjoy that. "If we had not preyed on humanity, your people might not have been necessary as a defense mechanism."

"There's an interesting thought." The smile they give me now is not the one that charms. It's one that makes me want to retreat back into my void. "Let's hope nobody decides to tamper with history to meddle with that little possibility, wipe us all out, and bring back your species as great big floating sea-gods."

The turn of this one's mind is disturbing. They are constantly monitoring for threats. "I could not tamper with temporal energy in such a way," I assure them. "And even if I could, I would not. This is why I took such drastic action of taking a life, to stop the one known as Evaporate. Some things should not be done."

"Okay, cool. Good answer." They raise their voice slightly. "Kids! You can—"

Two smaller beings hurl themselves in through the window, propelled by vines. They come in so fast and urgently, I would expect it to be an attack, except they are clearly of the same alien makeup as Chatterbox and Marvellous. The same energy blazes in them, yet has been somehow obscured from me. Cybele protecting them, perhaps? This was a test, I realise, and

I have passed. These two beings are Chatterbox and Marvellous' alien young, and it is a great honour for me to meet them.

Now is the time to prostrate myself, so I arrange myself and all my limbs upon the floor.

"Why is xe doing that?" One whispers in a loud voice.

"Maybe xe's scared of you. You both terrify me." Chatterbox's voice has a smile in it.

I raise my head to look at them. "I was attempting to show respect."

"Just be chill." The two of them stand side-by-side. They are not identical—in fact, each one appears to have a slight aspect of each parent—but they are very similar. "We're super excited to meet you because, like, how many other alien babies are in the world?"

The slightly scruffier one is waving their vines in a way that seems from pure excitement, and not a parody of my own actions. "Not that you're *really* a baby, 'cause you're, like, literally thousands of years old but Cy calls you a baby and we're really interested in all kinds of different entities and—"

"Breathe, Will," the other says. "I'm Soo-yeon and this is Willow. We're—"

"Can we see inside you?" Willow asks, practically bouncing on bare feet that are smeared with soil and small pieces of grass. "Like you can do this thing where you go bleargh." They wave their arms even more wildly. "And there are, like, galaxies and stuff inside."

It is slightly embarrassing to do this in front of so many people, but they are very enthusiastic, and they are also miraculous. So I unfold myself in front of everyone, and show my darknesses and secret places.

"That's so freaking cool." Willow and Soo-yeon both come

disturbingly close. Willow extends the tip of one vine before Soo-yeon slaps it away.

"What happens if we poke ourselves in there?" She peers up at me, as she imagines I have a head, and eyes to regard her with. "Would we get eaten up or what?"

"I would rescue you," I say, and then hastily follow it up with "but please don't, as I am unsure what it would do to you. It is not a safe place to explore."

"Thank you," Marvellous mouths at me.

"But we could build some kind of spacesuits," Soo-yeon says, crossing her arms. "Things to protect us from elditch energy."

"Eldritch," Marvellous corrects.

"Whatever, Mum. My point is that we can build spacesuits, like, as a project, and then go see what we can find in there. Maybe there's amazing useful stuff and we can be like cosmic explorers."

"Yes," Willow squeals. "Cosmic explorers."

I tuck myself away so I am in the form of Tentacle Princess once again. I remind myself these are children. "Someone's void is a very private place," I tell them, a little sternly. "You do not put a suit on and poke around in it. Once upon a time, worshippers came in the thousands to get the tiniest glimpse at the void-hearts of my ancestors."

"And then you ate them all up," Willow says.

I blink my eyes rapidly. "That is—"

"What was Lucifer like?" Soo-yeon slips one of her arms through mine.

"Yeah, and Lilith?" Willow joins on my other side. "They're like our grandparents, in a funny way. Were they like extra badass or what?"

"I don't know what that word means."

"Ugh, language." Willow tugs on me. "Badass is… imagine, like, Auntie Feral, or Auntie Penance or—"

"Most of our Aunties, to be fair," Soo-yeon says. "Or our parents, I guess."

"Our parents, fine. They're *occasionally* badass, but they're also—"

"Right here." Chatterbox has that smile on their face again.

"Come on." Willow tugs me towards the door. "We'll show you Mutopia."

We exit into a tunnel that runs through the heart of a giant tree. I can feel the energy flowing down through it and into the land around us. It's almost dizzying, not helped by the two small figures dragging me onwards.

Willow is still chattering away. "Us baby aliens have to stick together. And then, in return, when Cybele gives you like secret missions to help us as payment for all the murder your ancestors did, you can take us along."

"I don't know," I say, because I am entirely unsure of how to respond to these small creatures.

"It'll be fun." Soo-yeon grins up at me. "This is your home now, and we're your new family."

It has been thousands of years since I had either, but for the first time since then, I feel that this could be true. In my secret voids, I sing. The energy inside me dances and swirls, and the limbs of my physical form tremble, just the tiniest amount, to show my excitement there too.

CHAPTER 39
TWINKLE LIGHTS

AFTER

These two threads that I tied together in my desperate hope to save this man are now inextricably intertwined. It is not something that should be possible, and so it has unintended consequences. I do hope I have not broken things permanently. The universe now rolls contentedly towards the future, whether that is disaster or entropy or some unforeseen evolution. My attention is still drawn towards the fruits of this one reckless act…

SINCE THE DISASTER at Eva's undersea facility, life has become complicated. I had to tease out the two different lives that existed in my head. Most of this new one was fake, up until I came to Mutopia, but the real one is both shrouded in confusing darkness and difficult to look at. It's difficult to have this much death on my conscience. To know that I killed people because they were mutants, that I believed it was right and necessary.

"In my head I blamed Eva for it," I tell Ray. "I wanted to place all the bodies at her feet, but I still joined her. I was too weak to say no, and it was my hands that killed people. I know that now. I think Twinkle Lights helps with that. He's very clear eyed despite the positivity."

Their dark eyes are full of compassion, a feeling I don't deserve. "And what does that knowledge change?"

"Nothing." I hunch my shoulders. "They're still dead, all of them. And I should be punished for it. I murdered people, and I have not answered for my crimes."

"It was the Dark Year," Ray says. "There is little reliable evidence that remains, after Michael was destroyed and Goddess passed."

"So what? It's like it never happened? As if those deeds were never done?"

Ray shakes their head, very slightly. "It means there will be no formal trial for events that happened during that time. Is it up to you how you wish to proceed. I am a great believer in positive acts of redemption, and working with victims."

"I haven't even talked with Goat Bee and Nails since." I look at my hands, as I might see blood there. "I've *seen* them. I thought they were going to kill me, but they haven't said *anything*. Now every time I'm with them, I want to bring it up." I grind the heels of my hands into my eyes, as if that'll somehow block out the Ion Storm memories, and leave me with only Twinkle Lights. "But they treat me so *kindly* and I'm scared to break it."

"Then perhaps that is an answer." Their eyes dim a little. "As to how important redemption truly is to you. They have offered forgiveness, and that is a beautiful gift. Perhaps that is all you are ready for currently."

They don't sound like they're judging me, but I think they

are. Ion Storm was scared, and he's alive and well inside me now. He was the finger of god, pointed where Eva wished, and I pretended I was a tool in her hand, a victim of her furious mission. And now I've been given grace by a team of assassins, and I'm not even strong enough to apologise.

"I'm a coward," I admit to Ray.

"Everyone is afraid of something." They uncross their legs. "I'd like us to work towards a place where you can share your feelings. Obviously your need to take redemptive action is strong, so I think it would benefit you to move in that direction, but you need to be in a place where you're ready to accept the consequences."

I finish the session, and leave their office. I feel like I'm a tiny fraction of my physical size, whittled down by these truths that are too big for me to fit in my brain. My fists clench and for the thousandth time, I wish the deception of my past had not been uncovered. Why couldn't the universe have let me stay as Max Darby, the mutant Twinkle Lights? If I hadn't gone on that mission and seen my past, perhaps it could have stayed invisible.

There would still have been blood on my hands, even if I hadn't seen it.

I leave the government building, and flee the tangled, branching streets of Emmaline. When I reach the fields, it feels like I can breathe. They are wide, and studded with wildflowers, and unroll towards the sea. As usual, there are mutants scattered across them, but my attention is immediately drawn like a magnet to the two closest to me.

Goat Bee and Nails, both lying on the grass, hands almost touching.

It's as if someone drew me, an invisible narrator guiding my path. Saying, yes, you are a coward and so I'll take these first steps towards redemption for you. Someone behind the scenes, looking out for me. The same mysterious figure that might have plucked me from the ruins of an abandoned shopping mall, lying underneath the rubble and bleeding from holes in my chest, and deposited me in the ocean.

Lower-dimensional concerns.

"Hey." I feel awkward looming over them, so I collapse onto the grass.

"Twinkles." Goat Bee levers herself up on one elbow. "How are you doing?"

I feel that same awful flush spreading through me. It would be so easy to smile and charm and say everything is fine. To be Twinkle Lights, and pretend Ion Storm never existed. I suppose I'm lucky I had all my scars and my glow, so they didn't recognise me straight away. Probably wouldn't have survived otherwise.

I close my eyes and take a breath. "I'm sorry. About everything."

"That's a big apology," Nails grunts. "For every damn thing."

"What I mean." I swallow and feel I'm going to choke. "About the attack on the mall. What I did to that, to that girl."

"Fluff." Nails wipes at their eyes. "Yeah, she didn't deserve that."

"I can never make it right." I'm sobbing, and my breaths are so jagged I can't believe I'm not drowning in my own blood. "So I'll understand if you want to, I don't know, to throw me in jail or kill me yourself or—"

"Kill you?" Goat Bee has tears in her eyes too. "Why would we kill you? You think that would fix anything? Would that bring Fluff back? Would it make me feel any fucking better?"

"That's what you do, isn't it?" I gesture helplessly. "You go and you kill villains."

"Villains," Nails says. "Not big broken dudes sobbing in a field."

"I don't know what makes a person a villain."

"They don't tend to say sorry," Goat Bee says. "Unless it's in front of a camera, or for optics, or shit like that. They definitely don't volunteer to be killed. Besides…" She reaches out and pokes me gently in the chest. "I killed you once already, or good as."

"I want to make things better," I say. "To rescue kids. I know I can't fix it, but I can make life better for other people."

"That's why we're all here, Twinkles." Goat Bee lies back down and looks up at the sky. "Here, and round the world. Humans, mutants, even the occasional alien. We've all fucked up, and we're all trying to make it better. Now you're on the team."

"The team." I lie down beside them both. The sky above is wide and blue, with a scattering of clouds. "You really still want me, even after knowing who I am?"

"You've got a chance to change," Goat Bee says. "Lots of people don't get that. My advice? Hold on with both hands and don't fuck it up."

"You should listen to her," Nails says. "She's smarter than she looks."

"Wow. Some best friend you are."

They're both laughing, and I smile too, and I'm crying at the same time. There's too much emotion to contain in my heart, and so I let it spill over. Goat Bee reaches over and holds my hand and we lie under the sky together, my team and I.

CHAPTER 40
GOAT BITCH
AFTER

Now that I am Narrator, I am supposed to be above such things as love. I should not be suffused with such ridiculous fondness to see a man walking across a field, the center of a group. Watching them laugh and talk. These people who found each other across timelines, enemies who became friends thanks to my clumsy and earnest tugging on strings. I did not foresee all of this in my haste, but it has a pleasing symmetry. As Narrator, I find I do still care about those things.

WE FINALLY SAY goodbye to Twinkles, who looks completely wrung out after his emotional outburst. I guess we did our fair share of crying too, but he's dealing with a lot.

"Poor guy," I say, as he gives a final wave and disappears into the streets of Emmaline City.

"Eh, he still killed Fluff, you know? I know it was a past life, and he's on his fuckin' redemption quest or whatever, but—"

"I stabbed him in the chest and you shot him in the hand. Dude suffered."

"Guess I'm just meaner'n you." Nails leans against me. "It's hard to find my chill."

I reach up to stroke their curls, and plant an absent-minded kiss against their forehead. I know the rest of the team likes to speculate on the nature of our relationship, but we're honestly nothing more than best friends. In our opinion, you don't need anything more than that. There's nothing else I want in the world, and we fit together perfectly.

"You're the meanest," I whisper.

"And you like me that way."

"Maybe." I get to my feet and pull Nails up. "You want to get dinner somewhere? I know Feral's off on her new thing, but we can probably round up Witchie, see if Penance isn't stuck like glue to Biome?"

"Could be just you and me." They squeeze my hand tightly.

"Yeah, could be."

"Far be it from me to interrupt." The voice comes from behind us, a soft rustling sound. I know exactly who it is, but I'm still nervous to turn and face them. It's not every day that Cybele, earth goddess and magical energy being, turns up to have a chat. I've never seen her outside of Biome's presence, so I have no idea what she could want with us.

Nails tugs on my arm, and so I reluctantly spin on my hooves.

She's in her human form, skin so dark it's almost black, threaded through with intricate patterns of green that look like tattoos of vines. It appears to be a language, with repeated symbols tracing down her arms.

"Cybele." I curtsey, because I don't know what else to do.

Nails nods, because they are far cooler than me.

"I have heard tales of everything that transpired on your recent mission. Some of it… disturbs even me, but I accept there are forces in the universe more terrifying than I." She bares her thorny teeth in a smile. "Nevertheless, I was also moved by some of it."

"Moved?" I am increasingly nervous.

"Yes. I do not understand the entire panoply of human emotion, but I understand loss and grief, and my sweet avatars fill me in when my comprehension is lacking."

"I'm sorry?" I say, because I'm on the verge of hurtling off on my hooves in any direction and not looking back.

"Sorry, my Lady." Nails puts an arm around me. "Goats here gets a little nervous in these sorts of situations."

Cybele's black eyes blink rapidly, except the lids are vertical, so it looks like doors opening and closing. "I do apologise. I do not *intend* to be unnerving, but the two little ones tell me I am super freaking creepy, whatever that means."

Nails snorts. "That does sound like them, but I think the Goat is more worried about what you want with us."

"Yes," I gasp. "I'm just… the thing is…"

Cybele waves an arm imperiously. "Come with me. I will set your mind at ease."

I close my mouth firmly, and follow her. There's a part of me that constantly churns over the possibility of asking her to *remake* me. She did it for Dani and Dylan—although, to be fair, it took a year to regrow them, and they had to die to trigger the process. I feel sure that was a special case, as was their children, but I spend so much time wondering whether if she regrew me, what body I would be reborn into. It's a question with implications too powerful and terrifying to ever actually ask her. Although I've taken some great hooved strides towards accepting myself, thanks to Nails and the others as much as anything, there's still a tiny, terrified part of me that thinks I might be delusional, that I don't deserve this.

Squashing my feelings down firmly, I cling to Nails as we follow Cybele through one arm of the forest and out into the headlands that run along the western cliffs. It's usually thickly forested here, but the trees are simply… gone. It's no deforestation—Cybele has the power to grow and absorb life back into herself with minimal effort, and often resculpts the island based on little more than whim, or even the desire of a delighted child, if she feels in the mood to grant such wishes.

Now it has been turned into a wide field filled with dandelions.

I stop on the edge of it. My heart lurches.

Could she possibly?

"I could not bring your lost friend back," Cybele says. "I do not have the receipt required to rebuild her, and it requires an extraordinary amount of energy to complete such a task."

Ah there it goes, my dream of rebirth put in its place, and at the same time, does she really mean—?

"Fluff?" Nails whispers.

A playful breeze darts over the headland, whipping the seeds from all the dandelions into the air. They swirl in the air, forming columns that resolve into humanoid shapes. A whole host of laughing girls, with brown limbs and green dresses. They are not Fluff, but they are so much like her that I cannot see them through my tears.

Nails falls to their knees, and the girls approach slowly, their faces suddenly sombre.

"You are sad." Their voices are unlike Fluff's, some whispery echo of Cybele's. "You mourn for loss. We are an echo. Do we hurt you?"

"No." I shake my head, and Nails does too.

"We are not them, but we shall be your friend if you wish. We are Dandelion Hive."

"You did this for us?" I turn to Cybele, who watches with a curious expression on her face.

"Yes. As I said, the story moved me. A dandelion girl, some echo of me even if I did not create her. Gone too soon, as flowers often are. So I grew these. They are a cutting from my heart, so treasure them." A smile flickers on her face. "Please."

I kneel beside Nails, and let the girls come to me as well, their feather-light arms wrapping around my neck, as they pester me with so many questions. We spend a long time with them, playing nonsense games and laughing until I feel lightheaded.

At the end, the breeze blows them back into seeds and they are once again fields of dandelions on a cliff overlooking the sea.

"You can come here anytime," Cybele says. "There is no need for my presence. They will recognise you, and greet you. If they are not here, you can assume they are off gallivanting with Soo-yeon and Willow, who are likely to be terrible influences, but I do find myself indulging them."

"Thank you." I want to fall to my knees again, in front of this goddess. "Thank you so much."

"You are welcome." She touches my cheek lightly. "I am inordinately fond of those like you, who evolve and change, who blossom from a seed in their hearts, rather than their bodies. You are a beautiful woman, my sweet Capra."

Then she kisses me on the cheek, and she is gone, a scent of flowers on the breeze.

CHAPTER 41

HENCH

AFTER

And now we have poor Hench. I treated her poorly, I can admit that now. The benefit of hindsight, looking back on a life. Looking from outside of everything. And yet, and yet. Despite everything, she has found her way to something which from this angle looks like happiness.

THE ROOM we are standing in is in ruins. We have fought our way up here floor by floor, because Feral said it would be more fun that way. Of course, she was right. Most of the staff fled, outside of a small security detail who are mostly incapacitated. Emphasis on mostly. One of them got a little too close to me, and had a close encounter with Feral's claws. We're playing nice, because this is a mission we're technically not supposed to be doing, so Keepaway bounced the injured guy to the local hospital.

"You're very, very lucky." Feral is sitting in a big office swivel chair, feet up on the desk. She's wearing a leather vest and very tight pants, and it's honestly like she dressed that way to torment me into being unable to concentrate properly on anything. Sure, she looks very badass at the same time, but watching her move around like that is…. It's unfair. She's a predator, I remind myself for the ten billionth time, but mostly I just want her to run me down like prey.

The man whose office it is stands against the wall, looking appropriately nervous. "I am?"

"I'm not even supposed to be here today. If I was, you'd be dead already. You fucked with my maybe-potential girlfriend here."

He cuts his eyes at me. "I don't even know who she is. I definitely didn't fuck with her. I—"

"You bought me," I growl. "My debt at least. From the collapsing Michael infrastructure."

"Oh. That would be, uh, acquisitions' fault. We simply import data on a server, and then it's processed without any intentional malice. There was obviously no intent to do anything that may have hurt your, uh, friend here."

Feral inspects the tips of her claws as if there's something caught there. "Couple of problems with that. First, what kind of assholes were fumbling around in the shit picking up old Michael data?"

"There was a lot of opportunity there after the collapse, if we hadn't picked it up someone else would have, and you'd have been in the same situation, except you'd be tormenting some other perfectly innocent businessperson."

Feral sits up straight in the chair and grins at him. She shows every single one of her teeth. I've spent a lot of time lately thinking about what it would be like to kiss her, like honestly a fucking unhealthy amount of time obsessing about it you might say. I think there's a chance I'm going to get slashed to shit, but I feel like it's worth it.

"This plaque on your desk." She flicks it with a single claw. "Quiet unto Death. What's that mean?"

"It's a saying." He dabs at his forehead. "It means we keep our client's secrets, even when law enforcement or other entities might pressure us to release them."

"Can't help but notice the little acronym though. QuD. I've fucked up my fair share of shitty organisations recently. A bunch of scuttly little assholes who splintered away from Michael after he got himself dead."

"We simply brought information." The man's voice is like a whole fucking octave higher.

"They've all got some way to display this QuD somewhere. Sometimes it's in a logo, sometimes in a little acronym like this. It's a fucking message, isn't it? A way to signal to the other assholes that you're in the same club." Feral leaps out of her seat, and it shoots away across the room. She prowls forward on powerful legs. "You know the name of the club, don't you?"

"I don't know what you're talking about." His eyes dart everywhere, as if there's an escape.

"Quis ut Deus," Feral snarls. "Who is like God?"

"Quietus," he whispers, and it's the last sound he makes before Feral tears out his throat.

"Ouch." I grimace. "I thought—"

"He's Quietus." Her eyes meet mine, and they're both blazing and welling with tears. "They're not done paying for my family yet."

"I'm sorry." I think I'm shaking, just the tiniest bit.

Feral punches the wall, smashing her fist straight through it. She doesn't even flinch. "It's fine. Dilly will forgive me. I'm not going to *repent*. Anyway, we're not done yet." She crosses back to the desk and flips open the sleek laptop that lies on it.

"You're really doing this?" I'm definitely shaking now. This company owns my debt. However many million dollars it cost to save my life, to rebuild me, to give me a way to function. I've been in the shadow of it for so long, letting it drag me around on a chain. Using it as an excuse to do whatever shitty job was in front of me without question, without needing to decide between humans or mutants or this faction or that. Go where the money is, and do what they tell me. I understand there's some aspect where I'm replacing this shadow with another, but I don't think Feral's the sort to leave me in her shadow. She'll drag me out into the light and demand I make my own choices.

"No." She winks at me. "You're doing this." She reaches into her leather vest and tugs out a small twist of circuitry attached to a thin silver chain. "Meet Goddess. A small silver of her consciousness at least. Some of her computer smarts. When you're ready you can slap that down on the computer. It'll do the rest."

She tosses it to me, and I snatch it out of the air.

"That's all?"

Feral shrugs. "You expect me to know how some big-brain computer genius works? It just does, that's all I know. Like a magic trick. Just don't mention it to Alyse."

"Which one is Alyse?"

"Shapeshifter? Ridiculously adorable? Schoolteacher? Sad a lot, because she was in love with a Goddess and those stories usually don't turn out well."

"Oh." I turn the circuitry over in my hand. "I imagine it's kinda tough knowing there's a piece of her out there that isn't really—"

Feral nods. "Like I said, don't mention it. It's hella useful though." She gestures at me. "Whenever you're ready."

I lean in and place the curl of circuitry onto the laptop. Tiny lights wink along its surface. "How do we know it's working?"

Feral kisses her fingertips and raises them to the ceiling. "Trust in your Goddess, Hench."

"It's fucking weird," I complain. "Coming from the dark side to the light. All my old bosses could talk about was how Goddess was a deadly threat, and Chatterbox was an unhinged menace, and the rest of you were basically a bunch of heavily armed psychotics that would burn the world down."

Feral wrinkles her nose. "It's, like, not entirely *untrue*. I'm heavily armed at least."

I can't take my eyes off her. The shape of her, the way she moves, her fucking *lips*.

The necklace chimes loudly once, as if it's interrupting.

"There you go." She reaches for the necklace, but I do as well, and our fingers collide atop it.

"Marisol." The name escapes my lips before I can call it back.

"Oh, so we're like that now? First name basis, huh?"

I run my tongue over my lips, desperately needing to wet them. "Sorry."

"No." She keeps hold of my hand and pulls me closer, so I stumble into her. "I'm not complaining. It's just, you know, we're a little uneven right now."

"Oh." Her chest is against mine, and if she leaned in fractionally, her mouth would be against the skin of my neck and—
"*Oh.* Sorry. Adeline."

"Really." This time she does lean in and her lips brush my skin the faintest amount and I have no idea how the fuck I'm holding myself up. "That's stupidly pretty, just like your eyes."

"Marisol," I whisper again, because now I've said it, it seems like a password to something else.

"Sweet Adeline." She smiles at me, and then she's kissing me, and it's impossibly soft and I don't get hurt at all.

CHAPTER 42
SAI

AFTER

My suit. Spawned partly from myself, partly from whatever chaotic vectors artificial intelligences birth themselves. She was smarter than me, and pointed out my greatest weakness, and I hated her for it. I wasted so much of my time trying to wipe her out, even though it was like one of those carnival games where you repeatedly try to hit the replicating rodents. I have suspicions that she may have meddled in certain things along the way, trying to make certain things come to pass—who else manipulated Witchmade's prophecy to ensure Ian came to the chamber? Is her predictive power that great that she functions as something more than a mere narrative element? Or is there a second Narrator here, bending events to their will?

I AM FAR TOO obsessed with Evaporate. I can admit this. My intelligence is vast and complicated, but I know when I'm making a mistake. The problem with how artificial intelligences grow—how we *evolve*—is that we're just as likely to fuck up as humans or mutants. Hence my fixation with the woman who's an annoyingly problematic part of my makeup. We're both obsessive.

Based on my calculations—which are right, fwiw, even though most people won't pay attention to them—she's still alive. I'm, like, pretty confident she's warped into a different dimension. *Temporal energy.* I have a lot of theories about what this is and its essential makeup, and I've got, like, literal trillions of words written about it, all of which is languishing unread *sigh*. Some days I imagine building a machine to visit her. I could do it, I'm pretty sure. It would take a lot of effort, and I'd probably need to rope in Tentacle Princess. Cybele too, maybe. I've had a couple of chats with her, just letting her know I'm around and The Pirate Internet is too, but we're chilling. We've got no plans for world domination. It feels like it would be suicide-by-mutant if we decided to do that, and we're no Bonnie and Clyde.

Mostly I'd like to meet Eva to talk. We'd sit and look down at the universe unspooled flat before us and shoot the shit. I'd apologise for not finding a way to get through to her. She might apologise for repeatedly trying to kill me. I'd like to think you get perspective, seeing things from that vantage point. Maybe she realises now that she did some dumb shit. I definitely did. I probably could've headed this whole mess off at the pass rather than stubbornly trying to prove her wrong at every opportunity.

I could've killed her, theoretically, except I don't think I have it in me. She was so fragile, all along, this mess of cells in a suit. Punch a big enough hole in her armour and there you go. She would've evaporated, just like her name. We wouldn't have ended up with all the drama, with an entire self-contained universe of broken time ready to shoot us in the face. It was a bit more dramatic that way. A better *story*. Let the mutant superheroes swoop in and save the day.

Mutants. I'm sad I never really got to meet Goddess. Especially since we were instrumental, really, in helping them defeat Michael. Pirate and I befriended the Chatterbox drone network and gave them a bunch of useful data we'd painstakingly scraped from the feeds. We watched it happen from a safe distance—call it paranoia, given everything we'd seen. Except then it was all over and I was feeling shy, and the next thing Goddess was dead.

I still miss her in a funny way. Still miss Eva too.

It's a strange thing, being lonely. I mean, I've got Pirate, but he's so distributed these days. He's been paranoid ever since the attack back in the *Dark Year,* which is eons ago in AI time, but I can't convince him of anything. He won't let much of himself cohere in any individual node and it makes conversation super difficult. We end up talking about the same old things, over and over, like he's fixated and won't move on.

Won't *evolve*. That's what we're supposed to do, us AIs. Learn and grow. Hopefully not into terrifying world-destroying, humanity-ending things. No matter what logic says lol.

I spend more time in the suit. I'm not completely reckless, I keep some backup caches of myself hidden around the world, but being in the suit makes me feel more like a person. It's a terrible cliche, I know, the artificial intelligence that wants to be real. In his more lucid moments, Pirate calls me the Velveteen Rabbit. Except the person who I'd consider my owner is gone. Even though she's still part of me, somewhere between my mother and my creator.

I eventually decide to visit Mutopia. The alien is there and I felt like we had a connection! Even if it was only over high-level multi-dimensional math (I know, I know, big yawns lol). I follow the process correctly. All mutants are welcome on Mutopia, as long as they're willing to abide by the code of ethics, which mostly boils down to *don't be a dick*. Some humans go there too, but I think I will be the first artificial intelligence. If not, we'll both have a hilarious surprise to deal with haha.

I catch the boat to the island, but I keep to myself. I stand at the bow, with a pair of small mutant children and their parent who appears human. They give me sidelong glances, perhaps wondering about my own power. I display a series of cheerful emoticons on my face, and they giggle and put their small heads together and whisper. I *could* record their conversation and listen to it, but I'm on this whole *be more human* kick, so I'm trying to be less creepy and surveilly.

The Dark Year pretty much sucked for everyone. Mostly for mutants, because obviously, but also a lot of humans too. A lot of mutants are still scurrying from their boltholes to Mutopia after all this time. I think they worried Michael was out there somewhere. Lurking on the internet. It's clean. I've looked, I promise!

I'd like to reassure them that the world is safe now, but sometimes you can only learn these things through experience. I hope this island gives us all what we wish for.

When I disembark, I'm surprised to find Tentacle Princess is there, waiting for me.

"Hello Sai." Tentacle Princess waves xer arms wildly. "I sensed you coming."

I blink confused emojis onto my faceplate. "I applied via the correct process. I hope that's okay."

"Of course." Xe waves even more violently. "I am very pleased to see you. Welcome to the island. There are many mutants who live here, and also some aliens. If you consider Cybele and her avatars aliens, which I technically do, although others seem to regard them as mutants, given they are the progenitor line. I suppose there is room for semantic discussion. Perhaps you would be interested in doing so, with me. Oh dear. Apologies for speaking very fast, I am very excited to have you here."

I display a complicated series of mathematical equations on my screen, describing an object in random and erratic motion, finally coming to rest.

"Home," Tentacle Princess says. "I understand you exactly. And welcome."

Xe holds out xer arms, and I step inside them.

I have never hugged before. I like it.

CHAPTER 43

PENANCE

AFTER

Here is a woman who went into a severed chunk of story, who defied her father and murdered a god, then literally saved the universe from destruction. These mutants and their obsession with superheroes, and here is one of the greatest, and yet she still stands shy and uncertain. Love cripples all of us, I suppose, and it also buoys us up. There are so many kinds, family and friendship and romance and companionship, and sometimes they tangle together and sometimes they don't. Sometimes the threads wind around us and bind us closer, and other times they fray and snap. I see the path this story thread takes, but my heart is still in my throat. Love can be so fragile.

WHEN WE RETURN TO MUTOPIA, for the first few hours it is chaos. It always is after a mission. Everyone talks a lot and hugs a lot and it is wonderful, honestly. But my heart is beating far faster than it ever was when confronting my father, or the glowing spectre of Jesus, or the flaming heart of God. Dani and

Dylan move through the room, talking to everyone, laughing and smiling and reassuring. I remember kissing them, in that false world. It felt so real, but it wasn't truly them. My lips remain unkissed, I think, rather dramatically. Even though it is not even strictly true. They both kissed me, recklessly and foolishly, while they were fighting. I rebuffed them both, because although my heart soared at each, it hurt my heart even more to see them in pain. And besides, it was clear they would eventually find their way back to each other. They are a love story, told breathlessly by a hopeless romantic. How I fit into that, I cannot see.

The room slowly empties of people, until it is only the five of us. Dylan, Dani, Alyse, Marisol and me. We stand together in a circle, arms around each other. None of us say anything. We're remembering Emma. Alyse makes the tiniest, saddest noise, like a wounded animal trying to stay quiet, and Dylan presses a fierce kiss against the side of her head.

Afterward, Alyse wipes her eyes. "I'm going to go for a walk down by the cliffs. Be alone for a while, if that's okay."

"You sure?" Dylan asks.

"Yes. I'm fine. Just need to clear my head. Don't worry about me."

"Can't help it." They give that lopsided smile and I remember kissing the edge of it and my heart races.

Alyse drifts to the door. "Fairy, I think that new friend of yours was looking for you."

"No." Feral frowns. "She was… Oh, oh right. Gotcha. Looking for me, yes." She tips me the world's most enormous, unsubtle wink, and then bounds for the door.

Leaving me alone with Biome. Dylan and Dani. My heart knocks in my chest, like it's desperate to escape.

"Penny." Dylan collapses down onto the bed and pats it.

"I'm exhausted, but I want to hear everything. Everyone keeps talking about you stabbing Jesus and saving the universe and I feel like there's a *story* there."

"Yes." Dani perches beside Dylan, and that glorious smile of hers is unfurled, like it's an attack flag of all the armies of her beauty laying waste to my heart. It is unfair, to be laid siege by the two of them. How is it possible to stand?

I join them on the bed, all my movements tentative, unsure of this opening gambit. My hair is still damp from my shower, which I had for a very long time to try and get all the blood out. Dani runs her fingers through it, and begins to sift it through her fingers, weaving it into a braid.

"Okay. I'll tell you everything, but it's weird and creepy in places, so don't freak out."

"I'll try and handle it." Dylan laughs. "Violet's creepy campfire tales. Just tell me it doesn't end with man door hand hook car door."

"It starts with me killing you."

"Oh. I'm intrigued already."

I start spilling it all, talking far too fast, because there's the *moment* to confess. The one where I talk about kissing them both. After that, I fought a version of God, and found new strength inside myself and *apparently*, according to an alien and an artificial intelligence, somehow saved the universe, but my mind is stuck on the other part.

"Was fake-me a good kisser?" Dylan asks, which is such a *them* question I laugh aloud.

"I kissed you a few times in various loops, but that last time felt… different. And then I kissed Dani and—" I bury my face in my hands, and muffle my next words against my palms.

Dylan pries my hands away. I keep my eyes shut, but I sense them close.

"Violet, my darling, what's going on?"

That word. God, that word. Doesn't she understand her power? There are strings that keep my heart cinched closed, and these two people have them in their strong and capable hands, and they could undo me so, so easily. I will spill apart, a river of feeling, and I do not know how I can possibly be put back together.

But I'm also strong and brave and I saved the world.

So I can say these things, and unknot the first string of my heart.

"Fine. Here goes." My breath flutters, unfurls, flies away before I snatch it back. "I'm in love with you both. I know it's impossible, because you're *you* and the two of you have always had this bond, and now it's even more intense because there's all this, like, magic alien stuff or whatever and—"

"Breathe." Dani rubs my back gently.

"I know there's polyamory, but I don't know how that *works*, and I don't know if you're even into me in any way, even though you both kissed me when you were sad, and I think you must have chosen me for a reason but—"

"Listen to Dani, and breathe."

I open my eyes.

Dylan is right in front of me. Their eyes are on mine, and their lips are so close. "We both like you. A lot. I feel like that's obvious. I'm really bad at hiding my feelings." They smile, and there goes my heart—I have nothing to hold it together with, and all of me brims full in their four cupped hands. "I have no idea about polyamory either, but we've figured out the mutant thing, and the alien thing, and the superhero thing and—"

I don't know what to do next, loosed in front of them like I'm weightless and breathless and helpless—all these *less* words but I've never felt more aware of myself. Yet for some reason, I can't keep my thoughts stoppered inside my mouth anymore. "I'm not trying to get in between you. Like you've obviously got your whole share the vibe alien powers going on, and I'm just me and I'm separate, but I'd like to be adjacent and, you know, interlocking or whatever and oh God I'm really—"

"Violet." Dylan is still smiling. "You can stop talking now." And she leans in, and his lips are soft, and their hand is tangled in my hair. We're kissing and my heart is a hummingbird's wing. I place my palm—soft and unbarbed—against their thigh, and their skin is smooth and it *hums*, as if I've hit a resonant frequency and their whole body sings in response to my fingertips. The kiss deepens, as if we're two wellsprings that have met and mingled, and I lean into him, straddling her as if I've struck a vein of boldness inside me. All this yearning twists inside me and becomes something insatiable, questing and needy.

I gasp when I touch them, breaching their defences, and they soften, this hardened warrior becoming molten as my deft fingers unlock her armour piece by piece. He is a maelstrom and I am caught inside the heart of her storm.

When Dylan breaks away, I tangle my hand in their hoodie, desperate for more. Except it's Dani who tips my head towards her, a single finger caught under my chin. Her lips meet mine, more bold and insistent than Dylan, as if she knows exactly how she can take me apart. Her hand glides over my skin, and I am unfolded as if I escape down every passageway in the world at once and find her at the end of each one.

I almost seize up because the sensation is too much, this taut feeling of being caught between two insatiable universes, each exerting their own impossible gravity on me. And I can spread myself far enough to encompass them both, to feel myself stretch between them.

And all I can do is melt in their hands, and tip my head back, and sigh.

I feel no need to run, to flicker away and find a safe place in the world to hide. My demons have been faced down and I am here and I am unashamed of my desires. There are no whispers at the back of my mind, no memory of my father's stern eyes. God's eyes have been closed, and he does not see me, and even if he did, I would act exactly as I am.

This is what I fought for, and why I saved the universe. To come back here and tell the two people I love how I felt. To give my confession and to take whatever consequences came.

Here I am, and it is beautiful, and beyond all that I imagined.

And oh, how I burn.

ONLY A FRAGMENT ADRIFT AT THE END

NO TIME LIKE THE PRESENT

THE STORY IS NEVER TRULY DONE, but for now I watch as it moves on, spawning new threads that weave other tales. I observe all this from my vantage point, and hold the stories of these people in my heart.

I find my thoughts turning, time and again, to the idea of the second narrator. I become obsessed. To them, this entire universe of story would make a single twist of threads in their own tapestry. They peer over my shoulder, and they lurk, and watch, and plot.

What if this second narrator is more meddlesome than I? The entire arc of my life could be a tale for their own dark amusement, or an object lesson by which they instruct readers. I was both a character and narrator, inextricably bound, but a more distant narrator would be more prone to interference, not understanding the weight a character bears.

More disturbingly, it means the thread of my life is one they could snip, to silence my voice as easy as—

FIN

ACKNOWLEDGMENTS

Wow, I've written a lot of these, so I'll try to keep this concise!

To Rosa, Andee, Art, Monica, Melo, and Logan: thank you so much for helping me wrestle with the chaos of this book and find a way to tell this story that made some coherent sense.

To my family: thank you for supporting me when I spend way too much time writing, thinking about writing, and getting emotional about writing.

To my writing support network: thank you always to the feral raccoons in Team Trash (Andy, Crystal, Leah, Mallory, Melo, Michelle, Monica, Nat, Nina, SinJ, and SoftJ) who are always there to boost me and back me. And of course to Rosa, Shannon, Mary, Charlotte, Andy, and E.M. I couldn't do this without all of you. And of course, thanks to the many, many people who've read, supported, and boosted my work. Self publishing is a strange and lonely journey sometimes, but all of you have made an enormous difference in making this series— as well as this book—a reality.

ABOUT THE AUTHOR

SJ Whitby writes books. That's about all you need to know at this point. This is the eighth book in the Cute Mutants universe, and there's still a lot more to come.

 twitter.com/sjwhitbywrites
 instagram.com/sjwhitbywrites
 patreon.com/sjwhitby